"I believe I deserve
an explanation."

With that, Bess folded her arms over her chest.

"Don't get your neck hairs bristlin'," Jake said, smiling now. "I only meant that once you get your mind set on something...well, you just ain't gonna let it be, no matter what." A crooked grin slanted his mouth. "Are you?"

Her eyes narrowed. "So I'm stubborn. It's not a hanging offense, far as I know."

Her words left him cold. Jake knew she'd only been teasing, it was written all over her pretty face. Still, the words cut him raw, like a skinning knife. He'd developed a pretty thick hide these past ten years, or so he'd thought. "Men can be damned rude sometimes" was all he said.

"And one in particular," she countered, one brow high on her forehead, "is smart enough to evade an issue indefinitely, even if he has to pay himself to do it!"

Dear Reader,

'Tis the season to be jolly, and Harlequin Historicals has four terrific books this month that will warm your heart and put a twinkle in your eye!

We are thrilled to welcome author Loree Lough to Harlequin Historicals. Although this is Loree's first historical, she has published over twenty inspirational romances, including three for Steeple Hill's Love Inspired® line. Be prepared to laugh and cry while reading her gripping Western, *Jake Walker's Wife*. A good-hearted young woman who has cared for her father and brothers since her mother's death meets and falls for a dynamic Texas cowboy running from the law who helps them all to dream and grow—especially Bess.

In *Heart and Home* by Cassandra Austin, a young—and engaged—physician starts anew in a small Kansas town and finds himself falling for his beautiful and caring neighbor. Don't miss our special 3-in-1 medieval Christmas collection, *One Christmas Night*. Bestselling author Ruth Langan begins with a darling Cinderella story in "Highland Christmas," Jacqueline Navin spins an emotional mistaken-identity tale in "A Wife for Christmas" and Lyn Stone follows with a charming story of Yuletide matchmaking in "Ian's Gift."

If you want a Regency-era historical novel that will leave you breathless, be sure to look for *A Gentleman of Substance* by Deborah Hale. In this novel, a taciturn viscount offers marriage to the local vicar's daughter, who is pregnant with his recently deceased brother's child....

Enjoy! And come back again next month for four more choices of the best in historical romance.

Happy Holidays,

Tracy Farrell,
Senior Editor

Please address questions and book requests to:
Harlequin Reader Service
U.S.: 3010 Walden Ave., P.O. Box 1325, Buffalo, NY 14269
Canadian: P.O. Box 609, Fort Erie, Ont. L2A 5X3

Jake Walker's Wife

Loree Lough

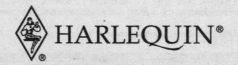

HARLEQUIN®

TORONTO • NEW YORK • LONDON
AMSTERDAM • PARIS • SYDNEY • HAMBURG
STOCKHOLM • ATHENS • TOKYO • MILAN • MADRID
PRAGUE • WARSAW • BUDAPEST • AUCKLAND

RECYCLED PAPER
RECYCLED PAPER

ISBN 0-373-29089-6

JAKE WALKER'S WIFE

Copyright © 1999 by Loree Lough

Visit us at www.romance.net

Printed in U.S.A.

LOREE LOUGH

A full-time writer for more than twelve years, Loree Lough has produced more than 2,000 published articles, dozens of short stories—appearing in magazines here and abroad—and novels for children ages eight through twelve. The author of twenty-five romances (including the award-winning *Pocketful of Love* and *Emma's Orphans,* and bestsellers like *Reluctant Valentine, Miracle on Kismet Hill* and *Just One Christmas Wish*), she also writes as Cara McCormack and Aleesha Carter.

A comedic conference speaker, Loree loves sharing in classrooms what she's learned the hard way. And since her daughters, Elice and Valerie, have moved into homes of their own, Loree and husband Larry have been trying to figure out why some folks think the empty-nest syndrome is a *bad* thing....

To Elice and Valerie, my beloved daughters...
and lifelong friends.

Prologue

Lubbock, Texas, 1840

The prisoner watched a beetle wriggling between his shackled ankles, its skinny black legs kicking frantically as it tried to right itself. It wasn't hard to empathize with the pitiful thing, struggling to survive in a world turned upside down. Reaching as far as the chain that bound his leg to the wall would allow, he set the bug back on its feet and watched it disappear between two, rough-hewn floorboards.

If only his own miserable life could be righted as easily.

His temporary, rolling jail cell was hot as an oven. He swallowed hard, trying not to think about his dry lips and parched throat. He'd asked for a sip of water as the deputy shackled him to the jail wagon wall. "Do you good to suffer a bit," Deputy Yonker had snarled, "like the Widow Pickett is sufferin' right now on account of you."

His thirst was forgotten as he recalled the way they'd hauled him from bed weeks earlier, shouting into the darkness, "How can you sleep after killin' a man in cold blood?"

Killing a man? his sleep-dulled mind had repeated.

But he'd been unable to protest aloud, for one of his captors had stuffed a sweaty neckerchief into his mouth as another hog-tied him. Thoughts flit like wasps, each with its own stinging barb: *Who's been murdered? And why do they think I'm the killer? I don't even like shootin' rabbits for the soup pot!*

Later that night, alone in the dimly lit, cramped cell behind the Lubbock sheriff's office, disjointed memories attacked through the long, restless night. In one dream, he was four years old again. Four years old and watching the cowhands brand cattle on the ranch his mama had inherited from her folks. Straddling the corral fence, he'd winced when the red-hot iron seared cowhide with a big, bold *W*. "Don't it hurt 'em, Pa?"

"Nah…"

"*My* name starts with a *W*, don't it, Pa?"

His father had scooped him up and said, "Yup. *W*, for Walker, in memory of your mama's daddy." He scanned the horizon. "Someday," he said, "this'll all be yours, son. That's why every one of them cows is gonna get a *W* burnt to his rump, so's folks'll know they're yours, too."

From that time on, whenever young Walker John Atwood rode the range, holding tight to the saddle horn as he nestled safely between his father's chaps, he'd point to the branded cattle and call out proudly, "Look, Pa, a *W*, see? Jus' like me!" He'd said it so often that his father took to calling his little boy W.C. The nickname caught on, and soon everyone, from the hired hands to his own mother, called him W.C.

His father had taught him many things, among them that "If you never lie or steal, you'll always do me proud." Even at the tender age of four, W.C. wanted few things more than making his father proud. "Don't worry, Pa," young W.C. had promised, "I'll never take anything that ain't rightly mine, and I'll always tell the truth."

He had hoped, as he lay on the lumpy jail cell mattress,

that when they came back to interrogate him in the morning, his pa's advice would see him through.

It had not.

"Guilty," the jury foreman had droned that fateful morning.

The judge's gavel had fallen with a sickening *thump,* and W.C. believed he'd hear the hollow echo of the man's monotone for the rest of his life: "I hereby decree that the prisoner, Walker John Atwood, be remanded to custody until next Tuesday at two o'clock, when he shall be hanged by the neck until dead."

And so now, as the wagon rattled toward the high, treeless ridge on the outskirts of Lubbock, Texas known as Dead Man's Hill, W.C. wondered if the townsfolk would gather at the gallows to watch him swing, or if he'd die with no one present but Smitty and Yonker, the two tobacco-spitting deputies up front.

A shudder passed through him, and W.C. did something he hadn't done in years:

He prayed.

His prayer was interrupted by the frantic voice of one of the deputies. "Hold it, man!" Smitty hollered. "That there's a rattler up ahead in the road!"

W.C. had spent every one of his eighteen years around horses, and knew without a doubt that if the men had seen the snake, the animals had seen it, too.

No sooner did he have the thought than the wagon's left side lifted. Higher, higher it rose as W.C. held on for dear life—what precious little was left of it—to the thick chain that tethered him to the rough-hewn interior wall. He held his breath, too, as the wagon teetered on its two right wheels.

He felt the rig pitch forward, heading down…into what, he had no time to guess. Anything but the river, he hoped, because he'd never learned to swim. But then, did it matter how he met his end? Better to meet Saint Peter by drownin', he thought as his body slammed into hard wood, than at the end of the hangman's noose!

The wagon skidded on its side as the high-pitched sounds of nails being ripped from boards and splintering wood mixed with the trumpeting of terrified horses and the shouts of panicked drivers.

When at last all was quiet, the chain that had tethered him to the big iron ring bolted to the wagon wall dangled from his left wrist, which was bruised and bloodied now by the rusting steel manacle still encircling it.

Slowly, he crawled from the wreckage and squinted into the bright Texas sunlight toward the thundering sound of horses' hooves. The big stallions were running full-out toward the flat, barren horizon, leaving nothing but a cloud of brown, sandy grit in their wake. Oh, how he envied their newfound freedom!

But why envy it, when he could *take* it?

Licking a droplet of blood from the corner of his mouth, he noticed both deputies, sprawled beside the wreckage. The steady rise and fall of their chests told him they had both survived the accident. From the look of things, they'd come to soon, compare their aches and pains, and cuss their bad luck as they headed back to Lubbock to round up the posse that would help them hunt down the escaped prisoner, W. C. Atwood.

For an instant, he considered sparing them the trouble, because if he lit out now, he'd be looking over his shoulder for the rest of his days. The shade of the overturned wagon looked mighty inviting. He could hunker down and take a short nap, if he'd a mind to, sipping cool water from one of their canteens until they woke up....

But W.C. didn't want to die. At least not at the end of a rope, and certainly not for a murder he didn't commit. He'd seen a man hang once. Took a full fifteen minutes for the poor fool to give up the ghost as the gathering crowed watched him twist helplessly in the wind, kicking for a foot-hold on his quickly ebbing life.

Like a bug on its back....

Smitty groaned softly, and W.C. knew he didn't have much time. First order of business—get rid of the iron man-acles that branded him a prisoner. He rummaged in Yonker's pockets for the key, and with trembling hands, unlocked the prison bands.

The blistering sun beat down, hot on his head. He'd die of heatstroke by day's end without his hat; they'd taken ev-erything, right down to his long johns, on the night they'd arrested him. But they didn't get his father's gold pocket watch. He'd had it since he was twelve, when his pa died, and he didn't want to part with it now!

Yonker's sweat-ringed hat looked mighty tempting now, more tempting, even, than the shade beside the wagon. Three water-filled canteens swung, pendulum-slow, from the wagon's cracked brake stick. He shook all three, took the emptiest, and limped over to where the drivers lay uncon-scious. And despite the fact that the watch he dug out of the deputy's pocket was in fact his own, W.C. would trade it for the hat.

For a moment, he stared at that gold watch, cradled lov-ingly in his open palm. It had been a wedding gift from his ma to his pa, and he dearly hated to part with it. But he hated the thought of stealing the deputy's hat even more. He'd promised his pa he'd live an honest life, and he aimed to keep that promise, even now.

W.C. pressed the button that popped open the case. He barely noticed the message his ma had paid the jeweler to engrave on the underside of its lid: *'Til the end of time.* Curlicue black hands pointed at twelve and three. *Quarter past noon,* he read, snapping the lid shut and closing his fingers tightly around the gleaming case.

Suddenly, W.C.'s eyes and lips narrowed. *I'd rather have*

my brain sunbaked like a biscuit than part with Pa's watch!
he thought, returning it into the safety of his pocket and
putting the deputy's hat back where he'd found it.

Slowly, he straightened to his full six-foot height, and
winced. He'd broken a few ribs in his day. Once, at eight,
when he'd fallen from the barn loft; again at ten, while
branding ponies. The searing pain in his lungs told him that
when the wagon hit bottom, he'd done it again. He looked
at the swollen fingers of his left hand. In all likelihood, he'd
broken a few of those bones, too.

But he'd faced pain—both the physical and the mental
kind—plenty of times before, and he'd beat it. W.C. poked
his chin out in grim determination, and started walking.

He wondered, as he limped along, how long it would take
them to find his trail. An hour? Two? *More'n likely, they'll
call in the Texas Rangers. The U.S. Marshals, even....*

He hitched the canteen's leather strap higher on his aching
shoulder. They were a determined lot, those U.S. Marshals,
and nothing riled them more than losing a prisoner. He'd
heard-tell of one bank robber who'd been on the run for
eight years before they managed to wrap a noose around his
neck. The thought made his own neck hairs bristle, and he
cast a furtive glance over his shoulder.

Better get used to doin' that, he told himself, stepping up
his pace.

The way his life had been going lately, he believed he'd
earned a kiss from Lady Luck. *Seems that li'l gal is always
puckerin' up for somebody else. Why not me for a change?*

Maybe, with her on his side, he'd be south of the Rio
Grande by this time tomorrow.

Chapter One

Freeland, Maryland, 1850

The distant sound of wagon wheels crunching down the gritty drive was swallowed up in a fog of memory as thick as the dust kicked up by the work horses' hooves. Sometimes, it seemed an eternity since the Beckley clan had buried their beloved Mary. Other times, like this one, Bess missed her mama so much it felt like only yesterday that she'd placed wild roses atop the burnished mahogany coffin.

The wagon and its passengers came into full view, waking Bess from her daydream. She waved as it rounded the last bend in the long, narrow lane that ribboned from the main road to the house, and returned her father's weary smile.

This year, as every other, she watched the newcomers' gazes flit from the two-story stone house, to the big red barn, to the acres of green, hilly fields beyond. Later, as the hired hands devoured their first meal at Foggy Bottom Farm, they'd ask the questions that churned in their minds now, and her father would, as always, let his own food grow cold to answer each one in turn.

And this year, like every other, one of the unmarried hands would try to woo Bess. Perhaps he'd pretend to love her, listing her beauty, her sweetness and her intelligence as reasons for his ardor, when in reality he saw marriage to Bess as the quickest cut to a slice of Foggy Bottom.

And maybe, he'd love her truly.

But it didn't matter either way.

There'd be no wedding bells in Bess Beckley's future! She'd vowed the day they lowered the fancy brass-trimmed casket into the ground that she'd never marry, because she honestly didn't believe she possessed the strength of character to withstand the demands of such a union. She'd seen how marriage had changed the boys and girls she'd gone to school with. If a wedding meant giving up her *self,* Bess would just as soon live out her life alone.

Besides, her father had been a fun-loving, high-spirited male while his dear Mary lived. But since her death, Micah rarely spoke, and smiled even less. If losing a beloved spouse could so drastically alter the character of a man as strong as Micah had been, well, how could she, a young woman with so few years of living behind her, even *hope* to withstand pain like that?

So this year, like every other, Bess would see to it that her so-called suitors returned home after the fall harvest…untethered, but with their male egos firmly intact. "I'm too busy taking care of Pa and the boys and the house and the books," she'd explain gently, "to be a proper wife to any man." That much, at least, was true.

Bess sighed. Maybe, this year she'd be lucky, and every man on the wagon would already have a wife and children of his own back home. And, if there was an unmarried man among them, she hoped he'd have a lovely fiancée waiting for him.

The wagon stopped in the shade of the giant oak beside the drive, halfway between the house and the barn. Micah climbed down from the driver's seat and took her in his arms. "Bess, darlin'," her father said softly, "you're sure a sight for sore eyes."

"Welcome back, Pa." She'd never grow tired of their now routine greetings. But it would be wonderful, Bess thought, to see Micah's wide, practiced smile reach his eyes for a change.

Forcing the wish from her mind, she stuffed one hand into her apron pocket. "Why don't you gents get washed up over there," she suggested, pointing to the pump beside the house. "I'm sure you're hot and tired after your long ride."

All five of them quickly climbed down from the wagon. As her twin brothers took turns introducing each field hand to their sister, Bess nodded politely. Her hope that they'd be married or engaged died, as it always did during this initial inspection.

They were drifters, every last one of them. Their eyes, dulled by years of hard luck, brightened slightly at the prospect of having a cot and three squares a day, if only for a few months. And their smiles, dimmed by a lifetime of misfortune, widened a bit as they reckoned with the fact that, in exchange for their hard work, they'd earn a fair wage. Where her father found these ragamuffins had always been a mystery to Bess. But each and every year, he managed to round up half a dozen or so misplaced wanderers, all so different, yet so much alike.

All but one, that is.

He stood out boldly from the rest. Not because he spoke more loudly—he hadn't said a word. Not because he wore a dapper outfit; his clothes, though rumpled, appeared to have been recently washed. Not because of his size, though he stood head and shoulders above the others. Rather, it was his *eyes* that captured Bess's full attention. Pale-blue and darkly lashed, they bored into hers with fierce intensity. Unconsciously, she took a small step backward. She'd never seen such eyes, except…

Bess remembered the day when, for her tenth birthday, her father had taken her to Baltimore. She'd been sitting on the bench outside the bank, waiting for Micah to complete his business when a commotion down the street caught her attention. The diminutive girl raced to the corner to see what had caused all the fuss and bother. She'd peered around men twice her size and spied a huge, iron-barred cage.

What had Amos Parker captured for his Traveling Wild Animal Show this time? she'd wondered, wending her way to the front of the crowd. Almost immediately, the pacing, panting wolf came into view. She stood near enough to run a hand through its shaggy gray coat—had she been able to summon the courage to poke that trembling hand through the bars. Instead, Bess had stood, silently awestruck, captivated by the creature's round, golden gaze.

It stopped its pacing, lifted its big head, ears upright and jaws clenched tight. The moment hung like a spiderweb— durable, yet delicate. And like a bug in that web, she stood shivering, trapped and transfixed. It seemed to Bess the beast was trying to send her a message on the invisible thread that had connected their eyes and hearts and souls.

This man who stood before her now, handsome though he was, wore the same wary, insightful expression as that beautiful, wild creature. And, as she had during her youthful encounter with the wolf, Bess shivered.

"There's the water pump, right over there beside the porch," Micah told him. The reminder, thankfully, rescued his daughter. "Feel free to freshen up whilst Bess, here, gets our grub on the table."

Her brothers headed the short, orderly line of men who waited their turn at the clean, clear water, chatting quietly, nodding, smiling.

Except for one.

"This here's Jake Walker," her father said, a hand on the big man's shoulder.

Jake Walker, she repeated mentally. Even his name sounded powerful. "Pleased to meet you," she said, fidgeting with the ruffled hem of her white apron. Difficult as it was, she tore her eyes from his and forced herself to look at her father. "I'll be in the kitchen if you need me, Pa."

She got an eerie feeling of being watched as she walked toward the back porch, then climbed the steps. One glance over her shoulder confirmed it. He grinned when she reached out and missed the door handle. Despite herself, Bess grinned back. Then, feeling suddenly silly and foolish, she hurried inside, letting the screen door bang shut behind her.

She needed to erase this feeling, so she poured cool water into tumblers, dipped hot stew into deep crocks, and set steaming bowls of butter beans and corn in the center of the long trestle table. But nothing blocked the memory of his penetrating stare. Something burned behind those ice-blue orbs. Something mysterious and—dare she even think it!— something dangerous.

Again, Bess pictured the wolf.

Again, she shivered.

Deep voices and masculine laughter interrupted her thoughts. "Pull yourselves up a chair, boys," Micah was saying as he took his seat at the head of the table. "Don't be shy, now. Help yourselves. Dig in and eat up."

While the others got situated, her brothers joined her in the kitchen. "Hey, there, Bessie-girl. Didja bake me a cherry pie, like you promised?" Matthew asked, kissing her cheek. "Why, I've been dreamin' 'bout it for miles."

Bess reached up to hug her younger brother. "You're big and strong as a man twice your age," she said, laughing softly, "but you don't behave a day over fourteen."

His twin, Mark, playfully shoved Matthew aside. "That's 'cause we *ain't* a day over fourteen…least not 'til tomorrow," he said, getting a sisterly hug of his own. "Are you gonna put a candle in the center of our birthday pie, and wish us a hunnerd more happy birthdays?''

Bess kissed the tip of his nose. ''Don't I always?'' She gave the boys a motherly shove. ''Now, get in there and eat, why don't you, and let me worry about the birthday party…if there's going to be a party at all.''

''Enough tomfoolery,'' Micah said, standing. ''It's time we said the blessing and let these hungry men eat. They've got a big day ahead of 'em tomorrow.''

Mark and Matthew obediently took their seats as Bess stood in the doorway, lowered her head, and folded her hands.

''Dear Lord above,'' Micah began, ''we thank You for our countless blessings…health and home and hearth. We especially thank You for our dear, sweet Bess, here, who made a tasty feast of this bounty You have so generously provided. We thank You for providing us with strong, honest men again this year, men who'll help us tend and harvest our crops. In Your most holy name, Amen.''

Micah pulled out the chair nearest his. ''Come, sit and eat with us, Bess.''

''Now, Pa, you know better—there'll be time enough for me to eat later,'' she said matter-of-factly.

Like a mama hen, Bess walked among the hands, each eagerly slouched over their steaming bowls of grub. ''Is it good, boys? Don't be shy now, there's plenty more!''

''Ain't you gonna set at the table with us, ma'am?'' the man named Jeremiah asked.

The only chair left was the one beside her father's, and directly across from Jake Walker's. A glance was enough to tell her he'd realized the same thing, for his mouth slanted in a wry grin.

''Why, we'd be right pleased if you'd join us,'' he drawled. And without taking his eyes from hers, added, ''Ain't that right, boys?''

The men stopped talking and chewing and reaching for food long enough to repeat Jake's question in their minds, then nodded and voiced their agreement. Matt, true to his nature, said, "But before you get all comfy, sister dear, how 'bout refillin' the biscuit basket?"

"We could use more taters, too," his twin added.

Jake stood, ignoring the dull squeal of his chair as it grazed the polished pine-planked floor. In an instant, he was beside her, one big hand pressed lightly to the small of her back. "Y'all just settle down there, Miss Bess. I'll fetch the biscuits and the taters for you," he said, pulling out her chair. Then, with what looked suspiciously like a sly wink, he added, "Is it all right if I call you Miss Bess?"

She forced herself to look away from his tantalizing smile and focused on her father. "'Miss Bess' indeed!" she repeated, grinning as she put her hand on Micah's shoulder. "Tell him the rules, Pa."

Micah cleared his throat and blotted his bearded face on a napkin. "We don't stand on ceremony around here, Jake. While you're at Foggy Bottom, you're family. I'm Micah. That's Matt and Mark. And this is Bess."

"Just plain Bess," she stressed.

Jake leaned close and whispered into her ear, "Nothin' plain about you, if you don't mind my sayin' so."

The nearness of him and the boldness of his statement caused her to inhale sharply. It amazed her that even after the long ride from Baltimore to Freeland, he smelled like fresh hay and bath soap. His compliment echoed in her mind. She'd always seen herself as quite ordinary, especially when compared to her mother's dark, natural beauty. But the way Jake looked at her made Bess feel anything but plain.

Not knowing what else to do, Bess dashed into the kitchen to fetch the biscuits and potatoes. When she returned, Jake was still standing where she'd left him, beside the empty chair. He took the bowls from her, put them unceremoniously on the table, and returned to his own seat. "So, will you be joinin' us or not, Just Plain Bess?" His words, his gentle smile, even his voice belied his flirtatious attitude.

For a reason she couldn't explain, her heart fluttered in response. "I...I think I'd best get busy scrubbing those pots and pans instead," she said, heading back into the kitchen. "If you gentlemen need anything," she added over her shoulder, "just whistle."

Before she even reached the kitchen pump, Bess heard the sweet, soft imitation of a songbird. Grinning, she wondered which of her ornery brothers had done it.

"Say, Jake," one of the men said, "when you're finished chirpin', how 'bout passin' the peas?" As she listened to the chorus of male laughter, Bess pumped water into the dishpan. *You're going to have to keep an eye on this one,* she warned herself, adding hot water from the kettle.

A mighty close eye...

Hours later, Jake lay back on his bunk, trying to remember when he'd last felt as contented. The bedsheets beneath him smelled like sunshine and spring air. Beside his cot stood a three-drawer bureau. He'd only needed the top one to stow his gear—man on the run had to travel light.

Smiling, he patted his full belly. Yes, he assured himself, his stay at Foggy Bottom was going to be pleasant, all right.

Though six months was a long time to stay in one place. Did he dare risk it?

He stared into the darkness for a long time, hands clasped under his head, thinking about Bess. She was beautiful, with a waist so tiny, he could have encircled it with his hands, and feet so small, he wondered how they kept her upright. The top of her head barely reached his shoulder, even in those high-heeled boots that had peeked out from beneath her lacy petticoats as she'd scampered up the porch steps.

He wondered if her hair felt as soft as it looked. Frowning, he tried to come up with a word that described the luxurious color. *Chestnuts,* he decided after a moment, with their muted browns and golds and pin-thin streaks of orange and black, explained it right well.

And those eyes, big and round as a fawn's. Jake didn't think he'd ever seen longer lashes. The sadness in her eyes confused him, though; Bess had a rich daddy, brothers who adored her, a home that was more mansion than house. What on God's green earth did she have to be sad about? he wondered.

Surely *she'd* never felt the hot sting of the buckle end of a belt, or spent half the day locked up in a dark root cellar. Certainly Micah had never forced her outside on a cold, windy night to teach her to appreciate the roof over her head. And Jake didn't suppose she'd ever been made to memorize Bible verses when she got the wrong answer on an arithmetic problem, or to stand in front of an entire congregation and admit she'd gone fishing rather than attend midweek services. She probably didn't know what it was like to sit at a food-laden table, yet not be allowed to eat because she'd nibbled at the crust of a pie without first asking permission.

She hadn't experienced any of those things because she'd grown up in the loving presence of a good daddy. Micah, Jake reasoned, had been everything his own father had been…good and decent and rock-solid. If the prairie fire hadn't taken his ma and pa, life would likely have been a mite different for Walker John Atwood, alias Jake Walker.

He'd worked for enough bosses in his ten years on the run to know a good one from a bad one, and Micah was a good one. If only he hadn't said that confounded prayer before they ate.…

Everything about the man, from his folded hands and bowed head to his tight-shut eyes, reminded Jake of his Uncle Josh, deacon of the King's Way Church.

Josh Atwood, his father's only living relative, had taken Jake in after the fire killed his parents. He had lived a happy, sheltered life to that point. Then, suddenly and mercilessly, the gentle, loving lessons of his parents were replaced with the harsh, sometimes brutal "disciplinary" methods of his uncle.

One month to the day after he'd buried his parents, Jake had been in the cemetery, standing between their tombstones when Uncle Josh joined him. "W.C.," the man had said, a firm grip on the boy's narrow shoulder, "startin' right now, you're going to begin earnin' your keep. There'll be no more mollycoddlin'. 'Spare the rod an' spoil the child,' the Good Book says," declared his uncle, raising the Bible high above his head.

"Are you gonna hit me with the rod...or your Bible?" the mischievous boy in him had asked, grinning.

His uncle failed to appreciate his humor, and he endured the first of many beatings that night. Jake couldn't help but wonder how two boys, raised by the same mama and papa, could have become such different men. His father had been so loving, so tender and kind, while Josh had been righteous and cruel.

Whipping and chastising his nephew didn't appear to satisfy his uncle. Ridicule and shame, it seemed, were as important in rearing a child as food and water. Jake had endured it, mostly because he wanted to believe it when his uncle said, "I'm doing these things because I care about you, boy."

He'd stopped believing, once and for all, when Josh testified at the murder trial that Jake had, indeed, killed the Lubbock banker Horace Pickett. "Heard him arguing with Horace that very afternoon," Josh had said. "He told ol' Horace if he ever caught him threatening a woman again, he'd break his fat red neck." Leaving the witness stand, he'd stood beside Jake and said with tears in his eyes and a sob in his throat, "May the Good Lord forgive you, W.C."

Jake hadn't been anywhere near Lubbock when the murder was committed, but who were the good people of Lubbock to believe...the angry young man who rarely attended church, or the good deacon who'd provided a home for his dead brother's orphaned son?

Jake had been twelve when his parents died. During his years with Uncle Josh, he sometimes had vivid dreams—memories of his parents' caring ministrations. Waking was heartbreaking, because then he was forced to admit that never again would he experience that kind of love.

And to Jake, the Beckleys seemed an awful lot like Josh Atwood, praising God for clean water and hot food, thanking the Almighty for bringing the hired hands safely from Baltimore to Foggy Bottom. They seemed to Jake too good to be true. If life hadn't taught him anything else, it had taught him this: when something appeared too good to be true, it was.

Jake rolled onto his side and decided right then and there, that here at Foggy Bottom, he'd keep his distance and leave as soon as the job was over. In the meantime, he'd earn his keep, just as he'd done on every ranch and farm between Freeland and Lubbock these ten lonely years. He'd exchange idle talk with his fellow bunk mates, with Matt and Mark Beckley. He'd show Micah the respect and courtesy due him as owner of the spread. And, last but not least, he'd exchange niceties with lovely little Bess—that would be the easiest part of his job. *Easy.* Jake couldn't remember when life had been easy.

He had very little to call his own. Family and home were mere words to him, as was his given name, Walker John Atwood. But Jake had his life, and he had his freedom—such as it was since the U.S. Marshals tacked pictures of him on every lamppost and fence rail and wall, it seemed, throughout the Southwest. Wanted, the posters said, Dead or Alive: W. C. Atwood.

He'd traveled about as far from Lubbock, Texas in ten years as a man could go on foot. And when things started looking too cozy in Freeland, Maryland, he'd head still farther east. Right out to the Atlantic Ocean, maybe. Then north, all the way up into Canada!

The Rangers' authority stopped at the Texas border, but U.S. Marshals could chase a "wanted" man from Maine to California if they had a mind to. And oh, but they'd had a mind to! So, he'd deliberately let his trail lead them southwest, from Old Horse Road, beside that battered, overturned jail wagon, into Mexico. For years, it seemed, the marshals believed he'd holed up with a pretty señorita.

But he wasn't that lucky.

Two years ago in Kansas, the same relentless marshals almost caught him. And they would have, if not for the outlaw gang that hid him in their shack on the outskirts of town.

Jake shut his eyes tight, hoping to block the horrible memories of running for his life, and when he did, Bess's beautiful face came into view. Her easy, honest smile. That lilting, lyrical voice. Those sad, doe eyes…she was everything he'd ever learned about angels, and then some.

His too-good-to-be-true rule gonged in his mind.

W. C. Atwood—Jake Walker—sighed deeply. He'd have to be careful here at Foggy Bottom. Very careful. He'd had women. Plenty of them. But he'd kept them at an emotional arm's length, because the surest way to jeopardize his freedom was to go and fall in love.

Chapter Two

Moonlight, slanting down from the heavens, reflected bright white from the corral fence. The black loam of the well-trod earth contrasted with the silvery coats of six horses, motionless, save the vapors of their soft, puffing breaths.

Bess didn't know how long she'd been sitting there, staring at them through her latched window. She only knew that this perch high above Foggy Bottom was one of the few places on earth where she felt truly happy. On nights like this, when sleep eluded her, this window drew her near. Of all the well-appointed rooms in the manor house, she liked this one best, because everything in it reminded her of her mother.

Her mama had sewn the ruffled white curtains that hung at the many-paned windows. She'd crocheted the lovely fringe that trimmed the canopy above Bess's bed, and had embroidered flower baskets from colorful satiny threads on the fluffy white pillows plumped against the window seat. Even the paintings, hung by wide pink satin ribbons from ornate black hooks near the ceiling, bore her mother's signature. And in the chiffonnier hung now too small dresses and skirts, jackets and shirts of every style and rainbow hue that Mary had designed and sewn for her little girl. The lovely frocks might be handed down to her own daughter one day...if Bess ever changed her mind about marrying.

If she married—and slim chance was there of that! But *if* she married, Bess would do things differently from other brides, right down to the sort of reception she'd organize. No pomp and circumstance for Bess Beckley! Her informally garbed guests would gather in the shady backyard to watch and listen as the bride and groom exchanged vows beneath the grape arbor. She'd wear her mother's wedding dress, and the ring Bess would wear for the rest of her life would be the one Micah had slipped onto Mary's finger on their special day.

String quartet? Absolutely not! Fiddlers, instead, along with a banjo player and a jug blower to make the music that would set folks' toes to tapping.

She'd serve none of those fancy finger sandwiches so favored by Baltimore's elite. Fried chicken and a spit-roasted pig would feed *her* hungry guests. Her mother would have loved a celebration like that, Bess knew.

Sighing heavily, she wondered what her mama would have thought about the handsome stranger who had arrived today. A romantic by nature, Mary would have been mesmerized by his soft Southern drawl. She'd have hidden a grin behind her dainty hand and whispered, "Oh, Bess, honey...isn't he a handsome devil!" And when the giggles faded, Mary's dark brows would have risen sympathetically as she commented on the sadness in his ice-blue eyes...and speculated on what might have caused it.

Bess snuggled deeper into the overstuffed backrest of her window seat and hugged a fat white pillow, her fingertips lightly stroking the tiny knots that made up the candlewicked bouquet. By now, Bess dreamily thought, her mother would have discovered the cause of the big stranger's woes, for she had such a way with people! Bess envied the ability she'd had to identify and soothe the pain in others.

It had been that very aspect of her gentle nature that had cost Mary her life. Leaning her forehead against the cool window glass, Bess closed her eyes and let the memory roll over her, like an angry wave at high tide.

On a cool March day, much like this one had been, Everett Thomas had sent his son to fetch Mary, the local midwife. She'd been baking bread, and a dozen loaves of spongy dough were waiting their turn in the oven when the boy burst into the kitchen, teary-eyed and panting. "M-m-ma's baby is comin', M-M-Miss M-M-Mary!" he'd stuttered. "Y-y-you gotta come, quick!" Mary had lain a flour-dusted palm against his fear-flushed cheek and kissed his forehead. "We'll stop at the barn on our way out," she told him, removing her frilly white apron and cooking cap, "and let Mr. Beckley know that a miracle is about to happen at your house." Her touch had been enough, Bess recalled, to ease the boy's fright. He was smiling by the time he and Mary headed for the barn, hand in hand.

The Thomas clan talked about it in excruciating detail at the funeral. Three times that night, Everett had said, Lizbeth would have died if not for Mary. Nearly twelve hours after she'd arrived at the Thomas house, Bess's mother gently lay a howling ten-pound, four-ounce baby boy in his mama's waiting, weary arms. Neighborly concern inspired Everett to invite Mary to stay the night. But she declined the friendly offer, saying in her playfully polite way that she'd rather brave the perils of the night than listen to newborn Daniel exercise his powerful little lungs for even one minute longer.

Birthing babies often took countless hours, so when Mary didn't return to Foggy Bottom before dark, her family hadn't given it more than a cursory thought. First thing next morning, Micah headed out to the Thomases'. As usual, his plan was to hitch his horse to the back of her buckboard, the way he often did when a woman's labor kept his wife away from home all night, and drive the wagon so that his exhausted wife could doze, head resting on his shoulder.

But halfway between Foggy Bottom and the Thomas farm, Micah had found her, lying still and pale alongside Beckleysville Road. He'd tearfully told Bess how he'd dismounted, scooped her up, and gently lay her atop the blanketed wagon bottom. All the way to the doctor's office, he'd said, he refused to believe that her cold, clammy skin and partially opened eyes were proof of the unthinkable.

"I never should have let her hitch that horse to her wagon," Micah whimpered at the funeral. He'd been trying for weeks to break the beast, but it was a spirited steed. "I told her he wasn't ready for range work just yet." Still, he'd let Mary convince him they couldn't spare the other horses for her mission of mercy at the neighbors' that day. She'd reminded him she was an able horsewoman, and that the short ride to Lizbeth's was the best use they could make of the newly acquired animal. And the despondent Micah had told his grieving young daughter that his decision to allow Mary to take that steed would haunt him for the rest of his days.

It had been decided, between the sheriff and the doctor, that Mary's horse had likely reared up, perhaps frightened by a rabbit or a raccoon, and sending Mary sailing into the underbrush. The doctor assured Micah she hadn't suffered, that she'd no doubt died the moment she hit the ground.

Bess was twelve when it happened, Matt and Mark barely walking. In the graveyard, Micah promised his children that they'd miss and remember Mary always. But he'd also promised that sadness would not haunt Foggy Bottom. "She's with Jesus now," he told his children, "and that's something to be joyful about."

She had taken comfort from the strength of his words. But

in the weeks and months to follow, Bess learned Micah hadn't believed them himself. If she'd known then what she knew now about her father's fragile emotional condition, she'd have been even more diligent about filling Mary's shoes.

Gradually, Bess took over more and more of Mary's duties. By the age of seventeen, she was running the house with organized yet gentle efficiency. She kept Micah's ledgers in better order than even he ever had. It was good, she told herself repeatedly, that the work kept her so busy, because, although her determination was genuine, Bess missed her mother more than she cared to admit. And of course, she couldn't admit it, for Bess sensed how much her father and brothers depended on her stubborn strength.

Only in her room did Bess allow herself to give in to loneliness and despair. Only here could she admit feeling tired, overburdened, deserted. Only in this peaceful, private place did she have the freedom to voice the whys and wherefores of death and dying, or dare to let tears fall. Surrounded by the things her sweet mama had so lovingly made especially for her, Bess did her most honest mourning.

Now, Bess took a deep breath and sat back, peering out into the dark, silent yard. A rabbit raced alongside the corral fence, a barnyard cat close on its heels. She said a little prayer for the bunny and glanced at the clock on her mantel. Nearly midnight. She could almost hear her mother's voice: "The breakfast bell rings early at Foggy Bottom. Get some sleep or you'll pay the price tomorrow!"

But not even the comforting weight of the afghan Mary had crocheted could soothe Bess's ragged nerves. Her mind swirled with thoughts of Jake Walker. Where had he come from? And what deep secret had darkened those beautiful blue eyes of his? He'd flirted blatantly with her during dinner. Why, he'd started flirting the moment he climbed down from the wagon! she admitted.

The thought made her smile a bit, and Bess stretched, yawned, closed her eyes. At the sound of whinnying horses, she opened them again. As a mother reads the meanings of her baby's cries, Bess knew her horses' moods. It wasn't like them to make such a racket at this hour.

She'd heard in town yesterday that rustlers had run off with a dozen of Abe MacPhereson's best quarter horses. *Well,* she determined, getting to her feet, *they won't get away with ours!*

Quietly, she scrambled across her mattress and, without lighting a lamp, stepped into her boots and buttoned them halfway. She belted a navy skirt atop her nightgown and shrugged into a red lamb's wool jacket, fastening it as she hurried down the stairs.

For a moment, Bess stood in the shadowy foyer and peeked through the bubbly leaded windows beside the door. Instantly, she recognized the tall silhouette. She threw open the door and half walked, half ran toward the corral. "Jake Walker," she whispered loudly, "what're you doing out here at this hour?"

He'd been leaning against the corral gate's top rail, and straightened at the sound of her voice. "Well, if it ain't Just Plain Bess," he said. "I might ask the same question...."

"I couldn't sleep," she said. "I was—"

"—looking out your window," he finished. "I know."

She glanced up at the house, and realized that from where he stood, he could, indeed, have seen her sitting in her window seat. Bess ignored her hard-beating heart. "Are you aware it's after midnight?"

His quiet chuckle punctuated her comment. "Don't you worry. Your daddy'll get his money's worth out of me tomorrow."

Bess gasped, and clutched her jacket tighter around her throat. "I never meant to imply—I only meant..."

He took a step nearer. "Whoa, there, Bess. Settle down. I was only funnin' with you."

She stared into his eyes. In the twilight, they looked silver-gray rather than blue. She thought again of the wolf, and hugged herself to fend off the unexpected chill. Blinking, she forced herself to say, "That's an interesting accent you've got there. Where are you from?"

"Texas."

The retort was short and deliberately evasive, so she pressed him for more. "I've been to Texas...."

He took another step closer. "Is that so?"

Bess didn't understand the worry lines that had creased his brow. It took all her willpower not to step back and put more distance between them. She felt a little afraid, a little curious, and a whole lot interested. So she nodded in response to his question. "Went with Pa to Houston, on business."

"Well," he drawled, smirking, "there's Texas, and then there's West Texas." He hadn't moved any closer, yet somehow, Jake's nose seemed only inches from hers. His eyes bored into hers with such fierceness that it made her pulse race, and Bess didn't understand why his mere nearness inspired such an intense physical reaction in her. Bess batted her eyes and smiled at him sweetly.

He nodded toward the corral. "Good-lookin' horses."

Her plan had been to make him feel so comforted by her friendly, nonthreatening demeanor that he'd start yakking and not stop until she knew his whole life's story. Instead, he'd looked into the corral and said "good lookin' horses." Tucking in one corner of her mouth, Bess sighed. "Oh, they're all right, I suppose." And then, to hide the disappointment in her voice, quickly added, "They're Arabians. Pa had them shipped here from Syria just over a year ago. He's hoping to breed them. They're as strong as they are beautiful, just as suited to pull a wagon as to seat a rider."

When he met her eyes, both blond brows rose high on his forehead. "It ain't often you meet a lady who knows her way around horses."

Shrugging, she stared at her feet. Until now, she hadn't realized how cold they were. "I don't know much about most horses, but I made it my business to know about *these*."

"Hmm." He spoke to the Arabian that was nuzzling his hand. "She's smart, pretty, a good cook. And honest, too. Hard not to like a woman like that...." Slowly, he swung his head around to stare into her face.

Unnerved, she struggled for something to say. "I've already forgotten where in Texas you said you're from."

His beautiful smile vanished like smoke. He stared into Bess's eyes. "I never said where I was from."

His closed expression warned her to stay out of his business. Out of his life. She got an or-else message from those dangerous orbs, too. *Or else what?* she wondered. Bess swallowed hard, hoping to repress the tickle of fear bubbling in her throat.

Well, food had always soothed the boys and Pa and the farmhands. "There's leftover chicken in the kitchen...."

That seemed to relax him some. He patted his stomach. "I ate enough at supper to last me two days."

She'd been around men all her life—never had a bit of trouble getting along with them. Bess didn't understand why *this* man rattled her so. "Pa tells me you're going to be an excellent foreman. Have you done much of that kind of work in the past?"

Jake nodded. "Ten years' worth. Hundreds of times, in hundreds of towns."

Hundreds? she repeated mentally. "I don't imagine your wife and children think very much of being without you—"

"Don't have a wife. No young'uns, either."

The flat, emotionless tone had returned to his voice. Bess

took a deep breath. She wanted to bring back the teasing drawl, the wonderful smile. "Maybe you'd like some cherry pie?"

Silence was his answer.

Exasperated, she blew a stream of air between her teeth. "Won't you sit with me, then, while I have a slice?" she asked over her shoulder as she walked toward the house.

His stony expression softened somewhat at her earnest invitation. "I reckon I can do that," he said quietly, falling into step beside her, "if you think you can rustle me up a glass of milk."

Without missing a beat, she winked. "Easy as…pie."

It had been easy to teach the new men her routine. Up at four-thirty every morning to perform barnyard chores. Wash up for breakfast, served at five. Out in the fields by quarter of six.

This day, the meal consisted of fried ham. Griddle cakes swimming in maple syrup. Eggs, sunny-side up. Honey-buttered bread. Hot coffee and cool milk. As Bess filled and refilled plates, the men ate and discussed the day's plans.

She'd saved the sticky buns, hot from the oven, for last. As she slid them onto a warmed plate, she heard Jake's quiet, authoritative voice. Not even her tasty surprise distracted the men from his instructions. They liked him, anyone could see. But more than that, they respected him. That fact alone told her he'd be one of the best foremen Foggy Bottom had ever seen, and Bess had seen enough foremen over the years to know a good one when she saw one.

In the month he'd been with them, Jake had gotten to know the farm almost as well as Micah knew it. Had gotten to know Matt and Mark. Got to know Bess pretty well, too, thanks to their late-night chats—some in the rockers on the front porch, some at the corral gate, some alone, over pie and milk by the soft light of the hanging kitchen lamp. Still, despite all the hours of gabbing they'd racked up, Bess felt she didn't know any more about him than she did on the day he'd arrived.

The eyes are the windows to the soul, or so the sages said. If Jake's eyes were any indicator of what lived inside him, she thought, he's about as good as a man can get. She sensed something in this man. Something honorable and decent.

And she'd had plenty of time to evaluate her feelings about him, since he seemed to be on her mind almost all of the time. Something told her Jake hid something painful behind that tight, careful smile. If she could only get him to open up, maybe she could help him put whatever it was behind him. It's what her mother would have done....

Bess was stacking the breakfast plates, hoping to find a way to reach his well-protected heart when he walked into the kitchen. "Lubbock," he said, leaning an elbow on the water pump. When she didn't respond, he said it again. "Lubbock."

She arched her left brow and grinned. "I don't know whether that's a very poor imitation of a frog, or if you have something stuck in your throat."

Jake chuckled. "It's my hometown."

Her heart skipped a beat, because he'd told her, in four simple words, that he trusted her, finally. Bess smiled. "So tell me, was the town named for a bullfrog? Or did the founding father have a frog in his throat when he announced its name?"

He threw his head back and laughed. She loved the music of it, hearty and deep and wholly masculine. Twice now, he'd treated her to the sound. Bess decided right then and there to make him do it again, and again, as often as possible. But before she could conjure up another joke to inspire a repeat performance, he saluted and grinned and left her alone with the mountain of dirty dishes. To her regret, Bess didn't see him again until dinnertime.

At least, she didn't see him *in person*. Bess saw plenty of him, though, whenever she closed her eyes.

Once she'd cleaned up the breakfast mess, Bess set some bread dough to rising near the warmth of the cookstove. Savory beef stew bubbled on the stovetop, and a batch of Apple Betty was baking in the oven. Just before the men came in, she'd whip up some potato dumplings and drop them onto the gently boiling stew. She tidied the house, then the bunkhouse. Clean laundry flapped colorfully on the clotheslines out back. The chickens had been fed and the eggs gathered. She'd save the mending and darning for evening, when she and the boys and Pa gathered around the parlor fireplace until bedtime. At last, her least favorite morning chores completed, Bess could indulge her other passion: ciphering.

Bess loved nothing better than adding up columns of numbers in her father's blue-lined ledger books. She'd learned precisely when to order seed, what kind and how much to order, and which peddler would give her the best price. She'd learned to wrangle a fair deal from old Samuel down at the livery stable when saddle cinches and blankets wore out, too. While other young women her age were having babies, organizing tea parties and crocheting doilies, Bess was busy running Foggy Bottom, and loving every minute of it.

Well, *almost* every minute.

Pastor Higgins told her after services one Sunday that she should pray hard about her future. "'A prudent wife is a gift from the Lord,'" he quoted Proverbs.

"'Even a child makes himself known by his acts,'" she returned, quoting the same book, "'whether what he does is pure and right.'"

The reverend's jaw sagged and his eyes bugged out. Bess

felt fairly certain that her retort stunned him sufficiently, and doubted he'd discuss marriage with *her* any time soon.

But later, at a church social, his wife did, however. "Don't you sometimes see your girlfriends with their little ones," Mrs. Higgins asked, "and wish you had a baby of your own?"

Years ago, when her friends began falling in love and setting up house, Bess thought maybe there was something wrong with her...that a maternal heart did not beat within her bosom, for she truly didn't yearn for a husband, a home, an infant to suckle at her breast. She'd shared her fears with the Widow Reddick, who owned the general store.

"Bess, my dear," the old woman had said, "babies and husbands are grand—and I've had a couple of each, so I know what I'm talkin' about—but babies spit up, and husbands, they just plain spit." The joke inspired a round of laughter to bubble from the old woman's throat, and once she'd regained her composure, the widow said something Bess would never forget: "If you follow those young hens, they might well lead you to a fox in the chicken coop. But your heart won't steer you wrong." She'd placed a withered hand upon Bess's sleeve and added, "When the right man comes along, you'll know it.

"Now, don't you roll your eyes at me, young lady, I'm tellin' you true! When the right man comes along, you'll *want* to make a home for him and give him children. Trust me, there's nothing you won't do...for the right man."

She'd been eighteen when she shoved that sage advice to the back burner of her memory. Four short years later, standing in the church basement facing Mrs. Higgins, Bess called upon the strength it had given her. "I have, at any given time," she told the pastor's wife, "as many as ten 'babies' to cook for and clean up after—if you add the hired hands to family members. Besides, I think I'm the best judge of when the Good Lord has called me to motherhood." From the look on Mrs. Higgins's face, Bess got the idea the pastor's *wife* wouldn't be discussing marriage with her again any time soon, either!

As she replayed the all too recent scene in her mind, Bess's pencil hovered above the ledger. In the blink of an eye, the memory of that Sunday, the pastor and Mrs. Higgins, vanished, and she thought of Jake Walker for the hundredth time that day.

Strong and handsome, he had all the outward qualities of the right man…of a husband…*if* she wanted a husband. Bess grinned at her own silly, romantic notions. *Why, Jake Walker is probably no more interested in you than he is in that hitching post out front!* she scolded herself. Then, giggling, she added, *It's not likely there's a* hitching *in his future!*

But he *had* blatantly flirted with her, right from the start. And he *had,* after all, often sought out her company. He'd hinted they were friends, and had entrusted her with the one piece of information about him she believed he had shared with no one else: his hometown, Lubbock, Texas.

Many a night, she lay awake hoping Jake would open up to her more, that someday he'd tell her why he'd left Lubbock in the first place. Bess could only hope she'd have the strength to be the giving, loving friend he'd need…if that ever happened.

Still, Jake got a faraway look in his eyes when the subjects of family or love were mentioned. He stood at the fringes of enjoyment, no matter how impersonal, as if afraid of the bonds that might develop if he got involved in the fun. Most curious of all, Bess thought, was the anger that strained his fine features as he watched the warm interaction between Micah and the twins.

Bess noticed all this, and said nothing.

She noticed all this, but went ahead and fell in love with him anyway.

Chapter Three

Matt, Mark, and Jake had left before sunrise to mend fences along the north side of Foggy Bottom. It had been a long, hard day, and the boys gladly bedded down when Jake suggested it. As they snored contentedly in their bedrolls, Jake took a deep, satisfied breath of early June night air as he stirred the coals beneath the coffeepot. After spreading his own blanket on the dusty earth, he lay back, fingers entwined behind his head, staring into the star-studded sky. As he peered through the branches of the yellow pine, Jake smiled, because the tree reminded him of the day, just last week, when he'd seen Bess heading for woods behind the big manor house.

He'd told himself he wouldn't follow. That she probably only planned to pick wildflowers for the kitchen windowsill. Or gather mulberries for a batch of sweet jam. He couldn't spare the time to traipse behind her as she did girlie things.

So Jake didn't for the life of him understand it when he found himself doing exactly that.

A gold eagle screeched overhead, but she didn't duck or lurch with fright. A raccoon scampered across her path, disappeared into the thick underbrush, yet her steps never faltered. It took a white-tailed doe, grazing beside a scrub pine, to alter her pace. Bess, walking slowly and deliberately, held out her hand and, speaking in low, even tones, invited the deer to share her sunflower seeds.

He'd been a cowboy all his life, and had seen his share of wilderness beasts, but he'd never seen one walk right up to a body. He could see her face from where he stood, hidden behind a locust tree. The way she smiled and crooned to the critter, Jake believed he knew how disappointed she'd be when the deer hightailed it into the woods. He also knew her disappointment would be short-lived. She'd likely shrug and sigh and carry on with her walk in the matter-of-fact way that was typically Bess.

But the doe hadn't run into the woods, as he'd predicted. Instead, it stepped—ears pricked forward and tail flicking cautiously at first—right up to her, and after a moment of careful scrutiny, nibbled seeds from her upturned palm. She filled and refilled her palm twice and, much to his amazement, stroked the deer's sloping forehead!

Grinning, he shook his head. He shouldn't have been surprised. Only the day before, he'd seen her in her rose garden, crawling around on her hands and knees, playing what appeared to be a game of hide-and-seek with a rabbit no bigger than her hand.

As a boy, his mama had read him *Snow White.* The pretty, dark-haired princess in the folktale was so sweet and kind that even woodland creatures recognized her goodness. Bess, with her creamy skin and chestnut-brown hair, reminded him of that fairy-tale princess. So lost in thought was he that Jake never saw the deer meander back into the woods. Never saw Bess turn toward him. Never saw her head in his direction.

"Jake Walker, what're you doing behind that tree?"

Her sudden appearance had startled him. He thought he'd hidden himself well, but she had him dead to rights, no doubt about it. He pocketed both hands and tried to come up with a reasonable explanation for his presence, but found himself speechless.

She'd crossed both arms over her chest, wicker basket dangling from one wrist. "Are you spying on me?"

"Course not," he'd said, shaking his head.

"Well, I certainly hope you didn't follow me because you thought I'd get lost. I'll have you know I could maneuver these woods blindfolded."

Fire and ice, his Bess.

Your Bess? What in tarnation are you thinking?

Now, as he lay on the cold ground staring up at the inky sky, the picture of her, standing there, chin up and shoulders back in proud defiance, made him smile. *She's some woman,* he told himself. *Some fine woman.* Feminine and delicate, she made every other female he'd known seem like boys by comparison. Bess refused to use her feminine wiles to get her way with the men in her life. She did not weep or whine or behave in coy and flirty ways. Instead, she faced life head-on in a straightforward manner. He liked that. Liked it a lot.

At the thought, his smile faded. *Where's your good sense, you hang-tailed coyote?* he raged mentally. Bess was sweet as molasses, and the years had made him bitter. She was innocent as a newborn, and he'd been convicted of cold-blooded murder.

She believed a little good lived in every being, and life had taught him the opposite was true. She had a doting father and brothers who thought she'd hung the moon, while the only family he'd ever known were cold in the ground…or cold and abusive. Surrounded by the warm arms of family and friends, she'd learned trust and love. Smothered by anger and bitterness, Jake had learned to mistrust and hate. They were as different as a mountain lion and a kitten.

Even if she had a mind to marry—and how many times have you heard her say she doesn't?—she deserves a man who's a long sight better than you, Walker Atwood! he told himself. *Besides, if you stay too long in one place, the marshals will catch up with you for sure.*

Jake wanted a home. A wife and children. Wanted those things as much as the next man…maybe even more. But thanks to his Uncle Josh's testimony in court, he'd live out the rest of his days alone. Long ago, he'd resigned himself to his sorry fate.

It presented a dilemma, all right: He'd fallen in love with Bess Beckley, and was powerless to do a blessed thing about it. Because in order to have chance at a life with her, he'd have to tell her *everything*. And having Bess know about his black past scared him even more than the prospect of dying at the end of a rope.

Jake rolled onto his left side, tugging the scratchy brown blanket closer to his chin. He tried to concentrate on other things. Like work. The weather.

The height of the moon told him it would soon be midnight. He'd warned the boys they'd rise before sunup and head out to repair the east boundary fences. *Practice what you preach,* he told himself, *'cause if you don't get some shut-eye soon, you're gonna have a powerful grouch on all day.*

He closed his eyes and tried to snooze.

Jake's muscles and joints ached from his long, hard day of riding the fences, and despite rawhide gloves, his hands and forearms were scratched and pockmarked from stretching miles of razor-sharp barbed wire and replacing rotting posts. *You're gettin' soft,* he scolded himself, groaning as he turned onto his back again.

Suddenly, he felt as ancient as Bess's father, though Micah was easily sixty and Jake hadn't lived thirty years yet.

Yes, he felt old. Old, and tired, and more alone than he'd ever felt in his life.

* * *

"You gonna sleep all day?" Matt asked, nudging Jake's boot with the toe of his own.

Jake yawned and blinked. "You better have a pot of coffee boilin'," he growled, "or you're gonna pay for that kick."

The boy snickered. "Coffee's been perkin' for half an hour. Thought for sure the smell of bacon fryin' would rouse you."

Jake levered himself up on one elbow. In the months he'd been at Foggy Bottom, he'd grown quite fond of these two young men. The twins seemed to sense they could learn plenty from Jake, and so they followed him, like adoring pups, and waited for whatever scraps of knowledge or advice Jake decided to toss their way.

And he'd taught them plenty since arriving at Foggy Bottom. They'd always been hardworking farm boys, but now they could cut a calf from a herd and hog-tie a heifer with the best of men. When he'd arrived, Matt and Mark could hold their own on horseback, but lately—partly because they tried to mimic his style, and partly because they'd developed a heap of self-confidence—they sat taller in their saddles.

Jake got to his feet and rolled his bedding into a tight cylinder. As he stowed it among his gear, he thought back several weeks, to the conversation he'd had with Micah.

"I've got to thank you for what you've done for my boys," the old man had said. "Since their mama died, I've sort of thrown myself into my work—gets my mind off missing Mary."

Micah had stared off into space, and Jake sensed the man wasn't focusing on the dense pine forest, or the contented cattle that grazed in the field beyond it, or the brown-board fences that hugged the property on all sides.

"I'm afraid I haven't been much of a father to them. What they know about farming they learned from the hired hands."

Jake remembered feeling a mite sorry for the man. But all too soon, pity was replaced by low-burning anger. He'd had a mind to tell Micah that it would have been better for the boys if he'd fessed up about his grief; honest sorrow, Jake reckoned, would have been easier to bear than the distance Micah had put between himself and the twins.

But he'd learned long ago that a man seldom spoke what was on his mind, and never spoke what was in his heart. So he kept silent his opinions, telling himself Micah had been as good a father as he knew how to be. Jake wondered how well *he'd* have borne up, if he'd lost the love of a woman like Bess.

Since that talk, Jake had given the matter a lot of thought, and in the end, he'd understood why Micah had avoided close contact with his boys. And that understanding had come the very next day, as he'd stood in Micah's parlor, staring at the row of silver-and-bronze-framed photographs on the mantel.

His favorite had been the tintype of the Beckley clan. In it, Matt and Mark looked like small, male versions of their mother. Jake assumed the likeness was simply too painful for Micah to look at in person, day in and day out. In the picture, the boys sat on a red velvet bench, wearing starched white collars and black ribbon ties, staring stonily into the camera's lens. Between them sat Bess, in a lacy dress, her dainty hands clasped in her lap. Behind them, Mary, in a dress exactly like Bess's, smiled softly. And beside her, Micah held his dark-bearded chin high.

Just a typical family portrait, folks might say. But Jake knew better, because he'd seen what went unnoticed by most: There, in the shadows behind their children, where they thought no one would see, Micah and Mary had clasped hands, their tightly twined fingers giving those who looked closely enough proof of their undying love and genuine affection for one another.

The photo had entranced Jake, and he found himself making up excuses to step into the parlor again and again, if only for a moment, to drink in the sight of true familial warmth. Sometimes, as he waited for sleep to rescue him from the snores and grunts of the bunkhouse, it was that picture, floating in his memory, that helped him drift off to sleep.

"What'd you do," Mark asked now, squatting down beside the campfire, "roll over and thump your head on a rock during the night?"

Jake shook off the last of his daydream and accepted the blue-speckled metal mug from the boy's extended hand. He took a sip of hot coffee and frowned. "What're you yammerin' about?"

Mark shrugged. "You seem a mite addlebrained this morning, is all."

Matt elbowed his brother. "Think maybe he's love-struck, little brother?"

Mark's eyes widened as he considered the possibility. "Sure looks that way to me." The boy drained the last of his own coffee, then faced his twin. "And if you call me 'little brother' again," he challenged, grinning, "I'll stick your nose in the dirt and plow the bottom forty with you! Just 'cause you were born two minutes before me don't give you no right to rub my face in it."

Matt tossed several pebbles at his brother's booted feet. "Wipe the ground up...with *me?* Ha! I'd like to see you try!"

It was invitation enough, and before Jake could open his mouth to forestall it, the brothers started wrestling in the dust like a couple of rowdy pups. He grinned, and wondered for a moment what it might have been like to grow up with a brother who really gave a hoot what happened to you, instead of coming to age in a house with no one but a man who despised you. Jake frowned to smother the fiery fury that always rose within him when he thought of Uncle Josh.

"You boys act more like four than fourteen," he said, forcing a sternness into his voice that he didn't feel. "I'll give you one minute to pack up this gear."

The playful jostling came to a grinding halt, and their dark-eyed expressions changed from young-boy-happy to young-man-wise. Jake swallowed the lump of guilt that formed in his throat at having caused the abrupt change, and pretended to busy himself by saddling his horse.

He listened as the twins stashed tin pots and metal plates and utensils into grubsacks and tied them to their saddles. "If we dig in good and hard," he said as he hung a coil of hemp rope over the saddle horn, "we can get this job finished up today."

"Good," Matt said, brushing dark curls from his eyes. "My belly is cryin' for some of Bess's corn biscuits."

"And a piece of her deep-dish apple pie," his twin added.

Jake would have settled for a glance at her pretty face. He stanched that mood before it could start. "Saddle up, boys, and let's head out. We're burnin' daylight."

They'd been riding for all of fifteen minutes when Matt spotted two riders on the horizon. "Who do you suppose that could be all the way out here?"

Jake stared hard at the spot where Matt pointed. Just as he caught sight of the distant silhouettes, one of the riders turned, and sunlight winked from something metal on his shirt. Jake's blood ran cold and his heart beat hard. The shiny thing, no doubt, was a badge. And it belonged, no doubt, to a U.S. Marshal. *So they've tracked you down again,* he thought miserably.

Neither man seemed to have spotted Jake and the boys yet, however. If the three of them headed back to Foggy Bottom at a fast clip, maybe the marshals would never know he'd been in Freeland at all....

Just then, Matt smacked his horse's rump and thundered toward the marshals.

"Are you out of your mind?" Jake hollered.

"I'm aim to find out who's been cuttin' through our property without permission, an' why," the boy shouted over his shoulder.

Jake spurred his own horse into action, yelling as he went. "That field is full of mole holes. Your horse is sure to—"

The warning came a heartbeat too late. Even before Jake completed his sentence, Matt's horse went down, pitching the boy head over heels. He landed with a quiet *thump* on a grassy knoll.

"Ohmigosh," Mark said, his voice a childlike whisper. "That's just the way Ma died...."

Bess had told Jake about the night Mary's horse bucked, overturning her wagon as she rode home after delivering the Thomas baby. The agonized tone in Mark's voice made Jake's heart ache.

In seconds, Mark and Jake were at Matt's side. They quickly dismounted and inspected the damage. The boy lay unconscious, his right leg bent at an awkward angle beside him, his right arm twisted beneath him.

"Looks like he busted himself up pretty good," Mark said, voice trembling.

Jake was far more concerned with the huge bump on the boy's forehead. "Get the canteen," he ordered, "and bring me my saddlebag."

As the boy ran for the supplies, Jake scanned the horizon once more. The commotion must not have attracted the marshals' attention, for they were heading in the opposite direction now.

Like soldiers, most U.S. Marshals could splint broken bones and tie tourniquets with the best of medics. As Jake saw it, he had two choices: run like the dickens, or stay put and see to it Matt got the help he needed.

Run, and avoid the gallows.

Stay, and save Matt's life.

Jake, still kneeling beside the boy's broken body, bowed his head. And then he unholstered his pistol, and fired a single shot into the air.

Chapter Four

"Trouble?" the biggest man asked as he reined in his beast.

"The boy's horse threw him," Jake explained, pulling his hat lower on his forehead to hide his face from the marshal's view.

Both men stared down at Matt's twisted body. "Good Lord Almighty," the first one said. "I ain't never set a broken bone afore." He looked at his buddy. "How 'bout you, Richie?"

Richie shook his head. "Nope." He met Jake's eyes. "Guess that's what you was hopin' when you fired that shot, eh?"

Jake nodded.

Only after the men dismounted did Jake realize they weren't U.S. Marshals at all, but two of Freeland's border farmers. And what he'd thought had been a silver star badge was, instead, the cinch of the smaller man's black four-in-hand tie.

Relief flooded Jake's veins and he exhaled the breath he'd been holding since he made the decision to put Matt's welfare ahead of his own.

The first man held out a big, callused hand. "Name's

Luke. Luke Elliot,'' he said. ''Sorry to make your acquaintance this-a-way.''

He pumped the man's arm. ''Jake Walker. This is Mark—'' Jake then gestured to Matt, who lay motionless on the ground ''—and Matthew Beckley.''

For what seemed like an eternity, no one spoke. Finally, Mark broke the endless silence. ''So what're we gonna do about Matt, Jake?''

Richie and Luke rubbed their bearded chins. ''Well, we could help you whack down one of those saplings over yonder,'' Richie said, nodding toward a thicket. ''Couple of blankets tied 'round 'em nice an' tight could make a passable litter.''

It was quickly agreed they'd build a litter to haul Matt home on. Jake placed a hand on Mark's shoulder. ''Stay here with your brother,'' he instructed, handing him the canteen and a neckerchief. ''Dribble a bit of water on his lips from time to time.''

Mark immediately fell to his knees and began drizzling water over Matt's forehead and cheeks.

The men walked several hundred yards due east in search of strong, young saplings. It took several whacks of Luke's hunting knife to cut the small trees down, but soon, they were back with the boys again.

After placing all their blankets one atop the other, Jake tethered them to the now branchless trees with strips of cotton he'd torn from his shirttails and cuffs.

Richie's contribution were two, long, leather bootlaces. Jake cut each in half, and used the four strings to bind the litter to his saddle girth. Once he'd tested it for strength and durability, Jake gently eased Matt's unconscious body onto the litter. Even out cold, the boy moaned with pain.

''In his condition, it'll take us a day just to get him back to the house,'' Jake said to the group. To Mark, he added,

"Ride on ahead and fetch the doc. See that he's waitin' when we get there, y'hear?"

Mark climbed onto his horse and gathered the reins. "Yessir!"

"And mind that you avoid those confounded mole holes!"

"Yessir!" the boy repeated, and rode off.

Richie and Luke mounted their horses, too. "We were on our way to Morris Meadows," Richie said. "We heard-tell that Isaac Junior had a wagon for sale. Luke, here, wants to buy it for his girl. They're gettin' hitched next week." Richie elbowed his friend. "He's gonna deck it out in baubles an' bows for the weddin', ain't ya, Luke?"

The bigger man nodded. "Thought we'd take us a short-cut across Foggy Bottom. Sure would save us a heap o' travelin' time."

Jake patted his horse's withers to keep the animal calm and still. "I'm foreman here," he informed them. "Anybody gives you any sass, you just tell 'em I gave you the go-ahead to cut through."

Each man saluted with a fingertip to the brim of his hat. "Thanks, man," Richie said.

"Hope the boy'll be all right," Luke said over his shoulder as they trotted off.

"So do I," Jake said to himself. "So do I."

Every few minutes, Jake looked back to check Matt's condition. When the boy finally woke up—nearly an hour after he'd fallen from the horse—Jake told him he'd have to work an extra half day to make up for this lazy afternoon nap. Matt, despite being drowsy and in obvious pain, chuckled at Jake's joke. He apologized repeatedly for causing so much trouble. "Pa is gonna be mighty upset," he said. "He's already got so much on his mind...."

Jake couldn't help but wonder if the pain in Matt's voice

was only due to his injuries or somewhat due to the distance Micah had put between himself and his sons. But the boy had lapsed back into unconsciousness before he could offer a word of assurance.

He'd been two years younger than the twins when his own parents had died. "Get down to the root cellar where you'll be safe," his father had ordered on that fateful day. "If I see your faces before I call for you, I'll tan your hides but good!"

Immediately, Jake had obeyed.

His mother had not. He'd never seen her cower at the sound of that deep, overpowering voice. So many times, he'd asked himself what she knew about his father that he didn't. What had she learned about the big man he so loved and respected that made her certain she could stoutly refuse to do as he'd instructed? Because on that day, if she'd gone with her son to the root cellar, as her husband had insisted, she'd have escaped the oncoming flames. More than likely, she'd be alive today, and so much about his own life would be different.

The thick wooden door of the root cellar had blocked out all light. All sound. Jake waited down there for hours in the dim glow of a single candle's flame, pacing the dirt floor as he'd waited for his father's signal—permission to exit.

Nearly half a day later, when Jake climbed up out of the sweet-smelling pit where he'd been surrounded by the dusty jars of peaches and beans and tomatoes that lined his mother's crude-built wood shelves, much of the smoke had already cleared.

There had been a prairie fire years earlier, and its hungry flames had greedily devoured the chicken coop and the hog pen before his pa got it under control. Remembering the destruction of that blaze, Jake ran for the house, yelling at the top of his lungs. "Ma! Pa!"

But no one had answered his call. Jake had balled up his

fists and fought the urge to cry. Turning round and round, the boy surveyed the silent, smoky world that had been his home.

Where the whitewashed barn had stood lay nothing but a pile of smoldering boards. The toolshed had become a blackened splotch on the earth. A small corner of the house had been spared, and young Jake had stepped through the rubble, carefully avoiding the tiny flames that still licked at table legs and bedding. "Mamma? Daddy?"

Hours later, his uncle had ridden in from town to investigate the ugly curls of dark smoke that churned above his brother's house and found Jake at the end of the drive, clutching his father's gold pocket watch to his chest. He'd wanted to say "'Tweren't my fault, Uncle Josh.'" He'd wanted to explain that he'd gone into the root cellar, as he'd been told. Wanted to say he'd found the watch where the kitchen used to be, and since it hadn't been permanently damaged, maybe, just maybe, if they dug around back there, they'd find his ma and pa in the same condition. He'd tried to tell them, but when he opened his mouth to speak, no sound issued forth. The doctor blamed his silence on smoke inhalation. But he'd wondered.

To this day, he wondered if one more pair of hands, fighting Mother Nature's fiery temper, would have made the difference between life and death for his parents? And even if he hadn't summoned the courage to leave the root cellar against his father's orders, could they have been there in the kitchen, buried under layers of wood and shingle? If he hadn't been so weak and cowardly, if he'd found his voice in time to tell them where to look, might his parents have been uncovered in time to save their lives?

Jake understood Matt's concern for his father, and heaped a little more contempt for himself onto the already heavy load of self-loathing he carried, because Matt, just two years older than Jake had been on the day of the fire, had put his concerns for his father ahead of his own fear and pain.

The boy woke, forcing Jake to shove the thorny thoughts aside as he groaned right along with Matt each time a bump in the road worried the broken leg or the injured arm.

It took nearly eight hours to get back to the manor house, and when at long last they arrived, Doc Hatfield, Bess, Mark and Micah were there to meet them. "You were smart not to try and splint these," Doc said once he'd inspected the boy's injuries. "That's a compound fracture he's got there. Repairing it is going to require some surgery."

Matt took a deep breath. "Surgery? Pa, do I really have to get an operation?"

Mark hovered in the background, wringing his hands. And Micah stood beside him, chewing his lower lip, seemingly unable to comfort his sons in any way.

Only Bess braved the sight of blood and exposed bone to step up close. She sat on the road beside her little brother, oblivious to the gravel and grit that soiled the pale-blue skirt of her dress. "Hush, now, Matthew," she crooned softly, patting his hand. "We're going to do whatever Doc says, 'cause he knows what's best, you hear?"

His big dark eyes swam with unshed tears of fear. "But Bess," he whimpered, "I'm scared to get cut...."

"Course you're scared, but there's no need to be." She leaned forward and pressed a gentle kiss upon his cheek. "Doc's scalpel won't do you near as much damage as I will if you don't lay back and keep quiet," Bess scolded gently, running her fingers through his dark, perspiration-dampened curls.

Her presence, her voice, her touch, seemed enough to calm him, and Matt nodded weakly. "Okay, Bess. Whatever you say."

Doc put a hand on her shoulder. "I'm going to need some help. Think you're up to it?"

Standing, Bess raised her chin and faced the doctor. "Just tell me what you need me to do."

His paternal, accepting smile said the doctor had known all along that she'd do whatever it took to help Matthew. "The dining room table will do nicely as an operating table," he said. "But it'll be dark soon. We're going to need light, and lots of it."

"Mark," she said, squeezing her other brother's hand, "round up every lantern you can find in the house and bring them into—"

"I'm on my way," the boy said before she could finish.

The doctor took off his suitcoat and draped it over a dining room chair. "I'll need bandages, and some hickory shakes will do for splints."

She lifted her skirt and started up the steps. "I've got a bureau drawer full of clean old sheets. I'll rip them into strips."

Doc looked at Matthew, pale and still, then turned his dark gaze to Micah's worried face. He led the father several yards away from the boy, who still lay limp and weak on the litter. "He's lost a lot of blood," he said, unbuttoning the cuffs of his shirt. "And there's a good chance infection has set in. I won't know what more I might find until I cut away the damaged tissue."

Micah's somber face paled. He ran both hands through his thinning, gray hair. "Will he..." He cleared his throat. "Will he lose the leg?"

"Not likely, but there are no guarantees, of course."

Micah glanced at his son. "He looks so young and helpless, lying there," he whispered, more to himself than to the doctor. "He will walk again, won't he?"

"Probably he'll be up and about and back to normal in a couple of months."

Micah shook his head. "Is there anything I can do, Doc?"

"Pray," said his friend. "Pray good and hard."

* * *

The makeshift operating room glowed bright with lamp-light.

Once she'd shoved all the chairs against the walls and drew the curtains, Bess covered the table with several thick, soft quilts, then draped line-dried sheets over them. After dipping Doc's surgical tools into boiling water, she placed each in order by size on the sheet-covered serving cart, which she'd rolled up beside the table.

She'd watched her mother assist once in delivering a baby when Doc performed a new technique known as a Cesarian section. He'd used dozens of rags to blot up the blood then; she presumed he'd need at least that many now. The old linen napkins in the buffet would do nicely, she decided, stacking the neatly folded squares near Doc's scalpels and clamps. Finally, a mountain of clean, white bandages, made by tearing bedsheets into strips, lay at the foot of the table.

Doc instructed Jake and Micah to position Matt on the table. They did, then stepped helplessly back into the shadows. Mark, still wringing his hands, stood between them.

"Get on out of here, all three of you," Doc bellowed. "Your sour faces are makin' me nervous." Pointing toward the door, he added, more gently, "We'll let you know when it's over."

They seemed almost too eager to obey, and immediately set to pacing back and forth across the front porch. Bess hoped they wouldn't keep it up for very long, because if the constant *thud thud thud* of boot heels striking wood distracted Doc like it distracted her—

She stormed to the front door and flung it open. "You boys take that pacing to the corral before you get Doc's hands to shakin' and he cuts something he didn't intend to!"

They were off the porch before the door closed behind her.

"This could get messy, Bess dear," Doc said when she returned. "You might want to protect your pretty frock."

She tucked in one corner of her mouth. "Since when have you known me to be afraid of a little mess?" she demanded, hands on her hips.

Smiling, the white-haired gent loosened his tie, rolled up his sleeves, and instructed Bess to copy his method of scrubbing up. Seeing this, Matt suspected what would happen next, and winced. Holding her now sterile hands aloft, Bess leaned over and kissed his forehead. "It's going to be fine, Matthew," she whispered. "It'll be all right."

"Promise?"

Winking, she forced a cheery, confident smile onto her face. "Promise," she said, kissing him again.

Doc dampened a cloth with a few drops of ether and draped it over Matt's nose and mouth. "Take a deep breath, Matthew," he said. "Start counting, backward, from one hundred."

"One hundred, ninety-nine, ninety-eight…"

Doc capped the small brown bottle and placed it on the table near Matt's head. "Every few minutes, put another drop on the cloth," he instructed Bess. "Not too much now, or he'll never regain consciousness."

Bess nervously licked her lips and nodded. Too little, and her brother would feel intense pain. Too much and—

"…ninety-four, ninety-three…" Matt's voice, slow and weak, waned. "Ninety-two, ninety-one…" By the time he got to ninety, he was sound asleep.

While she'd been comforting her brother, the doctor had fastened a tourniquet around the boy's thigh. "Doc, is that rawhide?"

"It is indeed," he said, pulling the last knot tight.

"But it's wet…."

He peered over his half glasses and frowned. "Yes?"

"When it dries, it'll be tighter still. Won't that hurt him even more?"

Straightening, the old man pursed his lips. "Yes. Yes, it could indeed." Shaking his head, he added, "But that's all I have to tie the—"

Bess lifted the hem of her skirt and began tearing the lacy ruffle from her petticoat.

"Surely we can find something else."

She branded him with a hard look. "Why should we waste time looking for something else when we have this, right at hand?"

Doc replaced the leather with cotton, then picked up a scalpel and said to his sleeping patient, "May God be with you," and made the first incision.

Two and a half hours later, Matt woke up in his own bed. He looked around woozily, blinked, and groaned. "Bess…?"

"I'm here, Matthew," she said, stroking his cheek. "I'm right here."

The boy winced. "It hurts, Bess."

"I'm sure it does." She reached for the bottle of tonic Doc had left on the bedside table, then guided a spoonful of the dark syrupy liquid between Matt's lips. "This will help some," she said, her thumb wiping away the drop that had escaped the corner of his mouth. "Go on back to sleep now, and you won't notice the pain so much."

He lifted his head and looked toward the foot of his bed. "Am I gonna be all right?"

Her heart lurched in her chest. Doc had explained every possibility. Matt's youth, the old man had said, was on his side. In all likelihood, the boy would recover. But…Matt could walk with a limp for the rest of his life, and infection, if indeed it had set in during the long ride home, might mean amputation sometime down the road.

Bess refused to think about that horrible possibility. "You're going to be fine, just fine."

He lay back, soothed by her promise, and closed his eyes.

Hoping her assurance rang with some truth, at least, Bess stood to leave.

Matt's eyes flew open. "Don't go, Bess," he pleaded, reaching for her hand.

She sat beside him on the bed and gently stroked his bandaged arm. "I'm here, sweet Matthew. I'm right here."

"Thanks, Bess," he murmured.

"I love you, Matthew," she answered.

He closed his eyes, and in moments, slept.

She didn't seem to notice the bloodstains on her favorite blue dress. Didn't seem to notice, either, that much of her dark hair had escaped the lovely braid she'd plaited that morning. Didn't seem to notice that her cheeks were streaked with sweat and her brother's blood.

But Jake noticed.

Only when she was sure that Matt slept soundly did she leave his side, and only then, to clean up the dining room. "Can't have Pa coming in here and seeing all this," she muttered, piling the bloodstained sheets and napkins and used bandages onto the serving cart. "It'll upset him no end." She seemed unaware that she was chattering like a chipmunk. "I'll just put these in a tub on the mud porch to soak," she added, scrubbing blood from the tabletop with one of the clean rags. "Tomorrow, once Matt's had a good night's sleep, I'll wash 'em up good and proper," she said, on her hands and knees now, wiping up the blood that had dripped from the table onto the wide-planked pine boards. She didn't hear the tremor in her voice. Didn't realize that her tears had mingled with Matt's blood on the floor.

When he couldn't stand to watch her suffering a moment longer, Jake grabbed her by the shoulders and brought her to her feet.

Immediately, she tried to drop back to her knees and resume scrubbing, but he held firm. "Bess," he said softly, "stop it. Stop your cryin', now."

She looked around the room helplessly. "But he's so young, Jake. And Doc said..." She bit her lip, then turned away from him, crossed her arms over her chest and cupped her elbows. "What if he...what if he never walks again?" She hesitated. Shook her head. "What if..."

He'd warned himself on his first day at Foggy Bottom to be careful. Even then, he'd known, somehow, that he could be drawn into relationships he couldn't afford to forge. And the proof of his rightness stood trembling in his arms now.

He'd never seen fear in her big dark eyes before. Had never seen that full lower lip quiver as she struggled to hold back her tears. She'd always been in complete control. Seeing her like this, looking so small and vulnerable, moved him like nothing ever had.

He'd have shifted heaven and earth at that moment to give her the solace she sought; to find the words to assure her that her little brother would be all right. But Jake had no such power, and he knew it. Why, he didn't even have the power to prove he hadn't killed a man!

Still, he didn't want *her* to know how weak and inept he was. So he held her tight and stroked her slender back and whispered softly into her ear. "He'll be fine. He'll be just fine."

"If he survives, he could have a limp for the rest of his life!"

Laying a hand against her cheek, he said, "I'd take on his limp, just to have a woman like you caring for me the way you care for that boy." He felt almost as helpless and useless as he had on the day of the fire.

In response to her wet-eyed silence, he added, "Doc said he'd likely be all right, didn't he?"

She nodded against his chest.

"And you trust Doc, don't you?"

Again she nodded, a little harder this time.

Jake could feel her warm tears seeping through the fabric of his shirt. He held her at arm's length and, for a moment, just looked at her. Her long, dark lashes clumped with glistening tears. With the pad of his thumb, he tenderly brushed the dampness away. He hated to see her this way, and searched his mind for a sentence, a phrase, a word, even, that would get her mind off Matt, even if only for a moment. "I don't suppose there's a slice of your famous cherry pie in the kitchen?"

She blinked, and the first hint of a smile tugged at the corners of her mouth. "I'm afraid you're too late for that." Still standing in the circle of his embrace, she brightened a little more, and added, "There's peach cobbler, though."

He didn't know what possessed him to do it, but without a second thought, Jake pressed a passionate kiss against her lips.

And much to his delight, Bess returned it.

Chapter Five

Almost from the moment he brought Matt home after the accident, Jake found himself spending a lot more time in the house than the rest of the hired hands. Though all of the men took evening meals at the Beckleys' dining room table, and felt at home in the parlor or lounging in the comfortable rockers on the front porch, none seemed so much a part of the family as Jake.

It had all started days after Matt's surgery, with Matt unable to get out of bed, even to bathe. Bess had tried to bustle in to get the job done; she hadn't given the matter a moment's thought, since she'd been mothering the boys since her own mother's death. Jake, who'd gone upstairs for his evening visit with Matt, had just stepped up to the bedroom door when the confrontation began.

"You can just put your old bar of soap right back where you got it," the boy insisted, tugging up his blanket in self-defense. "I'm fourteen years old, and I won't have my sister washin' where the sun don't shine!"

Bess rolled her eyes. "Well, you can't go the whole eight weeks of your recuperation without a proper bath!"

"I'd rather stink like one of Mr. Nick's hogs than have you see me buck naked."

Bess clucked her tongue and chuckled huskily. ''Why, that's just plain silly, Matt. I used to change your diapers and—''

He narrowed his eyes and scowled. ''That was when I was a baby, and couldn't defend myself. I'm nearly a man now, and—''

''Matthew, the longer you argue with me, the colder this water is getting,'' she scolded, thumping the rim of her wash pan.

''Doesn't matter if it's cold or hot, 'cause you're not bathin' me with it!'' Matt insisted.

She put the wash pan on the bedside table and propped her fists on her hips. ''There *will* be a bath, and if—''

''If Matt will let me,'' Jake interrupted, leaning on the door frame, ''I'll be glad to help him clean up.''

She'd looked at him with some surprise. ''You?''

Matt, grinning with relief, said, ''Yeah! Jake can do it!''

''Why would you want to do it?'' she asked Jake.

''I know how to rub down a horse after a hard day's ride, and what smells worse than horse sweat?''

Bess eyed Matthew slyly and crinkled her nose. ''My little brother, that's what,'' she answered, and neatly sidestepped the pillow Matt feebly tossed in response to her jibe.

As she remembered the scene, Bess grinned. Jake always seemed to show up, like the white knight in fairy tales, just in the nick of time. He'd bathed Matt that night, and every night afterward until the boy's arm healed enough to do the job himself.

Bess also remembered that when Matt finally seemed ready and able to begin the exercises Doc had prescribed to get his leg back into shape, it had been Jake's strong shoulder the boy had leaned on. When Doc said the time had come for Matt to get some fresh air, it was Jake who fashioned crude wooden crutches and taught the boy to use them, then walked slowly, patiently alongside Matt as he hobbled across the lawn. And when the boy seemed bored out of his skull from having nothing more physical than walking to do, it was Jake who taught him to play chess.

The men teased Jake mercilessly, their mocking falsettos calling him "Our hero!" But the serious tone behind their good-natured wisecracks rang true. Though she never told him so, he was *her* hero. Bess thanked God every morning and every night for him, for he'd saved Matt's *life*. And, he'd been the first person since Mary to offer her a moment of compassion or an instant of comfort…or to realize she needed either.

Bess thanked God for something else, too: finally, the boys had a man they could look up to.

Not that Micah didn't love his sons; Bess knew he'd have given his life for any one of his children if need be. But, since Mary's death, Micah had withdrawn from his sons and daughter, physically and emotionally. The man who had once showered his family with loving affection now seemed to believe that providing materially for them was enough.

She missed the man he'd been before Mary died. Fun-loving and kind, he'd had strong opinions—about everything—and didn't mind sharing them with anyone who'd listen.

With Mary at his side, Micah had been a man of un-bounded faith. Nothing worried or frightened him. Once, when a severe thunderstorm destroyed an entire corn crop, he's simply shrugged and said, "Well, thank God we had us a good potato crop this season." By comparison, just last week, when the skies over Foggy Bottom darkened, he paced from window to window, peering outside and sighing, stroking his gray beard. "What will become of us if those winds flatten the corn?"

Oh, he put on a mighty show for the farmhands, standing tall, strutting like a rooster, bellowing orders with the sure clear voice of a man in charge. But alone in the manor

house, where no one could witness his grief and misery—
except his only daughter—Micah's voice trembled with
doom and gloom.

Bess hoped the burden of grief would one day lift from
her father's shoulders. If only her pa would look around him,
he'd see he was surrounded by hundreds of things to be
thankful for. He had his own good health. The farm had
always been productive. The boys were healthy—why, even
Matt's injuries were healing faster than Doc had predicted—
and Bess had never suffered so much as an ingrown toenail.
His employees were honest and hardworking and devoted to
their boss. What more could he ask? Bess wondered time
and again.

She loved her father. But his behavior these past years
had been slowly chipping away at the respect and admiration
she'd felt for him while her mother was alive. Most of all,
she pitied Matt and Mark, for they needed a father who was
a pillar of strength, who could give them security, comfort,
and a man they could imitate as they grew from fine boys
into good men.

He hadn't been there for her, either. Take the night of
Matt's surgery, for example, when she'd been forced to assist Doc Hatfield and comfort Matt and Mark...and Micah,
too. If it hadn't been for Jake that night...

She'd stepped into Mary's shoes quite willingly. To say
it was difficult was beside the point. After all, Mary hadn't
chosen to leave them. And since her mother hadn't had a
choice, why should she?

Micah, on the other hand, *had* chosen to leave them. And
if the truth be told, his kind of leaving hurt far worse. There
wasn't a blessed thing anyone could do to bring Mary back,
but Micah...Micah was *alive!*

She resented his helplessness. Bess missed her mother,
too, yet her father's grief had forced her, to take on his
responsibilities in addition to Mary's. If Bess had refused to

assume those roles, bills would have gone unpaid, fields wouldn't have been plowed or seeded or harvested....

Many times, it took all the strength and self-control she could muster to keep from telling him, face-to-face, exactly what she thought of his self-pitying, hangdog ways. Ironically, Mary saved him even from that: "Your pa and me, we're just flesh and bone," she'd said, "and from time to time, we'll make mistakes, some of them big ones. When we do, it'll test your mettle, Bess my love, because that's when you'll find it hardest to treat us with respect."

Bess sighed deeply and set aside her exasperation toward her father. Her mother had been right, after all; Bess reminded herself that the Fourth Commandment didn't say "Honor thy father and thy mother *if* they deserve it."

She'd all but given up hope on Micah. And then Jake came along.

Bess sat in her window seat and stared into the darkened yard. A wistful smile on her face, she hugged the candlewicked pillow to her chest and sighed. Yes, she'd given "I love Jake" a thought or two, but she'd quickly dismissed the feelings as a silly, immature infatuation. Too many people depended on her, needed her, and she had neither the time nor the inclination for romance.

At least, that had been true in the past.

Jake's kiss had changed all that.

Bess put her fingertips to her lips and closed her eyes. Her heart swelled as she remembered the way his mouth lightly grazed her chin, her cheeks, her mouth. The way his big strong arms wrapped around her, gathered her close, made her feel safe and warm...and womanly.

If a man as handsome and available as Jake took a romantic interest in her, why, maybe she wasn't so plain and unattractive after all! She'd waved away such thoughts in the past, telling herself that vanity had put them into her head in the first place.

Surrounded by the steady strength of his embrace, he'd told her, without words, that it was all right to need others, at least once in a while, to take occasionally, instead of always giving. All these years, she'd been the family's sole source of strength. In all that time, she hadn't allowed herself to express fear, or worry or sadness. How could she cry over typical girlish concerns when it had become her responsibility to be mother, father and friend to her brothers…and Micah's rock as well!

Bess believed that when Jake wrapped her in that sheltering hug, he'd said in his quiet cowboy way that he loved her.

She remembered the Widow Reddick's advice, and now freely admitted how very ready she was to be loved.

Jake was a man who'd spent most of his adult life out of doors, so the long hours he spent under-roof, visiting with Bess and her brothers, had been hard for him at first. But each passing hour by her side felt more comfortable to him, until it seemed he couldn't stay away from the house.

Though he truly enjoyed playing checkers and chess with Matt and Mark, Jake had to admit the real reason he spent so much time inside the manor house: Bess.

He thought of her day and night. And that surprised him, because though he'd courted a few women in his ten years on the run, he'd never felt even the faintest stirrings of emotional involvement toward even one of them.

Jake remembered how he'd occasionally donned white shirt and black string tie, and escorted the prim and proper daughters of wealthy ranchers to fancy parties. He'd courted town girls in practically every city he'd visited. Spooned with the flirty girlfriends of other ranch hands. Why, he'd even bedded a few. But only if they'd invited him to, and only with the understanding he'd soon be on his way….

He'd lived on the edge because he believed that someday,

he'd die on the edge. Jake saw no reason to steal a woman's heart, saw even less reason to give his own. Because sooner or later, he'd have to say goodbye.

He resigned himself to a life alone. It got easier and easier to stick to his self-imposed rule as he watched frail little women make big strong men behave like well-trained lapdogs. If a gal set her sights on a trinket or a bauble, he wondered, why didn't she just come right out and ask for it, instead of pouting and crying until she got what she wanted? If her man did something to rile her, why didn't she just point-blank tell him what he'd done, instead of punishing him with the silent treatment until he puzzled it out?

There were scores of questions about life that he'd likely never figure out, but the only thing he *did* understand about women was that all the way back to the days of Adam and Eve, they'd been troublemakers, liars, users. That's what he'd believed....

Until Bess.

Pretty and petite, she could have used her gender and diminutive size as a shelter from hard work. Instead, she challenged her curvy little body to perform chores that would have given most men pause. She didn't flutter her long, thick lashes and giggle to gain attention. Rather, Bess let the importance of what she had to say command the notice it deserved. He'd seen plenty of girls leap onto chair seats or hide behind their boyfriends at the sight of a field mouse. Not Bess. She'd grab a broom or a mop and chase the furry critter outside with a stern warning that if she caught sight of its wooly little butt in her kitchen again, it'd be mashed flatter than a griddle cake.

She laughed easily and ate heartily. And the only time he'd ever seen her cry had been the night of Matt's accident. Even then, she'd been embarrassed that he'd seen her tears, and apologized profusely for them, as though they'd been a symbol of some great character flaw.

When he pulled her near that night, he'd wanted to say something to soothe her ragged nerves. Wanted to assure her that her brother would be all right. Wanted to promise nothing bad would ever touch her life again, not if *he* had anything to say about it. But, frustrated by his inability to express what he felt, Jake could only hold her tighter, hoping to let her know with his actions—since his words had failed him so miserably—that he'd be there for her any time she needed him.

When she melted against him, her tears dampening his shirt, she'd moved him as nothing ever had. She had always seemed so strong and secure and sure of herself, so her sudden vulnerability touched him deeply. *That's* why he'd kissed her, he told himself later.

But deep in his heart, the truth lived…and grew.

He'd kissed her because he'd *wanted* to. And he knew that he'd *been* wanting to kiss her since the first time he set eyes on her. And, if he was honest with himself, he'd done it because he'd needed to.

She was a remarkable woman, all right. She'd been mother and father to Matt and Mark. She'd kept Foggy Bottom running, almost single-handedly. She'd done all the womanly chores anyone could have expected of her, plus a few most tried to foist on their menfolk. Beautiful and talented and honest, she'd somehow remained untouched by life's viciousness.

Bess was sweeter than any woman he'd ever known. She made him feel smart and important, decent and *good*. He liked the way he felt around her.

Liked the way she felt in his arms, too, because while other women had made him feel virile, he'd never before felt *wanted;* others had made him feel lust, and Bess made him feel *loved*. If he didn't have a death sentence hanging over his head, he'd ask her to marry him, right now!

That's why it had been a bad idea to take her in his arms,

an even bigger mistake to kiss her. Having her that close felt so right, and so very good.

Yes. Kissing her had probably been the stupidest thing he'd done in ten years.

Because now that he'd had a taste of what real love could feel like, it would be hard, real hard, to leave it behind.

Chapter Six

For weeks now, Jake had been listening to Bess complaining that her pantry supplies were low. One night, out of the blue, she announced that first thing next morning, she'd be heading into Baltimore to restock the dry goods.

As it happened, Micah had asked Jake to ride into town to pick up Bess's surprise birthday present. But over supper that evening, it was Micah who surprised them all. "Take Jake with you," the old man told his daughter.

Bess had nearly come clean out of her chair. She'd been to town dozens of times, Bess had pointed out, and had never needed a chaperone before!

"You'll take Jake with you or you won't go at all!" he'd said, his voice uncharactersitically stern. Softening a bit, he'd added, "The bigger that city gets, the more dangerous it becomes."

Bess stifled any further protestations, but Jake could tell she hadn't done it willingly.

Now, as he rode beside her in the wagon, Jake wondered how long it would be before Bess registered her objections aloud.

Less than ten minutes into their five-hour journey, Bess said, "I really don't understand Pa's attitude. I've gone to

Baltimore plenty of times, all by myself. It's insulting, that's what it is, the way he made me take a chaperone along.''

"He's just looking out for you, Bess," Jake said without taking his eyes from the road. "Can't say as I blame him. If you were my—"

"Well, I'm not your daughter," she interrupted.

He looked at her then, a wry smile sparkling in his blue eyes. "I was about to say," he continued calmly, "if you were my woman, you wouldn't go *anywhere* alone."

If you were my woman, he'd said. She liked the sound of that, and grinned. "Why wouldn't you let me go anywhere alone? Do you see me as a needy, helpless female?"

Jake focused on the team. "Needy and helpless? *You?*" He chuckled. "Hardly."

His sideways flattery made her sit up a little straighter, but she decided it was time to change the subject. "Matt's doing well, don't you think?"

Jake nodded his agreement. "That boy's bound and determined to be fully mended before the harvest." His eyes met hers again. "I reckon stubbornness runs in your family."

She smiled. "I'll just take that as a compliment, Jake Walker."

He'd been wearing the name for ten long years, yet he still bristled every time he heard it. Jake wondered what the proper and pretty Miss Bess Beckley would think if he told her he'd been convicted of murder. If he told her a jury had decided he should swing for the crime. If he told her he'd been on the run for ten long years, changing towns like most folks changed socks, always looking over his shoulder for the next U.S. Marshal or the next bounty hunter.

He believed he could predict her reaction. Her big dark eyes would widen with disbelief and fear. She'd gasp with surprise. Those strong yet delicate hands would fly protectively to her throat. Then she'd lick those full pink lips of hers, throw back her slender shoulders, saying, in effect, that she wasn't the least bit afraid of him, a convicted killer. Not Bess Beckley!

He wanted to hug her for that.

Several minutes ticked by, and neither of them said a word.

"Why so quiet all of a sudden?" she asked.

He tugged at the brim of his hat, bringing it to rest lower on his forehead. "Guess I just don't feel much like talkin'."

From the corner of his eye, he saw her stiffen in response to his gruffer-than-intended response, as if to say, "Well fine, then, if it's silence you want, it's silence you'll get!" Jake breathed a sigh of relief.

She folded her hands primly in her lap, held her head high, and stared straight ahead. Try as she might, Bess did not understand this man. He angered and aroused and frightened her, all at the same time. She wondered for the hundredth time what horrible secret he hid, and if, when exposed, it would explain his quicksilver mood swings. So lost in thought was she that Bess never noticed he'd increased the horses' pace.

Jake was deep in thoughts of his own. He hadn't meant to hurt her feelings. But then, he hadn't meant to let himself get this fond of her, either. Jake remembered how helpless he'd felt when the jurors made their decision. He didn't have much left at that point, but at least he'd managed to stay in full control of his emotions through it all. He never begged for mercy, even when the judge's gavel slammed hard on the bench and sealed his fate. Never whimpered, even as they shackled and chained him like a rabid dog in the smelly jail wagon. Never shed a tear, though he knew his young life was about to end. The way he saw it, he had all eternity to cry about the unfairness of it. He'd show those so-called good Christians what pride and dignity were all about!

So why couldn't he control his feelings for Bess?

For the next two hours, the silence was broken only by the *clip-clop* of the horses' hooves and the crunch of road grit beneath the wagon's huge iron-rimmed wheels. Now and then, as they passed a clump of trees or a thicket, they heard bugs buzzing and birds chirping.

Several times, he opened his mouth and took a breath, thinking maybe he'd say the first thing that came into his head, to get things back on track. But, just as quickly, he'd clamp his teeth together. If he didn't know what had gotten them *off* track, how in the hell did he expect to get them back *on* again?

Besides, in this frame of mind, he didn't dare start bumping his gums. Dozens of times, he'd seen her zero in on the only sad face in a room full of people. She not only knew how to find out what caused the sour expression, but managed to say exactly the right thing to sweeten it, too. *Nope,* he told himself, *in this mood, you're better off stayin' mum.*

Begrudgingly, he admitted it had taken every bit of strength to keep his past a secret from her this long. He yearned for some of the peace and comfort others seemed to take from her caring concern. Why, if he had a penny for every time he'd nearly spilled his guts during one of their long, friendly conversations, he'd have a couple of extra dollars in his pocket for sure.

He wasn't accustomed to admitting fear, but this strange power Bess seemed to have over him scared him, and Jake didn't like it one bit.

Suddenly, he was distracted by her rummaging in her black velvet drawstring purse, angrily mumbling under her breath…something about a place for everything and everything in its place? He dared not ask her to repeat what she'd said.

After a moment, she pulled a pocket watch from the bag. He heard her cluck her tongue, then heard the watch case pop open. "It's nearly eleven," she said, snapping the gold case shut. "Hungry?"

Slowly, Jake faced her. "I could eat, I reckon," he said, shrugging as he returned his attention to the horses.

"That's not what I asked, Mr. Man-of-Few-Words."

With that, he looked her square in the eye. It surprised him to see the wide, friendly smile on her face. Surprised him even more that he was smiling back, despite his foul mood. "Yeah, I'm hungry."

A note of disappointment rang in his heart as she bent to retrieve the wicker basket at her feet, because in doing so, she'd deprived him of looking into her eyes. *A man could drown in those big brown eyes,* he'd told himself on more than one occasion. *And you'd best be careful, Jake ole boy, 'cause you've never been a particularly strong swimmer.*

She peeled back the red-checkered tablecloth that lined the wicker basket. "Fried chicken. Corn muffins. Apples." She met his eyes to add, "And lemonade, but it's warm, I'm afraid."

And why not warm lemonade? he wondered. It would go perfectly with his warm cheeks. His warm palms. The warm sensation that swirled from deep in his chest to his gut to his groin every time she cut a glance in his direction.

"Shall we stop, or do you think we should eat as we go?"

He couldn't think of anything he'd like better than to curl up on a blanket with her under some big ole shade tree. But they had a good two hours' ride ahead of them yet, and at least an hours' worth of business to tend to once they got to Baltimore. If they stopped now, even for half an hour or so, it'd be dark before they got back to Foggy Bottom. And he didn't want to risk driving the team along these ruddy roads on a moonless night. Not with Bess's birthday surprise from Micah lashed to the back of the wagon.

After handing him a golden-fried chicken leg, Bess

grabbed the reins. "I'll drive while you eat," she said, matter-of-factly. "We'll make better time if we take turns."

She looked straight ahead as she spoke, and he marveled at her ability to read his mind. Marveled at her ability to control the team, too. Jake took a bite of a crisp drumstick. He hadn't quite finished it when she handed him a corn muffin. Just before he polished that off, she gave him a shiny red apple. Bess seemed to enjoy waiting on him, doing for him, taking care of him. *A man could get used to this kind of pampering,* he said to himself, grinning.

His bad mood disappeared as quickly as the warm lemonade.

He dropped her off at the bank and promised to return for her in an hour. Her birthday surprise, Micah had confided to Jake, was a player piano. According to the bill of sale, it would be waiting for him on Dock C at the Baltimore harbor. "Just look for the biggest crate there," Micah had said, slapping Jake's back. Sure enough, a huge wooden box labeled Beckley stood just inside the warehouse door.

As Jake steered the wagon as close to the opening as possible, he noticed a big man leaning against a piling on the pier nearby, frowning at him from beneath a dingy sailor's cap. "Don't mean to bore holes through ya," he said, squinting through the blue-grey haze of cigar smoke, "I'm just tryin' to recollect why you look so familiar."

Jake didn't have to figure out why he looked familiar to the man—last time he'd seen that ruddy face, it had been unconscious on a deserted road just outside of Lubbock.

Climbing down from the wagon seat, he pulled his hat low on his forehead, walked a wide circle around the former deputy, and handed the bill of sale to the warehouseman. "I'll give you a hand getting that monster into the wagon," he said, grinning and gesturing toward the crate. He tried hard to sound jovial and matter-of-fact, like a man who'd simply come here to pick up his piano...like a man with nothing to hide.

The foreman followed Jake's gaze. "Yep. Gonna take a couple of strong backs to load that one," he agreed jovially. "Jasper," he hollered into the bowels of the musty warehouse, "get your sorry ass out here an' help us, why don't ya?"

Jasper, wiping his hands on a grimy rag when he rounded the corner, took his time crossing the dusty floor. "What's in the box?" he wanted to know.

"None o' your bu'iness," his boss said. "Just grab that cart over there and let's get the beast loaded."

Jasper seemed in no hurry to wrench his back, and took his time delivering the metal-wheeled skid. Jake pretended he'd forgotten all about the ex-jailer, and focused on Jasper. On Jasper's boss. On the boxed piano. But he couldn't help wondering what Yonker was doing so far from Texas. Couldn't help wondering what would happen if the man should remember who he was....

Jake and the dock workers slid the huge crate onto the skid, then rolled it up a makeshift ramp into the wagon. Half an hour later, after a fair amount of huffing and grunting, the piano was safely secured to the wagon and ready for its long ride back to Foggy Bottom. Jake shook each man's hand and thanked them for their help, then climbed back into the driver's seat and breathed a sigh of relief. He thought for sure the Texan would put two and two together, but it seemed he'd been spared—this time.

He released the brake stick, and just as he prepared to flap the reins to spur the team forward, the big man sidled up to the wagon. Jake held his breath. His heartbeat doubled and his palms grew damp as he waited for the inevitable to begin.

"I'd recognize a Texas drawl anywhere."

Jake swallowed hard.

The ex-jailer laid his hand on the brake stick and stared, as if trying hard to remember.

Jake licked his lips. "I'm from Texas, you've got that much right," he said, smiling nervously. "Jake Walker," he said, extending his hand. "Don't run into many folks from back home way out here," he added, increasing his drawl.

"Where you from in Texas?" Yonker asked, suspicion glinting from his dark beady eyes.

"Eagle Flats," Jake lied smoothly, withdrawing his still unshaken hand. "Little town just—"

"—east of the Mexican border," Yonker finished, as if to brag he knew the big state like the back of his hand.

Jake nodded. "You?"

"Lubbock." Warning and danger mingled in his deep, gravelly voice. He spat a stinking wet wad of tobacco onto the dusty dock and put a finger to the corner of his mouth to dam up the black liquid oozing from the chaw of tobacco bulging from his cheek. "I gotta tell you…you're the spittin' image of a man we tried to hang back there."

Jasper whistled. "Hang? For what?"

"Because he was a mangy, no-good dog," Yonker answered. "Jail wagon overturned on the way to the gallows, and the polecat ran off and left us out there to die in that heat."

But he hadn't left them to die; he'd left them with two full canteens!

"We lost our jobs for lettin' him get away. Why, I been huntin' him for more'n ten years now. If there weren't a fat reward for draggin' his sorry bones back to Texas, I'd hang him myself, wherever I found him."

The ex-deputy grabbed a coil of rope, hanging from a piling on the dock, and swaggered toward Jake. "I bet that bounty has doubled by now," he said, forming a lasso with the rope. "I bet I'll be a hero when I bring in W. C. Atwood.'' The Texan's harsh laughter echoed, then faded, into the deep, dark bowels of the open warehouse.

Jake had been wrongly accused of murder, and it had altered the course of his entire life. He'd hated running from the law all these years, because running had made him look guilty as sin. But he hated the idea of dying for a crime he hadn't committed even more. In one moment, he wondered if he hated it all enough to kill this man, if it came to that, to guarantee he could continue to live his life…miserable as it was.

In the next moment, he had his answer.

He would.

The guard doubled up his fist. ''Y'can't fool me, At-wood,'' he growled, reaching for Jake's shirt.

''I don't know what you're yammerin' abo—''

''Get your sorry ass down here so I can hog-tie y—''

''You don't wanna do that,'' Jake warned, his eyes mere slits, his voice dangerously low as he grabbed Yonker's wrist.

''Why, you low-down back-shooter,'' he said malevolently, grabbing Jake's neckerchief.

''I never shot a man—not even in self-defense, not here, not in Lubbock.'' He increased the pressure on the deputy's wrist. ''But if I did,'' he snarled, glaring into the man's fear-widened eyes, ''a man like you'd be smart to watch his *own* back, don't you reckon?''

Jasper had summoned a constable at the first signs of a fight. ''What's goin' on here?'' the officer demanded. Sun glinted from the polished brass buttons of his dark-blue jacket.

''This here fella is a killer,'' the Texan growled. ''Been on the run fer ten years.'' Facing Jake, he repeated, ''You're W. C. Atwood, and you killed Horace Pickett in Lubbock. And if you laid the wanted posters with your face on 'em end to end, you could walk on 'em, all the way back to

Texas. You *deserve* to swing." Without breaking eye contact with Jake, he told the policeman, "The Texas Rangers *and* the U.S. Marshals will back up my story. Just wire the sheriff in Lubbock if you don't believe me."

"That's the smartest thing anybody has said so far."

At the sound of her soft, musical voice, every man's head turned toward Bess. How long had she been there? Jake wondered. How much had she seen...and heard?

She faced the uniformed officer and, hands on her hips, said, "This appears to be a clear-cut case of mistaken identity. If a telegram will clear the entire matter up, then I think we should send it." She glared at the dirty, burly Texan and added, "Immediately."

She turned to Jake. "Well, have you done what Pa told you to do?" she asked, forcing a bossy, sassy tone into her voice. Without waiting for his response, she rolled her big eyes at the officer. "Good help is *so* hard to find these days." She smoothed her skirts and daintily tugged at her high, lacy collar. "He was supposed to come down here to fetch a delivery for my father, not pick a fight with the likes of *him*," she said, her voice icy and deliberately haughty. Suddenly, Bess was all sweetness and light again. "Do you know my father?" she asked the policeman. "Micah Beckley?"

The constable stood a little taller in response to what appeared to be blatant flirtation from the pretty young woman. "Course I do, miss," he said. Then, with a jerk of his thumb, he gestured toward Jake. "You say this man works for your daddy?"

With a tired sigh, she nodded. "He's worked for my father for years...since he was practically a boy."

The Texan began to protest.

"He's from Texas, I'll give you that much." And cutting a glare in the deputy's direction, she added, "He never managed to lose that low accent, I'm afraid."

A moment of tense silence passed before she said, "Well then, shall we head on over to the telegraph office?" she suggested. "I'd like to get home before dark, and that'll never happen if we stand here bickering like children all afternoon."

"That won't be necessary, Miss Beckley." The constable removed his high-domed hat and tucked it under one arm. Then, grinning, he added, "It is *miss,* isn't it?"

Bess smiled and fluttered her long, dark lashes. "Why, yes, it is. But please, it's Bess. Just plain Bess." She avoided looking at Jake's eyes when she said it, but could see by the way he shook his head that, despite the heat of the moment, he, too, remembered how he'd teased her on his first day at Foggy Bottom.

The policeman blushed and grinned and twirled his night-stick.

She stepped up to him and hid her mouth behind a white-gloved hand. "I don't want that filthy man bothering my foreman for another moment," she whispered. "It's hard enough to get an honest day's work out of him without a lot of unnecessary distractions."

The officer glared at the Texan. "I don't recall seein' you in town before."

The beer-bellied ex-deputy retrieved his cap, slapped it against his thigh a time or two to shake off the dust, then plopped it onto his head. He pointed to a ship, docked a few piers down in the harbor. "I'm a merchant marine, takin' a tour of your fine city, officer. That's all." Then, almost as an afterthought, he tensed. "Hey, why are y'all treatin' *me* like the criminal. *I'm* not the one who was s'posed to hang for murder."

"Hang? *Murder?*" Bess echoed, her voice trembling almost as much as the hand pressing against her forehead. "I'm afraid all this shouting and violence makes me feel as if I'm going to swoon...."

The constable was beside her in an instant, one arm around her slender waist, one hand supporting her elbow. "You're upsetting the lady," he growled at the Texan. "Now, get on out of here, or you're gonna get a tour all right—of the inside of the Baltimore jail!"

As he lumbered toward his ship, the Texan leaned close to Jake and rasped through clenched tobacco-stained teeth, "Keep your back to the wall, Atwood, 'cause one of these days…"

Splinters of steel glinted in Jake's eyes, but he said nothing.

Bess didn't know what had been said during the quick, heated exchange between the men, but Jake's narrowed, hateful glare frightened her more than she cared to admit.

She had waited for him in front of the bank for ten minutes, and couldn't imagine what could be taking him so long. It was a beautiful, breezy day, and since it was only a short distance from the bank to the harbor, Bess decided to walk to the dock and save him having to steer the wagon back through the bustling city streets.

She'd heard the unmistakable sounds of an impending fistfight long before she saw it. Worse, she'd heard that horrible man say, "You're Walker Atwood, and you killed Horace Pickett in Lubbock."

The man insisted Jake looked like the fellow he'd been hunting for…for ten years, and Jake had been away from Texas…for ten years. Mistaken identity? Coincidence? Bess didn't think so.

It was going to be a long ride back to Foggy Bottom, that much was certain.

She thanked the officer for his assistance as Jake helped her onto the wagon seat. They rode in silence toward the main road, and she couldn't help but notice that Jake hadn't looked her in the eye once since she'd arrived on the dock. Just as well, she told herself. After Bess had seen the way he'd looked at that Texan, she didn't know what she'd do if he aimed the murderous glare in her direction.

She wondered when he'd explain himself—*if* he'd explain himself. As they rode along, she thought about all the odd and peculiar things that made up this man named Jake Walker—or was it Walker Atwood? The sullen silences. The distant, forlorn expressions. The unexplainable mood swings. That occasionally frightening, angry look in his eyes.

Suddenly, she felt very far from home. Very alone, and very unprotected. Bess wondered if she'd done the right thing in helping him out of that mess. After what she'd witnessed there on the dock, she honestly didn't know what to think anymore.

So she prayed.

She prayed she'd been right when she told herself something good and decent lived inside this man.

Mostly, though, she prayed she hadn't made the worst mistake of her life when she allowed herself to fall in love with him.

Chapter Seven

Bess couldn't get the scene on the dock out of her mind.

Jake's dark, malevolent look had been frightening, as if he had it in him to kill the Texan.

If that man had been telling the truth, Jake had *already* taken a human life. Was he capable of such fury?

She sat quietly beside him on the wagon seat, fiddling with the drawstring on her purse, wishing he'd fill the uncomfortable stillness between them with some explanation of what she'd seen and heard.

Bess didn't like rumors. An individual's privacy, she'd always insisted, must be respected. On more than one occasion, she'd scolded acquaintances—young females, usually—for passing along tidbits of hearsay they'd acquired. But the look on Jake's face when confronted by that awful man… How could she keep this to herself?

Telling her father and brothers wouldn't be gossip. In fact, didn't she owe it to everyone at Foggy Bottom to let them know that a dangerous man could be living among them, a man who may very well be a convicted murderer?

Bess shook her head. The idea was ridiculous enough to be laughable. He'd been so gentle with Matt. So gentle with *her. No!* she insisted. *It can't be true!*

Then that look of his came to mind again, that rough-tough expression that lifted his mouth in a vicious snarl and turned his blue-eyed gaze hard and mean.

If it were true, she told herself, then surely he had a good reason to kill the man. Perhaps it had been in self-defense. Or maybe he'd been defending a woman's honor. Had he interrupted a robbery?

Despite the goodness she saw in Jake, her mind conjured that venomous glare, the deadly stance that gave him the appearance, at least, of a man who was capable of savagery.

She felt the hard hammering of her heart and the rush of blood pounding at every pulse point. Biting down on her lower lip, Bess fought the thoughts that flit through her brain. Why not just *ask* him!

As if on cue, Jake cleared his throat. Startled, Bess chanced a peek in his direction. The sun, dappling through birch and willow branches that umbrellaed Oakland Road, slanted across his face. Her stomach fluttered with an odd mix of fear and fondness, and she forced herself to look instead at the wild roses growing alongside the road.

But neither the delicate scent nor the velvety petals could distract her from his presence, for in that quick glance, she'd seen far more than his worry-rumpled brow and tension-clenched jaw. She'd also taken note of shining waves that poked out from under his wide-brimmed hat. The manly curve of his aquiline nose. Lush black lashes and high, angular cheekbones.

He leaned forward, rested his elbows on his knees, causing the fabric of his blue cotton shirt to tighten over his bulging biceps, one powerful hand coming to rest on his meaty thigh as the other casually held the reins that controlled the big, creaking wagon. That same hand that had gently brushed the hair back from her forehead after Doc left that night…and tenderly pressed her own to his cheek, as if sensing that her tears would not be quieted or comforted with mere words.

Those were the hands that had built a makeshift litter for Matthew. She could almost picture him, gently laying her little brother onto it, and just as gently draping a blanket over the boy.

And those were the hands that had hovered so near the Texan's throat just hours ago on the Baltimore dock.

Could those same hands have *killed?*

Now she heard him sigh, a long, lingering inhalation that wrapped round her like the hauntingly sad notes of the whip-poorwill's song. Bess glanced over just in time to see him run the tip of his tongue over his full, almost-pouting lips.

Those soft lips had touched hers that night, fanning the flickering flame that had sparked the moment she'd first seen him. It was Bess who sighed now, because, try as she might, she could not remember a single moment with any man that could even begin to compare to—

You're behaving like a silly schoolgirl, she chided, *thinking about a kiss when you could be sitting beside a cold-blooded murderer!*

Bess took a deep breath, gave a little nod of her head. *Well,* she admitted, *the kiss is a far more pleasant memory than that scene on the dock!*

Exhaling slowly, Bess slipped off her gloves, one white-cottoned finger at a time, and stuffed them into her purse. She removed her hat, too, and tucked it under the wagon seat. She should have taken more care to put it in a safe corner, folding the broad satin ribbon inside the bonnet to prevent wrinkles. But her mind couldn't have been farther from proper headwear care.

A strange thought began pinging in her mind: What about Jake? *Surely he's been with a woman in a…in an intimate way. Why, if it's true that he's been on the run for ten years, it's entirely possible he's been with dozens of women.*

Immediately, Bess suppressed the angry, envious mood awakened by the picture of Jake in the arms of another woman. *What in God's name are you doing?* she demanded of herself. *How can you be thinking such thoughts, when that awful man on the docks all but accused Jake of…of murder?*

She rubbed her eyes, hoping to destroy the image of him, standing there on the dock, fists clenched, facing his opponent. Nothing *but* murderous thoughts could have turned his warm blue eyes cold as ice. Nothing *but* deadly deeds could have changed his cool, detached grin into an vile and vicious scowl.

Immediately, Bess blinked away the ugly sight. Without turning her head, she looked at the flesh and blood man beside her.

Without turning her head, she looked at him again. He sat tall and straight now, blond brows drawn together in a serious frown, the muscles of his broad jaw clenching and unclenching, the reins wrapped so tightly around his big hands that the leather seemed part of his bronzed skin.

Suddenly, Bess felt an incredible urge to cry—not tears of fear, for something deep inside told her Jake would never harm her—but tears of sadness. She didn't want to believe he'd committed a crime, especially one so heinous as *murder.* But it went far deeper than that, far deeper: Bess didn't want to believe that falling in love with him had been a mistake.

It's your own fault that you feel this way, she scolded herself. *If you'd stuck to your plan—never to fall in love, never to wish for marriage—you wouldn't be sitting here now feeling…*

Exactly what *did* she feel?

A little angry, for one thing, that Jake seemed to have no intention of telling her what the fight on the dock had been all about. They'd been on the buckboard for hours now; if

Jake had intended to tell her, wouldn't he have done it by now? Hurt, too, that his silence meant he didn't trust her enough to tell her the truth about his past. And that evoked a sadness, an incredible, unmeasurable sadness.

Mostly, though, she was afraid. About as afraid as she'd ever been in her life.

Because *if* the filthy Texan hadn't been mistaken—or lying—if Jake had been convicted of the murder and sentenced to hang for it, her dreams of a future with him would remain just that. And the mere thought of losing him, even for a reason like that, woke an ache inside her that she'd thought long buried, a pain as cutting and as deep as Mary's death had caused.

Almost immediately, grief became guilt. How could she sit there and compare what she felt about this man she barely knew with the feelings of loss she'd experienced when her mother died! *Get hold of yourself, Bess, and do the right thing. Confront him, and force him to explain what happened back there.*

The huge box on the wagon bed shifted, groaning slightly as Jake guided the horses around a soft bend in the road. It reminded her how, even before he'd even climbed up onto the wagon seat beside her, she'd asked him what had been housed in the mammoth container. He'd said he didn't know what was in the box. But that hadn't been the truth; she could tell because his pupils had constricted and his lips had thinned, just the way Matt and Mark's always did when she caught them in a fib.

The knowledge that she'd be able to tell if he ever told her another fib...or an outright lie...lifted her sagging spirits a bit. She *would* confront him about what had gone on back there on the dock. *And while you're digging for information,* she thought, grinning, *you may as well see if you can get him to tell you what's in that blasted crate!*

Several more moments passed in total silence before Bess took a deep breath.

"Thanks for taking my part back there," he said.

The time was ripe. "We both know you owe me an explanation. I won't feel better until you do."

He'd just *chick-chicked* to quicken the horses' pace. Her question seemed to hit him like a bolt, and his hands froze in midair. Jake cocked his head and gave her a halfhearted grin. "Feel better?" Raising one blond brow, he added, "About what?"

After another exasperated sigh, she said, "About what that awful man said, of course."

She probably wouldn't have said "spit and vomit" with as much disdain in her voice as she'd said "that awful man." Jake had only known her for three months, but in that short time, if he hadn't learned anything else about Bess, he'd learned this: for all her stubborn determination to appear in charge and tough, she was more sensitive and tenderhearted than anyone he'd ever known. He knew the almost-brawl had troubled her...scared her, even....

"That man threatened you," she was saying. "He said—"

"That man," Jake interrupted, "doesn't know what in Sam Hill he's talking about!" He said it with such ferocity that Bess drew back slightly. Immediately, he regretted his harshness. "That man is nothing but a drunken sailor, spewing a lot of horse manure."

She flexed her hands. Smoothed her skirt. Tucked a loose tendril of hair behind her ear. "You don't really expect me to believe all that fuss and bother was nothing more than a case of mistaken identity...."

This woman could never play poker, he thought.

Bess ignored his quiet chuckle. What should have been a rapid-fire inquisition never happened. She sat back and stared straight ahead, one dainty finger tapping lightly on her knee. "So you're saying he *was* mistaken, then? He's got you confused with some *other* fellow from Lubbock…a fellow who killed a man and escaped before they could hang him for it."

Ordinarily, her straightforward way of putting things was admirable. For a reason he couldn't explain, the way she'd put *that* unnerved him more than he cared to admit.

As they'd left the docks, Jake told himself if she didn't ask about what happened, he wouldn't volunteer any information. But a nagging voice inside him kept saying, *You know better than that, Jake ole boy.* The only surprise, really, was that she'd waited this long to ask the question. He'd known full well that, as she sat there beside him, fidgeting with her purse and fiddling with her hat, she'd been reliving the scene, word for word. And he'd known why, too.

Bess didn't want to believe he'd done anything so contemptible as to take a man's life. It was part of her character to look for even the dimmest glimmer of good in every situation, in every person; her sighs, the shoulder shrugging, the nervous toe tapping, Jake realized, were evidence that she was building a case, a defense of sorts, to excuse what he'd done…if indeed he'd done it.

Too bad you weren't in the courtroom that day, Bess! he told her silently. *Things might have turned out a mite better if you'd been on my side.…*

That voice in his head had saved his hide a time or two on the trail because he'd had the good sense to heed it. He should have listened to it earlier. Because if he had, he'd have had the good sense to come up with an explanation that would ease her mind and soothe her fears. Not knowing for sure if he'd killed a man or not was driving her to distraction.

"Well…?" she said, interrupting his reverie.

Part of him wanted to stop the wagon, right there in the

middle of the road, tell her the whole damned story. She deserved to hear the truth, the whole truth, and nothing but. Maybe, if he fessed up, he'd find out it didn't matter one whit to Bess that somewhere, far from this idyllic place, a judge and jury had branded him a murderer and a thief. Knowing her, once he'd told his sordid story, she'd wrap her arms around him and insist he couldn't possibly have done harm to another human being.

But the lone, dark-spirit part of him warned him that was exactly why he must never tell her the truth. Because what if, after he'd told it all, instead of acceptance, instead of understanding, he saw fear—or worse, disgust—in those big brown eyes of hers? It would cut right to the bone, that's what. He'd survived snakebites and gunshots and a knifing, but Jake didn't believe any of those wounds had hurt as bad as Bess's rejection would.

"Men amaze me sometimes," she huffed, turning slightly in the seat to face him. "You can be such a gentle man, Jake. But if looks could kill, that Texan would be stone cold dead right now."

"Gentle? *Me?* You don't really think that...." His voice was so soft, he wondered if she'd heard him.

Bess rested her hand on his forearm. "No. No, I guess not."

He frowned, because her admission hurt.

"I don't *think* you're gentle, I have *proof* that you are. What you did for Matthew, for starters...."

His heart swelled with relief and gratitude—a surprise in itself, under the circumstances. "Oh. That." He shrugged. "I just did what any man would have—"

She squeezed his forearm. "Tell me about it, Jake."

He didn't answer.

"Jake," she huffed. "What about what that *man* said!"

He might have done it, then and there, if only he'd known where to begin.

"So, did you?"

"Did I what?"

Another sigh. "Have anything to do with that murder in Lubbock, of course!" She paused, then added, "Does he have you mixed up with some other Texan? Or...or..."

Her voice trailed off, and he thanked God for that small blessing. Jake tilted his face toward the sky and prayed for the strength to ask her to drop the subject, to simply trust him. Because her line of questioning made him feel as if he were back in Texas on the witness stand, listening to the nonstop inquisition of the state's attorney. For the first time since he'd met her, Jake wished Bess was a mite dumber. Grinning and frowning at the same time, he said, "Well, now. Ain't you just like a puppy to the root?"

She squeezed his arm again. "Land sakes, Jake! Don't try to confuse me with one of your Texas witticisms. I put my reputation on the line—Pa's, too, for that matter—to defend you back there. I believe I deserve an explanation." With that, she folded her arms over her chest and tapped one booted toe on the wagon's board floor. " 'Puppy to the root,' indeed. Now, out with it!"

"Don't get your neck hairs bristlin'," he said, smiling now. "I only meant that once you get your mind set on something...well, you just ain't gonna let it be, no matter what." A crooked grin slanted his mouth. "Are you?"

Her eyes narrowed. "So I'm stubborn. It's not a hanging offense, far as I know."

Her words left him cold. Jake knew she'd only been teasing, it was written all over her pretty face. Still, the words cut him raw, like a skinning knife. He'd developed a pretty thick hide these past ten years, or so he'd thought. "Men can be damned rude sometimes," was all he said.

"And one in particular," she countered, one brow high on her forehead, "is smart enough to evade an issue indefinitely, even if he has to pay himself an insult to do it."

She was sitting there on his right side and, as she had on the trip into Baltimore, she'd left a good foot of seat between them. Now, however, intense curiosity caused her to sidle closer. So close, in fact, that he could feel as well as hear the rustle of her many-petticoated skirts against his hip, could feel as well as smell her sweet warm breath against his cheek. He liked having her this near. Liked the way the toe of her tiny boot touched his big one. Liked the way her calf brushed his, the way her hand rested daintily, almost possessively, upon his thigh.

Jake had never seen her in anything but modest dresses made of sturdy fabrics, but he could imagine the lovely curves hidden beneath muslin and cotton. And, judging by the skin of her hands and throat and face, her thighs and calves, too, would be creamy and white as the pearls his mama wore to Sunday services.

Not wanting to do anything that would cause her to move away, Jake shifted the reins from his right hand to his left.

Smart enough to evade an issue, even if it means paying himself an insult, she'd said. Smart, indeed! If he *were* smart, he'd take her in his arms and—

"Bess," Jake whispered hoarsely, "I'm not a smart man. You can bet your last dollar on that."

She leaned nearer still and said softly into his ear, "Lucky for you, I'm not a betting woman. My mama used to say that gambling is evil."

Sitting there, her face lit by the bright yellow light of the setting sun, he noticed tiny green-and-gold flecks in her brown eyes. And the lashes he'd believed to be black as coal were, instead, the color of mink. He wondered if the long ride or the intensity of their conversation had heightened the pink in her cheeks. Most of all, he wished she'd stop pursing those full, kissable lips of hers.

"Penny-ante gambling ain't evil," he returned. *At least we're on a more pleasant subject than my date with the gallows....* "It's good clean fun, long as it doesn't get out of hand."

She shrugged. "Mama wasn't talking about the gambling that takes control of folks, of *course* that's wrong. She was talking about ordinary, everyday bets. Penny ante isn't evil you say? Well, *I* say it's wrong, because for one person to win, someone else has to lose—the winner's good fortune comes at the expense of a relative, a friend, a neighbor."

Jake smiled wistfully, wondering, *Would you take a gamble on me, Bess?* So lost in her lively eyes and animated gestures was he that Jake forgot for a moment how the subject of gambling had come up in the first place. And when he remembered, she flashed him an enticing, mischievous grin, all but making him lose track of what he'd intended to say about the subject. Smiling, he finished his thought. "*If* I were a smart man, I'd hitch this team to that tree over there," he said, nodding toward a big maple beside the road. "I'd lift you down from this old wagon and set both your pretty little feet on the ground."

He turned on the bench, so that only their knees touched now. "I'd give you the biggest hug you've ever had," he added, his thumb pushing up the brim of his hat, "then I'd kiss you like you've never been kissed before." He could feel her soft breaths, could see by the gentle rise and fall of her chest that she was breathing a mite faster than she'd been breathing before. Jake focused on her lips, then licked his own. "And I wouldn't stop kissing you until you agreed to be my girl."

He watched her dark eyes flutter as her eyes widened with shock and surprise. Smiling gently, he added, "But I'd never do any of those things, Bess. And do you know why?"

Her lips parted slightly as slowly, slowly, she shook her head.

He could have kissed her right then and there, if he had a mind to, for their noses were nearly touching. But this wasn't the right time for a thing like that. *Hell,* he grumped inwardly, *it may never be the time.* Frowning, he said through gritted teeth, "I'll tell you why," he rasped. "'Cause I'm *not* a smart man, that's why."

Bess blinked once, twice, three times, ran her tongue over her lips and took a deep breath. Squaring her shoulders, she said, "So the man on the dock mistook you for someone else?"

For a long moment, all he could do was stare, disbelieving, into her beautiful face. He'd just announced, in his clumsy way, that he loved her. And how had she responded? *Puppy to the root!* he told himself.

Gathering the reins in both hands, Jake threw back his head and laughed, long and hard.

He is the strangest man, she told herself. Hours earlier, she'd seen evidence that Jake might be capable of some dark deed. She'd pressed him to the wall for details about the Texan's accusation. If anything would have invited one of his sullen moods, the scene on the dock and her insistent questioning about it should have. Instead, Jake had sat there, laughing like a hyena, shaking his head, and muttering some nonsense about puppies and roots!

For several miles, Jake didn't speak. And Bess, determined to not give him more evidence to prove his puppy-to-the-root theory, wondered silently what might be going on inside that handsome head of his.

"What's on your mind, Jake?"

Several seconds ticked by before he said, "There are a whole lot of things you don't know about me, Bess, but I can promise you this—" again, he moved the reins to his left hand and grabbed her wrist with the right "—I promise I've never killed a man in my life."

His pale-blue eyes bored into her brown ones, and Bess drank in the look, like a refreshing rain hungrily absorbed by the rich dark earth. She had the distinct impression he was searching for proof that she trusted him. He seemed to need her to say that she believed him, that she believed *in* him. His strong, lone spirit needed her approval, she realized, and that could only mean one thing.

He loves me!

Bess ignored her fluttering heart and squeezed the hand that held her wrist. "If you say the man on the dock was mistaken, I'll take you at your word."

For a long moment, he only stared at her, a soft smile gentling his rugged features. "You don't know how much it means to hear you say that."

But she did know. She saw such sadness in the depths of those crystal-blue eyes, and wanted, more than anything, to take it away, to make him forget whatever had put it there in the first place. Bess didn't know what possessed her to do it, but she reached out and pressed both palms against his cheeks. The summer sun had warmed them, and the hours had stubbled them with bristly whiskers. Her thumb traced the contour of his lower lip.

"Ahh, Bess," he rasped, combing his fingers through her hair. "My sweet, sweet Bess..."

She'd always liked her name, but never more than at that moment.

Chapter Eight

How her father and brothers had managed to plan such a gathering without her knowledge flabbergasted Bess.

They'd decorated the yard with ribbons and bows, spit-roasted a steer and a turkey and several fat hens, too. They'd seen to it that some of the ladies brought side dishes, and made sure Bernie, with his flattop guitar, and his brother Bennie, the fiddler, showed up to make the festive music that was always such a part of Freeland get-togethers.

After the partyers had eaten their fill, Micah invited everyone inside, and as they crowded into the parlor, he rested a beefy arm on a huge, sheet-covered box.

It looked amazingly like the crate she and Jake had retrieved in Baltimore…the one Micah had insisted be stowed in the barn the moment the pair arrived home with it. How long had it been here in the parlor, Bess wondered, and how had they managed to get it inside without her noticing?

"Like her mama," Micah said, interrupting her reverie, "my darlin' Bess was blessed with a musical soul. Why, sometimes, when she sings as she goes about her chores, I'm convinced she's an angel, on loan to us from Heaven."

"Pa," Bess said, blushing, "please!"

Micah winked at their friends. "…an angel, 'til she goes

and says something to prove how very much a human woman she is," he said, winking at her.

"As you all know," he continued, "Bess has been the heart and soul of this family for many years. Without her, we'd likely have lost the farm, and we all would've starved to death."

"By the looks of your old man, you've done a fine job of keepin' the wolf from the door, Bess," hollered one of the hands.

Micah chuckled and patted his ample belly. "Keep a civil tongue in your head, Sammy, or I'll eat your share of the birthday cake!" he teased good-naturedly. "Why," he continued, "we'd have worn dirty, tattered rags. Would've been forced to kick our way through rubbish and debris just to get from one side of the house to the other!"

Again, the laughter of the Beckleys' friends filled the cozy, crowded room.

"Most of you knew my dear, sweet Mary. Those of you who did couldn't help but love her. She was a wonderful, giving woman." Micah stopped speaking for a moment. Took a deep breath, then swallowed hard. "I loved Mary more than life itself. For a while there after she died, I believed she took the best part of me with her."

He gestured for Bess and the boys to join him. Draping an arm over each twin's shoulder, he smiled fondly at his daughter. "A good friend helped me to see that, in reality, she left the best part of me, right here." He tugged his boys closer.

Micah held up a hand to silence the heartfelt sighs that filtered around the room, then laid that same hand upon Bess's cheek. "Your mother was a wonderful woman, my darlin' girl, but life was easy for her. From the moment Mary was born, she never had a worry in the world. You, on the other hand, have lived a hard life. A life that's—"

"Pa," Bess interrupted, blinking back hot tears, "hush now, why don't you?"

Micah thrust out his chest in defiance. "I'll not hush!" he insisted, loosing his black string tie. "I've been doing a lot of thinking these past months, about something my good friend, Jake Walker back there, said." Micah nodded toward the front door, then focused on his daughter again. "He helped me see that you pretty much single-handedly saved our bacon."

Paternal love glowed in Micah's damp, gray eyes. He coughed and cleared his throat. "The Bible tells us that to do a good deed in secret is to secure ourselves a place in Paradise. Well, Bess, my darlin', there's not a doubt in my mind you'll have a home up there some day, because you've devoted your life to giving us a taste of heaven, right here on earth."

The tears she'd been trying to blink back now rolled freely down her cheeks. Very few of their guests' eyes were dry, either. Matt and Mark stared at Bess, obvious adulation glowing on their fresh young faces. The Widow Reddick nodded her head in agreement. Pastor and Mrs. Higgins smiled approvingly. But Bess didn't see them, not because of the tears that blurred her vision, but because she only had eyes for one person...the tall, muscular man in the back of the room who leaned against the doorjamb, casually maneuvering a blade of grass from one corner of his mouth to the other. Lord help her, she loved that man!

Bess didn't know for certain if he'd committed a murder or not, but she knew for certain that Jake was a thief...for he'd stolen her heart.

She had no idea what gift Micah had hidden beneath the white sheet. She didn't know what might be in the boxes her friends had tied up with bright ribbons and big bows. But it didn't matter, because the best gift had already been presented: she had her father back!

She saw in Micah's gray eyes the once familiar loving smile, and on his bearded face, a serene expression. The way he stood there, tall and strong and proud, told Bess that her prayers had finally been answered. Her father had at long last set aside his grief over losing his beloved wife, and decided to start living, *really living* again.

He'd said flat out that Jake had been responsible for the magnificent change. Bess didn't think she'd live long enough to receive such a more meaningful gift, and she had Jake to thank for it.

Her heart throbbed at the mere sight of him. She wanted to run across the room, throw her arms around his neck and kiss him soundly. She wanted to tell him what she ought to have told him on the way home from Baltimore, when he'd said he would hug her and kiss her until she agreed to be his girl: *I am your girl!*

"You've been the only music in our lives for eight long years," Micah was saying. "So the boys and I decided it was high time we put some music into yours." With that, he stepped aside and whipped the sheet from the box. "Hand me that crowbar, Matthew," he instructed, grinning.

Board by board, the box was dismantled, and bit by bit, the lovely instrument appeared.

Bess ran her fingertips lightly over the smooth ivory and ebony keys, stroked the polished mahogany of the upright piano. Her voice trembled when she whispered, "Oh, Pa, it's…it's so beautiful."

"Not half as beautiful as the lady who'll play it," said a deep voice from the back of the room.

All heads turned to see who'd issued the compliment.

Bess knew without even looking up who'd spoken. She'd have recognized that wonderfully masculine voice anywhere. Much to her disappointment, when she turned toward the place where she'd last seen him, Jake was gone.

* * *

For a brief moment, he'd clung to the hope that Bess had fooled the ex-deputy, and he could live at Foggy Bottom with her forever. But reality set in as he watched the birthday festivities, and he couldn't bear to stand there a moment longer, looking at the woman he wanted…but couldn't have.

Jake turned slowly and headed from the house, and though he moved at a slow, deliberate pace, he was running again, and he knew it.

It seemed he'd been running from one thing or another most of his life…Sheriff Carter and his deputies, Texas Rangers, U.S. Marshals, bounty hunters, the hangman…and now his love for Bess.

During those long, lonely years, he'd been shot at, kicked and punched, survived cattle stampedes, border wars between ranchers. He'd seen death and dying more times than he cared to remember, and felt the scrape of the Grim Reaper's scythe a time or two, himself. But none of what he'd lived scared him half as much as what he felt for Bess.

One short month from now, his job at Foggy Bottom would be done. The corn and soy crops would have been harvested. The fences would have been mended. The outbuildings would shine under fresh coats of white paint. Jake knew if he wanted it, he'd have a position here at Foggy Bottom for the rest of his life. And the Good Lord knew he wanted it.

But sadly, Jake admitted he couldn't have it.

The Texan had walked off—as if he'd made a mistake in identifying Jake as a wanted man. But Jake had heard beyond the words, had seen the shrewdness in the man's eyes. He'd come back, and when he did, he'd bring trouble with him—trouble Jake could not afford to expose Bess to….

No fine words would satisfy the greed and bloodlust of these lawmen-turned-bounty hunters. Men determined enough to travel fifteen hundred miles through wilderness and over hardscrabble roads to hunt him down would be satisfied with nothing less than their thirty pieces of silver.

The thought made his heart ache. Leaving here, in his mind, could be compared to a slow, torturous death. Even the hangman's way was more humane than that. He would stay and face the music, and hope for the best, if he could predict the outcome. But the scuffle that was sure to take place when the Texan showed up to claim his man would likely require loaded guns. Only a shoot-out would buy Jake his freedom. Freedom, but at what cost? He would not put Bess and her family in the line of fire, not even for that. The Beckleys had been good to him. Had invited him, open-armed, into their family.

Yes, soon his job here would be done. And when it was, he'd pack his meager possessions, saddle his horse and quietly go.

If only there was a way to prove he hadn't killed Horace Pickett, he might be free again. Free of the hangman. Free to love Bess, to spend the rest of his life, happy beside her. But the only witness who came forward to testify about anything that had happened had been his own uncle.

Jake had been in Lubbock that fateful day, running errands for his Aunt Polly, when Horace Pickett stormed into the general store. "Francine," he'd bellowed, "just the little lady I want to see."

Francine Miller had lost her young husband a year earlier, and had been struggling ever since to keep up with the payments on their fifty-acre spread. But the banker, greedy and demanding, snapped mercilessly at her heels. Horace didn't seem to care that in the year since her Billy's death, Francine had worked so long and so hard that she looked sixty instead of thirty. Didn't seem to care, either, that she had three young children to feed and clothe. Or that she had no family to turn to for assistance.

"Francine," Horace had repeated, cornering the terrified

young widow in the middle of the store, "you're three weeks late with your September payment."

"I know, Mr. Pickett, I know," she said, her voice quaking with quiet fear, "and I'm right sorry. But I'm about to harvest...." Francine wrung her hands pitifully. "I ran out of money and had to let my hired hand go last week, so the young'uns an' me, we're gonna have to do it by ourselves. It's gonna take a mite longer than I hoped, but it'll get done. I promise you that. And when I've sold the crops, you'll get your—"

"Making excuses again, eh, Francine?" Horace had shouted, glowering. "Well, save your breath. I've heard so many of your promises, I'm deaf to them. I've had it up to here," he'd barked, slicing a hand across his throat, "with your whining and whimpering. You owe a debt, and it's your responsibility to honor it." He curled his lip in disgust. "It's not my fault, is it, that your spineless husband didn't plan better for your future before the fever took him."

Francine was crying hard by then. She'd heard it all before. Jake could tell that much by the way she nodded and mumbled "Yes, Mr. Pickett. I'm so sorry, Mr. Pickett."

Everyone in Lubbock knew that since her husband's death, Francine had made every payment late. Other shopkeepers made allowances, knowing that eventually, she'd honor each and every debt, even if it meant that in addition to running the farm, Francine would have to take in laundry and ironing. Even if it meant she'd have to clean the hotel and wait tables to earn a few extra dollars. Why couldn't Horace cut her the same slack? Jake wondered. It wasn't as though her measly payment would make or break his beloved bank.

It had been during the finale to Horace's tirade that Jake recalled a conversation he'd heard some weeks earlier. A Boston investor had come to town looking for suitable property on which to build a cannery. He'd visited Horace, knowing full well that the banker would have firsthand information regarding suitable properties.

The Miller spread, Jake had reasoned, was perfect for the Bostonian's business. Not only would it provide an ample water supply, it also had easy access to town by way of the main road. Rumor had it the man from Boston had said, "Money is no object."

Suddenly, standing there listening to Horace berate Francine, Jake realized that the banker's ranting and raving had one purpose: to intimidate Francine so badly she'd crumble, for if that happened, she'd lose hope and the will to work night and day, and wouldn't make any payments at all. The Miller farm would revert to his control and...

"Why don't you take this conversation to a more private place?" Jake had said, stepping between Francine and Horace.

"Why don't you mind your own business, boy?" Horace shot back.

He may have only been eighteen then, but thanks in no small part to his uncle Josh, it had been a long, long time since he'd felt—or behaved—like a *boy*. Jake narrowed his eyes. "There's nothin' worse than a bully, Horace. Exceptin' maybe a bully who'd attack a defenseless woman."

Horace had straightened and doubled up his fists. "I won't say it again, W.C., mind your own damned business!"

Jake crossed his arms over his chest. "Seems to me you're makin' it my business—makin' it *everybody's* business—bellowin' like a bull." He'd focused on Horace's crotch. "Mooin' like a cow, I shoulda said," he'd added, snickering, "'cause no *real* man would terrorize a wo—"

Horace shook a fist under Jake's nose. "Back off, man, or..."

His smile had vanished as he took a confrontational step forward. "Or *what?*" Jake demanded, his voice dangerously low.

In anticipation of a brawl, the store emptied. Even Francine slipped away from what was threatening to become a full-fledged fistfight. Later, she testified at Jake's trial that she'd left the store to fetch the sheriff. "I didn't want Jake gettin' on Mr. Pickett's bad side on account of me. I been there long enough to know he kin make a body wanna lay down an' die...."

Though well-intended, Francine's testimony hurt Jake more than it helped him, because in the end, the jury had focused on his anger and his threats instead of on Jake's attempt to protect her from the shame and anxiety induced by Horace's wrath. Jake could only thank his lucky stars she hadn't been present to witness the meanest part of his dispute with Horace:

"I've a mind to—"

Jake's harsh, angry laughter had interrupted Horace's sentence. "You hardly have a mind at all, Horace. But I'll tell you what you'd better remember in that pea brain of yours...if I ever hear-tell you're threaten' Francine again, it'll be the *last* damned time you threaten a woman!"

Horace swallowed and took a step backward. "You threatening me, W.C.? 'Cause if you are..."

"No, sir, it wasn't a threat—it was a *promise*."

"Who do you think you are, telling me how to run my business?"

He'd followed the banker outside, onto the porch. "Maybe I didn't say it plain enough—pester Francine again, and I'll break your fat red neck."

Horace grit his teeth, whirled around, and began stomping toward the bank. "You don't scare me, W.C.," he'd repeated. "Don't sca—"

"Boo!" Jake had hollered, stomping his boot on the board walkway outside the store. And then he'd laughed out loud as he watched the tiny clouds of dust Horace kicked up as he hotfooted it to the other side of the street.

"That mean streak of yours is gonna get you in a heap of trouble some day, son."

Jake hadn't known his uncle was in town, let alone there beside him on the steps of the general store. "Uncle Josh," he'd said, forgetting about the joke he'd played on Horace, "I'm gonna have to put a bell around your neck."

"This is no laughing matter, W.C.," his stern-faced uncle said. "You've got to learn to exercise some restraint. The Good Book says—"

Jake held a hand up to silence the man. It had been years since he'd tolerated a whipping from the man; he wasn't about to listen to a lecture. "Spare me the sermon, Uncle. You've been singin' that same old tune since I was twelve. Well, I'm a man now...."

Josh muttered several unintelligible sentences before snorting. "Threatening to kill someone doesn't make a man of you. Praying for the wisdom to solve problems as Jesus would have solved them. *That's* what a man...a *Christian* man would do."

Jake walked down the steps and hoisted himself onto his horse's back. "You took me in when my mama and daddy died, put food in my mouth and a roof over my head, and I'm grateful for that, Uncle." He made no mention of the scars he'd wear on his back and legs for the rest of his life...scars inflicted by leather straps and tree branches when Josh believed Jake hadn't behaved "right." He'd heard enough fire-and-brimstone sermons, both at his uncle's home and at the church, to last him a lifetime.

"I know I've been a burden," Jake had continued, "but I've always tried to earn my keep. I've got nearly a hundred dollars saved up. In a few weeks, I'll be leavin' here for good. You'll have one less mouth to feed, and one less worthless soul to try to save." With that, he rode off.

The next time he saw his uncle, Josh was in the witness chair beside the imposing figure of Judge Talbot. Jake had listened in stunned silence as Josh told a packed courtroom that, yes, he'd heard his nephew threaten to kill Horace Pickett, and yes, he believed the boy capable of such violence.

Later, deputy Buddy Smith had run into the sheriff's office, gasping and panting that he'd found Horace's body in the alley between the bank and the post office. The banker's pockets had been turned inside out, he'd been savagely beaten and his neck was broken. And, whoever had killed Horace had run off with the pocket watch his wife had given him on their wedding day.

After the arrest, they'd shown Jake's watch—the one that had been his father's—to Mrs. Pickett. It had taken nearly a week, after finding it in the wreckage of the prairie fire, for the orphaned boy to polish away the soot. But once cleaned, it kept perfect time and shined like the sun, and from that day forward, Jake had never gone anywhere without it. On the outside, the watches looked exactly alike. It was no surprise, when they showed her Jake's timepiece, that she'd sobbed into her brother's chest, "That's it. That's Horace's watch." And so the thing that had been such a comfort to Jake since losing his parents and his home and his peaceful, loving life became the one piece of evidence that linked him to Horace's murder...and marked him a killer and a thief.

He hadn't been well-versed in the law back then, but in his time on the run, Jake had puzzled out a thing or two about his so-called case. His watch should have been held by the sheriff, as evidence. But the Lubbock lawmen hadn't needed physical proof of Jake's guilt. In his opinion, all they'd needed was someone to pin Horace's murder on. And who better than a hotheaded young man like himself? They'd let him keep the watch to torture him in what would have been his last hours...if the jailer's wagon hadn't overturned....

It was an ugly little story, and the ten long and lonely

years that had passed since that night hadn't made it any prettier. And since there wasn't a blessed thing Jake could do about that, he made a decision.

He'd leave Foggy Bottom after the harvest.

And as always, he'd leave alone.

Because this was no life for a woman. He loved Bess far too much to subject her to looking over her shoulder, of worrying that maybe around the next bend, or in the next town, the hangman would be waiting.

Chapter Nine

Bess hadn't seen Jake in hours.

She'd looked for him as Pastor Higgins said a blessing on those gathered on the occasion of her birthday. Looked for him as her guests sampled the Widow Reddick's apple butter. And an hour later, when the pastor's wife dished up the peach pies she'd baked and brought to the party.

Halfway through the festivities, Micah announced they'd gather in the parlor in an hour to watch Bess unwrap the remainder of her presents. Overwhelmed by the surprise party—and Micah's extravagant gift—Bess found herself needing a moment to gather her thoughts.

She headed for her favorite spot on the Beckley property, her "thinking place," she'd come to call it, where she went when the trials and tribulations of being mother and father and overseer threatened her sometimes precarious hold on calm. Without exception, she'd always left the rocky precipice overlooking Freeland's wide valley feeling that all was right with the world. As she neared the path that would take her to the huge boulder, she felt the peace of the place embrace her.

The serenity was short-lived, however, interrupted by deep, mournful wailing. Quietly, she tiptoed closer, closer, until a silhouette came into view. There, between the leaning pines that flanked the big rock, sat Jake, his broad shoulders lurching with each agonizing sob.

She hadn't intended to eavesdrop. But once she'd gotten that far, Bess couldn't think of a way back down the incline without alerting him to her presence. She'd spent her whole life around men, and knew that he'd sooner die than let anyone see him in such a state. So Bess stood stock-still, scarcely breathing, lest she give her position away, and listened.

"Lord," said the cracking, rasping voice, "it's been a long time since you and I have talked." Head in his hands, he continued. "I'm no saint, but I'm none of the things I've been accused of, either."

The burly arms lifted slightly, then dropped in a gesture of defeat and dejection. "You're a harsh God—I never did anything to deserve a life like the one I've lived, yet You've let me live it for ten long years. If I knew why, maybe—"

He drove both hands through his hair, swiped angrily at a tear that rolled down his cheek, then held his breath for a long, silent moment. "I suppose Uncle Josh would say You're trying to teach me some kind of a lesson." Jake punctuated the idea with a short, bitter laugh. "What am I to learn…that if I live a life of looking over my shoulder, I'll be better company for You and the angels? That if I live out the rest of my days without Bess…"

Without Bess? It was all she could do to keep from running up to him, wrapping him in a comforting hug, and promising he'd never have to live another day without her. But how could she do that…and spare him the humiliation of having a witness to his grief?

Still, Bess couldn't bear to listen to another moment of his torment. Carefully and quietly, she picked her way back down to the roadside. Once both feet were on firm soil again, she made as much noise as possible going back up. "Jake?

Are you up there?'' She took her time getting to the top, intentionally stepping on crisp leaves and unearthing as many rocks as possible. ''They're going to cut my birthday cake soon,'' she was saying as she reached the rim. ''You don't want to miss that, do you?''

Bess heard him clear his throat, then cough. He'd gone around to the other side of the boulder, and now stood beside one of the huge pines.

Very deliberately, she faced the wrong direction, to give him as much time as possible to get hold of himself. When she turned, she put on her brightest, happiest smile. ''So *there* you are!'' she said, forcing a cheeriness into her voice that she didn't feel. ''I see you've found my secret place,'' she added, heading toward him.

He was sitting on the boulder now, elbows resting on his knees, staring straight ahead.

Bess stared straight ahead, too. ''Suffering from a summer cold?'' she asked when he sniffed.

''Must be.''

''Pity,'' she said, ''because they're the dickens to shake.''

Jake nodded. ''That they are,'' he said softly, still staring at the horizon.

''It's an amazing view, isn't it?'' she asked, shrugging. ''I've been coming here for years, when sanity eludes me....'' She sighed. ''So tell me, what do you think of the place?''

He took a deep breath, let it out again. ''I like it. I like it a lot.''

''I was about six years old when I first found it.'' Bess joined him on the big rock. ''Even then, before I was old enough to truly appreciate the magnificent view, I loved it up here.'' She looked toward the Gunpowder River Valley beyond them. ''I feel as if I can see forever!''

She took his hand in hers. ''Isn't it beautiful?'' Bess didn't wait for a reply. ''When I was a little girl,'' she continued, "I did some of my most serious contemplating here. Funny, but I remember coming up here on my eighth birthday, too. I was sitting right here when I decided I would *not* marry Tommy Lucas," she said, giggling, "even if his daddy did own the only confectionary for miles and miles."

It did her heart good to hear his warm chuckle. "This is the perfect place for soul-searching." She squeezed his hand, content to keeping up the idle banter until Jake felt ready to join in. "I spent a whole lot of time up here right after Mama died. I felt close to her up here, maybe because it seems so close to heaven."

Bess shook her head. *This isn't working.* And then it dawned on her. *Maybe,* she told herself, *what he really needs is silence. Just the quiet assurance of a friend.*

Jake leaned down and scooped up a handful of pebbles, cast them, one by one, into the murky water far below. Side by side, the two listened to the tiny rocks' distant *blips* and *plops.* After a while, Jake said, "Folks are probably wondering where you are."

"Let them wonder," she replied, lifting her chin in challenge. "And speaking of 'folks'…how long did you know about this shindig?"

Jake shrugged. "Just about from the get-go, I reckon."

"You could have given me a hint, at least."

"And spoil your surprise? Now, why would I go and do a dang fool thing like that?"

"Because if I'd suspected a party was afoot, I'd have worn my new dress, instead of this old thing." She patted the blue gingham that covered her knees.

"You'd look just as beautiful in a burlap sack."

"Stop," she teased, nudging him with her shoulder, "you'll make me blush." Bess made no mention of his red-rimmed eyes. Said nothing about the catch in his otherwise smooth, controlled voice. Instead, she simply sat, his hand sandwiched between hers.

"Thanks, Bess."

It was the second time in as many weeks he'd said those same words. She faced him. "Thanks? For what?"

Jake hesitated, as if unable just yet trust himself to speak. Then he gave her a crooked grin and draped an arm across her shoulders. "For being you," he answered.

She thought of the scene on the dock, the things he'd said about her at the party, and everything that had come before. Somehow, Bess knew the moments she'd treasure most were these, shared here, in this special place.

She'd witnessed Micah, grieving for Mary. Had seen various farmhands cry at the loss of a friend or loved one. Matt and Mark had shed tears when a beloved pet breathed its last. But she'd never seen—or heard—a man as miserable as Jake had been moments ago.

What kind of life had he lived before coming to Foggy Bottom? she wondered. What tragedies had he survived, what losses had he suffered? He was an amazing mix of tough and tender, and she wondered what experiences had made him so....

When he'd learned that she loved daisies, he picked them wherever and whenever he found them. Yet, when he saw one of his men haphazardly brushing a mare, Jake severely reprimanded him in plain sight of his co-workers.

When he'd discovered she enjoyed guitar music, he taught Bess to play Micah's beat-up old instrument. But when he caught a farmhand trying to steal a saddle blanket, Jake fired him on the spot.

When he'd heard that blue was her favorite color, he bought her a whole bolt of cobalt satin, and told her that a dress made of the stuff would bring out the muted blue that ringed her dark-brown irises.

You're a harsh God, she'd heard him say. She wanted to know about every harshness he'd suffered and survived. Wanted to know every detail, from the moment he was born to this very one, about the man she'd come to cherish so deeply.

Her mama had been a woman of great faith, but since Mary's death, Bess hadn't done much praying. Still holding Jake's hand, she bowed her head and closed her eyes. Yes, he'd stolen her heart, but he was no murderer. She would stake her own life on it, if it came to that.

Lord, she prayed silently, *show me the way to help heal his heart-wounds. Teach me how to love him as he deserves to be loved.*

At Foggy Bottom he felt, for the first time since losing his folks, that he belonged. In the ten years he'd been running from the law, he'd never called a place his own. But here, where towering pines shadowed grasslands that rolled like a wide, wind-rippled river, he felt *home.*

Likewise, in the years he'd been dodging Texas Rangers and bounty hunters and U.S. Marshals, Jake had never allowed himself to become attached, not to a place, and certainly not to the people in it. Many folks for whom he'd worked had invited him to stay on, indefinitely. With genuine gratitude, he'd declined their kind offers, and headed out, giving no explanation for his departure and no reason why he wouldn't stay.

Because in truth, he *couldn't* stay, despite the fact that he admittedly missed a few of those places and people. Caring about a town—or anyone in it—was a luxury he couldn't afford. Not if he wanted to avoid the dreaded hangman's noose.

Often, as he traveled from one place to the next, Jake ruminated on those invitations, figuring they'd been extended because he'd given his employers their money's worth and then some. Not once did he consider they might have asked him to stay because they liked *him* rather than the hard work and dedication that made him worth his pay.

Now, sitting here, in Bess's private place, Jake glanced down at his thigh, where her tiny hand rested in his callused palm. Now and then, she'd sigh, or tuck a wayward tendril of dark hair behind her ear, or incline her head toward a bird's song. Time and again, she'd squeeze his hand, or sigh and point across the valley at a hawk or an eagle, soaring high on a sultry summer air current.

Jake thought he knew how those winged creatures felt, coasting way up there in the clear blue sky, where the wind caressed the treetops and held billowy white clouds aloft. The big birds could glide from lofty nests and survey the landscape below, or slip silently by, or slow their flight should something catch their eye. And when their mighty wings grew tired, they could rest on a bouncing birch bough. Remain in flight, or pause in some protected perch: the choice was theirs, for this was their home, and here, they were free.

Until coming to Foggy Bottom, Jake hadn't allowed himself to taste freedom. Glorious as it was, he'd spent his entire adult life in the shadow of it, knowing full well that he'd never bask in the warmth of that hard-earned, elusive thing.

Until this place, Jake hadn't recognized how much he *wanted* to belong, to call one place home. And until Bess, he hadn't admitted, even to himself, how much he yearned to be enveloped by the unconditional love of a woman, *this* woman.

He glanced over at her, sitting there, thick dark hair blown back from her pretty little face, long lashes curling up from her high cheekbones as she surveyed the vast valley beyond.

In recent years, the thought had crossed his mind a time or two that letting the marshals catch up with him might just be a blessing. Why had he been running all this time, after all? In truth, lately, the longer he ran, the less he feared the end.

But since Bess...

How still, how hushed she sat! he acknowledged, smiling to himself. Ordinarily, she'd be chattering like a chipmunk. Jake knew what her silence meant. It meant that she'd sensed his need for quiet, just as she'd sensed his need to pretend she hadn't seen his tears or heard his sobs. And he loved her all the more for that.

"Have you opened all your birthday presents?"

She blinked a time or two before facing him, then sent him a smile he could define only as serene. "All but yours."

He looked into her teasing, smiling face. "How do you know I even got you a present?"

The grin faded into a slow, small smile of certainty. "I just know." Just as quickly as it had disappeared, the mischief in her eyes reappeared. "I only hope you didn't spend *all* your pay on me...Pa's birthday isn't all that far off, you know...."

If he'd earned himself a fortune in his years on the run, it wouldn't be enough, because what he wanted to give her couldn't be bought with money. Jake wanted to give her his true name: Walker John Atwood.

The worst of his torment behind him now, Jake grinned. "Folks are going to wonder where you are," he repeated.

Bess lifted her chin and raised both brows. "Let them wonder," she said again in her matter-of-fact way.

This time, it was he who squeezed her hand. "They've gone to a lot of trouble to make a fine party for you."

She'd lowered her head to hide her thoughts from him, he realized. But she hadn't done it quickly enough. For in that instant before she focused those incredible eyes on some unknown spot between her tiny boots, Jake had read her lovely face, and saw that she'd already had the same thought.

Without releasing her hand, he stood. "Let's head on back," he drawled, "before Micah rounds up a posse to hunt us down."

Bess sat for a moment, looking up at him through those lush, black lashes. She'd never said she loved him straight out, but he'd long suspected it.

She didn't iron the *other* hired hands' shirts, or darn their socks, or polish their boots. She'd never invited any of them to join her on the porch after supper to sip cool tea and enjoy the breeze.

He'd never heard her ask any of Micah's other employees what their favorite color was, and if their answers had been "red," he'd never seen them sporting bulky red sweaters she'd knitted to warm them when winter's cold winds blew through the valley.

Never had she studied the others as they ate, to determine a food preference, then whipped that favorite dish into a tasty lunch the very next day, wrapped in a line-dried napkin.

No, she hadn't told him how she felt—she'd *shown* him instead.

And he loved her for that, too.

"C'mon," he said, tugging her arm until she stood beside him, "or they'll cut into the cake without you."

Love still sparkled in her eyes when she grinned. "They wouldn't dare."

Jake knew he shouldn't have pulled her into that tight embrace. Knew he shouldn't press his mouth against her waiting, parted lips. He'd known he ought to keep his callused fingers out of those satiny waves. But the swell of emotion that rose inside him at the lovelight in her eyes gave him no choice.

All right. So he'd weakened on that score. But Jake was determined to exhibit strength elsewhere.

He mustn't let her know how good it felt to have someone as warm and wonderful as she in love with him at all! Mustn't ever allow her to discover that he'd never held another woman as tenderly, or kissed another woman as passionately.

Bess could never know that she aroused in him a physical desire like no woman before her ever had...or could. And she would never know that he loved her more than life itself, more, even, than his precious freedom.

Because to be with her night and day as husband and wife, he'd gladly forsake his precarious hold on freedom. If she'd have him, he'd wait out the marshals. *Any* length of time would be long enough, for he'd have those months, or days, or minutes to carry him through eternity.

But no. He loved her too much to subject her to that kind of pain. Jake loved her enough to sacrifice those precious moments rather than subject her to the agony of yoking herself to a wanted man.

Leaving her would be harder than anything he'd done to date. Harder, even, than burying his parents, for they hadn't left him by choice, as he'd be leaving Bess.

Another eagle screeched overhead, reminding Jake of the creature's freedom to come or go or stay, as it chose. Suddenly, he no longer felt quite so envious of that great, wild bird.

Hungrily, he kissed her, clutching her to him in a desperate attempt to blot out thoughts of being caught, of leaving Foggy Bottom, of losing Bess. She responded to his hunger by pressing closer to him, until every inch of her clothed flesh touched his. Jake could feel her heart beating hard against his chest, felt her fingers combing through his hair. A gnawing need ached in him as she returned his kisses with wild abandon.

He took her face in his hands and tore his lips from hers, fully expecting to read fear and shame in her soulful doe eyes. Instead, Jake saw the same need to love and be loved that pulsed in his own heart...and groin. But Bess was a true lady, innocent and untouched. He'd stirred the embers of passion inside her with his greedy need; it was up to him to cool her fires, to protect her from the likes of him.

Inhaling deeply, Jake looked up into the pale-blue sky and shook his head. He'd never felt more important or cherished than when in Bess's arms. Was it wrong to want her on every human level? To want to bed her, make her his own in every earthly way?

Not wrong, perhaps, but not right, either.

And so Jake took a careful, if not reluctant, step back.

But Bess took a step forward, and snuggled close once again. Then, in a move that seemed anything but innocent and untouched, she slid her hands up his chest, slowly and deliberately, until her fingertips rested lightly upon his shoulders. Her dark eyes bored into his with an intensity like none he'd ever seen, telling him, without words, that she wanted *him* in every earthly way, too.

Jake groaned quietly, uncertain what to do next. Should he press his lips against that inviting, enticing mouth? Run his hands down her narrow, curvy back? Or break free and run like hell, before he did something they'd both regret?

Bess didn't give him a chance to decide.

She slipped her slender fingers behind his neck and drew his face near, nearer, and when it was but a whisper away, closed her eyes and tilted her face, waiting, waiting, for his kiss.

He felt as he had when the jailer's wagon overturned, and he'd walked for miles under the blistering Texas sun once his water ran out. Even that powerful thirst couldn't compare to the one he felt now, looking at the mass of chestnut curls that framed her delicate face. At the well-arched brows, and the dewy lids of her dark-lashed, closed eyes. And perfectly shaped, slightly parted lips. Lips that begged him for more.

And so he kissed her. Soft, so soft at first. Then, more fiercely, grinding his lips against hers as if to say, *You're my woman, Bess Beckley!*

Again Bess responded in a heated flurry of sighs and gasps and moans that weakened his knees and set his fingers to trembling. She was by far the strongest woman he'd ever met, yet she felt like a tiny bird in his big muscular arms. He loved her. Wanted her. Needed her. But it couldn't, shouldn't be this way. "Bess," he rasped into her hair, "we've got to quit this."

"Why?" she asked in a small, vulnerable voice.

He quaked, from his feet right on up to his hair, then looked darkly into her eyes. He had no answer. At least, none he cared to speak at this moment. And so he kissed her again, harder this time. The moment was a fragile thing, frail and invisible as a soap bubble floating on a gentle breeze. He knew if something strong—God, Mother Nature, her father—didn't stop him now, he'd have her, right then and there.

The moment beat in hot silence. Then, settling her gently upon a bed of pine needles, Jake lay down beside her.

Her fingertips seared his skin wherever they roamed. She arched toward him as his hands gently caressed her breasts, gasped softly as his fingers slipped behind the ruffled neckline of her dress and tweaked the rosy peaks, then moved down to hold her buttocks. The V of her gowned crotch was hot when his palm cupped it, and Bess ground herself against his hand.

But how could he take this, her most precious gift, knowing he'd be leaving her soon?

Groaning again, Jake rolled onto his back, then lifted himself onto an elbow and stared into her love-flushed face. "You drive me plumb loco," he growled, "do you know that?"

In a move he could characterize only as wifely, Bess plucked a pine needle from his hair, then tenderly kissed his chin. "*I* drive *you* loco?" Bess gave his shoulder a playful shove, sent him a flirty, sexy grin and tilted her head seductively.

Clearly, the invitation remained open; if he wanted her, she was ripe for the plucking, those huge, sparkling eyes said. And how he wanted her. Wanted her more than he'd ever wanted a woman in his life.

He reminded himself he'd be leaving Foggy Bottom soon. Too soon. He'd meet his share of lusty women in the towns and farms that dotted the trail, women with whom he could satisfy his manly urges. He'd ignore the throbbing in his pants—for now—for the best gift he could give her was the very thing that had eluded him all these years....

Freedom.

Clumsily, he got to his feet and held out his hands to her. "When you cut that cake," he said, tenderly tidying her mussed hair, "I expect an extra big slice."

"An end piece," she agreed, tidying the collar of his shirt, "with plenty of frosting."

Whether it was shame or anger that darkened her velvety eyes, Jake couldn't be sure. Either way, whatever she felt couldn't possibly equal the regret coursing through his veins.

Chapter Ten

Bess had been waiting years for an opportunity like this. She'd accompanied her father on a number of trips out west, watching closely, listening carefully as he bargained with Texas ranchers for the best-priced cattle. She had Jake to thank for this chance of a lifetime, for he'd been the one to convince Micah that Bess could cut a smart deal.

Much to Bess's amazement, Micah had agreed to let her try. She knew full well the implications of her trip to Philadelphia: if she did well this year, Micah might just let her go it alone next year...out west!

It was important to pack light for this three-day trip north. Important, too, to outfit herself like a woman who understood a thing or two about negotiating.

Her practical, low-heeled shoes would match what Micah teasingly referred to as her "do business" dress. Richly trimmed in deep green cotton, the folds of its sea-green skirt shimmered in light and shadow. The three buttons that graced each wide cuffs were covered in the same dark green fabric, as were the two that held the glimmering golden throat clasp on its collar. When her mother had worn the dress, she looked to Bess like a goddess. No such aura came to mind when she donned it herself, however. Even in the beautiful gown, Bess saw only a plain young woman looking back from the mirror.

She'd never viewed herself as pretty. Her mother had been one of those rare beauties who needed no rouge on her lips or high cheekbones. Her luxurious, waist-length brown hair shone with lustrous red-and-gold highlights. And her skin, so pale it was almost translucent, reminded Bess of the fragile china that her mother reserved for special feasts.

She'd never recognized the similarities in her face and her mother's. Nor did she see the likeness between her own delicate frame and Mary's. She had no way of knowing that every time he looked at Bess, Micah was reminded of his beloved wife, or that the striking resemblance was a daily reminder of a painful fact: Mary was gone to him, forever. Bess could not have known that this fact caused him to hold his daughter at arm's length, avoiding her when he could...avoiding her dancing brown eyes when he couldn't.

So when Jake had jokingly dubbed her J.P., for Just Plain Bess, it had been all too easy to believe. Not until he began to show genuine interest in her—not as the boss's daughter, not as someone who could help him carve out a wedge of Foggy Bottom as his own, but as wholly woman—did Bess begin to see herself as more than "just plain."

She remembered the first time she'd come face-to-face with the fact that she did, indeed, look very much like her beautiful mother.

She'd been in the dining room, polishing the silver, when she heard a noise in the parlor. Leaving her cleaning supplies behind, Bess tiptoed across the foyer's Persian rug to peek through the velvet curtains that hung on either side of the wide doorway.

Jake had stood before the fireplace, one big hand gripping the mantel on either side of the gilded frame that housed the tintype of her family. He'd seemed entranced by the images, captured forever by the photographer. Sensing her presence, he turned. For a fleeting moment, Bess saw naked vulnerability in his blue eyes. But in a blink, the warm, sweet look was gone, and in its place, Jake's usual, guarded expression.

"Didn't hear you come in," he'd said, pocketing both hands.

"I was in the next room," she'd explained, feeling oddly like an intruder in her own home. Bess walked across the thick bloodred carpet and stood beside him. "Would you like me to introduce you to everyone?" she asked, gesturing at the other pictures that lined the mantel.

Jake gave her a half smile. "Maybe some other time," he said, glancing at the family portrait again. He looked at the clock, nestled there among the frozen, somber faces of Beckleys past and present. "It's time to—"

"Oh, surely you can spare a moment...."

Bess took his hand, then faced the fireplace. From left to right, she identified grandparents, aunts and uncles, and cousins, saving the family portrait for last. Lovingly, she held it in her free hand. "The boys favor Mama, don't you think?"

Jake took the picture from her, then gently put it back where it belonged, nodding his agreement. Taking her other hand in his, he'd added in a voice that was scarcely a whisper, "Matt and Mark do take after your mother, but I can see her likeness in you, too."

"Oh, no," she'd protested, "Mama was beautiful...."

"With all due respect, you could be her twin." Ever so gently, he brushed the backs of his fingers across her cheek.

The remark had confused her, she recalled, as he'd gone on to say, "Met a man in Kansas City once. Said he'd been all the way across the ocean, where he'd spent time in sunny Italy. Told me about these beautiful statues, carved by Michelangelo. And he described paintings by a man name of Lorenzo Ghiberti."

She remembered how impressed she'd been to learn that

Jake, rough-and-tumble cowboy, knew so much about foreign art. But what it had to do with her being proof there was a God, she hadn't known....

And then he'd drawn her into a sweet embrace. Looking into her eyes, he explained: "No painter or sculptor could create a work of art as magnificent as Bess Beckley. It took a being as powerful as God to do that."

With that, he'd kissed her.

It was no kiss of comfort. No kiss to share a friend's joy. This was an openmouthed invitation that told her, in no uncertain terms, that he needed and wanted her. Like a hummingbird dips into a flower, his tongue reached tentatively into her mouth.

Immediately, he'd stood back, gazing lovingly into her eyes for a long, silent moment, then bent low, his lips coaxing hers apart. Her mouth sought his out, like a dry riverbed seeks rainwater. He smelled so good, fresh and clean and manly. Her fingers had combed through his soft, golden waves, and he'd slipped his arms around her waist. A slow heat churned deep in her belly, and with each insistent press of his lips to hers, it burned hotter, higher, until it roared in her heart.

Bess had felt his own heart, beating hard against her chest. Heard his insistent sighs and groans of pleasure. Suddenly, without warning or reason, Jake had lifted his head and looked at the ceiling, closed his eyes and drew a deep, shuddering breath.

His lips had parted slightly, and three whispered words floated on the near silent air toward the candle scones that flanked the mantel. It had sounded like *I love you....*

Her heart hammered wildly, happily. "What? What did you say?" she'd asked, surprised at the lusty huskiness of her own voice.

Jake held her at arm's length and met her eyes. She read warmth and compassion in those sparkling blue spheres. Unshed tears glistened on his long, dark lashes. One corner of his mouth twitched involuntarily, as if he were trying to fight back the emotions roiling inside him. Bess watched as he blinked once, twice. She'd looked deep into those wolfish eyes as he gently traced her lower lip with a fingertip. Then, resting his chin atop her head, he'd said, "I'd better get back to work."

And just like that, he left her in the parlor to admit that without him, she felt cold and empty, and very much alone.

Even now, Bess's heart fluttered, just thinking about that magical moment. She supposed folks would call their escapade at her secret place far more intimate, but *that* would be the kiss she'd dream of, that she'd remember as she went about her chores, that she'd look forward to experiencing again…and again.

But no opportunity presented itself for that next kiss to happen these past few days, for Jake had much to do, overseeing the harvest, and she had plenty to keep her busy, too, preparing for her meeting with the Texas cattle rancher in Philadelphia.

Excitement bubbled inside her in anticipation of this, her first real business trip. After lunch, Bess hummed contentedly as she straightened the rows of canned goods she'd stored on the pantry shelves. Soon, the humming escalated to under-her-breath singing as she stacked neatly folded, line-dried sheets and pillow slips in the linen closet. By the time she hit the backyard, where she was beating rugs, Bess's song could be heard clear across the yard.

"'Amazing grace,'" she sang, "'how sweet the sound…'"

Of all the melodies she could have chosen, Jake wondered why Bess sang *that* particular hymn. It was his uncle's favorite, sung morning and night…and as he beat Jake for whatever infraction, and before and after every lecture. By the time Jake turned fifteen, he'd come to hate that song with a vengeance.

Always before, hearing it had conjured painful memories in his mind. Raised doubts and awakened the suspicions that he kept so carefully hidden under layers of protective, pretended sternness. Christians, he'd come to believe, were all the same, good on the outside—and out of the house, when decent folks were in plain sight, but mean and evil on the inside—and behind closed doors, where no one but family could see.

His aunt Polly had endured nearly as many whippings as Jake had over the years. Several times, in trying to rescue her from yet another lash of Josh's thick, leather strap, it was Jake's skin that rose with ugly, red welts. "In the name of the Lord God," Josh would thunder, "you will obey me! It is His law that, as head of this household, you will do as I say!" And after each beating, once Josh grew calm and quiet, he would insist that Jake and Polly join him in praising the Lord by singing his favorite hymn, "Amazing Grace."

This time, strangely, the song didn't conjure angry, bitter feelings. Bess's sweet, angelic voice trilled with meaning and intent, and for the first time in his life, Jake actually heard the *words*.

"'Through many dangers, toils, and snares,'" Bess sang, "'I have already come. 'Twas grace has brought me safe thus far, and grace will lead me home.'" Suddenly, she saw him standing there, and lurched with fright. "Goodness gracious. You nearly scared me out of my boots!"

"Sorry," he said, walking closer and taking the rug beater from her hands. "I was just enjoying your song. Please don't stop."

She grabbed the tool back and gave the rug a good wallop. "I'll sing, but only on one condition."

He tipped back his hat and crossed his arms over his chest, waiting for her to name her terms.

"You have to join me."

Jake laughed. "Me?" He pointed at a nearby tree, where several chickadees perched on a low branch. "What'd they ever do to you?"

Bess's merry giggle was punctuated with a wink and a bright smile. "I've heard you sing. You have a beautiful voice, and you know it."

Jake shrugged. He supposed his voice was pleasant enough, but he'd always thought of it merely as a way to soothe the cows on moonlit nights.

Bess sat on the rough-hewn wooden bench alongside the flagstone walk and patted the empty space beside her. When he joined her, their backs to the white-picketed kitchen porch, she took his hand. "'Oh, Lord, my God,'" she began softly, "'when I in awesome wonder, consider all the worlds thy hands have made...'"

With a gentle poke of her elbow to his ribs, she nudged him. "Come on now, sing with me."

"Can't," he said. "Don't know that one. But it's beautiful. Don't stop."

Her brown eyes bored deep into his blue ones, as if in search of the truth. Then she closed her eyes and began again: "'Oh Lord, my God...'"

Jake stared at her lovely profile, reveling in the feel of her soft, warm fingers nestled in his callused palm. The moments sped by, and disappointment rang loud in his heart when she sang the last line, "'How great thou art, how great thou art.'"

She sighed. "I've always loved that one."

"Is there anything you *can't* do?"

Bess giggled again. "Can't seem to get any work done when you're around. You're a very distracting presence, Jake Walker."

He stiffened. *I'm not Jake Walker,* he ranted mentally. *My name is Atwood. Walker John Atwood!* He was proud of the name his parents had chosen for him, but regrettably, he hadn't been able to use it, not once these past ten years. More regrettably, he knew he'd probably never be able to look a man square in the eye, grasp his hand in friendly greeting, and say, firmly and without hesitation, "Name's Atwood. Walker John Atwood."

By the startled, almost frightened expression on her pretty face, Jake realized he must have been grimacing something fierce. He forced a friendly smile.

"Aren't we friends, Jake?"

Such a simple question, yet Jake didn't know how to answer it. Yes, he admitted, she'd been a friend. The best he'd ever known. Why, he'd told her more about himself than he'd ever told anyone. Somehow, she'd wrangled out of him that he'd lost both parents in a prairie fire when he was scarcely twelve, and that he'd spent the next seven years with his aunt Polly and his uncle Josh. Somehow, she'd managed to get him to talk about the horrible abuse he'd suffered at Josh's hands, and had convinced him that surely goodness and mercy lived *somewhere* in his uncle's heart. It was her point-blank question, fired in exactly the same way as she'd fired every other, that made him remember the precise moment in time when his uncle Josh changed.

Jake had been ten years old on the Sunday when his parents, along with his uncle Josh and aunt Polly, had been invited to a neighbor's spread for dinner. Just as Josh picked up his fork to dig into the delights prepared by their hostess, Bob Martin held up his hands and said, "Before we eat, we must thank God for our bounty."

"Thank *God?*" Josh had countered, smirking. "If you want to thank somebody, thank your pretty little wife Marta, here, who slaughtered the hen and roasted it, who peeled the spuds and snapped the beans, with her own two hands."

Jake recalled Josh's words with startling clarity. Recalled, too, that Bob had simply shrugged and said, "I suppose you've got a point, there." At that, he picked up his own fork, as did everyone at the table, and began eating without saying grace.

Two days later, or so the story went, while in the barn helping Bob repair the sickle's broken handle, Marta had reached out to steady the workbench, and when she did, the sharp blade of the sickle slipped from the vise, nearly severing her hands. The doctor had stopped the bleeding in time to save her life, but not quickly enough to save her fingers. And though Marta learned to manage quite well with her thumbs-only stumps, Josh felt responsible for the accident, as if his careless, Godless words had caused it.

He refused to listen to reason, and found solace only in his Bible, believing it to be the only way he could rectify the awful thing his blasphemy had provoked. Day by day, nose in the pages of the leather-bound Good Book, his anger and bitterness grew, for no matter how many verses he memorized, no matter how well-acquainted he became with God's word, Josh couldn't undo what he believed his words had done. He was dead certain that his lack of faith had started the series of events that led to Marta's deformity. His callous, faithless words had been directly responsible for the mishap that meant she'd never again comb her long fingers through her children's flaxen hair, or hold their tiny faces in her hands to soothe away their tears and fears.

Josh intended to repent, and did so by burying himself in his faith. He spent every spare moment at the church, earning first a position as elder, then a deacon. Finally, when the pastor passed away, Josh was chosen by the brethren to take his place, for they knew no man more devoted and devout than Josh Atwood.

What they didn't know was that Josh had become a tortured, tormented soul. Every time he saw Marta and her fingerless hands, he was reminded again of what he considered to be his greatest sin.

He was hard on his parishioners, demanding pure and abiding faith in all things. He was hard on his wife, expecting total surrender and submission, which he claimed was the Lord's way for wives.

He was hard on his brother's son, determined to make a strong follower of him, to ensure that his nephew would never have to suffer the pangs of faithlessness Josh himself had suffered.

But, Jake remembered, Josh was hardest of all on himself. He allowed himself no human pleasure. Allowed no errors, no lapse in judgment, no time for anything but God. Instead of the Godly lessons turning him warm and loving, Josh's constant self-abuse turned him stone-hard and cold. He had no love in his heart, no mercy in his mind, no forgiveness in his soul for typical human mistakes, least of all his own....

Bess's simple questions had freed Jake of the years of resentment and hatred he'd harbored against his uncle Josh. By making him take a long hard look at *why* his uncle had become a spiteful, angry man, she'd lifted that heavy burden from his shoulders, and he was able, for the first time since the murder trial, to think almost fondly of the uncle who had opened his home to a frightened, orphaned youth.

Yes, he and Bess were friends, that much was certain. But in the months since he'd been at Foggy Bottom, Jake had come to realize she was far more than that. She was the first woman he'd ever truly loved. The woman he'd marry, if his miserable past would allow it. He wanted her to be the mother of his children. Wanted to grow old beside her, and watch their grandchildren play in the yard as he rocked beside Bess on the porch of the humble house he'd build for her, board by board, with his own two hands.

But he'd never be able to tell her any of that. He'd never be able to ask her to marry him and share children—*life*—

with him. He'd grow old, all right, but not beside Bess. Because she deserved more, so much more than he could offer, running and hiding to stay one step ahead of the hangman.

"Aren't we friends?" she asked again, squeezing his hand, as if unsure he'd heard her question the first time.

"Course we are," he whispered. *And that's all we'll ever be.*

"Then why don't you tell me what's made you so sad all of a sudden?"

When she let go of his hand, his own felt so cold and so empty that Jake thought his heart might break. *Better get used to that,* he thought, for it was only a sample of how life would be…when he left her.

"Maybe someday," she said quietly, getting to her feet, "you'll trust me enough to tell me whatever has hurt you so badly." She headed for the house, but paused halfway there. "You *can* trust me, you know. With anything." She stared hard at him from across the yard. "Do you believe that?"

He trusted her with his very life, so why couldn't he admit that he'd been tried and convicted of murder, that he'd been sentenced to hang for a killing he'd never committed?

Undaunted, Bess tossed her head and made her way to the porch. "Whenever you're ready to talk," she said, stepping through the screen door, "I'm ready to listen."

He didn't know how long he'd sat there, alone on the bench beside her rusty rug beater, staring after her. It wasn't until a barnyard cat brushed against his boot that he realized the sun was setting.

It would be suppertime soon, and he'd get to watch her bustling about in the kitchen, walking up and down behind the hands, refilling their plates and the biscuit basket. He'd revel in those moments, for there would be painfully few of them before he'd be forced to leave.

Jake rose slowly and headed for the bunkhouse to wait for the dinner bell to ring.

Chapter Eleven

Bess leaned back and sighed, oblivious to the towns and farms that whizzed by as the train sped over the polished tracks. "Aren't we friends?" she'd asked him.

Hiding behind both hands, Bess wondered how she could have said such a thing, especially after that kiss in the parlor! When his lips touched hers, a tenderness tempered the passion but did not cool it, rather, honed it to a keener point, like the heat from a stoking furnace tempers steel to take a finer edge.

Nearly every time she closed her eyes, she pictured him, big and broad and brooding. But oh, how his handsome face changed when he smiled! Bess sighed softly at the mental image of his wide grin. His sparkling blue eyes. Honey-gold hair that curved and curled beneath his wide-brimmed hat.

Her smile grew as she pictured that hat, for before Jake had come to town, Bess could have counted on one hand the number of fellows who sported western-style headwear. Now, she'd need ten hands to count them all: all over Baltimore, men strutted in what they called "ten galloners." Foggy Bottom field hands claimed to have purchased their chapeaus because it made good sense, since the height of the crown allowed air to circulate and cool their heads, while the width of the rim protected their necks and faces from the blistering effects of the sun. Matt and Mark, however, made no bones about it. "Hey, Pa," they'd exclaimed when Homer Jensen stuck one in the window of his Baltimore haberdashery, "we'll clean the barn twice over in exchange for a hat like Jake's...." Her father hadn't said yea or nay. Instead, he quietly paid for two white toppers for his twins...and plunked down enough cash to buy a gray one for himself as well.

And the mimickery hadn't stopped on their heads.

Most Freelanders had never seen a cowboy before; these men who'd never worn dungarees for anything but field work now emulated Jake's style, from silver-buckled leather belts to pearl-buttoned plaid shirts to snakeskin boots. It didn't matter that the purpose of the boots' pointy toes was to make it easy for a cowboy to slide his foot into his saddle's stirrups, or that the slanted heels held them tight once in place.

Before Jake came to town, his quiet presence commanding the respect and admiration of Freelanders, bushy beards, muttonchops, and handlebar mustaches had been all the rage. And now? Bess put a knuckle between her teeth to suppress a giggle. Now, she saw far fewer sideburns and a whole lot of clean-shaven faces. She wondered if the men copied Jake's "look" because they genuinely liked and respected him, or if their womenfolk had talked them into it. If so, Bess wondered, did their ladyfriends get the same reaction from their men's kisses as she'd gotten from Jake's?

She knew how hard he'd tried to stay in the background, unnoticed. And after that scene on the dock, Bess understood *why*. A slight smile of fondness crossed her face as she thought, *If he'd known he'd make such an impression, maybe he'd have passed right on by Freeland, rather than chance being recognized by the likes of that ghastly Texan!*

Immediately, her thoughts returned to his kiss, and the

way he deliberately teased her with his lips, grazing hers slowly, then pressing, ever so softly at first, exerting more pressure as the heat between them intensified.

Stop this nonsense, Bess scolded herself, *you're behaving like a wanton hussy!* She tried to focus on fences and trees, farmhouses and barns, silos and fields that whizzed by on the other side of the train's lace-curtained window.

She tried counting the number of minuscule rosettes that made up the trim of the white cotton gloves that poked neatly from the opening in her drawstring purse. She adjusted the folds of her skirt, and retied the bow on her bonnet.

Why, Bess even went so far as to pull her latest knitting project from her sewing bag. But nothing, it seemed, could distract her from thoughts of that kiss. Because truth was, Bess had enjoyed it. Not just *it,* but every other hot, throbbing sensation it had stirred inside her as well.

The way her heart raced, for example. Why, it hadn't even beat that hard or fast when she'd chased the twins into the barn for putting a garter snake in her clothespin bucket!

And the way her breaths became ragged little gasps. As a very small girl, she'd had pneumonia. Even *that* hadn't affected her breathing the way Jake's kiss had.

And his huge, hard body, pressed tight to hers, so tight she could feel the tautness of every lean muscle....

Bess especially liked the way his massive hands soothingly, sensually stroked her shoulders and back, and pulled her closer, closer, as though, strong as he was, he doubted he possessed the power to hold her close *enough.*

His heart had raced, too. She'd felt it against her breasts, jostling her innards like the big bass drum in the annual Freedom Day parade. Jake's warm breaths, ragged and deep, fanned her cheeks. And the quiet moans that began, it seemed, in the pit of his stomach, had echoed upward toward his throat, reminding her yet again of the caged timber wolf she'd seen as a girl, growling low and soft from behind iron bars.

But what had touched her most were the tears that welled up in his beautiful eyes at the conclusion of their sweet union. That he'd allowed her to see them at all meant he trusted her, at last. And for that, Bess gave thanks, because the giving of his heart couldn't be far behind. In fact she thought she had heard him declare his love that very moment. It had been a tactical error, she realized too late, to ask him to say it again. She'd been around enough men to know that matters of the heart were most times impossible to discuss, and always harder to admit.

But what else *could* she have done? The man she loved more than anyone in the world had just admitted that he loved *her,* too. It was only natural, she thought in an effort to comfort herself, that her delight in hearing those three lovely words would make her want to hear them a second time. And if he hadn't so deliberately and carefully avoided her those last days before she left for Philadelphia, she'd have told him flat out that she loved him, too.

Well, perhaps it had been for the best that Jake hadn't restated his proclamation. And maybe it had been best that she hadn't had a chance to return the words. Because, in truth, she wasn't absolutely certain he'd said "I love you"— though it had certainly *sounded* like those were the words he'd spoken....

One way or the other, she intended to make it her business to find out where she stood with him. The moment she got back to Foggy Bottom, she'd seek him out...whether he wanted to be found or not. One look into those wonderful eyes, and she'd know.

The farm consisted of nearly five hundred acres. Oaks, maples and pines, Micah's ever ready lumber supply, flanked Foggy Bottom on the north and the south. In the valley between its densely forested borders, on grassy hills that rippled and crested like a verdant sea, Black Angus and Hereford cows grazed contentedly.

The grand plantation, split down the middle by Beckleysville Road, stretched in all directions as far and as wide as the eye could see. It was a big spread to manage, and not an hour of daylight passed without something—a stray animal, a sagging fence post, a fallen tree—demanding Jake's attention. With all that to occupy his mind and body, he wondered why couldn't he get involved enough in any project to distract him from memories of Bess.

He'd deliberately put himself as far from the stone house as possible on the morning she'd left for her trip to Philadelphia. What would the men have said if they'd seen him "aw shucks-ing" like some addlebrained schoolboy at the prospect of being apart from her for a few days? They'd have badgered him relentlessly, that's what! The moment Jake learned when she would depart, he devised a plan to be absent, because he knew full well he couldn't have stood there and watched her ride away from him.

Not after that kiss...

He'd been chomping at the bit to get that close to her since...well, since damn near the first moment he'd set eyes on her. He didn't count the night of Matt's operation, figuring her hungry kiss was mingled with relief that her brother's operation was finally over and had gone well. Didn't count the afternoon of her birthday party, either, though her heavy-lidded smoky gaze and kiss-swelled mouth told him she wanted him in anything *but* an innocent, reassuring way.

But he sure as hell counted that afternoon in her parlor.

It had been like nothing he'd ever experienced. Bess's sweet lips roused a raging fire in his loins...and a gentle warmth in his heart. Her loving hands, tenderly combing through his hair and stroking his cheeks, reminded him how good a simple touch, dispensed in genuine affection, could feel. And those lips, velvety and yielding, loosed soft murmurs of pleasure between his kisses. True, he'd been excited as never before. But she'd reached a part of him that no woman before her had reached.

It reminded Jake of his stay in Kansas, where his boss's wife was a renowned and gifted harpist. Several times, when no one was about, he'd pulled at the massive instrument's taut strings, each time wincing, amazed that anything so beautiful could produce a sound so offensive. Only when Mrs. Scott strummed and plucked at the oversize lyre did Jake understand what Heaven might sound like.

Before Bess, he'd never confused lust and love. But until now, he'd never understood that the two, mingled with friendship, could produce a comfort such as he had never known…or hoped to know. Man-woman love, in his experience, had been about taking, never giving. Why, he wouldn't dare have dozed after a bed battle, for it would likely have cost him his wallet, his boots, the shirt right off his back!

Man-woman love began and ended with lies. If he told a woman she was beautiful, desirable, her body would be his, at least for a moment in time. And while she was his, she'd tell him she'd never met a stronger, handsomer, more virile man, because saying so, she hoped, might earn her furs, jewels…at the very least, dinner in town. It was a hard-edged, no-rules game that boasted no winners.

And yet, without schoolbooks or slate or chalk, Bess had taught him that the exact opposite was true. Love was not frightening or threatening. It did not shout its presence, nor announce itself with loud, lusty sounds. It was not a stalking beast, ready to pounce and steal a man's property…or his freedom. He'd gone through his life believing he neither needed nor wanted love, that he couldn't afford to want it.

But that day in the parlor, when Bess stood in his arms

and looked up at him adoringly, and touched him soothingly, and kissed him tenderly, he realized love was a lot like Mrs. Scott and the music she made with her harp: it had simply taken the right woman to make his heart sing.

A crow cawed above, waking him from his daydream. Jake looked around. He'd started riding north at sunup to check on the men's progress. Somehow, he'd ended up far east of the cornfields.

Chuckling under his breath, he reined in his horse and turned her in the right direction. "I'm trustin' you to keep me on the straight and narrow, Mamie," he said, patting the filly's withers. Jake stared hard at the horizon. *Concentrate,* he told himself, *and maybe you'll get where you want to go, straightaway this time.*

Concentrate? How could he concentrate on anything but that kiss!

She'd surprised him that day by slipping into the parlor, quiet as a cat.

She'd looked so elegant, standing between the deep-red curtains that festooned the doorway, despite the fact that she'd worn a plain brown dress beneath her ruffled white work apron. Her dark hair, curling around her delicate face like a softly furred frame, shimmered with gold-and-red highlights in the sunlight that slanted through the French doors, and her chocolate-brown eyes sparkled with girlish innocence.

Oh, but her kiss hadn't been that of an innocent girl! Quite the contrary, in fact. Raw, demanding need pulsed from her core to his when their lips and bodies pressed together so tightly that not even the sweet summer breeze could have passed between them.

She'd willingly opened her mouth at the slightest insistence of his tongue, inviting him to enter and explore and enjoy. And when he'd backed off to allow himself a glimpse of her beauty, she'd stared up at him, and blinked, and in so doing, willed him near again with nothing more than the silent draw of those long-lashed, inky eyes.

The moment he'd slipped his arms around her, he knew.

Knew that if he *could* settle down, it would be with this petite yet powerful woman. Knew that when his life-style forced him to leave her—and all too soon it would—his heart and soul would be far emptier than his arms had been when he left the parlor that day.

He'd lived a rough, rugged life and had bedded rough-and-rugged women, because he'd had neither the time nor the inclination for love. He couldn't afford to fritter away even one precious moment seeking something he could never have. And so he'd guarded his heart with extreme caution. Built a sturdy wall to protect himself. If he couldn't accept love, why bother to give it? *Like a puppy to the root, she burrowed under that wall.* He laughed softly to himself, shaking his head ruefully.

But Foggy Bottom had changed his mind. Changed his belief that church-goers were phonies, that friendship was phonier still. Changed, more than anything else, his notion that he could walk through life untouched by love. Oh, he'd built a wall around his heart, all right, but he hadn't built it nearly tall enough or strong enough—to resist Bess.

That day in the parlor, when she'd looked into his face, he realized she saw him as the man he'd always *wanted* to be. No need for a fancy suit or a Boston education. No need for lies and pretense, or pretty words, either.

On that day, when she'd caught him staring at her family's portrait, she seemed to sense how alone he felt in this miserable world. Seemed to know how much he needed to feel that he belonged. Jake marveled at that, because until she'd dispensed her love, like warm, soothing salve, *he* hadn't even known he'd needed it.

Damn if she ain't some kind of woman, he told himself.

*Li'l gal whose head barely reaches your shoulders makin'
you feel that special!*

The breath caught in his throat as he recalled the sensation
of her slender fingers weaving through his hair. Her whisper-
soft sighs had floated into his ears as she responded to his
touch, and her heart—the same heart that beat hard and angry when faced with life's injustices—had thumped wildly
against his chest as he held her close.

He'd asked himself time and again since that day why
he'd said those three words. And each time, he'd shrugged,
thinking that when a man had thought a thing a thousand
times, wasn't it natural to say it out loud, at least once? He'd
spent all his adult life avoiding those words, which, until
Bess, had been fearsome and damnable. Still, they'd linked
together and rolled off his tongue so easily and so naturally,
all he could do was hope they'd spilled out quietly enough
that she hadn't heard them.

What did you say? she'd asked, her voice husky and lust-
laced.

He couldn't very well repeat it, now could he? It wouldn't
have been fair to either of them, since he knew full well he
wouldn't be staying on after the harvest, no matter how
much he'd meant what he'd said.

What did you say? had been her quiet, honest question.

Jake wouldn't have hurt her for all the world. He'd rather
die than cause her a moment's pain. So he'd stood there,
trying to conjure up a similar-sounding phrase that would
satisfy her, painlessly. No matter what he said, *he'd* be hurt.

If she hadn't branded him with that loving, longing look
as she traced his lips with her fingertips right then, creating
a soft *W*, Jake might have summoned the strength to pull it
off. "Look, Pa, a *W*, see?" he'd said to his father. *If you
were with me now, Pa, you'd see this little gal has her brand
on me, just as sure as you branded our cows. You said it
didn't hurt 'em, but you were dead wrong. It's a powerful*

pain, and that's for sure. He'd almost made a clean getaway. But that intimate yet innocent gesture was the final hammer stroke to the already crumbling wall he'd built around his heart.

He'd never let anyone see him cry, not since he'd buried his parents. Not even the threat of death by hanging had pushed him that far. But gazing into her eyes and seeing the purity of her love looking back at him woke emotions long asleep. And once awakened, those feelings boiled up and bubbled over like a too hot stew pot. He'd never wanted anything in his life more than he wanted her...and her pure, unconditional love.

But he could never have either, and the grief at admitting that had hit him like a tidal wave, so hard and so fast that Jake hadn't had time to mask it.

So he'd gathered her close, closer, whether to hide his tears from her or to hide her from his tears, he didn't know, and rested his chin amid her mass of soft chestnut curls. "I'd better get back to work," he'd said, his voice gruff and hard from biting back a sob. Then he'd walked away, just like that, without a backward glance or a by-your-leave.

And he hadn't seen her since.

Now that he'd exposed his most vulnerable self to her, he didn't know if he could face her, especially during these last weeks before he must once again hit the road, knowing she'd seen his weakness. Jake had fretted about it for two whole days, and avoided her by skipping meals and staying far, far from the house.

But he soon learned Bess Beckley was not a woman who would be avoided.

On the third morning after their kiss in the parlor, she sent Mark to the bunkhouse to deliver a large, overstuffed envelope to Jake. "You're to sort through it all," the boy explained, "and deliver the payments next time you go into town."

No surprise there. Jake had often been "the Pony Express" to Foggy Bottom debtors since taking over as foreman. Imagine his surprise, when, tucked among the invoices, he found a neatly folded sheet of scented ivory stationery:

Dear Jake

I realize you've been terribly busy, what with preparing for the harvest and all, but I couldn't leave for Philadelphia without saying goodbye. I hope you'll take proper care of yourself while I'm gone to choose the new cows for Pa's herd—so far this week, you've missed two dinners and two breakfasts—because I'd hate to come home and find you've keeled over from exhaustion. I'll have enough work to catch up on without having to nurse you back to health! I know if you could fit it into your schedule, you'd wish me a safe trip. And you'd probably wish me good luck, too, in making a smart deal on Pa's behalf. So I thank you in advance for your thoughtful well wishes, and I wish you a productive harvest in return. I'm sure you know that you're always in my thoughts and prayers. And I intend to think and pray even harder now that I know you're undernourished! Believe it or not, I'm going to miss you a lot while I'm gone, Jake Walker!

And it was signed, "Just Plain Bess."

He'd read the note twice more before tucking it into his shirt pocket. Read it half a dozen more times that same day, and the day after that, too. And each time, he chuckled softly at her typically humorous way of making the men in her life toe the line, smiled at her ability to read his mind, strived to still his hammering heart as he read the implicit messages of love written between her lines.

The steady *thump-thump* of Mamie's hooves meeting the tall grass kept time with his heartbeat as he continued north toward the cornfields. He slid the note in his pocket. By the position of the sun, he guessed it to be nearly eight in the morning. She'd been gone almost a week already, and had no doubt arrived in Pennsylvania by now.

Regret tugged at his heart. He wished he'd sent her off with a proper goodbye, for if he had, he'd have *that* kiss to recollect, too, as he drifted off to sleep, alone each night.

Wearing a wan smile, he looked at the vastness of the Foggy Bottom horizon, with its gently rolling hills and pasturelands. Once, it had been a place of raw and natural beauty. Now, tamed by the powerful hand and determined will of man, Mother Nature's acquiescence was evident.

And without Bess, the land seemed forever forlorn.

Chapter Twelve

He'd been at it since dawn, trying to get the north fences repaired before nightfall. Hard work, Jake told himself, could take his mind off the fact that soon, he'd be forced to leave this place.

But no matter how demanding, the chores couldn't blot Bess from his mind. Hard work *and* singing, he discovered, lessened the chance that she'd come to mind.

"'Oh, don't you remember,'" he crooned, "'a long time ago, there were three little children, their names I don't know…'"

His grandfather had taught him the ballad, about three youngsters, kidnapped from their home. "'They were stolen away on a bright summer's day, poor babes in the woods I've heard people say…'"

The eerie tale had been put to music by his grizzled grandpa and, according to the gap-toothed old man, true to the very last word. As a young boy, the song had terrified Jake. Even now, fully a man, its story haunted him, because for a child to be stolen from his folks was about the scariest thing he could imagine. Ironic, Jake often thought since reaching maturity, that just like those innocent babes in the wood, no one knew what had become of him, either.

"'…they cried and they cried, how bitter they cried. The moon went down and the stars gave no light…'"

He could almost picture those children, huddling in a teary embrace beneath the black, oppressive canopy of the forest.

"'…and when they were dead, the robins so red, took strawberry leaves and over them spread…'"

How had they died? Jake had asked the question every time he heard the song as a boy—asked it each time he sang it, even now. Had they suffered some awful torture at the hands of a madman? Had exposure to the elements sucked the life from their frail bodies? Or had despondency caused them to simply lay down their little heads and hand their innocent souls over to their Maker to spare themselves another bleak, frightening night, parentless in the dark woods?

"'…and sang a sweet song, all the day long. Poor babes in the woods, now you've heard my song.'"

He'd always hated the abrupt ending, and often asked his grandpa to think up a more satisfying conclusion. But the gray-bearded man refused. "That's the way it happened, boy," he'd insist, talking around the stem of the corncob pipe he held between his snaggled, yellowed teeth. "Life ain't no fairy tale. Sometimes, there ain't no happy ending."

Jake hadn't fully understood the wisdom of those words until he'd been on the road nearly two long and lonesome years. Rational and practical by nature, he couldn't help but agree that the story should be told, if indeed it were true, exactly as it had happened. Still, the same sadness that, as a boy, inspired him to yearn for a happy ending, made full-grown Jake yearn for the very same thing. He'd tried on one occasion to add a verse or two of his own. But knowing he'd altered the tale left him feeling even less satisfied than he'd been with his grandfather's more sorrowful version.

So he'd taken to singing the beginning several times over, once he'd sung the end, to leave himself with, if nothing else, a sense of hopefulness.

"'Oh don't you remember,'" he began again, "'a long time ago—'"

"Now there's a lullaby if ever I heard one."

The deep voice startled Jake so badly that his right hand automatically gripped the carved wooden handle of his pistol. Life on the road had made him jumpy and watchful, but it had also taught him that patience almost always paid off. This wasn't the first time his caution had saved a man's life. "Hell, Micah," he complained, "you likely shaved another ten years off the tail end of my life, sneakin' up on me that way."

"*Another* ten years? You've had ten years wasted already at your age?"

But the older man seemed not to have noticed that Jake's revolver was cocked and ready. "You're going to work yourself into an early grave," Micah said matter-of-factly. "I don't believe I've ever seen a man push himself harder. Never seen a more fidgety man, either." He leaned both forearms on the top rung of the wagon wall. "What're you running from, son?"

Jake replaced the gun in its holster and faced the father of the woman he loved. "There's a lot to be done around here, Micah. Seems there aren't enough hours in the day.…"

Micah rested a hand on Jake's shoulder. "Son, you're the best foreman I've ever had, and I've had a few, so I know what I'm talking about. But there's something about you, something—" The older man frowned hard, took a deep breath, and shook his head. "There's something dark inside you."

Jake opened his mouth to object, but Micah's raised hand silenced him.

What if, he wondered, *Micah had somehow seen one of the wanted posters set about by the U.S. Marshals? What if—*

As if he could read Jake's mind, Micah said, "Whatever

it is, it's history, far as I'm concerned. You've earned every dollar I've paid you, and then some. I like you, boy.'' Laughing softly, he added, ''Why, if I weren't so young myself, I'd say you're like a son to me!'' He gave Jake a hearty clap on the back. Then, in a more serious tone, added, ''You befriended my boys when they needed a man to guide them, and taught them more'n I could have, in my sorry state of mind. There's not enough money in all the world to repay you for that.''

Jake wished he hadn't taken off his hat; the shade of its wide brim might have helped hide the flush that warmed his cheeks. ''I'm right fond of Matt and Mark, Micah,'' he said, putting the hat back on. ''There's no need for this kind of talk.''

Micah shook his head. ''That's where you're wrong, son. Somebody's done you a powerful wrong, and I'm sorry about that, truly I am. But it's eating you alive, like a cancer.'' He dropped another slap on Jake's back. ''Let it go, boy, before it kills you!''

No one had ever dared tell him what to do…and gotten away with it. But then, no one had ever told him what to do in *friendship* before. Jake didn't know what to make of it, let alone how to respond to it. Clumsily, he moved the hammer from his right hand to his left and back again. ''We're burnin' daylight,'' he said. ''I'd best get back to work.''

Micah sighed. ''All right, then. But if there's anything I can do, just say the word. If it's money that'll dig you out of the trouble you're in, I've got plenty of it.'' Then, adjusting the top button of his white, collarless shirt, he coughed. ''But if it's just a friendly ear, well…you were a friend when I needed one.''

Staring at the toes of his dusty boots, Jake remembered the day, not long after he'd arrived at Foggy Bottom, when he'd gone into the barn for a shovel. He stumbled across

Micah, huddled in a back stall, bawling like a baby, a half-empty bottle of whiskey at his side. The older man's obvious grief stunned him, and oddly, shamed him, too. Because to survive the life he'd been forced to live these past ten years, Jake had had to teach himself to live simply, and with few rules: Hide your money in your boots. Travel by the river roads, and only after dark. Keep your canteen full.

Micah's unrelenting sobs had made him wish for a rule that went something like, "Never ask a man what's wrong." Because when Jake asked him what was wrong, Micah had poured out his heart. Later, when the man blamed his temporary insanity on a sizable consumption of whiskey, Jake pretended to believe it. But both men knew full well that missing his Mary—not alcohol—had inspired the rib-racking sobs that echoed between the stalls.

Jake had pretended to believe Micah's rendition of the story because he understood exactly how the man felt. True—he hadn't shared more than a few hot kisses with Bess. And true—they would never share a bed, let alone a lifetime—but he didn't have to live the life to know how much he wanted it, to know he'd remember Bess Beckley until he drew his last breath.

"…and I don't soon forget a kindness," Micah was saying.

Clearing his throat and frowning, Jake blinked himself back to the present. "Micah, look here now," he began, "it was nothing. Anybody would have—"

But one look at the stubborn expression on Micah's wizened face told Jake he could talk until sundown and not change the man's thinking. So he clamped his jaw shut.

It had been said a time or two that he had a stubborn streak of his own. It surfaced as Jake gripped the hammer tight and struck the nail he'd been pounding into the wagon's sideboard when Micah interrupted his work. But when he raised the hammer in preparation for yet another blow, Micah grabbed the tool midswing.

"Don't be a fool, Jake...look at me when I talk to you!"

Like an obedient child, he did as he was told.

"You're young and healthy, so I guess it's natural for you to think you have all the time in the world. But let me tell you a thing or two," Micah said, wagging an arthritic finger under his nose. "Time is precious."

His voice grew softer as he gazed at some unknown spot, far off in the distance. "She was a good woman, my Mary. She gave me three young'uns, made me a fine home. Getting out of bed each morning was pure pleasure, because I knew she'd be there, smiling that sweet smile of hers, telling me to hustle my ornery butt down into the kitchen before my eggs and ham got cold...."

Shaking his head wearily, Micah took a deep breath. "God, I miss her," he admitted, his voice gruff with a held-back sob. He blinked. "Time," he repeated, "is a precious thing." His eyes bored hotly into Jake's as he aimed his advice home. "Hold fast to what's important, because you never know when your *time* will be up."

He turned, as if to go, then quickly faced Jake again. "I'll tell you this—if I'd'a known I would lose her so soon, I'd'a done a lot of things differently." He sighed and shrugged and held his hands out in front of him, saying, without words, how helpless he'd been since that fateful moment in time.

Jake watched him move slowly toward the house. He figured that, when Mary lived, Micah had probably walked straight and tall. Now, it seemed to be a great effort, just shuffling along, as though he bore the weight of a thousand lifetimes upon his once-powerful shoulders.

Determined to put Micah's speech out of his mind, Jake focused on his task. It wasn't that he didn't appreciate the kindness that had inspired the lecture; Jake recognized the well-meant advice and—and agreed with every word. *Point is,* Jake told himself, *it's useless information.*

He looked toward the horizon, at the invisible something that had so captured Micah's attention earlier. *The U.S. Marshals, or worse—bounty hunters—could be out there right now, like mountain lions, waiting to pounce…chompin' at the bit to slip a noose around my neck.* "Time is precious," Micah had said. "Hold fast to what's important.…"

Jake knew *exactly* how precious time was! He'd lived life, for the past ten years, minute to minute, never knowing when he'd have to saddle up and head out. He knew how precious his time at Foggy Bottom had been, just as he knew he'd like nothing better than to settle down here forever, marry his beloved Bess and raise a passel of kids. Why, he'd do it in a heartbeat…if he thought for even a moment he might actually be able to live a real life with her.

Oh, Bess would try to make a real life for them, he knew, telling him that what happened in Texas didn't matter one whit to her. He knew she'd be willing to spend whatever precious little time God chose to give them by pampering and spoiling him, just as he knew he'd treasure every blessed second of it. And when that dreadful day finally came—as it surely would—she'd stand beside him, chin poked out in proud defiance, determined to prove to him and the rest of the world that their time together had been blissfully well spent. At the gallows, she'd gather him close, straighten his tie and shirt collar, telling him she'd miss him mightily and love heartily him until the day she died.

He knew all this as he knew his name was Walker John Atwood. He knew it from watching her give love and care without ever asking for or expecting anything in return. He knew it from seeing the way she did the right thing, even when weary or frightened or out-and-out furious. He knew it from listening to her musical voice bolster the sagging spirits of the men in her life, giving them the strength to carry on, even when things seemed unbearably grim.

He knew it from her gentle touch, her sweet kiss, her tender embrace.

Mostly, he knew it from the light that began somewhere deep in that huge heart of hers, and shimmered from her velvety brown eyes every single time she looked at him.

Yes. Micah had been right. Time was precious. So very precious.

Which was exactly why he could never tell her.

Not about his past. And certainly not that he loved her. He wouldn't allow her to waste a moment of *her* precious time on the likes of him.

Chapter Thirteen

"I'm busy," he whispered into the teller's ear.

The banker's young assistant adjusted the black armbands cinching up his white shirtsleeves. "But Mr. Cramer, she's been waiting nearly thirty minutes already. She says she had a nine o'clock appointment with—"

Cramer proved his impatience by exhaling a loud sigh. "I'll get to her when I'm good and ready," he said through his teeth. "No woman ought to be traipsing around the country doing a man's bidding, anyway. If she doesn't know her place in proper society now, she'll know it by the time I'm finished with her, by God!" He punctuated his statement by lifting his head slightly, then bringing it down with a snap.

"Yessir, Mr. Cramer." The young man glanced in Bess's direction and shot her a weak smile.

Bess did not return it. She'd heard every word, loud and clear. What business was it of Cramer's to dictate who would make this deal on Micah's behalf? But she wouldn't allow him to read on her face that he'd riled her. No, Bess would much rather *show* him instead.

The teller stood before her, licking his lips while folding and refolding his hands in front of him. "I'm sorry, Miss Beckley...."

His distress at being forced to deliver such rude news might have touched her if she wasn't so angry at being slighted this way. Still, standing, she placed one white-gloved hand on his forearm. "Don't you worry another minute about it," she told him, smiling.

And then she burst through the swinging wooden gate that separated the bank officials from patrons.

"Wait," the teller said, one finger in the air as he hurried after her. "You can't go in there, Miss Beckley!"

She turned, her hand still on the gate. "I believe I've already done it," she announced, grinning.

Bess then turned her attention to the banker, marched straight up to his desk and sat in one of the two red leather chairs in front of his desk.

Cramer looked up from his paperwork. "What's the meaning of this?" he demanded, glaring at his terrified employee.

"I tried to stop her, sir," the teller said. "But she—"

Bess, smiling sweetly, looked up at the young man. "I'd very much appreciate a glass of water...."

He blinked. Cleared his throat. Flushed. "Well, I— Um..." He looked to his boss for guidance. "Mr. Cramer?"

"Oh, go and get the little lady some water, Anderson," the man snapped. "And be quick about it. I haven't got all day." He gave Bess his full, undivided attention to ask in a falsely syrupy voice, "What is the nature of your business, missy?"

Her polite smile still in place, Bess leaned forward slightly. "My father wired you that I'd be here. Micah Beckley. Perhaps you've heard of him?"

Cramer leaned back in his creaking wooden chair and folded his hands across his black brocade vest. "Yes...yes, of course I've heard of him. He's one of our depositors."

"One of your *biggest* depositors, you mean!"

The banker's eyes narrowed, but he did not respond.

Tilting her head to one side, she sighed. "As you probably know, my father has spent the past several years trying to build up a respectable herd of cattle that will enable him to compete with Virginia ranchers. His research told him the very best bulls are born and bred right here by the Amish. That's why he's been doing business with Mr. Shelby."

The banker rolled his eyes and sighed with exasperation. "Your family history is of no concern to me, Miss Beckley. Now, I'm a busy man. I have a lot to do and—"

"—and I'm sure you can see it makes good sense," she continued, "to keep enough cash on hand, right here, where the business takes place, to make the transactions as efficient as possible for my father and Mr. Shelby alike."

He sat forward and this time, folded his hands on his desktop. "I'm not accustomed to doing business with womenfolk. I'll have you know that right up front."

Anderson showed up with her water just then, and as she accepted the glass, Bess said to Cramer, "And I'm not accustomed to doing business with arrogant, overbearing old fools—"

"Now, see here, Miss Beckley, I—"

Smiling, she continued, "Which is exactly why my father has sent me to do business with *you,* Mr. Cramer." She looked up at the teller, who was drying his water-dampened hands on the seat of his pants. "Thank you so much," she said, her smiling sweetening.

"You're quite welcome, Miss Beckley." He grinned and shuffled from one foot to the other before departing.

Cramer's narrowed eyes flashed with anger and the top of his bald head glowed bright-red as the teller retreated, chuckling under his breath.

"Need I remind you that my father has a considerable sum on deposit in your little bank?" Still smiling frostily, Bess paused before adding, "Which is precisely why I insist upon doing business with you directly, Mr. Cramer. You are, after all, the man in charge, aren't you?''

Blinking innocently, she took a sip of the water and focused heavenward. ''Correct me if I'm wrong—'' when Bess met his eyes again, she was not smiling ''—but isn't the whole idea of banking to earn more money for the institution by making use of cash on deposit?''

Frowning, he coughed and cleared his throat. Just as he opened his mouth to respond, Bess put the water glass on the edge of his desk and cast him a withering glare. ''My father's dollars won't work less efficiently on your bank's behalf simply because it has come into contact with—'' she daintily wiggled her fingers ''—womenfolk's hands.''

He put his agitation aside in exchange for outright anger. ''I don't believe I need a lesson in banking from the likes of you, young lady!''

''Perhaps not,'' she snapped, ''but you most certainly *could* use a lesson in customer relations!''

She gave him no time to respond. Bess stood, calmly flattened both hands on his desktop, and leaned into his face. ''Mr. Cramer, do you respect my father?''

''Why, yes. Yes, of course I do,'' he said, running a thick finger around the inside of his collar.

''Do you believe he's an intelligent man?''

His reddened face glistened slightly with a sheen of perspiration. ''Well, yes. Naturally. But I—''

''You're confident, then, that he is completely capable of making wise decisions regarding the running of his businesses and the handling of his money?''

Cramer was standing now, too. ''Really, Miss Beckley, I fail to see what any of this has to do with you.''

She rested both fists on her hips. ''Well, then, allow me to spell it out for you, Mr. Cramer. If you wish to continue doing business with my father, you have no alternative but to show me the same courtesy and respect you'd show him, since putting me in charge of this transaction was *his* wise and intelligent business decision.''

Bess sat again and straightened the folds of her skirt. Once Cramer had settled into his squeaking chair, she said in a soft but firm voice, ''Now if you don't mind, I'd like to make a withdrawal.''

Cramer knew he'd been bested. And by a woman young enough to be his daughter, no less! He bristled for a moment as he considered his next move.

''Does that ledger contain a listing of your present accounts, Mr. Cramer?'' Bess asked, blinking innocently as she pointed to the thick leather book on his desk.

''Yes.''

''I suggest you open it, then, to refresh your memory as to exactly how much of my father's money I have total control over here today.'' She reached into her purse and withdrew an envelope. Tapping it lightly, she said, ''This letter is my power of attorney. It gives me permission to withdraw any dollar amount I see fit.'' Nodding at the now open brown ledger, she added, ''Please don't give me reason to believe I must withdraw *all* of it....''

He'd been frowning until she said that. Suddenly Cramer's dour expression turned friendly, and he gave her his best bank manager's smile. Opening his desk drawer, he pulled out a withdrawal slip. ''Just how much *will* you be taking...taking from the...from your account today, Miss Beckley?'' he asked, grinning nervously as he dipped his pen into the inkwell.

Bess held out her hand. ''Won't you let me fill that out for you, Mister Cramer?''

She was in no mood for more manly dominance. If Ernest Shelby thought he was going to give her the same hard time the old banker had, well, he had another think coming, Bess decided.

The moment she'd arrived in town, Bess sent word by way of messenger to Shelby that she'd see him at his convenience. One of his farmhands delivered a note that very afternoon, indicating Shelby would meet her at Gracie's Restaurant on Porsmouth Street, three o'clock sharp.

Bess peeked at the watchbob that dangled from a silver chain around her neck. Already, he was more than fifteen minutes late. She detested tardiness. But far more important than that, she didn't like carrying such a large sum of cash.

"Well, now, haven't you gone and grown up pretty?"

Startled, she turned toward the gruff but friendly voice. Bess would have recognized Ernest Shelby anywhere. She'd met him years ago, when she'd traveled north with Micah to purchase those first dairy cows. Shelby was by far the biggest man she'd ever seen. Even from all the way across the room, he reminded her of the stuffed grizzly Homer Jensen kept in the front window of his Baltimore haberdashery.

Bess stood and held out her white-gloved hand to him. "Mr. Shelby, it's a pleasure to see you again."

"Pleasure's all mine, little lady," he said, shaking it firmly.

"Would you care for some coffee?"

"Don't mind if I do," he said, dropping his huge bulk onto the seat of a cane-backed chair. "Sorry I'm late. One of my cows had a breech birth this mornin'. Took nigh on to four hours to get that damned little calf born."

She smiled, for his voice was as large as frame. Bess could almost picture the big man gently tugging a tiny cow from its mother's womb. They spent the next few minutes catching up on family gossip. Then, suddenly, Shelby shoved his mug away and said, "So you're here to buy two of my bulls, eh?"

Bess nodded and squeezed the money-stuffed purse in her lap. "Pa said there'd be no need for me to ride out and inspect them. Said he trusted you to choose two of your best to—''

Shelby nodded. ''Ain't never cheated a man in all my life,'' he said, male pride glittering in his pale-blue eyes, ''and I sure as hell ain't gonna start now, when I'm this close to meetin' my Maker.''

''You needn't convince *me* of your impeccable reputation, Mr. Shelby. I trust you completely to make the best selection.''

Shelby's satisfied smile beamed from his ruddy face.

''...but I'm sure you won't mind telling me *why* the bulls you've chosen for my father are what you consider to be the very best you have to offer.''

The next half hour was filled with a detailed discussion of bovine quality, during which Bess cornered Shelby into a description of the bulls he would ship south to Baltimore. Exhausted by her inquisition, Shelby leaned back in his seat and took a deep breath. ''Well, now, I'm sure you're anxious to get back home to your daddy.''

Bess smiled, a hand against her chest. ''That I am.'' *Pa may trust you implicitly,* she thought, *but he's plunking down an awful lot of money for that trust.* She wouldn't insult her father's friend, but she wouldn't chance that he *was* Micah's friend, either. ''May I share a secret with you, Mr. Shelby?'' Looking left, then right, Bess leaned forward and whispered, ''I've always wanted to watch as the branding took place. Do you suppose that could be arranged?'' She sat back then, still grinning, and added, ''Kill two birds with one stone, as they say—my little adventure will be fulfilled, and there'll be no chance for confusion at time of shipment.''

Shelby, taken aback by her businesslike acumen, grinned sheepishly. ''I, ah, well, I'd be happy to arrange that.''

''Thank you, Mr. Shelby! I just knew you'd understand!''

His relieved laughter filled the eatery, drawing curious, momentary glances from other patrons. ''Hold it down over there, Shelby," the man in the corner booth hollered. "You're curdlin' the milk in my tea!" ·

"Save it, Boone!" Shelby hollered right back. "The milk curdled the minute it looked up from the cup and got a gander of your ugly face!"

Everyone seemed to find that funny, including Mr. Boone. Everyone but Bess, that is. She was far too busy reading the posters tacked to the board outside the restaurant's wide window. There would be a church social this Sunday, one flyer said. Amos Mossman's wagon was for sale, said another. There was a Wanted poster. But it was the sketch of the white wolf that had captured her attention, its wily, wary eyes boring into hers in much the same way the timber wolf had all those years ago in Baltimore.

"I didn't know there were any wolves in Pennsylvania," she said.

"Ain't. Not in the wild, least-ways. That one there," he said, pointing to the poster, "was on her way to a zoo up in New York City when the train derailed. That there she-wolf is responsible for killin' more cows'n I can count," Shelby said, realizing where her attentions had been focused. "She's got herself a roving spirit, and by golly, I'd like to be the one who stills it. Why, I'd kill her for free, just for the pleasure of hangin' her hide on my wall!"

Bess couldn't take her eyes from the animal's portrait. She was a farmer's daughter, and fully understood Shelby's reaction to any animal that threatened his breeding stock. Still, it seemed a shame that this beautiful, one-of-a-kind creature should pay with its life for doing what came naturally.

"Now, iffen it was *money* I wanted," Shelby added, nodding to the Wanted poster beside the wolf's, "*there's* the animal I'd go after."

Bess looked at the Wanted poster again. Really looked at it this time. Above a face that looked amazingly like Jake's, big black letters said Wanted, Dead or Alive. And beneath those words, the same bold type spelled out W. C. Atwood. On the last line, behind the huge dollar sign, Bess read the amount of the bounty. "Five hundred dollars! What on earth could he have done to—"

Shelby proceeded to fill Bess in on the killer's vicious crime: he'd beaten a man to death, and all he'd gotten for his trouble was a gold watch on a chain. As the story went, the killer had outrun dozens of Texas Rangers, had outfoxed twice as many U.S. Marshals since his escape. "Seems every lawman between Maine and California is huntin' him. Can't set foot in a post office or a bank these days without havin' to look into his haunted eyes...."

He leaned forward and said, "I heard-tell of one marshal who came back empty-handed from huntin' Atwood—they say he came mighty close to baggin' his prey. Seems the slippery fella got clean away, again, but not before promisin' to run every lawman ragged. Said it'd be easy work, too, 'cause not a-one of 'em had the brains or the brawn to out-last him."

According to Shelby, the challenge, if indeed one had been issued, rankled every man with a badge, and even inspired a few of the badgeless to vow they'd see W. C. Atwood hang...or die trying. So far, Shelby said with more than a hint of admiration in his voice, W.C. had outwitted them all, making himself a legend of sorts for having dodged first the Texas Rangers, then the U.S. Marshals, Pinkerton detectives...for more than a decade.

"But five hundred dollars," Bess echoed. "Surely dozens of murders are committed every year. Why is *this* man worth so much?"

Shelby shrugged. "The man he killed...his widow put the money up. Rumor has it she said at her husband's funeral that she wouldn't rest 'til she could see his killer swing." Winking, he added, "Been a long time since that woman's had any rest. Maybe the Good Lord has been on W.C.'s side.''

"Why would God help a killer?"

"Atwood said from the get-go that he never kilt nobody, that he never stole no watch, neither. Me? I believe him."

"You do? But why?"

Shelby shrugged. "Well, for one thing, if he kilt the man for the watch...why'd he leave it behind?"

Bess glanced at the crudely drawn portraits again, and couldn't help thinking that the wanted man and the hunted beast had a lot in common, right down to those icy, wolfish eyes.

Bess's heart beat harder, and she didn't even know why.

All during the train ride from Philadelphia to Baltimore, Bess thought about the amazing likeness between the man in the Wanted poster and Jake Walker.

Jake was a Texan. He'd told her he hadn't been home in more than ten years. And he'd been mighty evasive about where he'd been and what he'd been doing all that time. It had been like pulling teeth barehanded, she recalled, to get him to talk about any aspect of his past....

Matt and Mark were at the station to meet her. She was thrilled to see them, yet her heart sank. She'd hoped that, after reading her note, Jake would realize he needn't avoid her—especially not for a reason as silly as letting her see that seldom-viewed sensitive side of himself. His absence at the station told her, in no uncertain terms, that his male pride stood between them.

The twins chattered all the way home about the things Jake had taught them while she was gone. They'd learned to birth a breech calf. How to mount a moving steed. When to administer medication to a sickly horse. And when to stop saddling a pregnant mare.

Bess sighed and smiled and thanked God for Jake. Her

brothers had been little more than boys when he showed up early last spring. In these few months, they'd begun to show signs of turning into men, thanks to his patient influence and tutelage. Before Jake had come to Foggy Bottom, she'd regularly had to threaten to tan their hides just to get them to wash up for supper. Now, in an attempt to emulate their hero, they came to the table squeaky-clean, on their own.

Not so long ago, it took no fewer than three requests to get them to make up their beds in the morning. Now, Bess couldn't remember the last time she'd had to ask them to tidy their rooms. And schoolwork! She recalled the nagging and pestering it used to require to get those boys settled at the dining room table to complete their lessons. These days, a sideways glance from Jake encouraged such an immediate response that the curtains hanging at the French doors fluttered from the breeze of quickly opening books.

He'd affected Micah's life, too, in his quiet way. The change had been more slow and subtle, but the man who, until Jake's arrival, had been sullen and withdrawn, began to shed his gloomy spirit. The smiles she remembered as a girl were back again, and so was the jovial, high-spirited daddy who tickled and teased, and hugged with abandon.

And there was no denying the impact Jake had had on Bess's life. He'd never come right out and told her how capable and efficient he believed her to be, yet she knew it's what he thought. He'd said it often, with his smile and the genuine respect in his eyes. She'd never considered herself pretty, yet without ever having said it in so many words, he'd convinced her that she possessed a beauty rare and fair.

Until Jake, she'd resigned herself to being a spinster. Like old Martha Willis, who at eighty-one still cooked and cleaned for her younger siblings, Bess always believed she'd be caring for her brothers until they married and moved into homes of their own. And after that, she'd care for her father until he—or she—drew that last breath. She had to grin, just thinking about the wedding dress she'd sew if Jake ever screwed up the courage to ask her to be his wife!

But...first there had been the man on the Baltimore dock, and now there was the matter of that Wanted poster....

She'd slipped outside after her meeting with Ernest Shelby and, when no one was looking, untacked the poster from the board and stuffed it into her purse. Bess guessed she must have taken it out and looked at it a hundred times between Philadelphia and Baltimore. The black-and-white rendition of the murderer *did* bear an uncanny resemblance to Jake as he might've looked when he was younger. The man in the picture had longer hair, wore muttonchops and a mustache. There were no laugh lines beside his pouting mouth.

But those eyes...

Pale and slanting and darkly lashed, they captured her attention in exactly the same thrilling yet terrifying way the timber wolf had all those years ago in Baltimore.

Behind her closed bedchamber door, she'd unpacked her bag and emptied her purse. Petticoats and stockings in need of a good laundering lay in a heap beside her dusty black boots and bonnet. But she paid them no mind. It was the crumpled poster that captivated her.

Gently, Bess smoothed the wrinkled paper with the palm of her hand. Then, perching on the edge of her bed, she held it this way and that, to catch the light in varying ways. No matter how she looked at it, the drawing still resembled Jake.

Bess lay back, snuggled into her plump feather pillow, and pressed the poster to her breast. *It can't be Jake,* she thought, biting her lower lip. *He simply couldn't be a thief and a murderer!*

She thought of all the kindnesses she'd seen him perform. Of all the thoughtful things he'd done—none of which had anything to do with his job as foreman—since coming to Foggy Bottom. Of his deep masculine voice, its powerful tremolo floating over the yard as he sang ballad after ballad on sultry summer nights, unaware that he had an audience of one. *Could a man who sings like an angel be a cold-blooded killer?*

She held the picture aloft, so that the man in the poster was looking down at her in much the same way Jake had that day in the parlor. She stared long and hard into those wolflike, icy eyes, at the firm set of that broad jaw and the grim line of his mouth. Even the slight rise of that well-arched left brow was exactly like Jake's.

Sighing, Bess hugged the poster again and fought the bitter tears that stung behind her eyelids. Much as she hated to admit it, Jake did have a hot temper. And he had behaved mighty mysteriously on occasion. The incident on the Baltimore docks, for example, when the Texan had said Jake reminded him of a man by the name of W. C. Atwood. And what about the time she'd found him in her secret place, shoulders heaving as he begged God to explain why he'd been doomed to living life looking over his shoulder?

Bess dried her eyes with the backs of her hands and all but leaped from the bed. Trembling with fear, she haphazardly folded the poster in half, in half again, and tucked into her apron pocket. Crossing the room in purposeful strides, she leaned close to the mirror above her dresser and pinched both journey-paled cheeks, then tucked a stray wisp of hair behind her ear.

Could she really have been so wrong about him? Were all his kindnesses merely a ruse to hide his true identity? If so, then she was the biggest fool this side of the Mississippi!

Suddenly, fury replaced self-pity. Bess stood straight, threw back her shoulders, and marched toward the door. There was only one way to find out.

Chapter Fourteen

Bess charged down the stairs and through the foyer, propelled by a full head of steam. *I'll get to the bottom of this if it takes the rest of the day!* she insisted as she barged through the front door and onto the porch.

"Bess Beckley, where are you off to in such an all-fired hurry?"

The deep, resonant voice startled her badly, and Bess stifled a scream. "Pa," she said, clutching her throat. "I didn't see you sitting there." As her heartbeat returned to normal, Bess studied her father's handsome, gray-bearded face. "All right," she said, standing near his chair, one hand on his shoulder, "out with it. What's wrong?"

He smiled a bit. "Nothing. I'm right as rain," was his quiet reply.

"Don't give me that. There's something on your mind...."

Micah only shook his head and stared across the lawn. "Remember the day your Mama planted those trees?" He nodded toward the clump of white birch just beyond the drive. "Everybody insisted they'd never grow in heavy soil, but Mary didn't believe them. Not for a minute."

Grinning, Bess knelt beside his rocker and laid her hands

atop his. She, too, gazed at the clump of birches. "Ma always did have a mind of her own, didn't she?"

"'Deed she did." He faced his only daughter, took her hands in his. "I visited her grave this morning."

"Oh, Pa," Bess interrupted. "Why didn't you tell me? I'd have gone with you. I know how upset it gets you to go there alone."

Gently pressing a callused fingertip against her lips, he shushed her. "Do I look upset?"

She studied his face for the usual signs of distress—furrowed brow, trembling lips, tear-dampened eyes. It surprised her to see a smile playing at the corners of his mouth. "Quite the contrary," she said warily. "In fact, you look like the cat that swallowed the canary."

He laughed softly, then stared off into space again. Shortly, Micah leaned forward, slid an arm around Bess's waist and drew her near. "How will I ever make it up to you, my sweet girl?"

Unfortunately, she knew exactly what he meant.

This wasn't the first time he'd apologized for his years of emotional absence. But it did seem the first time he'd been sincere about it. Sometimes, she'd been tempted to stamp her foot and tell him it was high time he realized what his whining had put her through. But mostly, like now, Bess's love for her father made her want nothing but to see him smile again. Bess rested her head on his shoulder. "There's nothing to make up for, Pa."

Micah kissed the top of her head. "Oh, but you're wrong. There's so much…" He inhaled deeply before continuing. "From the moment your mother left this world, you've been ma and pa to the boys. Been my lifeline, too. Wasn't fair of me, heaping all that on your shoulders. You were barely more than a child when Mary died." He paused, took another deep breath. "I'm ashamed of myself. I ought to have been there for you."

He got to his feet, and Bess joined him, she on the top step, Micah on the one below her. And for the first time in a decade, father and daughter saw eye to eye.

"I was happy to help out, Pa."

One hand on each of her shoulders, he gave her a gentle squeeze. "'Help out!' You did far more than just 'help out!' Believe you me, I know what you did for us…for me. And not once did you complain." His gray eyes misted, and he quickly blinked back the traitorous tears. Frowning slightly, he gave Bess a little shake. "You're made of some mighty sturdy stuff, Bess m'girl. Why, I don't believe I ever saw you shed a tear."

She focused on that trio of birches that formed a giant white *W* beyond the drive, because if she allowed Micah to look into her eyes at that moment, he'd know in an instant that she *had* cried, thousands of tears, alone in her dark room during these ten, long years.

No. It hadn't been easy. Not easy at all, being mother and father to the twins, being caretaker to Micah, keeping the farmhands fed and the ledgers in order, the house tidy, the shopping, the mending, the laundry…. In fact, it had been so hard that sometimes, as she cried herself to sleep, Bess wondered where she'd find the strength to do it all again come morning.

But without fail, as if in answer to her tearful prayers, Mary's voice, gentle and reassuring, would whisper in her mind, promising that tomorrow would be a better, brighter day. And there, in her room, surrounded by the loving and meaningful gifts her mother had made for her, Bess grasped that promise tight, like a drowning woman clings to a life preserver.

What would be gained, after all, by letting Micah know that she'd suffered because of his grief-induced weakness? What possible good could come of admitting he was right…that his years of wallowing in self-pity had robbed her of golden girlhood? Either way, those precious years were gone, and she'd never get them back. Why, right this moment, faced with the dilemma of Jake's identity, Bess didn't know if she *wanted* them back! Being a clear-minded full-grown woman, unfazed by childish dreams, would no doubt help her cope with the truth...whatever it might be.

Bess sighed shakily and wondered what her mother would have done in a similar situation. Immediately, the answer began to bubble in her heart. Love, Bess realized, would have prompted Mary to reach out to her father, would have compelled her to soothe his shattered spirit and ease his wounded pride. And that's exactly what Bess had done. Knowing her mother would have approved of her actions made them all that much more bearable.

"I was happy to do it, Pa," she repeated, shaking a forefinger under his nose, "and I don't want to discuss it, ever again." With that, Bess smiled brightly. "I saw some lemons in the cupboard. Now, why don't you keep me company while I squeeze us a pitcher of lemonade?"

Micah didn't respond to her invitation. Instead, he stood there, looking from her eyes to her hair, from her cheeks to her mouth, to her eyes again. And then he whispered, "Do you realize how much you look like your ma when you do that?"

His piercing gaze and intense tone surprised her, and Bess flinched almost as noticeably as when his voice startled her moments earlier. "When...when I do what?"

"When you throw back your shoulders and lift your chin that way...as if you're prepared to take on a mighty enemy, single-handedly." Gently, he stroked her hair. "I'd hate to be that enemy, Bess, m'girl." Winking, he added, "Because you look determined to win."

Grinning, she kissed his cheek. "Well, Ma always said—"

"—'no sense doing anything halfway,'" they quoted in unison, laughing.

Micah held open the screen door. "We'll talk business and gossip at dinner, when Matthew and Mark are back from the fields. Right now, I'm far more interested in hearing where you were headed in such an all-fired hurry a bit ago."

Bess stepped over the threshold and headed for the kitchen. She wouldn't tell Micah—or anyone else, for that matter—what she suspected about Jake. Because if she was wrong, if he *wasn't* W. C. Atwood, his life could be ruined forever. No, she would confront him alone. And if her suspicions turned out to be facts... Well, she'd just cross that bridge when she came to it. "I was looking for Jake," she told her father, choosing her words carefully. "I wanted him to bring me up to date on...on the harvesting."

"Ahh." Nodding, Micah crossed both arms over his chest. "The harvesting. Yes. Of course."

"And exactly what does *that* mean?" she asked in response to his wink and sly grin.

"It means Jake has been mooning around here like a sick calf ever since you left. Seems every other word out of his mouth these days is *Bess*. And don't think I haven't noticed the way you two look at each other when you think nobody's paying attention." Micah snickered. "I could do worse, I suppose...."

Bess wrinkled her brow. "Pa," she interrupted, "I haven't any idea what you're talking about."

"...could do worse than Jake...as a son-in-law, that is," he concluded.

Her heart skipped a beat at the sound of it. *Son-in-law*. It had a magical, musical ring, because in order for Jake to be Micah's son-in-law, he'd have to be her husband!

If it had been Mary standing there, wearing that silly smirk, wiggling her eyebrows, Bess wouldn't have been at all surprised, because her fun-loving mother had often seemed able to read her mind.

But her father hadn't paid enough attention to her since Mary's death to know she'd *had* secret thoughts, let alone try to read them. At least, that's the way it had seemed to Bess all these years.

"For your information," she began, feigning a good-natured grin, "Jake has no romantic designs on me." It was a bold-faced, blatant lie, but a necessary one until she forced a showdown about the Wanted poster. "And I have no romantic notions about him, either, for that matter." Bess turned on her heel and headed for the kitchen.

"Mmm-hmm," her father said, pocketing both hands as he followed her. "And the sun doesn't rise ever' morning...."

Long after she'd cleaned up their lemonade and cake snack, Bess thought about her father's pronouncement. *I wonder how eager he'd be to have Jake for a son-in-law if he'd seen that Wanted poster?* she asked herself, putting the cut-glass tumblers back onto their doilied shelf in the hutch. She hung the neatly folded tea towel over the wooden dowel beside the sink and headed for the barn.

She had procrastinated long enough. One way or another, she would have an answer to her question by suppertime.

This time when she stepped into the bright sunshine, there was no head of steam propelling her, no righteous indignation urging her onward. Because if Jake admitted to being W. C. Atwood, she'd be forced to make a choice:

Stand with him...or stand apart.

As she neared the red-sided building, Bess heard the unmistakable *chit-schr-r-ring, chit-schr-r-ring* that told her someone was in the loft, forking hay into a stall below. Hoping it was Jake, Bess took a deep breath and grabbed the rusting iron door handle. The hinges squealed mercilessly as she pulled the heavy wooden door and slipped through the narrow opening.

A bright shard of sunlight sliced across the board floor, broadening as it slanted into the darkened interior of the barn, and in its center, Bess saw her own shadowy silhouette. For an instant, she stared at it, mouth agape, for the daystar's gleam made her dress appear to have a long, billowing train. Her hair seemed have taken the form of a flowing, filmy veil. And the poster she'd wadded in her left hand looked like a bouquet of posies. *If only it could be so,* she thought.

But reality called, waking Bess from her reverie as surely as the cock's crow woke her every dawn. Swallowing hard, she shook her head, hoping to shake away the ridiculous notions of herself as a bride as well. *It was Pa who put that idea in my head,* she told herself, *with all his talk of sons-in-law....*

The breeze gave the door a gentle shove, and it creaked slowly shut, blotting out the sunlight, and the beautiful mirage. With a huff, Bess stuffed the Wanted poster back into her apron pocket, wondering when—and *why*—she'd taken it out in the first place. Then, licking her lips, she looked up toward the loft, fully prepared to call out his name.

Sunshine, slanting in through the window beside the door, climbed the ladder and slithered into the loft. And there, in the center of its bright, golden light, stood Jake.

Had he been there all along? Had he seen her looking at her shadow and read her mind, as he'd done so many times before? If the lusty expression on his face was any indication, he knew exactly what fanciful thoughts had been dancing in her head—and in her heart—as she stood there like a schoolgirl, stunned into silly silence by the image of herself as a bride.

"Somehow, when that door opened, I knew it'd be you," he said softly.

He looked like an angel, all aglow in the pale-yellow light. Sunlight gleamed from his hair and his lashes and the buttons of his shirt. And it sparkled in his eyes...in those untamed, wolfish eyes....

Bess pressed a hand to her chest, hoping to still the furious beating of her heart. *But how had he known it would be me?* she wanted to ask. But when she opened her mouth to voice the question, no sound issued forth.

"It's good you're home."

She cleared her throat. "It's good to *be* home."

The silence that followed their brief exchange fell slowly, heavily, the way darkness drifts down from on high and spreads over the earth at day's end. Bess heard a cricket chanting merrily in the corner stall, harmonizing with the hungry mews of newborn barn cats. Outside, birdsong competed with locust chirps and horse whinnies, as though this were any ordinary afternoon, as though she would not soon face him with that awful question.

A thought flashed through her mind, paralyzing her: She should have stayed in her room, behind its closed door, Bess realized, until she'd plotted a sensible way to talk to him. She should have drawn up a plan. Written out a script. Considered how she'd deal with the question...and his answer.

But you went off half-cocked, as usual, she scolded herself, *and jumped in with both feet without testing the water first.* With a sigh and a frown she added, *It'll serve you right if you're scalded in the process!*

"Your pa showed me the telegram," he said at last.

If anything burned her, it would be his smoldering gaze, she acknowledged. "What telegram?" she managed to ask.

"Did you send more than one while you were in Philadelphia?"

The teasing sarcasm of his tone stunned her out of her daze. "As a matter of fact, I wired Pa twice."

Jake chuckled. "Then I'm referring to the one about your

meeting with Shelby.'' He hunkered down into a squat and grinned. ''Micah says you cut a better deal with that farmer than he could've on his best day.''

Though it was cool in the semidarkened barn, she felt hot from her toes to her scalp. Bess unbuttoned her top collar button. ''If I did well in Philadelphia, it's because I learned at the feet of a master.''

He shook his head. ''I do declare, I've never met anyone like you.''

The heat in her cheeks increased, and she undid the buttons of her shirtsleeves and rolled them up. ''I'm getting a crick in my neck standing here talking to you.''

''So stop standing there.''

Bess hoped Jake couldn't see that the heat of his challenge—and seductive scrutiny—had reddened her cheeks. She loosed another collar button and issued a challenge of her own. ''Come down here and talk to me, or I'm coming up there.''

He didn't move, save the narrowing of his eyes. ''If that's supposed to be a threat,'' he said, his grating drawl deepening, ''you'd better try again.''

That does it! Bess thought, setting her jaw. Hitching up her skirts, she marched toward the ladder. She paused a moment to tuck the hem of her dress into her belt, then headed up the narrow, rough-hewn ladder.

He stepped closer when she reached the top rung. ''Took you long enough,'' he said, leaning his pitchfork against the loft's back wall.

She only had to swing her foot over the rail to be on solid ground again. But she made the move a bit too quickly....

''I'd like to see how fast *you* could climb straight up on a rickety old ladder—in a skirt!'' she dared. ''Why, I've a mind to...*ouch!*'' Wincing, Bess stuck her fingertip into her mouth.

The mocking grin disappeared from his face, immediately

replaced by an expression of concern. "Bess, are you all right?"

Rolling her eyes, she said around her pinky, "Ith only a thmall thplinter. I think I'll thurvive."

Ignoring the lisp, Jake grabbed her wrist and examined her injury. "Hell, the way you downplay everything, you might have a log in there and not admit it," he said, frowning.

How was she supposed to answer that, when he held her so tenderly, so possessively? How was she to defend herself, when he looked into her eyes as though he'd protect her until his dying day? "I don't downplay anything. I just don't believe in making mountains out of molehills."

Bess tried to retrieve her wounded hand, but Jake held tight. He pressed her finger to his lips. "More like molehills out of mountains. Now hold still. We've got to get that sliver out of there before you swell up like a pregnant whore."

Giggling nervously, she tried again to free herself. "Why, I've half a mind to wash your mouth out with lye soap, Jake Walker!"

His left brow lifted. Well, she had reasons of her own to behave like a stern parent! She'd come here to shove that Wanted poster under his nose and force him to admit or deny that he and W. C. Atwood were one and the same man. First, he'd sidetracked her with provocative taunts, shooting her full of that sizzling stare. And now he was using a minuscule wood fragment to distract her from her cause.

Bess was about to insist that he turn her loose when she saw him slip a small knife from a leather sheath tied to his belt. Her eyes widened and her jaw dropped when sunlight sparked from its well-honed blade. Suddenly, it seemed swordlike in length and width. "Wha-what do you think you're going to do with *that?*"

Calm as you please, Jake raised both brows. "I'm going to cut out that splinter, that's what."

And before she could protest, he'd removed the offending chip. "There." Jake examined the flake that now rested on his own fingertip. "That got it," he said, resheathing the knife.

A tiny blood droplet formed where the splinter had been. Instinct made her move to stuff the fingertip into her mouth.

But Jake was quicker. In an eyeblink, he'd slipped an arm around her slender waist and pulled her near. One tender touch of his lips to her fingertip, and the puncture was forgotten.

For what seemed to Bess an hour, they stood, eyes fused by an invisible current of heat as powerful and intense the red-hot coals in a potbellied stove. He'd pressed her so close against him that she could feel the furious drumming of his heart against her rib cage, could feel his warm breath against her cheeks, could feel the raw need throbbing deep inside him.

She hoped he couldn't sense her own urgent desires....

Too late, she wished for the strength to move away from the commanding, passionate embrace, for Jake had drawn her nearer still, crinkling the Wanted poster in her apron pocket and reminding her why she'd come into the barn in the first place.

"I've missed you," he rasped, his lips grazing hers.

Bess inhaled deeply, searching for the courage to do what she'd come here to do. She wriggled this way and that, but rather than liberating herself from his iron-strong arms, her maneuvering only served to give him more leverage, and he held her tighter yet.

She'd been embraced, dancing at church socials, and had experienced the gentlemanly end-of-evening farewells of young beaus. Pleasant enough experiences, she'd thought at the time. But no touch, no kiss, had made her want to abandon all ladylike decorum, because no touch, no kiss, had aroused a craving like the one simmering inside her now.

Just as a raging blaze begins with a single spark, Jake had set her soul afire long before he'd ever touched her.

And he'd done it by simply looking at her.

"Seemed you were gone forever," he said, his voice thick with emotion, his eyes glinting with feral fervor. He filled both hands with her hair and almost savagely forced her to look at him. "Did you miss me?"

Blinking with surprise at the wild, primal gleam in his eyes, she licked her lips. She could see in the glittering blue orbs that he *wanted* her to admit she'd missed him; *wanted* her to admit their time apart had seemed like years instead of days. So in a hoarse whisper, she admitted it. "Yes...."

Her quiet confession became the key that unlocked emotions he'd hidden away all those years on the road. But Jake needed to be sure, before he exposed himself further, that she could be entrusted with that instrument of freedom. He pressed a palm to each of her cheeks, his thumbs drawing slow, lazy circles on her jaw as he probed for the lies he'd read in every other woman's face. He continued to study the lovely, angelic features, convinced that upon closer examination, he'd find deceit hiding somewhere in her...beneath the finely pored, pale skin, perhaps, or on those full, pouting pink lips, or in her dreamy, dusky eyes. Soon, it became clear that he could spend a lifetime inspecting every inch of her without finding a trace of dishonesty.

It pleased him that Bess didn't bristle under his examination. Instead, she smiled, and gently traced the backs of her fingers across his jaw, letting the fingertip he'd repaired linger on his lower lip. "Yes," she said again, dark eyes blazing with trust and love, and with that simple word, loosed the floodgates of his lonely soul.

But he didn't believe he deserved the devotion of one so fine, so pure, so innocent. Didn't believe he deserved the loyalty of a woman so good that even the animals in the forest sensed they were safe with her.

Even the animals in the forest...

He'd been like an animal these ten years, like a god-damned mole! he rued, always seeking shadows as he moved from place to place in search of safety, in search of peace. Survival of the fittest, he'd heard, was the law of the land. Well, he'd survived, but to what end? To find safety and peace in Bess's arms, only to leave it behind?

He'd learned to accept the fact that he'd never have a permanent home. A family. The love of a good woman. But could he learn to live without Bess's love, now that he'd tasted the sweetness of it?

Yearning, he understood now, was an emotion born of having experienced perfection; yearning, he understood *too late,* would be his only friend, his traveling companion, his bunkmate for the rest of his days.

Despair made him wish he'd never begun this dangerous game with her, this flirtation-turned-fondness-turned-love. Suddenly, that despair made him wrap both arms around her, holding tight this fragile flower who had planted the seed of her love deep in his heart, just as the wild rose vine plants its seed in the craggiest outcropping of a snow-covered mountaintop. He would hold tight to perfection for as long as he could, so that he'd have this moment to remember when the powers that be ordered him to let her go.

A sob ached in his throat, and he buried his face in the crook of her neck, for he couldn't bear to have her remember him this way when he was gone...and all too soon, he feared, he would be long gone.

But, like the angel she was, Bess read his heart. Placing one tiny hand on either side of his face, she brought him out of hiding. Tears shimmered in her eyes and glistened on her long, lush lashes when she said, for the last time, ''Yes, Jake. Yes.''

She pressed her lips to his, softly at first as she combed delicate fingers through his hair, more urgently then, as those dainty fingers clutched at his shoulders, his back, his neck, with a strength that belied her size. Oh, how he wanted this woman. Wanted her with every echo of his solitary soul, with every beat of his lonely heart.

He'd been in Southern Illinois years ago when a levee collapsed and the muddy Mississippi threatened to devour every building and barn, every mortal and mammal for miles. The awesome power of the surging river humbled him as it sluiced through the streets, hissing like a giant turbid snake. If the mighty Mississippi had been a god, Jake would gladly have genuflected before that venerable authority in the hope its gluttonous hunger would soon be sated.

What emanated from Bess, who felt so small and helpless in his arms, was far more powerful than the river's rage. And though she couldn't have known it—and certainly wouldn't have intended it—she stirred more fear and apprehension in him than the roiling waterway had.

Jake had survived numerous near-fatal experiences, but with nothing to live for or look forward to, death had no authority over him. Even the hangman's noose didn't terrify him as much as this tiny woman in his arms, who waited to hear his truth.

And much as he wanted to claim her as his own, Jake would not subject her to a lifetime of waiting and wanting, of yearning for what could never be. His soul, his life, belonged to others; he could not belong to her until he'd freed himself of those "others." The only way to loose the ties that bound him was to prove himself innocent of the murder in Lubbock. And how likely was that? Bess deserved a normal, complete life. A home. Children. And a husband who loved her more than life itself.

Because she loved him.

He could see it in her eyes, in her smile. Felt it in her touch. Tasted it in her kiss. Jake knew that if he told her everything, right now, and asked her to run off with him, she'd do it.

But if he loved her, truly loved her, he couldn't ask... *wouldn't* ask.

And oh, how he loved her, more than life itself!

Jake looked inside himself for the strength to turn away, right now, and wrapped his hands around her waist, intent upon gently pushing her away.

They were strong hands. Hands that had hammered nail and tightened barbed wire, hands that had turned almost as tough and leathery as the rawhide tethers he'd used to rein in the snorting thunder of many a wild Appaloosa. Those hands had not wavered, no matter how strenuous the task. And yet, when he put those work-hardened hands on this tiny woman to put time and space between them, they trembled, as a crisp autumn leaf shivers at winter's first icy blast. He knew he must let her go, must *make* her go, for his sake as well as hers.

He looked into her eyes then, and read the love there.

He'd let her go.... Soon. But not yet. Not just yet....

Hesitantly, he ran his hand down her back, and when he did, his rough skin caught on the finely woven fabric of her housedress. He stopped, pulling abruptly away, embarrassed that his big clumsy hand had damaged the pretty frock.

Yet again, Bess read his heart. "It's all right," she whispered.

But it wasn't all right. Nothing would ever be all right again. Because he loved her like he'd never loved anyone, Jake knew he was doomed.

Before Bess, he could easily outrun and outwit the U.S. Marshals. Now, memory of her, of loving her, of knowing that she loved him, would haunt him all the days of his life. The memories of what was, and of what might have been, might distract him....

She pressed the offending hand to her chest. "See? I'm afraid, too."

Jake felt the wild thrumming of her heart, felt it vibrate through his palm, past his wrist and elbow, straight to the core of him. They were connected, for the moment, by hard-beating hearts, by desire that coursed from her into him and back again.

In a move that stunned and surprised him, she boldly reached out and grabbed the bandanna wrapped round his neck, drawing him near as surely as his artfully tossed lasso had drawn runaway calves back to the herd, her soft yet insistent kisses imprinting on his heart as surely as his branding iron had seared ranchers' seals to cattle hide.

His knees buckled and his mind whirled as a sweet, soft moan sang from deep within her, its music moving over him like wind ripples on a still pond. Like a dormant volcano, long-repressed needs erupted, and he returned her kiss with equal ardor.

Suddenly, she was on her back in a bed of straw, the billows of her white petticoats encircling them as he blanketed her with his hot, throbbing body. Between deep, urgent kisses, his thick, fumbling fingers struggled to undo the pearl buttons of her dress.

It was as if she sensed that his need was far more than physical, for she wrapped a small, warm hand around each of his big, cool ones. "Easy," she sighed, "easy...."

Misunderstanding her intent, Jake immediately withdrew. Bess read the hurt and humiliation burning in his eyes. "I said 'easy,'" she smiled mischievously, "not 'stop.'"

His left brow quirked as the blue eyes flared, and his smile slanted slightly as cautiously, carefully, he undid the next button, and the next, exposing the creamy white swells of her breasts. He stared for a moment, dumbstruck at the sight. His ears grew hot and his eyes began to burn as dizziness settled in, for he'd forgotten to breathe.

And was it any wonder? He'd bedded barmaids and whores, bored housewives and entertainers—some of whom deserved to be called beautiful—but not one of them, not even the most professional and practiced of them, could compare to the vision that was Bess Beckley.

The long, slender neck sloped gently downward until it blended gracefully with her breasts. Beneath them, her narrow waist curved delicately into softly flared hips.

Jake couldn't tear his eyes away. Looking at her, lying there nearly naked beneath him, reminded him of a passage in a book he'd read years ago. It told of Aphrodite, goddess of love and beauty. Worshipped throughout Greece, she was the embodiment of purity and spirituality, of marriage and family, the essence of earthly, sensual love. But Aphrodite, the book said, possessed strength to match her enchanting comeliness, strength that had inspired the adoration of sailors and warriors throughout the land.

A statue had been carved in her honor. *Venus,* the sculptor had named it, and the marble rendition of her had been discovered just a few decades earlier, on the island of Melos. As he'd read, Jake had found it impossible not to stare at the artist's black-and-white illustration of the statue, of Aphrodite: she stood before God and all mankind, unashamed of her womanly attributes, just as Bess lay beneath him now.

"You're beautiful," he breathed.

And for the first time in her life, Bess *felt* beautiful.

Soon, his scrutiny became too much to bear, and she stirred. "Didn't your mother teach you it's not polite to stare?" She caught her breath and raised her fingers to her mouth, amazed at her brazenness.

"No, thank God," he breathed, the hint of a smile tugging at the corners of his mouth.

As his face neared hers, he growled softly, and the fierce sound of it sent a shiver down her spine. His lips parted hers as he slung a leg over hers.

"I may have had the upper hand earlier," she whispered, wiggling the injured pinky, "but you definitely have a leg up right now...."

Again she considered pushing him away, protecting her virtue. Jake had made no promises to her, after all. And while she believed he loved her, too, she had no guarantee that, once he'd had his fill of her, here in the sunbathed hayloft, he'd be around to pick up the pieces of her shattered reputation. She'd be the talk of the town.

Bess looked at him then. Really looked at him. The blue of his eyes had intensified, not from passion, she sensed, but from need. Not the kind of need that drives a man to bed a woman, but the kind that turns a manly expression into the pleading supplication of an long-orphaned boy who is offered his first warm, nourishing meal in years.

So let her be the talk of the town. Let him leave on the morrow and never look back. She would concentrate on Jake, on what he needed. Because, foolish though she might be, Bess believed he *did* love her, and that the dark secret he'd harbored for so long simply wouldn't allow him to admit it, aloud.

She loved him. Oh, how she loved him!

But did she love him enough to give him memories that would comfort him when he was alone? Did she love him enough to think of his needs rather than her own, so that when he left this place, he could think of this day and believe in his own innate goodness, in his true worth? Did she love him enough to put his best interests ahead of hers, so he could remember, on cold dark nights, that once upon a time, he'd been loved as no man had ever been loved?

Did she love him enough to risk this moment, knowing it could be the start of a tiny human, made in the image of Jake...and her?

Yes, she did.

Bess closed her eyes and surrendered her heart to him, an

easy gift to give, really, for when he left her—*if* he left her—
she would find solace in the arms of her father and brothers.
They would stand beside her, even if a child was born of
this union without benefit or blessing of sacrament or ceremony. She would always be embraced by the strong, loving
arms of her family; who would Jake turn to when the hard
road ahead beckoned his spirit and called him back to his
roving life-style?

Yes, she loved him.

And she would show him. She would prove it in the only
way she knew how.

Arching her back, Bess tenderly wove her fingers through
his golden waves and gathered him near, inviting him to
suckle at her breast, inviting him to take all that was hers to
give.

Chapter Fifteen

It was almost midnight when Jake strolled from the bunk-house, hands in his pockets. He'd tried to sleep, but images of that afternoon wouldn't allow it.

Mamie pawed the dirt and whinnied, commanding his attention. Smiling, he sauntered toward the corral. Absent-mindedly, he lifted the coil of barbed wire he would need at first light and slung it over his shoulder. "What's the matter, girl?" he said softly, leaning over the gate. "Jealous?" The horse bobbed her head, as if to answer in the affirmative. Thoughtfully, Jake stroked her nose. "Don't you worry. You'll always be my best girl...."

But Bess...Bess will always be my woman, he added silently, looking deep into the starry sky, where Orion and Perseus winked at him from the inky darkness. *Silver in velvet,* he told himself, *like Bess's eyes.*

He turned as Mamie nudged his chest, and when he did, Jake's nose brushed his shirtsleeve...the same shirtsleeve where Bess had rested her head mere hours ago. The clean, sweet scent of her still clung to the fabric, and he closed his eyes, filling his nostrils with it.

She had given herself to him wholly, a gift he would never be able to forget—or repay. Why he had allowed her to give that gift, or why he'd so hungrily accepted it, Jake didn't know. But he'd known, even as his trembling hands had slowly removed the dress, the petticoats, the stockings and bloomers that hid her loveliness, that he should have told her "git...whilst the gittin's good."

As though she'd sensed his apprehension, as though she'd read his heart and knew why he had hesitated, Bess let him know with loving looks and gentle touches and tender kisses that she had no desire or intention of 'gittin.'

He grinned a bit, remembering that, despite her good intentions, she *did* leave him during those blissful moments that united them as completely as only love can bind man to woman....

She'd buried her fingers in his hair and, after sending him a silent message by way of those hypnotic, alluring eyes, whispered, "Yes." The action, and the single word accompanying it, had taken him back in time to days when, as a helpless babe, he'd nuzzled at his mother's breast, drawing nourishment and warmth from her steady, dependable love. Jake had known that it had *not* been his mother who held him tight there in the hayloft. No, it had been *Bess* whose fingers moved slowly, sensuously through his hair, as if attempting to match his tongue flicks across her areolas stroke for stroke. Still, it had been a dizzying, heady mix of eroticism and solace that had him sucking greedily at her nipples as his hands caressed every inch of the satiny skin he'd so clumsily exposed.

He chanced a peek at her from time to time, amazed with every glance at the way she threw herself into the lovemaking. Head back and eyes half-closed, her lips had parted and her breaths came in shallow, panting gasps. Her chest heaved and her back arched as those feminine, curvy hips swayed and rocked, slowly, slowly....

"Yes," she'd hissed, gritting her teeth as those long black lashes fluttered. It had shocked him, the way she responded to him. So intense had her yearning been, so deep her hunger, the thought flashed through his mind that such open expression of desire could only mean she was an experienced woman—a woman who had gained that experience in the arms of another man—perhaps in the arms of many men. It had been one thought and nothing more, quick as an eyeblink.

Yet it burned in his mind like a fever.

As though sensing his doubt, Bess had lain a hand on each of his cheeks. "I've never done anything like this before," she'd said, her beautiful eyes glistening with unshed tears. "I hope—I hope you won't be disappointed...."

He could only shake his head at the absurdity of her suggestion. "Disappointed? Not a chance on God's green earth." He'd smiled then. "Just between you and me, I've never been with a woman...who's never been with a man before."

It was as though his teasing words were the magic that shattered the last remnants of fear wrapped so tightly around her. Her lilting laughter cast a seductive spell of its own as she flung her leg over his. "Then we start out on even ground, don't we?" she murmured, drawing him nearer....

Sudden and intense pain pierced his chest, penetrating his reverie and abruptly snapping him back to the reality of the here and now. Jake looked down, puzzled at first by the dark circular stains rapidly spreading over the tight weave of his blue cotton work shirt. Instinctively, he drew his palm across the bloodstained garment, only to discover that his palm, too, had been punctured by the razorlike barbed wire he'd flung over his shoulder earlier. The memory of Bess in the hayloft, he realized, had produced an intensity of its own.

But he paid his wounds little heed, for the physical discomfort paled by comparison to the ache in his heart: someday, soon, he'd be forced to leave Bess behind for good.

He jolted when a warm hand rested on his shoulder.

"What in tarnation happened to you, Jake? You're blood-ier'n a newborned calf."

I'm losing my edge, he told himself. Before Bess, the old farmhand wouldn't have gotten within thirty yards without being detected; ten long years as a fugitive had conditioned him well. "Guess I got a little careless with the barbed wire," he explained, grinning sheepishly.

The grizzled fellow shook his white-haired head. "Way I hear it, you've had yourself a mighty tough day," he muttered over his shoulder as he headed for the bunkhouse. "Better wash up them there cuts."

Jake hated to admit it, but the old codger was right. From the cock's first crow, it *had* been a difficult day. His shin still smarted from the sharp kick of the unbroken horse he'd carelessly approached from behind, and his left thumb still throbbed from a misplaced hammer blow. He'd sliced through his trousers with the baling hook, nearly impaling himself instead of the hay bale in the process, and pulled a muscle in his shoulder while heaving a hundred-pound sack of grain.

Woodenly, Jake walked toward the watering trough, stripped from the waist up, hung his shirt on top of the pump, and proceeded to wash the blood from his hands. Soaking his neckerchief in the cold water, he daubed gingerly at numerous tiny, stinging punctures on his chest.

He knew he should bunk down, for another hard day would begin at sunup. But as much as he tried, his thoughts would not let go of Bess and their quiet hour, alone in the barn....

In giving herself to him, she had put her well-being, her heart, her mind and body and soul into his hands. She had told him, with every buck and pitch of her beautiful, responsive body, that she trusted him, even on this, her first venture into the world of desire.

And so it was that mentally, Bess left him there in the

loft for those precious moments, to savor what his hands and his lips…and his manhood…could give her. And glimpses into her passion-pinked face told him she had no intention of returning to reality until she'd experienced every last ounce of it all. She unabashedly, unashamedly gave of herself, and she had accepted *his* offerings, too.

Even as he was still throbbing deep inside her, she'd gently nipped at his lower lip, then bracketed his face with both hands, and made him look at her. Tears had shimmered in her eyes, and when she said his name, it was with the reverence and awe reserved for prayers. "Oh, Jake…"

Misunderstanding the reason for her tears, he'd rasped, "I—I'm sorry. I didn't…I never meant to hurt you.…" He looked away, cursing the self-centered *need* that had turned him into a greedy, pounding brute.

But she would not remove her hands from his face, and forced him to meet her eyes. "Do I look like I'm in pain?" she'd asked huskily.

There had been no misunderstanding her loving smile *then!* "No," he'd whispered, giving the tip of her nose an affectionate kiss. "As a matter of fact, you look very—"

"—content?" she finished for him, her smile widening to a mischievous grin.

"Content. Yes," he agreed, kissing her cheek. "And maybe a little—"

"—eager for more?" With that, she'd winked.

Jake had laughed softly and hugged her closer, then reared back to study her lovely face.

As she looked at him, her sassy smile had slowly faded, and in its place, a smoldering, bewitching expression proved her eagerness. He kissed her then, long and hard, to prove an eagerness of his own. But, mindful that it was her first experience with love, with sex, he'd told himself to proceed carefully.…

His pa had drummed an old saying into his head, one Jake

had memorized long before his father died: "When you give a gift with no expectation of getting one in return, you get back far more than you give." It hadn't been a difficult piece of advice to understand, even when he'd been eight or ten, but Jake had never experienced the impact of its meaning quite as he had, alone with Bess, on that crude bed of hay. Putting her physical needs ahead of his own had not only sent her soaring, but drew him along on the same wondrous current, and together, they'd reached a fulfillment he'd never known possible.

When it ended, she'd snuggled close, her fingers sketching lines and circles in his chest hair, sighing as his hands skimmed over her perspiration-slicked skin. "I'm sorry for frightening you," she'd said quietly.

Jake had laughed, drawing her nearer. "You did a lot of things to me just now, darlin', but frightenin' wasn't one of 'em."

Levering herself up on one elbow, Bess said, "Well, you sure *looked* afraid...when I cried...."

Her tears *had* scared him. Thinking he'd physically hurt her had terrified him, if the truth be told. "Then why *were* you crying, if I didn't hurt you?"

She'd straddled him, pressed her palms to his chest. "Because...I was happy."

Again he'd chuckled. "Happy? You cried because—"

Bess leaned close and squinted. "Don't you dare make fun of me, Jake Walker. A woman is entitled to a bit of—" she sat up again and closed one eye, searching for the right word "—she's entitled to a bit of dampness at a moment like that."

He'd never asked a woman to share the lusty secrets of her soul with him; hadn't even thought to ask. But Jake had a feeling that, with Bess, he could ask, and would be told, exactly what the lovemaking had been like for her. His shrug, he hoped, would encourage her to continue. "I don't get it."

She shook her head, sending dark curls ruffling like the summer breeze ripples the leaves in the trees. "I don't know if I can explain it...." Bess slid off him, nestled against his side, and nonchalantly propped her head on her palm. "It was as though," she began, "my mind left my body, and everything—every sound, every touch, *everything*—was intensified." She kissed his cheek. "It wasn't at all what I expected."

From the corner of his eye, he watched as she bit her lower lip. Watched as the blush crept from her throat to her cheeks.

"What *had* you expected?"

"Well, I didn't expect to like it," she'd whispered hoarsely. "But I did." Flopping back onto the hay, she flung both arms out beside her and smiled serenely. "I liked it *a lot!*"

He'd gathered her in a hug, pressed a kiss to her temple, pleased—and more than a little grateful—that she didn't seem in the least ashamed or uncomfortable. "Then I'm happy to be of service, ma'am," he'd said with an exaggerated Texas drawl.

She'd sat up and began to retrieve her clothes. "You must be a warlock," she whispered, smiling. "You've cast a spell on me, and it's made me abandon all ladylike decorum." Bess stared straight into his eyes. "The only other human being in the entire world who ever saw me bare-naked was my mama."

Jake stood and stepped into his trousers. "I'm honored to be in such fine company," he'd said, winking. As he watched her wriggle into her petticoats, his smile faded at the sight of the bright-red blotch that stained the white ruffled garment.

Bess followed his gaze. A moment of surprised puzzlement crossed her face until realization set in. Lifting her left brow and the hem of the garment at the same time, she sent him a challenging grin. "Is there any doubt in your mind now, Mr. Walker, that you were my first...and my only?"

He'd smiled when she said it, and he was smiling now as the night breeze riffled his hair. The meaning and intent of her words rang in his heart, and warmed him so that he scarcely noticed the chill wind that raised gooseflesh on his wet, naked torso.

Jake bowed his head and, taking a deep breath as he grabbed his shirt, headed back to the bunkhouse. It took every ounce of reserve to keep from looking toward the second floor of the farmhouse, because if he saw Bess there in her window seat, smiling at him, nothing would keep him from breaking down Micah's front door, taking the stairs two at a time, and barging into her room. He wouldn't have asked to repeat what they'd shared in the loft. To lie in her arms, cheek against her milk-white breasts, listening to the thrumming of her heartbeat until slumber wrapped round him like a mother's hug, would be his only request.

It would be his only dream.

As it would be, all the days of his life.

Lubbock, Texas

"I tell you, it was him!" The burly Texan jabbed his meaty finger into the seated man's chest.

Sheriff Chuck Carter examined the tip of his toothpick, then stuck it back into his mouth. Crossing one booted ankle over the other on the corner of his battered desk, he folded his arms across his chest. "You saw W. C. Atwood, all the way out East?" Carter shook his head and snickered. "You don't really expect me to believe that one!"

"You're a fool. A damned fool," Yonker bellowed, pacing like a caged tiger. He threw both hands into the air. "Here's your chance to be a hero and make some easy money in the bargain."

Carter didn't move, save to flick his toothpick into the trash barrel across the way. Through narrowed eyes, he glowered at the bigger man. "When I hunt a man down, I go it alone."

Yonker stopped his frantic stepping. "Without me," he challenged, bending until he was nose to nose with Carter, "you'll never find him."

Grimacing and leaning as far back as the chair would allow, Carter waved a hand in front of his face. "When was the last time you washed out your pie hole, Forrest? Smells like somethin' crawled down your throat an' died."

In response to the reference to his rotten breath, Yonker's back straightened. "You want Atwood or not?"

Casually, Carter dropped both feet to the planked floor in a single *clunk*. Yonker was at least three inches taller and outweighed him by at least fifty pounds. Still, the man took a step back when the sheriff stood. "You owe it to me to tell me where W.C. is—*if* you know—since it was you who lost the thievin' murderer in the first place. Besides," he added, almost as an afterthought, "if you don't, I'll arrest *you*."

"Me?"

He gave it a moment's thought, then shrugged. "Aiding and abetting a fugitive, for starters. If you know where he is and don't tell me, it's the same as lettin' him hole up in your house."

Angry defiance thinning his lips, Yonker poked the sheriff's badge. "I don't owe you a goddamn thing, way I see it," he snarled. "A snake spooked the horses, *that's* why the wagon overturned. Weren't nobody's fault he escaped, least of all mine. But you went and fired me, all the same.

Atwood's the reason for it all, so the way I see it, the bastard deserves to swing.''

From the other side of the room, a voice asked, ''For what? He never kilt nobody.''

Though toe to toe, both men cut angry glances toward the man who'd interrupted their verbal sparring. The bedraggled fellow continued to push a broom across the jailhouse floor. After a long, silent moment, the sheriff cut him a scathing glare. ''You've been singin' that song for ten long years, Joe Purdy,'' he growled. ''Nobody believed you the night W.C. killed Horace Pickett, and nobody believes you now.''

Leaning on the broom handle, Purdy gave an exaggerated shrug. ''If you hang him,'' came his slow, soft drawl, ''you'll be killin' an innocent man.''

Carter pinched the bridge of his nose between thumb and forefinger and shook his head. A second or two ticked by before he sighed and said, ''That may be, Joe. That may be. But the evidence said otherwise, and it got him convicted. It's my job to find him, see he pays the price…not second-guess the jury.'' Frowning, he added, ''Now get back to your sweeping or there'll be no whiskey money for you today!''

Reminded of his purpose, Purdy licked his lips. ''You hang W.C., you'll be killin' an innocent man,'' he repeated as the broom *whisked* past the sheriff's boots. ''Wouldn't want that on *my* conscience.…''

Yonker had heard about all he cared to hear from the town drunk. ''Ain't nobody interested in what you got to say, Purdy.'' Then, facing the sheriff once more, he snapped, ''You want to get W.C., you get *me*.'' Snickering, he punctuated his statement by adding a last poke to Carter's shirt.

In the wink of an eye, the sheriff was behind Yonker, one big hand filled with shirt collar, the other firmly gripping his manhood. ''The man ain't been born who can wriggle out of this here bouncer's grip,'' Carter said calmly. ''You poke that finger in my chest again, I'll break it off and shove it down your throat. You got that?''

Squealing like a stuck pig, Yonker nodded. ''Didn't mean nuthin' by it, Sheriff. I swear to—''

''Smartest thing I ever did was to fire your sorry, lazy ass. You were trouble ten years ago, and I can see time hasn't changed a hair on your ugly head.'' In Carter's powerful grip, Yonker was little more than a willing puppet. He walked on tiptoes in his futile attempt to climb out of the sheriff's painful hold on him. With a rough shove, Carter released him, then turned him around. ''If I get W.C.—and I think we both know I will—it'll be on *my* terms.''

''But…but you don't know where he is,'' Yonker whimpered, wincing as he rubbed his crotch.

Casually, Carter slipped another toothpick from the shot glass on the corner of his desk.

''I know *exactly* where he is,'' Yonker bragged.

''You don't know his whereabouts, either. Dumb as you are, if you did, it would-a been the first thing out of your mouth.''

Yonker patted his hip pocket. ''Got me fifty dollars here says otherwise.''

Shaking his head, Carter smirked. ''Yeah. And Joe over there ain't a drunk, neither.''

The ex-deputy's face reddened and his shoulders hunched with pent-up rage. ''If you was half as smart as you think you are, Carter, you might just be dangerous. I *do* know where W.C. is, by gum!''

Carter shuffled the papers on his desk. ''I ain't got time for your fairy tales, Yonker. Now get on outta here, before I—''

''Why you—'' Yonker's fists doubled up and he blurted, ''He's in a town name of Freeland, north of Baltimore, working as a foreman on a farm called Foggy Bottom.''

''Hot damn, Yonker,'' Carter said, laughing, ''when you

spill your guts, you don't fool around, do you?'' When the snickering ebbed, he added, ''Hey, Joe, put that broom away and get a mop, sop up this mess ole Forrest made.''

Grinning at the sarcastic joke, Joe only shook his head.

Carter sauntered toward the door, nodding as he went. ''You a card-playin' man, Forrest?'' he asked, opening the door wide.

His reckless confession had humbled him, and like a disobedient pup trying to earn back his master's approval, Yonker followed.

''Do yourself a favor,'' he said, pushing the ex-deputy onto the boardwalk, ''and stay away from the poker tables. You ain't got the *stomach* for it!'' With that, he slammed the door and sauntered back to his desk.

The old chair squealed in protest as the sheriff slid onto its burled wood seat and leaned back, resting his boot heels on the corner of the desk once more. Unsheathing the hunting knife that hung from his leather belt, Carter began to trim his fingernails. ''Like I said the day you ran off, W.C., you can run,'' he whispered, moving the toothpick to the other side of his mouth, ''but you can't hide.''

As old Joe continued to sweep, his frown deepened....

Forrest Yonker headed straight from the sheriff's office to the general store, where he bought himself passage on the next stage leaving Lubbock. Once he got to Kansas City, he'd buy a one-way train ticket to Baltimore, find some farmer with a nag for sale, and the rest would be like taking candy from a baby.

Atwood hadn't been much more than a boy the day the jailer's wagon overturned. But time on the run had sharpened his wits, had toughened him up. Yonker had seen that much in Atwood's eyes.

Alone with his own thoughts, he didn't mind admitting that Atwood scared him worse than any imagined monster.

He'd come at him like a madman, teeth bared like a wild animal, bloodlust in his eyes. According to the stories, Atwood was sly, had outslicked every lawman who'd come looking for him. If those stories were true, he'd earned his nickname: "Widowmaker." Yonker didn't have a wife, but he didn't relish the idea of being planted six feet under beside the married men who'd tried to make a name for themselves by bringing in the elusive W. C. Atwood.

So he'd headed straight back to Lubbock after the altercation on the dock, thinking that half the reward money was better than no money at all. *Let Sheriff Carter figure out a way to get Atwood back to Texas,* he'd told himself. *Let it be Carter's bones they bury out behind Calvary Baptist...whilst I count the bounty money.*

But, like the child whose fear of ghosts and ghoulies in the dark abates with the morning light, the passing of time had a way of easing a man's fears.

Bravado now fully intact, Yonker scowled as he tucked a brand-new box of shotgun shells into his rucksack. *When are you gonna learn to keep your big mouth shut?* he asked himself, slamming a fist into his open palm and cursing his own stupidity for having tipped Carter off.

The Wanted poster said Dead or Alive. *He'd* rather be dead than admit what the thought of becoming another of Atwood's victims did to him. *Why risk it when you can take him down with one well-placed bullet, fired from a safe distance?*

What difference did it make if Atwood died at the end of a rope or at the business end of a shotgun? *Dead's dead!*

His strategy was simple: find Foggy Bottom, hunt down Atwood, and kill him.

The telegram arrived the evening after he turned Bess Beckley into a full-fledged woman. Jake had known immediately the message meant bad news. What else *could* it mean, since only one man knew what name he'd been using since coming to Baltimore?

His heart clenched with dread. Another man knew: deputy-turned-merchant marine-turned-bounty hunter, Forrest Yonker.

Jake accepted the envelope from the boy on the pony and handed up one silver dime. "Gosh, thanks, mister," the boy said, grinning at the generous tip.

But Jake didn't hear him, for he'd already headed for the porch. Slumped in one of the twin rockers that flanked the wide, oak doors, he read the name on the envelope. *Walker,* it said, and nothing more. Heart hammering with fear and dread, he tore it open and read: Carter and Yonker headed East—Stop—Purdy.''

For as long as Jake could recall, Joe Purdy had been Lubbock's resident vagrant. Most of the time, the man had been too drunk to do much of anything useful, but he'd managed to sober up just often enough to push his big boar-bristled broom around town and earn enough cash to buy his next bottle.

Once, the old sot saved Jake from his uncle's wrath by putting himself between the man and the boy. Why Joe had deliberately accepted the single lash of Josh's meaty leather belt in his stead, Jake had never quite figured out, but the action earned Joe a place in his heart....

Between the ages of twelve and fifteen, he shared school lunches with the man. From the time Jake finished school until the day he left Lubbock for good, as Joe slept off his latest binge, Jake replaced soured shirts and socks with the ones he'd secreted away the week before and washed down at the creek. It had given him a certain satisfaction, believing Joe didn't have a clue who was responsible for the acts of charity. But on the night of Horace Pickett's murder, he learned differently.

"I know you, boy," Joe had whispered through the barred

jailhouse window. "Anybody who treats a good-for-nothin' drunk the way you've treated me all these years ain't no killer!"

When he arrived safely in Acapulco, Jake had sent an unsigned telegram to the only person who'd ever seemed to give a damn about him. "Joe—Safe south of the border— stop—Hope you're changing your socks." Would the telegraph operator deliver his message to the town drunk? And if he did, would Joe be sober enough to decipher his message? For all Jake knew he'd been communicating with a dead man all these years.

Still, in every new town, he'd plunk down his hard-earned coins to get a message to old Joe Purdy, because he needed to believe that someone, *somewhere,* knew where he was.

Now, Jake glanced at Joe's telegram and said a quick prayer of thanks that the old man was still alive. It was proof that not only had he known who'd been sending the telegrams, but that he'd taken care, all these years, to protect the sender. That had likely cost him more than the price of this telegram.

Jake reasoned that Joe had likely been in the sheriff's office, pushing that old broom of his when Yonker blew in to announce who he'd tangled with on the Baltimore docks.

Sheriff Chuck Carter had never been one of Jake's favorite people, but he was an honest man who took his job seriously. He hadn't shackled Jake to the jailhouse wall ten years earlier because of a personal vendetta; he'd done it on account of evidence that said it was the right thing to do. Jake would much rather have Carter on his trail than Yonker any day. At least with the sheriff, he'd get a fair shake....

Jake folded Joe's message and slid it into his shirt pocket. Then, to ensure it couldn't slip out and fall into the wrong hands, he buttoned the pocket's flap.

With grim determination, he set his jaw.

He'd known since walking away from that overturned

wagon in the Texas desert that the day of reckoning would eventually dawn. Jake took a deep breath and surveyed the horizon, possibly his last chance to enjoy the beauty and tranquility that was Foggy Bottom.

He rose on shaky legs and headed for the bunkhouse. He'd pack, and saddle Mamie—his final "pay" from Micah—and head north, into Canada.

But first, he had a message of his own to write.

She'd dreamed of rose bouquets and long flowing veils and ruffled white dresses. He hadn't come to dinner the night of their interlude, but then, Bess wasn't surprised. Jake had always been a bit remote and distant, particularly when folks got too close.

And the day before yesterday, she remembered, smiling serenely, they'd gotten as close as two people could get.

For the second day in a row, she made all his favorite things for breakfast: eggs and thick-sliced ham, jam and bread, fried potatoes and honey buns. She'd brewed the coffee extra strong, just the way he liked it, and added a dash of pepper to the biscuit batter, because she'd so often seen him spice them up at the table.

Bess had never minded the womanly chores that involved caring for the men of Foggy Bottom. But she'd never enjoyed it quite so much as when she prepared the food that would sustain Jake throughout his long, hard day.

Bess whistled as she set the dining room table, hummed as she put big steaming bowls of food in its center. By the time she stepped onto the porch to ring the bell, Bess felt like singing at the top of her lungs. Jake loved her! What more proof did she need than what had happened between them in the barn?

Bess knew the male mind well enough to understand that terms of endearment—and commitment—were difficult to speak. No matter. Jake had told her in other ways what his heart had spoken in silence, and that meant as much to her than anything he could have said.

She rang the breakfast bell, and one by one, the men filed into the dining room. Plates began to fill as serving platters were passed up and down the long, narrow table. How could Jake miss yet another meal, she wondered, and continue the hard pace he set for himself?

Once the hired hands had everything they needed, Bess strode determinedly into the kitchen, flung her apron onto the table and slipped quietly out the back door, carrying the plate she'd fixed him. She would deliver it to the bunkhouse, and didn't intend to leave until she'd watched him eat every last bite!

When Bess knocked on the door, she heard the sounds of chair legs scraping across the wood floor. ''Who's there?'' he called.

''It's me, Bess. I've brought you breakfast.''

Silence. Then, ''I'm not hungry.''

But how could that be? He hadn't had a real meal since breakfast, two days earlier. ''Jake Walker,'' she scolded, ''I'm going to count to five, and then I'm coming in. So you'd better make yourself presentable.''

She tapped her foot on the flagstone walkway outside the bunkhouse. ''One, two, three,'' she said, her free hand on the tarnished brass doorknob, ''four, five!''

Ordinarily, she did not enter the men's quarters except to change their bed linens and mop the floor, and only then, while they were at work in the fields. She believed they deserved as much privacy as this crowded, eight-bed space would allow. It felt odd to be inside while the men were still within shouting distance; odder still to be here with one of them present.

''I told you,'' he said angrily, standing when she entered the room, ''I'm not hungry.''

''Well, you don't have to get all uppity about it. I *thought*

I was doing you a favor. I *thought* you might enjoy a nice hot meal, since you haven't eaten in so long...."

Jake couldn't take another minute of watching her lovely face, pinched by the hurt his harsh tone had caused; couldn't take another minute of listening as she struggled not to cry. He crossed the room in three long strides, but stopped short of where she stood. He pocketed both hands and stared at the toes of his boots. "I didn't mean to bark at you," he said softly.

When she'd knocked, he'd been sitting at the rickety old desk, trying to explain why he had to leave her. Six sheets of paper, wadded up and tossed into the corner, proved how inadequate words could be at a time like this.

As he'd sat there, trying to pen his goodbye, he found himself angrily swiping at his eyes. What would Matt and Mark have thought if they'd seen him, snuffling like an old crone as he tried to write the note that would allow him to sneak away from Foggy Bottom without having to face her directly?

She continued to stand there, napkin-covered plate balanced on one hand, the other fisted on her shapely hip, blinking back tears of her own. He could tell by the set of her shoulders and the tilt of her jaw that she sensed he'd started construction on a wall that would separate them; the quivering of her full lips told him she had no idea *why* he'd started building it.

If only he could tell her everything, from that strange and terrifying night when he was arrested in Lubbock for a murder he didn't commit, to the overturned jailer's wagon that freed him from the hangman's noose, to the years he'd moved from city to town to keep ahead of the U.S. Marshals. If he could set the record straight, maybe she'd understand why he couldn't stay. Maybe then she'd realize that if he didn't go, she and Micah and the twins would face the same danger *he'd* faced these long, bitter years. If only he could explain that *love* was driving him away.

He closed his eyes against the "if onlys" and steeled himself to do what had to be done. She could never be told, because for Bess, the truth would set her every way but free.

Jake took the plate from her, placed it on the corner of the desk, then took the hand that had held it. Her fingers were still warm from the heat of the food, and he stroked her palm, knowing it would probably be the last time he'd touch her in any way. He closed his eyes and sighed. *God, but life can be hard.*

"Jake…what's wrong?"

If he looked into her face, into that trusting, open face, he'd lose the last vestiges of self-control. And he dared not give in to self-pity, though he'd held his emotions in check for so long that his muscles were permanently taut and hard, making him bone weary. If he let himself, he'd likely fling himself into her comforting arms, bury his face in the crook of her neck, and unleash a flood not unlike the one he'd survived on the Mississippi.

She lay a hand alongside his cheek. "I dreamed of you last night," she said, her voice whisper-soft and sweet as fresh-pulled taffy.

And I dreamed of you, he admitted silently.

Bess tilted her head, tucked in one corner of her mouth. "You aren't ill, are you? Not that I'd be surprised, the way you've been skipping meals…." She pressed her palm to his brow, then frowned. After a moment, she took a step closer and linked her fingers behind his neck, drew him near and kissed his forehead. "It's a foolproof way to tell if someone has a fever. The lips are far more sensitive than the hands, you see, and—"

Why was she torturing him this way? He should tell her to leave, so he could finish writing the goodbye letter, and pack and— "Bess," he moaned, "I've never been sick a day in my life. It's just...I have to...I..."

It was no use. He'd never be able to tell her, face-to-face, that he must leave. As long as she was there, studying him with those *eyes* of hers, he'd stammer and stutter like a simpleton.

Jake was certain she sensed something awful was about to happen, yet there she stood, shoulders back, prepared to take it on the chin.

"Your breakfast is getting cold."

He heard the tremor in her voice, and felt like a heel for being the one who had put it there. "I'm—"

"—not hungry. So you said."

She sounded angry and hurt. And why shouldn't she be? After what they'd done in the loft, she had every right to expect him to propose marriage. At least, she had a right to expect him to stick around.

Jake drove a hand through his hair, nodded toward the plate. "Thanks for thinking of me, though. It was mighty—"

With no warning, Bess threw herself into his arms. "Oh, Jake. It's all right," she mumbled into his chest. "Whatever it is, we can work it out, *together*." She looked at him. "Because...because I love you, you big galoot."

Groaning with frustration, he gathered her close. *Why* did she have to say it out loud? *Why* had she forced him to hear the very words he wanted to say, but couldn't?

He would berate himself later, once he was long gone. Jake would punish himself severely for being so selfish, so self-centered that he'd allowed his own yearnings to prompt him to take what she so generously, so willingly offered: herself.

But right now, he had to find a way to make her understand. To make her see that he was no good for her, so that she'd have no regrets, once he was gone. Jake closed his eyes. "Bess," he began, "I—"

"Shh," she whispered, a forefinger against his lips. Her eyes glittered with love and devotion when she added, "You don't owe me any explanations." She glanced away, but only briefly, as if searching for the courage to continue. When she met his eyes again, it was to say, "You don't owe me anything."

Oh, but you're wrong, my sweet Bess. I owe you everything.

She had given him a reason to live. A reason to hope. Had made him believe in himself, by making him see W. C. Atwood, alias Jake Walker, through *her* eyes. But before he could put those thoughts into words, she was kissing him, hugging him, promising to love and stand beside him forever, no matter what. And by saying those things, she'd awakened that old longing he'd so carefully hidden deep in his soul. Jake buried his face in her hair, closed his eyes and inhaled, as if to memorize its scent; ran his fingers through her thick curls, as if to imprint its texture on his brain.

Bright light dappled through pinholes in the oilcloth window shade, peppering the left side of her face with sunny freckles, illuminating the soft curve of her cheek, highlighting her full lips, glinting from eyes that gleamed and glittered with unconditional love.

This is how he would remember her, always.

When Jake took her in his arms, she melted against him like honey on a hot biscuit, and all rational thought fled his mind. As he guided her onto the thin, straw-stuffed mattress of his cot, he felt her shiver. "Cold?" he whispered.

"No."

"Nervous?"

"Why would I be nervous? I'm an old hand at this, remember?" She punctuated the question with a playful wink.

Remember? I'll never forget! A slight smile tilted his

mouth. *I'm gonna miss you, Bess,* he thought. "Afraid, then?"

She rolled her eyes and shot him a mischievous grin. "The only thing I'm afraid of is that you're going to keep asking questions, instead of—"

It was all the prompting he needed.

In moments, their clothes lay in an untidy heap on the crude board floor. And as their limbs and torsos tangled on the narrow mattress, it dawned on him that all too soon, he'd be alone again, as he'd been when the prairie fire took his parents, and when the jailer's wagon overturned, forcing him to run…or die.

But he wasn't alone yet.

So he would revel in the sweetness of her soft breaths and the satiny smoothness of her face. He would concentrate on every innocently seductive movement of her curvy, naked body, and commit to memory the syncopated rhythm of the sighs that could inspire composers to put notes to the music of her voice. This precious tick in time would become his treasured keepsake, his reminder of their short-lived love affair, a cherished souvenir he could take out and examine at length any time life on the trail threatened to squelch his will to survive, as surely it would.

When the icy snows and cold rains and blustery winds chilled him to the marrow of his lonely bones, he would reflect upon this instant of complete freedom and perfect love, and hold tight its warmth.

She had been a virgin before he'd touched her, and though he'd bedded countless women, he'd never *made love* before.

When the interlude ended, Jake held her close, to cherish the moment. Like a drowning man reaches for a life preserver, she was the ring of life that had saved him. No matter where he went from this day forward, her love would live inside him. "Ahh, Bess," he rasped, "you're way too good for the likes of me.…"

She rose up on one elbow and kissed him full on the mouth, looked him straight in the eye and said, "You're full of stuff and nonsense, W. C. Atwood. But I love you anyway. And I always will."

Chapter Sixteen

"**W**hy all the secrecy, Jake?" Micah, head bowed and hands clasped at the small of his back, paced back and forth behind his desk. Suddenly, he stopped and jabbed an arthritic finger into the air. "I don't mind sayin' it pains me that you feel I can't be trusted with the truth."

The older man's red-faced anger, Jake knew, was born of frustration; he couldn't condone what he didn't understand, and he couldn't understand what Jake wouldn't tell him. "What you don't know won't hurt you," was all he'd say.

Micah turned his back on Jake. Though his foreman's response didn't satisfy him, it seemed to be one Micah could resign himself to. Nodding somberly, he asked, "Have you told Bess?"

Jake cleared his throat, shrugged. "I'm not much for conversation, Micah, and if I know your daughter, she'll want to talk this right into the ground. Frankly, I don't have the time or the patience to tell her what she wants to hear, so it'll be easier all-round if I just lit a shuck out as soon as—"

Mouth set in grim determination, Micah walked wordlessly past Jake and slid the pocket doors shut, effectively closing the rest of the world out of his oak paneled office. "So what you're telling me," he said, sitting on the corner of his desk, "is that you already know she'll react badly to news of your...sudden departure."

Jake ran his a hand through his hair and nodded. He'd given the matter a great deal of thought. There would be a fair amount of ranting and raving, and one helluva lot of her "puppy to the root." She'd give him a piece of her mind, all right. *And why not? She's given you her heart....*

And *that* was the nub of it: she loved him enough to set aside her own hurt and rejection and concentrate on doing what was best for *him*. He could handle her anger. He could handle tears, if they came. But to watch as she suffered in silence, for him...

"Now, I've had dozens of foremen over the years," Micah was saying, "and some of 'em were worth every dollar I gave 'em." He shook his head. "But *you*—" a long sigh punctuated his comment "—you put your shoulder to the wheel and your nose to the grindstone, as they say. But there's something...something *different* about the way you work, has been from day one. You couldn't convince me in a month of Sundays that it's just for the pay. This place *means* something to you."

Jake couldn't deny the truth of Micah's words, and so he didn't try. He'd been standing there, hat in hand, staring sullenly at the toes of his boots, but the older man's speech forced him to make eye contact.

Micah's scowl gentled to a near smile. He held up one hand to fend off further comment from his younger counterpart. "Son, as I said before you may be running from something—and I do believe you are—but I can tell you I've learned the hard way, there are some things you just *can't* outrun...." An expression of remembered pain flickered across his face as he swallowed.

"This farm is what it is today, in part because I'm a better-than-average judge of a good horse. Well, I'm a pretty good at sizin' up *people,* too. I figured you for a good man right from the get-go.'' He pursed his lips, narrowed his eyes, and aimed that bent finger at Jake again. "You don't think for one minute I would have looked the other way while you courted my daughter if I didn't think you as worthy of her as any man could possibly be...."

Jake's heart beat hard and his palms grew damp.

"No need to look so guilty, son. I've seen the way you two behave when you're together." He tucked in one corner of his mouth. "Believe it or not, I remember a thing or two about love."

When he'd left other farms, other towns, no one had tried to stop him. No one had seemed to give a damn one way or the other whether or stayed or went. Why couldn't Micah be like that, Jake wondered, accept that he had to go, and leave it at that? "I've spelled it out as best I can," Jake said, taking an envelope from his shirt pocket.

Like smoke, the paternal smile vanished from Micah's face. Silently, he accepted the note and gave it a cursory glance. The look on his face was more disappointment than disbelief, and it cut Jake to the quick.

"I know it seems cowardly," Jake said, nodding at the envelope, "saying goodbye that way." He held Micah's steady gaze. "It isn't the telling that scares me...it's what the telling will do to her." Shaking his head, he frowned. "I've grown mighty fond of your daughter, and I wouldn't hurt her for all the world."

"Well, you're going to hurt her, leaving this way."

"Won't make me any too happy, either."

Micah slipped the envelope into the breast pocket of his jacket. "So when are you headin' out?"

"Soon as I get my gear stowed."

He frowned as a sputtering cough escaped him. "Today?"

Jake nodded.

Shaking his head, Micah sighed heavily. "I suppose you want me to wait 'til you're gone to give Bess the note."

Another nod. "I think it'll be easier that way."

There was a moment of profound silence, which Micah broke by saying, "For Bess...or for you?"

He didn't hesitate to say, "Both."

Pressing the pads of his fingertips together, Micah tried a new tack. "I'm not a rich man, Jake, but I'm far from poor. Let me help you."

Wasn't it bad enough that he had to leave Foggy Bottom...and Bess? Did the man have to pour salt into the wound by extending his hand in friendship? A sob ached in Jake's throat, and for a reason he couldn't explain, it riled him. *Should've written two notes,* Jake decided, *so you could ride out of here with some dignity....* "Goddamn it, Micah, I don't want your money. That isn't what I need to take with me."

"Well, I have friends in high places. Maybe—"

Exasperated, Jake blew a stream of air through his teeth. "I'm mindful of what you're trying to do for me, and I'm properly grateful, Micah, but not even your rich and powerful friends can get me out of this mess."

Micah stood and resumed pacing, head down and fingers linked against his backside. After a moment, he stopped. "Then Godspeed, son," he said, giving Jake's shoulder a meaningful squeeze, "and take our prayers with you."

Jake had just cinched the saddle when he heard the thundering hooves. Dust billowed all around the big palomino, hiding its rider from view. He continued to watch as the man dismounted and tethered the beast to the hitching post near Micah's front porch. It wasn't until the stranger removed his hat that Jake recognized him: sheriff Chuck Carter.

If he'd left last week, as he'd planned, he'd be in Canada

by now. But Jake had put it off, and doing so had put the Beckleys in the line of fire; just as surely as he could predict Bess's reaction to his leaving, Jake knew that any one of them would do whatever it took to protect him.

The very least that could happen if they got involved in this mess was that they'd be charged with aiding and abetting a fugitive. The worst? Jake preferred not to think about that.

But he knew this: his miserable hide wasn't worth putting them at risk.

Hidden by Mamie's generous rump, Jake saw Mark answer Carter's knock. A moment of chitchat was all it took to inspire the boy to invite the stranger inside. As soon as the door closed behind them, Jake climbed into the saddle and rode quietly from the barn. If he could make it as far as the north fields without being spotted, he might just be able to avoid a confrontation.

Better still, he could protect Bess from seeing it.

Mamie loved a full-speed run, and needed very little urging, once he'd gotten safely out of earshot of anyone in the house, to go full out. When horse and rider reached the crest in the hill beyond the field, Jake stopped and looked back. Without dismounting, he stared through the spyglass Matt and Mark had given him and zeroed in on the manor house.

A painted pony now stood beside the palomino.

He swiveled the spyglass left just as the front door opened. Jake wouldn't have needed the visual aid to name the second man. Forrest Yonker.

He gave a sarcastic chuckle. *If Carter was hopin' to put the two-heads-are-better-than-one theory to the test, he's in for a letdown, 'cause Yonker doesn't have half a brain!*

The men had what appeared to be an angry exchange. *That's odd,* Jake thought.

Movement just inside the door caught his attention, and he fixed the glass on it. Through its polished, curved lens, he saw Bess looking at him. How she'd known where he'd be, Jake didn't know. But the expression on her face was unmistakable: *Go!* he read in her wide, frightened eyes, *go, and don't look back!*

It came to him in a blinding flash that he'd misunderstood Joe Purdy's warning. Yonker and Carter hadn't planned to arrive together to arrest him, hadn't planned on sharing the bounty. Quite the contrary. Jake had become the prey, stalked by two hungry predators...separately.

He likened his fate to that of a longhorn sheep, soon to be mounted over some dogger's cabin door, for the bounty had become the prize for whichever hunter could drag his "trophy" back to Texas first. Jake knew he'd have to do some mighty fancy footwork if he hoped to escape this time.

He would never know what made the sheriff turn in his saddle and look north. Had he followed Bess's terrified gaze? Or was it instinct?

In one second, Jake and Carter sat in their saddles, locked in an eerie, distant eye contact. In the next, the lawman had whirled his horse around and urged it forward. Jake didn't have to see it happen to know that Yonker soon joined the chase.

He urged Mamie into a full gallop and headed for the cave where Mark and Matt had spent many boyhood days. It seemed ordinary enough on the outside as its mouth yawned big and black in the mound of dirt. But inside, dozens of deserted mine shafts aimed in all directions, like the spokes of an ancient wagon wheel.

It would be a good place to hide.

He'd take the tunnel that led east, toward the Gunpowder River. From there—if he was lucky—he could slip into the grove of pines that grew thick as wheat, then follow the B&O Railroad tracks along the river. If he made it that far without being spotted, he'd could turn north, and disappear into the dense woodlands of Pennsylvania.

Mamie seemed not to notice the thick lather that coated her withers as she obeyed Jake's every command. Much as she enjoyed a fast run, she was a farmer's horse, accustomed to carrying her master for long distances—at a leisurely pace. Her breathing had become ragged and labored, and the usually surefooted beast began to stumble. If he didn't let her rest, she'd likely die.

But Yonker and Carter were hot on his trail. If Jake allowed her that rest, *he* would die.

Hunkering low in the saddle and hugging her neck, he said through clenched teeth, "Just get me to the edge of the woods, girl. To the edge of the woods…"

Mamie served him well, and carried him far from Foggy Bottom. He rode her hard until they entered the woods, then slowed her to a trot. Jake held her to the fast pace until it became impossible to maneuver between the close-growing pines. Though he could tell by the way her muscles tensed under his thighs that she didn't like the feel of the bark scraping against her shoulders and thighs, Mamie, head bobbing and ears flicking, continued to obey. "Atta girl," he urged, his voice raspy and low, "nice and easy."

Up ahead, he could see a break in the trees. "We'll pull up soon," he assured. And as though she understood his words, Mamie's tight muscles and labored breathing relaxed a bit. She needed food and water, and if the truth were told, Jake wouldn't mind a good long rest, himself. That clearing up ahead was looking better and better.

When at last they reached it, Jake dismounted and stroked Mamie's neck. "Good girl," he whispered appreciatively. He'd pushed her hard, harder than she'd ever been pushed, and yet she'd gone full-out without once breaking stride. She'd earned a leisurely meal, but he couldn't risk letting her stand out in the open to graze her fill. So, while the horse nibbled absently on the leaves of the blackberry bush he'd tethered her to, Jake set about the business of gathering an armload of the knee-high field grass that grew aplenty on the outskirts of the woods.

In the years he'd been "heading for sundown," Jake had been forced to hole up and hide more times than he could count. Blending into the landscape was, by now, second nature to him. Being a fugitive all these years had taught him two things: never stray far from water and, if you're lucky enough to have a horse, treat her like a best friend, 'cause that's exactly what she is. He was ever more grateful for Micah's generous gift.

He moved slowly and carefully, never stepping too far from the protective shadows of the trees, always scanning the high rim that ran alongside the woods, whacking at the grass with his big bowie knife…one of the few things Jake had managed to keep with him over the years.

He'd come by the weapon passing through Arkansas during his first year on the dodge. He'd stumbled onto the campsite of a hide rustler who'd been on the run far longer than Jake. Equally startled by the surprise meeting, the high-strung men unholstered their weapons in a heartbeat. The two of them had stood in frozen fear for half a minute before Jake said, using the six-shooter he'd taken from the Lubbock deputy as a pointer, "I got five beans in the wheel…how 'bout you?"

"Same," the rustler had answered.

"Don't rightly know which chamber's empty," Jake admitted.

"Me, neither." Shrugging, the man reholstered his gun. "You look a might stoved up." Nodding toward the camp-fire, he added, "Ain't much, but you're welcome to a bite of that rabbit on the spit.…"

It had been the scent of roasting meat that had drawn Jake toward the cookfire in the first place. Licking his lips, he put his weapon away, too. "I'm down to my last chip," he'd admitted, tearing a thigh from the carcass above the fire. Seated now, he said around a mouthful of the tender meat, "Much obliged."

The stranger shrugged and tore off the other thigh. "What you doin' prowlin' about in the dark?"

Chances were fair to middlin' that his host and Jake were in the same fix, so he told the truth: "Had me a run-in with the law back in Lubbock."

Nodding, the man said, "Abilene for me." Grinning a bit, he added, "Little matter of whose cows those was that I took to market." He inspected the bone for last shreds of meat. "How 'bout you?"

"They say I killed a man." He'd made the mistake soon after his escape of telling a gang that he'd been wrongly accused of murder. They'd called him everything *but* a human being, and threatened to string him up by his short hairs for whining like a woman. It hadn't taken long to figure out that, if he got any help along the trail, it would come by way of men who, like himself, were just one step ahead of the law; men who, unlike Jake, were guilty of murder, robbery, rape....

Without looking up, the stranger continued to gnaw on the small bone. "What'd you kill him for?"

"They say I did it for his pocket watch."

His narrow, glinting dark eyes met Jake's. "You kilt a feller for his timepiece?" Clucking his tongue, he licked grease from his fingers, then wiped them on his shirt. Flapping his saddle blanket over his dusty trousers, he lay back and rested his grizzled head on his bedroll. "Maybe I'll just sleep with one eye open tonight," he said chuckling. Grunting, he turned his back on Jake. "He'p yourself to what's left of the huckeydummies...."

Jake would have a sweetened biscuit, maybe two. But he had no intention of hanging around long enough to fall asleep in this old man's camp. With his bad luck of late, the

fire and the scent of rabbit had likely alerted whatever lawmen were hot on the rustler's trail. He didn't wish the man
any bad luck, but he didn't care to become a souvenir of the
lawmen's hunt, either. So once he'd eaten his fill of rabbit
and raisin biscuits, Jake would head out, find someplace else
to slumber.

He'd almost downed his second cup of coffee when the
first soft notes filled the air:

"Oh, you'll be soup for Uncle Sam's Injuns;
It's 'beef, heap beef,' I hear them say.
Get along, git along little dogies,
You're going to be beef steers by and by.
Whoopee, ti yi yo, git along little dogies,
It's your misfortune and none of my own."

The stranger's song, sung sad and low, hung in the wind
like the mists that hovered over the Rio Grande in the early-
morning hours.

He hadn't seen the river or her mists—or anything else
Texan—in a long, long time. The man had been right; Jake
was bone tired. Tired of hiding, tired of walking, tired of
wondering where his next meal would come from, tired of
worrying if, next time he lay down to sleep, the marshals
would find him.

Jake drifted off to sleep as the rustler sang the next verse
in his ode to the cattle, and dreamed of his stint as a cowboy.
He'd been born on a ranch, had lived his first twelve years
riding the range. Working the ponies and punching cows
came as naturally and as easily to him as counting money
was to a banker. He'd participated in a dry drive or two
before the fire took his parents and destroyed the ranch. His
pa and the ranch hands often passed the long, lonely nights
singing sweet and low to keep the cattle calm…and the cowboys awake.

When he woke, the stranger and his horse were nowhere in sight. But he'd left a few of his belongings behind.

He'd no sooner had the thought than Jake spied a piece of wrinkled brown paper poking out from between the knife and its leather sheath. "Had me two of these," was all the gritty, printed message said. The old fellow hadn't seemed the type who'd know how to write, or the type who would have known Jake would be able to read what he'd written.

Shaking his head in wonderment, Jake lifted the heavy-handled knife and turned it over and over in his hands. Even then, long before he'd had call to use it, he knew he'd be eternally grateful to the rustler for the generous gift.

Now, he whacked at the knee-high grasses that he hoped would fill Mamie's belly. Once he'd gathered a hefty armful, he dropped the load near her front hooves. Because she'd always been a fussy eater, Jake stood and watched...and hoped. She preferred barley, wheat and hay to wild grass, and he wasn't at all sure she'd accept his offering. With her nose, Mamie shoved the grass to and fro, as if searching for something more appetizing beneath it.

"Don't rightly know what I'll do if you decide to get all persnickety on me now," he said when she lifted her head to nuzzle his cheek. "Tell you what," he said, scratching her nose, "if you eat that mess, I promise to buy you the biggest bag of oats I can find first chance I get."

Almost immediately, her pliable lips brought the grass into her mouth, chopped it into pieces with her hard incisors. Nostrils flaring, her thick pink tongue tossed the food to the back of her mouth, where it was ground down by her powerful molars.

He wanted to unsaddle her, give her a brisk brushing, allow her to roll around on her back as horses are wont to do after a long, hard ride. But he couldn't chance it. No telling how soon Yonker and Carter would catch up to him—if they did. And though Mamie surely wanted her rider's seat removed even more than the rider wanted to remove it, she continued to chew the grass he'd brought her. "You're a bone-seasoned filly, I'll give you that."

Jake plucked a few ripe blackberries from the nearby shrub and popped them into his mouth. Chuckling, he said under his breath, "Bess would whale me good if she could read my mind right now...."

He'd been standing there, one hand on his horse's rump, the other acting like a bowl for the blackberries, thinking how much Bess and Mamie had in common: strong, hard-working, willing to go the extra mile for anyone they'd taken a liking to. Sleek and hard-muscled and—

The comparison ended the moment he pictured Bess's legs, shapely and milky white, wrapped tight around his waist....

The memory of her, lying under him on that too narrow dicehouse cot, was torture to him now. Would be torture to him until he could hold her in his arms again.

If he could hold her again.

No, not torture, he corrected himself, *comfort.* He'd made her no promises, and she'd made none to him. Still, he knew he wouldn't bed another woman—wouldn't *want* to. Because it was Bess that he wanted, and no other. *'Cause she loves you.*

The thought made him smile. *She loves you even though she knows the whole damnable truth!*

"I love you, W. C. Atwood," she'd said last time they'd been alone, "and I always will." It must have taken all the willpower she could muster not to press him for all the gory details, and he loved her all the more for that. Someday, maybe he'd be able to sit her down and spell it all out.

She knows, he repeated in amazement, *and still she loves you!*

It wouldn't be easy, moving farther and farther from the warmth of love like that, but he had do it, as much for her safety as his own. Maybe in a year or two, God would have pity on him, give him the information he needed to clear his name. Then he could go back to Foggy Bottom, where she'd likely be rocking on the big covered porch, watching the horizon. When she spotted him riding toward her, she'd run like the wind until she reached him. And he'd stand beside Mamie, holding the reins in his hands, waiting, waiting....

Laughing and crying at the same time, she'd throw her arms around him, kiss him soundly, and press every curve of her beautiful little body against him.

Mamie snorted and shook her long-maned head, as if to say, "You have more important things to worry about right now besides cuttin' your wolf loose...."

He gave her an affectionate pat. "Keep thinkin' things like that, and I might just have to wash your mouth out with lye soap," he drawled. And taking a few steps away from the trusty beast, Jake sat with his back against the gnarled trunk of a yellow pine. No matter where this journey took him, no matter how long he stayed away from Foggy Bottom, he'd carry the farm—and Bess—in his heart and mind.

Other women had said they loved him, had begged him not to go—oftentimes with tears in their eyes. But their words hadn't been any more honest than their accompanying sobs, and he'd known it. Still, he'd held them tight and dried their tears and echoed their empty promises. Then, without the slightest pang of guilt, he'd left them as easily and as quickly as their tears had dried.

Not so this time! This time, though Bess had confessed her love in every womanly way, she had not asked him to stay. She had given herself over to him, knowing somehow that he would carry her memory in his heart forever.

Afterward, as their heartbeats and breathing returned to normal, as he had held her tight, her tears spilled into the crook of his neck. "Got something in my eye," she'd insisted when he tried to blot them with the corner of the bedsheet. He'd written his goodbye on a thick sheet of butcher's paper; that tear, he reckoned, had been *her* goodbye.

Mamie pawed at the loamy woodland soil, searching for more chow. Sighing, Jake stood to get it for her. As his bowie knife hacked at the yellowing stalks, Jake wondered if Bess had read his final farewell yet, and if she had, how she'd reacted to it. He wished he could be there, to hold her close and comfort her, to tell her that for the first time, *leaving* caused an ache inside him that ran deep and strong.

As in answer to a prayer, her beautiful face appeared again in his mind, along with that *look*, that courageous yet terrified look....

Though he hated himself for feeling it, Jake thanked God for that look, for it told him she'd be as miserable without him as he'd be without her.

At least, he hoped that's what it meant.

Jake had experienced real fear before—fear of being orphaned, of being on the receiving end of his uncle's wrath, of being on the business end of a loaded pistol, of facing the hangman's noose. None of it had scared him like the thought that she wouldn't be waiting for him if—*when*—he returned.

God, how I love her! his miserable heart shouted. *You should have told her oftener. Should have told her sooner.* Perhaps the words would have given them both some sort of comfort, some sort of guarantee.

Life doesn't come with guarantees, he reminded himself.

The admission put him on his knees. There, on the sun-dappled forest floor, he bowed his head, knife hand hanging limp at his side. He'd asked the question a thousand times since that jailer's wagon overturned on the dusty trail outside Lubbock: *Why, God, why* me! He ran down the litany of "ifs," knowing before he cited the first "if" the futility of the exercise:

If he'd left Lubbock a month earlier, as he'd planned, he wouldn't have been in town on the night Horace Pickett had been murdered.

If his uncle hadn't harbored such a deep-seated hatred for him, the testimony wouldn't have cinched the rope around his neck.

If he'd been caught anywhere between Texas and Maryland, he'd never have met Bess.

And *if* he hadn't met her, leaving Foggy Bottom wouldn't be so goddamned hard!

He'd started out on the farm as he'd started out in every other town…looking forward to the day he'd move on…and out. But he hadn't wanted to leave this time.

I left because I love you! was the silent, tormented shout that echoed in his soul.

He could only hope Bess knew and understood that, for this was the first time putting a place behind him had caused *his* tears to dampen the dusty earth.

Chapter Seventeen

Bess had been out back, humming to herself as she picked sheets and pillow slips from the clothesline, when the ruckus started.

"I seen 'im first, Carter, you got no right to him," shouted the first voice.

Bess rounded the corner as the second man bellowed, "Like hell I don't! I'll see *you* swing a'fore I let you—"

In a single, sweeping glance, she took it all in: Matt's stunned expression, and the fury between the man on the porch and the man still astride his horse. Hitching up her skirts, she ran up the porch steps and wrapped a protective arm around her brother. "What's going on here?" she'd demanded, scowling for all she was worth.

Her ire seemed to have temporarily quieted their wrath.

Matt spoke first, pointing a forefinger at the man on the porch. "He rode up, asked if a man by name of W. C. Atwood had been around these parts." Aiming the digit at the man on horseback, he added, "Whilst I was tellin' *this* one I ain't never heard of any such person, *that* one rides up and starts barkin' orders, sayin' he'd followed that galoot's trail right to our door, and if I didn't tell him where I was hidin' that fella, he'd hog-tie me and—"

Standing beside him, Bess hugged Matt a little tighter. Ever since that afternoon on the Baltimore docks, she'd known this day would come. The presence of these two angry men explained Jake's agitation earlier that morning. She didn't care *what* they threatened—no one at Foggy Bottom would help them slip a noose around Jake's neck! Lifting her chin and raising her left brow, she said, "Will one of you…*gentlemen*…please explain why you're on Beckley property, making threats?"

Her long dark hair had been tucked under a bonnet that day on the docks, and she'd been wearing one of her best Sunday dresses. Unless he was doing a good job of faking it, he hadn't recognized her….

"Didn't mean no harm, ma'am," said the first. With his thumb, he shoved his hat farther to the back of his head. "Name's Carter. Chuck Carter, and I'm the sheriff in Lubbock, Texas."

Her whole body stiffened at the mention of the town. She could only hope the sheriff hadn't noticed her reaction.

"I'm here to collect a prisoner," he continued, his elbow resting on the saddle horn. "Ever hear-tell of a man by name of W. C. Atwood, ma'am?"

She frowned. "No, no…the name isn't at all familiar, I'm afraid." Bess had brightened a bit to add, "There's a family down the road a piece," she said, pointing east, "whose name is Atkins. Maybe you've got your names mixed-up."

The sheriff grinned and shook his head. "No, ma'am," was his patronizing reply, "there's no mix-up."

Bess aimed a glare at the man on horseback. She would have recognized him anywhere. He was the filthy sailor who'd picked a fight with Jake that day on the docks. "I suppose you're looking for this Atkins fellow, too?"

"His name's Atwood, ma'am. W. C. Atwood. And yes, I'm huntin' him, too."

"Why?" Matt wanted to know. "What's he done?"

''Killed a man with his bare hands...broke his neck,'' said the man in the saddle.

Under her hand, Matt's shoulder tensed. ''In Lubbock?''

''That's right,'' the sheriff said. ''He was about to pay for his crime when he escaped.''

''P-pay?''

The man on the horse snickered. ''Another hour or so, he'd'a been lookin' up a limb. Ain't that right, Sheriff?''

Carter stared hard at the man. ''Shut up, Yonker,'' he growled, ''can't you see you're scarin' these nice folks?'' He poked around in his shirt pocket for an second or two, then withdrew a many-folded sheet of paper. Leaning forward, he handed it to Bess. ''That there's the feller we're lookin' for, miss,'' he said. ''He look familiar to you?''

She held in her hands a Wanted poster exactly like the one hidden in beneath the desk blotter in her room. Matt peered over her shoulder; surely, the striking likeness to Jake wouldn't escape his scrutiny. Her voice was thin as she said, ''I'm sorry, but I've never seen this man before in my life.''

Bess quickly summoned the strength to aim a carefree, friendly smile in their direction. Just as quickly, she realized it had been an exercise in futility, for their visitors no longer had any interest in anything she had to say.

Sheriff Carter had turned slightly in the saddle to face north, a steely, determined expression on the handsome face that was shaded by a wide-brimmed hat. What had so completely captured his attention? she wondered, following his gaze.

In the fleeting moment that ticked by, Bess and Carter had seen the same thing...the silhouette of a horse and rider. She guessed the distance to be a mile away or more, yet she'd have recognized the way he sat a saddle anywhere. *Run, Jake!* was her silent warning. *Run as fast and as far as you can!*

Somehow, she must distract them, and give him the head start he needed. But *how?*

"Here's your Wanted poster, Sheriff," she said, holding it out to him.

Her words seemed to have fallen on deaf ears, for Carter was already in the saddle, tugging the reins so tightly that the leather squealed against the snaffle rings. The hackamore bridle tightened as the horse responded by rearing back its mighty head, ready and willing to obey his master's next instruction.

In an eyeblink, Carter had whirled his stallion around, and was bulleting toward the shadowy figure on the horizon. "You ain't goin' nowhere without me," Yonker shouted, pressing his own horse into action. "I aim to get my fair share of that sum-bitch!"

She and Matt huddled in stunned silence, blinking into the gritty fog kicked up by the horses' hooves.

"I always wondered why Jake kept to himself so much," Matt said when the dust cleared. He nodded at the Wanted poster Bess still clutched in her hands. "Now I know...."

"He didn't kill that man in Lubbock."

Matt only shook his head. "I never said he did, Bess." He gave the poster one last worried glance, then jammed his hat onto his head. "I promised Jake I'd clean the barn this morning," he said, and headed out.

"Where's Mark?" she asked as he crossed the yard.

"Mixin' feed for the horses, just like Jake told him to do," he hollered over his shoulder. When the boy reached the barn, he slid open the wide double doors and faced the house. "Hey, Bess!"

One hand on the door frame, the other over her hammering heart, she looked his way.

"You think he'll be all right out there?"

The hammering beneath her hand escalated. For the first time since Mary's death, she felt no inclination to lie to protect her younger sibling. "I hope so," she'd said to Matt. *God in heaven,* she'd said to herself, *I hope so....*

After supper, as Bess was scouring the skillet she'd fried their chicken in, Micah joined her in the kitchen. "Hey, Pa," she said without looking up, "there's hot coffee on the stove."

He crossed the room in three long strides and took a heavy pottery mug from the open cupboard shelf. "Matt told me what happened this morning."

The last time she'd heard him speak in that gritty, glum tone of voice had been on the day they'd buried her mother. Bess set the pan aside and dried her hands on her apron. She took the mug from his hands and filled it with coffee, poured a cup for herself, and followed him to the table.

With thumb and forefinger, he repeatedly stroked his bearded jaw and shook his head. "Guess it was just a matter of time 'til they came for him."

All day, she'd been fighting tears, but staved them off by throwing herself into her work. Though the silver hadn't needed polishing, she'd shined it up anyway. Only two days earlier, she'd dragged every rug outside and hung it over the wire clothesline out back, but she'd done it again today, beating the carpet nap with every ounce of energy she had. She'd taken down the kitchen curtains and soaked them in a tub of lye, despite the fact that she'd done the exact same job just last week. Even tonight's planned menu—chicken pot pie and buttermilk biscuits—had turned into a Sunday feast, complete with mashed potatoes and gravy, butter beans and turnip greens.

Ever since Mary's death, Bess had been putting on whatever face her father and brothers needed her to wear, regardless of her own moods or feelings. Even now, as she watched Micah's worried frown, she wondered what she could do or say to comfort him, to ease his concern....

"He'll be fine, just fine," she said, forcing a cheeriness into her voice that she did not feel. "I'm sure he's found a good hiding place by now."

Micah sighed deeply. "Bess," he said, reaching into his coat pocket, "I have something for you." He held the envelope in his left hand, and covered her right hand with his.

Blinking back hot tears, she stared at the envelope and folded her hands in her lap. "It's from Jake, isn't it?"

Micah nodded. "He gave it to me first thing this morning, and asked that I—"

"Why didn't he talk to me himself?" she demanded as a sob welled up in her throat. Fingers flexing nervously, she looked at the note. "Why did he feel he needed to say good-bye...*that* way!"

"He said he gave it a lot of thought, and figured this way would be least painful for you."

She thought of what they'd done that morning, remembering with crystal clarity the way he'd held her, breathed into her ear that he'd never loved a woman as he loved her. "You've given me something to live for, Bess," he had whispered. "I swear to God, I'd give my life for you...."

Less painful! she repeated mentally. *He's gone for good. How can anything make that less painful?*

Glaring, she met Micah's eyes. "And you believed him? He decided to take the coward's way out, and you *let* him?" She stood so quickly that her chair tumbled backward and clattered to the floor. "What kind of father are you?" she demanded. "How could you let him just walk away?"

Micah calmly got to his feet and wrapped her in his arms. "I swear to you, Bess, I tried to stop him. But Jake believes his leaving is best—and safest—for all of us." He tightened his hold on her to add, "And under the circumstances, I'm bound to agree with him."

As surging floodwaters slowly erode a dam, her careful control began to wear away. It started as a slight tremor in her fingertips that ebbed up, and out, until every inch of her quivered with fright and dread. She was utterly helpless to bring Jake back, to prove him innocent, to make things right. Frustration born of feeling that he'd abandoned her pulsed inside her, flared from her heart, heating her cheeks and causing her ears to burn, and burst from her lips as a dry, guttural groan.

Bess gripped her father's shoulders, the scratchy wool of his jacket reminding her of Jake's work-hardened hands. Would she ever feel his gentle touch, or hear his heartfelt proclamations, or see the lovelight glowing in his ice-blue eyes again?

Habit, more than anything else, warned her to get hold of herself. Habit—and fear that once the floodgates opened— there would be no stanching her tears.

Hard as it was, she drew away from her father's embrace. It had felt good to be surrounded by his protective arms again. Perhaps too good....

It would have been better if he hadn't exhibited this moment of strength and sureness, for it only served to remind her of the man he'd been when her mother was alive. After her death, self-pity had made him weak and timid, had blinded him to the needs of his children, whose loss had been every bit as painful as his own.

Bess would not allow that kind of selfishness to do to her what it had done to her father. And so she gritted her teeth and squinted hard, and reached into that now shallow well of self-determination for one last ounce of control. "Let me have the letter," she said, extending a trembling hand.

"I'm sorry, Bess," he said, handing it to her. "I wish there were something I could do to—"

"There *is* something you can do, Pa," she said matter-of-factly, folding the envelope in half and tucking it into her apron pocket.

Micah stood near the door, waiting for Bess to spell it out.

She rolled up her sleeves and drove both hands into the sudsy water to tackle the skillet again. "You can find Matt and Mark, and help them understand why Jake had to leave...us." She hid the catch in her voice behind a tiny cough. She couldn't bring herself to wound Micah with the truth; in place of "father," Bess said "brother": "It won't be easy—he's been like an older brother to th—"

"I expect I'll find them in the barn," he interrupted.

She nodded, understanding that he'd done it to spare her any further pain. One hand on the screen door, he said, "I'll be in my study later, reading...in case you want to talk...."

She dared not meet his eyes, for fear she'd see evidence of sympathy there. It wouldn't take much to bring the last of her self-control tumbling down. Bess continued to attack the frying pan as though the answers to all her problems were hidden beneath the layer of crisp, cooked-on chicken fat. "Enjoy your book, Pa," was all she said as the door closed with a muffled *thud*.

An hour later, after she'd swept the porch and scoured the table and chairs, the cookstove, the pine-planked floor, Bess wearily climbed the stairs and locked herself into her room. Covering her shoulders with the cream-colored crocheted shawl that had been her mother's, she took off her apron, settled into the nest of pillows Mary had long ago stuffed into the window seat, and hugged it to her breast.

The stiff envelope crinkled between her hands and her heart. Sighing, she removed it from the right-hand pocket. In the silvery, shadowy light of the moon, she slowly lifted the flap and withdrew the single sheet of paper that had been folded from top to bottom, from bottom to top. Pressing it against her lap, she smoothed away the neat creases.

Then, tilting the letter so that a shard of moonlight illuminated the bold, masculine handwriting, she read:

September 28, 1850
Dear Bess,
It might seem this is the coward's way…leaving a note instead of facing you head-on. It isn't that I'm yellow, it's just I want your last memory of me to be a good one. You deserve a stronger man than me. Maybe someday, the Good Lord will tell me what I did to deserve even a few months with you.

I told them in Lubbock I never killed Horace Pickett. Even folks who knew me all my life didn't believe it. I don't rightly give a damn what the rest of the world believes. You believe me. Nothing else matters.

You can believe this, too, Bess: there's a hefty price on my head, and there are men out there who aim to collect it. If anybody gets in their way, they'll shoot first and ask questions later.

I won't let my past harm you in any way.

My plan is to head north, then double back to Texas. Who knows? I could get lucky, find Pickett's real killer. One thing's sure: I can't come back to Freeland 'til I know it's safe for you to be around me. Could take a long while, darlin', so don't wait for me. If love comes knocking, you answer that door, you hear? 'Cause I love you more than life itself, and I don't want you pining away over the likes of me. Just don't forget me, Bess.

Yours truly,
Walker John Atwood

She read the letter three times before sliding it back into its envelope and tucking it into her desk drawer. She hesitated near the chair for a moment, uncertain whether or not to lift the blotter and withdraw the Wanted poster. Biting her lower lip, she did, and carried it to the window seat.

The artist had not created a very good likeness of Jake.

In the drawing, the wanted man's hair was mostly black, as was the mustache above the slanting, smirking grin. The chin was too narrow, the nose too broad, and the cheekbones too flat and far apart.

But the eyes…those piercing, crystalline eyes…

Even if all she'd seen on the billboard that day in Philadelphia had been the eyes, she'd have immediately recognized the man as Jake Walker.

Correction. W. C. Atwood.

Wanted for Murder, the blotchy black letters said, Dead or Alive.

The bounty was high, encouraging lawmen and lawbreakers alike to take out after him, in the hopes of collecting it. What chance did he have against their greed?

Bess pressed her cheek to the picture of the wanted man's, and closed her eyes. Of all the things Jake had told her his father taught him, "the truth shall set you free" echoed loudest in his memory.

She didn't believe for an instant that Jake had killed anyone, and yet he was being hunted, just as surely as that white wolf. Bess wondered if the bounty hunters had bagged their prey and collected their prize money…or had the beautiful creature managed to find a home with her brethren, eluding her two-legged predators?

Something told her the wolf still lived, wild and free. If the she-wolf could escape men armed with powerful rifles, perhaps Jake could outrun *his* enemies, as well.…

She told herself the Texas lawmen would not find him. As he'd been doing these ten long years, he'd outwit them again, and return to Foggy Bottom. If the wolf could survive, surely a man with as much spirit as Jake could, too.

Perhaps he *would* get lucky, as he'd said in his letter, and Horace Pickett's real killer would be caught. If that happened, Jake could take rightful claim of his given name once again. But even if that never happened, it didn't matter to her whether she whispered "W.C." or "Jake" into his ear.

He'd written "Don't forget me." *As if that's possible!* she thought.

She ran back to the desk, gathering the poster and the letter to her bosom, and hurried back to the window. He was out there, somewhere. Bess *knew* it. And so, eyes closed, she inhaled deeply, as if drawing his wandering wolflike spirit into her.

Immediately, she was filled with joy and peace. Smiling serenely, she closed her eyes and pictured Jake. Though his quest for safety might take him hundreds of miles from Foggy Bottom, he would never be more than a breath away.

She made him a promise, right then and there: every morning before her day began, and every night when it ended, no matter the weather, no matter her mood, she would stand in this window and draw him into her.

And then she would search the horizon, and pray she'd see the familiar silhouette that would tell her he had come home.

Chapter Eighteen

The best place to hide, Jake had learned, was in the most obvious place. Yonker and Carter would expect him to continue heading north, following the Allegheny Mountain rivers and trails.

For a while, he allowed them to think just that, and thanks to Mamie's stubborn determination, he managed to plug along, staying several miles ahead, despite the fact that the ex-deputy and the sheriff were coming at him from opposite directions. Jake left markers along the trail—a bent twig here, ashes there—to fool them into thinking he was trying hard to disguise his makeshift campsites.

Then, after more than a month of zigzagging through the thick Pennsylvania forests, he did an abrupt about-face and headed south, skirting territory already covered. Another week or so of that, he figured, and it would be safe to move west, toward Texas. No telling how many years or how many jobs there'd be between here and Lubbock....

For more than a decade now, he'd been what cowboys sometimes called a waddy, meandering from ranch to ranch, from farm to farm, filling in during the busy seasons. But Jake never felt more like a drifter. At least his drifting had a purpose this time: he'd clear his name so he could return to Maryland, to Foggy Bottom, to *Bess*.

Boredom had seldom been a problem for this man on the run. He'd accepted his solitary status stoically, if not easily, for it fit well into his resolve to dodge the hangman. Oh, he had a gregarious side, to be sure. Everywhere he'd been, folks liked him. And Jake had wanted it that way, because being accepted made his plan to elude the noose all that much easier. Still and all, it was a dangerous undertaking, walking that tightrope between being charming and friendly…without being too memorable.

He hadn't had to play that game at Foggy Bottom. There, surrounded by Matt and Mark, Micah and the other hands, and his sweet Bess, he'd been free to be *himself,* and he missed that.

Missed *them.*

Jake estimated the loneliness had set in at just about the same time Foggy Bottom was out of sight. Leaving when he did had put a safe distance between him and the men hunting him, but that's also when old, cold habits replaced the comfortable sociable mannerisms he'd adopted at the farm.

Distractions of any kind could be deadly. Jake knew full well that he couldn't afford to wallow in this self-pity born of loneliness. And so to put it out of his mind, he'd taken to whistling and humming, much to Mamie's dismay. Her ears, it seemed, twitched twice as often as usual as the notes pulsed from his parched throat.

Both horse and rider were tired of their diet of berries, bark and wild grasses. Jake yearned for a hot, sit-me-down meal, and knew Mamie was panting to plow into a nose bag full of oats.

So in the next town they came to, Jake pulled up. Beyond the narrow Main Street, in a place called Gettysburg, it was farmland, far as the eye could see. He tethered Mamie and sauntered into the granary. "Howdy," he said when the men who'd gathered at the counter turned to face him.

"Howdy, yourself," answered a small, wiry fellow. "Been on the move quite awhile, from the looks of you."

"That I have," Jake said, dusting his hat against his thighs. He knew when to give just enough information, and when to give a lot; when to tell the truth…and when to lie: "Had me a farm down Richmond way. Drought's been real bad down south this year. You fellas having the same trouble up this way?"

"Nah," said another man, "been a good season."

"Praise God for that, Henry!" a third added.

He knew how to get in their good graces. "Well, to make a short story shorter," Jake continued, "the bank up and foreclosed on my loan. Booted me off my own land."

"Tarnation!" the first man sympathized. "You got a wife and young'uns?"

His thoughts turned immediately to Bess, and a knot formed in his heart when he said, "No. Never did take a wife." Forcing a grin, he added, "Just as well, 'cause what I know about women, you could put in one eye."

The men laughed heartily. "They are a puzzle to figure out, ain't they?"

"So," Henry said, "you lookin' to settle down in these parts?"

"Could be." Jake shrugged. "For now, at least. That is…if you know of somebody who could use a hardworking hand…?"

The wiry man scratched his chin. "Seems to me I heard-tell the Widow Parker was looking for a man to run her spread awhile back."

"When cows climb trees!" the biggest said. "All Beula's lookin' for is a man to spread her *legs* an' keep her warm at night."

The laughter following this joke doubled the last in volume and duration. When it waned, Jake said, "Didn't think old women liked to be, ah, 'spread.'"

"Old? Beula might be a bit used up, but she ain't old," Henry explained. He wiggled his eyebrows. "She was a hurdy-gurdy girl up New York way." And in a louder voice, "Tell him, Archer."

"That's right. 'Bout a year ago, that 'ceiling expert' opened up her own house, right here in good old Gettysburg!"

Jake frowned. He couldn't imagine what work a woman like that would have for him. "Well, maybe you've heard-tell of a farmer in these parts who's lookin' to hire a—"

"What's the matter, boy?" Chuckling, Archer dropped a hearty slap on Jake's back. "Y'ain't bashful, are ya?"

Jake reconsidered his options. He doubted the born-and-bred Texans on his heels could survive a cold, Pennsylvania winter. The minute Yonker and Carter could see their own breath, they'd likely turn tail and head home, with a plan to take up the hunt again when spring broke. *But if they do stick with the hunt, what better place to hide out than a whorehouse!*

"So tell me, boys," he said, smirking as he rubbed his palms together, "which way to Beula's?"

Beula hadn't asked a single question about Jake's work history. Instead, she had given him a quick once-over with those heavily made-up eyes of hers and said, "There's a cot in the hayloft. Tend to your horse while my girls rustle you up a bite to eat. We'll talk later."

Jake hadn't been in any position to question her kindness. And so he had turned, wordlessly, and followed Beula's instructions.

In the barn, along with six beautiful palominos, Jake helped himself to everything he would need to groom Mamie. He hung her saddle over the stall wall, hooked her bridle and bit over the saddle horn. All her gear was in need of a good cleaning.

But, first things first.

Gently, Jake cooled and massaged her tired legs with a good, wet brushing. The coarse-bristled brush rid her coat of the dirt and sweat of the trail, and the softer hairbrush cleaned her mane and tail. Last, he used the hoof-pick to scratch dirt and grit from her hooves. He spent a good hour massaging her big body with the tools, with his hands, speaking softly to her as he worked. Then he backed her into an empty stall and forked a mound of fresh hay onto the floor. After hanging a bucket of mixed grain from a peg in the wall, he latched the stall door.

Jake was about to head on over to Calico House when he realized he'd ridden the same trails Mamie had. *No tellin' what you smell like,* he thought, frowning as he dug through his pack for a change of clothes and a bar of soap. "You're a lucky bunch," he said to the horses. "Old Beula's even put a pump in the barn for y'all!"

He worked the handle until a coarse stream of water issued from the spout and filled the gray metal tub beneath it. Tossing his soiled outfit in a heap near Mamie's saddle blanket, he cleaned up and changed into the dungarees and flannel shirt Bess had washed for him.

Right now, all he really wanted was a couple minutes of shut-eye in a place where he didn't have to worry about a cougar…or a bounty hunter rousting him out.

"You have a kitchen in this place?" he asked in response to her invitation to join her for supper, grinning as Beula hung his hat on a rack near the door.

"Sweet thing, anything you can dream is possible in this place." Beula squinted around the smoke of a hand-rolled cigarette. "So tell me, honey, what's the law want with a handsome cuss like you?"

His heartbeat doubled as he seated himself on the chaise opposite hers.

"Oh, now don't get your neck hairs a-bristlin', sugar. Seems kinda funny—in a coincidental kind of way—that not two days ago, big ugly fella stopped in here askin' if I ever met a man name of…" She narrowed her eyes and tapped a stubby fingertip against her chin. "W. C. Atwood, I believe he said."

Beula took a long pull from the cigarette. "And the day before that, a good-lookin' fella wearin' a six-star badge come struttin' up my steps, askin' the same question." She exhaled, watched the wispy gray-white smoke curl toward the ceiling, then fixed that icy stare on him again. "They say you killed a man—broke his neck to get his watch." Beula raised a brow, but not her voice. "Is that true?"

Jake shook his head. *Goddamn it,* he ranted mentally, *can't even find a moment's peace in a whorehouse!* "No. It isn't true."

"Why *did* you kill him, then?"

By now, Mamie would have eaten her fill of the oats and barley in the stall. She'd been watered and brushed, had rested for a few hours. There was no reason he couldn't saddle up and head for parts farther north…except that he could smell that something mighty delicious was happening out there in this calico queen's kitchen.…

Jake frowned as he ticked off his options. He had three choices, as he saw it: lie outright; come clean and hope she'd let him leave here with a full belly; or come clean and appeal to her mercies…and keep letting her fill his belly until it was time to hit the trail again.

"Look, Miss Beula," he began, leaning forward and resting his elbows on his knees, "I won't insult your intelligence by feedin' you a row of manure." He linked his fingers together. "You've likely heard every lie in the book, so I'm gonna tell it to you straight.

''More'n ten years ago, a fella got himself killed in Lubbock, Texas. That much is true.'' He lifted both shoulders in a gesture of helplessness. ''The evidence pointed straight at me.''

Ice-blue eyes met ice-blue eyes as Jake continued. ''Now, I ain't sayin' I'm guilty, and I ain't sayin' I ain't. I'll just say this much, no self-respecting Texan would do a man in for his pocket watch.''

She broke the intense eye contact to study the glowing tip of her cigarette before the cold blue stare fixed on his face. ''So the question is, are you a self-respecting Texan?''

Jake let the slight narrowing of his eyes form his answer.

''Been on the run, all this time?''

He took a deep breath.

Beula smiled. ''Then we have something in common, I see.''

His left brow rose high on his forehead. ''And what'd that be?''

''Well,'' she said, casually inspecting the fingertips of her free hand, ''you don't stay one step ahead of the U.S. Marshals for ten long years if you're stupid....''

When next their eyes met, hers no longer gleamed with aloof, businesslike detachment. Rather, a hungry warmth burned behind the blue spheres. ''You know how long it's been since I've had me a man with brains?''

I ain't even gonna hazard a guess, Jake answered mentally, *but you damned sure aren't gonna have one tonight.* He'd made a promise to himself to be true to Bess, no matter how long it took to clear his name, and he aimed to keep it.

Beula's red lips parted to tell him exactly how long it had been when her girls entered the room. Two carried huge silver trays, and one held a matching swan-necked coffee pot. They placed the articles on the table nearest Jake.

The first, a girl with flaming-red hair, poured steaming

coffee into a delicate china teacup. "One lump or two?" she asked, holding silver tongs above the sugar bowl.

Smiling, he held up a hand. "Straight up, but—"

A blonde lifted the lid from a golden charger plate, and slid it under his nose. "I hope you like steak and eggs...we're all out of chicken."

His stomach growled and his mouth watered. "This'll do just fine," he told her.

A brunette stepped up and held out the salt and pepper shakers. "Say when," she singsonged, sprinkling seasoning over his food.

"Whoa," he said, chuckling, "you'll have us all sneezin'."

The girls giggled dutifully as Beula looked on. She nodded, and a second blonde filled a cut-crystal goblet with bloodred wine and placed it beside Jake's plate.

Before he could utter a polite "thank you", a second brunette draped a white linen napkin over his thigh, and the redhead tucked another under his chin.

"Ahh...thanks," he managed to say.

"Well, what are you waiting for?" Beula asked. "Go on, eat!"

The steak knife weighed nearly as much as his six-shooter, the fork as much as his bowie. Something told him that even if he hadn't made that promise to Bess, there'd be no nighttime acrobatics for him; if Beula could afford silver this solid, she charged far more than he could afford! He carved off a slice of steak and popped it into his mouth. Jake closed his eyes and slowly shook his head, savoring that first bite.

"What's wrong?" Beula demanded. "Don't you like it?"

He opened his eyes to find her sitting on the edge of her chair, leaning forward slightly.

"We'll fix something else. Corn fritters. Mashed potatoes.'' Waving her hands in the air, she said, ''Anything. Just name it, it's yours.''

''Ma'am...I mean Beula...there ain't a blessed thing wrong with this meal. In fact, it's downright dee-lightful.'' He stuck another hunk of meat into his mouth. ''It's the first real food I've eaten in over a month,'' he said around the bite. ''I'm just tryin' to give it its due, is all.''

The girls and Beula exchanged puzzled glances. ''You haven't had a meal in more than a month? But...but what have you been eating, then?'' the boss-lady wanted to know.

''Nuts. Berries. Wild fruit.'' Jake shrugged. ''You know...trail food.''

Beula settled back on the chaise and repositioned her pose. ''No, I wouldn't know.''

Something in her attitude told him that, while she hadn't eaten on the run, she knew what it meant to be hungry. And something in those glittering azure eyes said she'd gone without *more* than food.

From the corner of his eye, he watched as she draped the feathered robe over her shapely calves and exposed just the right amount of cleavage for his benefit. He buttered a biscuit, took a sip of the wine. *You're a good-lookin' woman, Beula,* he told her silently, *but you ain't my Bess.*

The smile he sent her, he hoped, said ''I ain't interested.''

The smile he got back clearly stated ''*interest* isn't what I want.''

Jake cleared his throat, dipped the biscuit into the egg yolk. *Yep, it's gonna be an interesting couple of days, all right.*

Chapter Nineteen

After the hot, satisfying meal they'd made upon his arrival, Jake didn't know how he'd managed to keep his eyes open through the quiet conversation in front of the fire. Somewhere along the line, he'd gotten into bed. *What* bed, and *where,* he wasn't sure. But the sheets were clean, the mattress soft, and the pillow slips smelled like the soap powders his mama once used.

Mind and body numbed by the jug wine Beula's girls kept pouring into the thin-stemmed goblet, Jake rested easy for the first time in the six weeks since he'd left Foggy Bottom. One thought swirled at the outer edges of his drunkenness: the sheriff and ex-deputy might figure out his scheme to double back on his own tracks. But even if one or both of them found him, at least he'd have caught a good forty winks first.

Bess's pretty, smiling face hovered in his mind. "'I love you,'" he drawled, quoting what she'd said the last time they'd been alone together, "'and I always will.'" To have her beside him now, in this satin-sheeted, flower-scented brass bed would have been like a dream come true.

But Bess is wa-a-y down in Freeland, and you're wa-a-ay over in Gettysburg. Frowning sadly as he burrowed his whiskered cheek deeper into the pillow, he added, *Dreams don't come true.*

Or did they?

The corner of the covers lifted, the mattress dipped, and the unmistakable curviness of a soft-skinned female form pressed tight against his side. "Say, handsome," sighed the husky voice, "I wouldn't have figured you for the type who sleeps in his birthday suit."

Jake tried unsuccessfully to pry one eye open. "Wha-a?"

She giggled and pressed a finger against his lips. "Shh. You'll wake the whole house." Taking his hand in hers, she placed it atop her bared chest. "There, now," she whispered, "isn't that nice?"

Without opening his eyes, he smiled crookedly. "Mmm." He nodded. "Real ni—"

Her openmouthed kiss blocked his words. Slowly, tantalizingly, she swept her mouth from his cheekbones to his chin, then gently caught his lower lip between her teeth.

Jake realized in a flash of lucidity that his hand was resting on a naked breast...and that the rest of the naked woman lay stretched out beside him.

Bess? he wondered. *But—but how...?*

What did it matter *how* his sweet Bess had gotten here! "I've missed you," he admitted, accepting her advances...and making a few of his own. He wrapped her in his arms. "How I've missed you."

Raucous laughter began in the pit of her, bubbling up and spilling out. "But we've only been apart for a few minutes, you naughty boy."

Minutes? Smiling drunkenly, he said, "Seems like a helluva lot longer than that!" And as the fire within him raged, his heart ached with love for her. How *good* it felt to have her this close again. How *good* it was to hear her saying she wanted him, too.

Jake combed his fingers through her hair...and wondered

why it wasn't as silky as he remembered; kissed her lust-swollen lips…and asked himself why they didn't seem as innocently inviting.…

Through the jagged edges of sobriety, he viewed fragments of the past—Bess's eyes, her luxurious hair, her loving smile. Then, quick as they'd appeared, the images were gone.

Thankfully, *she* wasn't.

Grinning with boozy mirth, he gathered her closer. "You're still here. Thank God."

"Thank Him if you like, sugar," she said, her voice husky with passion as she climbed on top of him, "but I have to admit it seems a little sacrilegious."

"Huh?"

"Tell you what, handsome," she panted, "why don't you just lie back and hush, and take ole Beula for a ride? And maybe—"

Jake reached up in the darkness, filled his hands with her breasts, and squeezed. "'Take ole *Beula* for…'?" he interrupted, repeating her last words.

"—and maybe *I'll* leave a two-spot on the bureau for *you*," she purred, arching her back and raking her fingers through his chest hair.

His heart called *Bess,* but something told him she would not answer. Jake lifted his woozy head and forced his eyes open. Still perched upon him, head tilted back and throat exposed, a woman. A very pretty woman.

But not Bess.

The effects of the liquor still swirled in his mind, and yet, he sensed that something was wrong. This woman's torso was too long, her hair too dark, her breasts too soft to be Bess's. But then, he *had* swallowed a lot of wine.…

If only she'd meet his eyes, *then* he'd know for sure.

With trembling hands, Jake reached up and placed a palm on each of her cheeks, gently coaxing her to look at him.

A sliver of moonlight squeaked between the velvety drapery folds, streaking across the woman's face and illuminating lusty ice-blue eyes.

The sight sickened and shamed him. "Beula..."

That quick, it seemed, he was sober. Too late, he wondered, to prevent...?

"What's wrong, sugar?"

"Tell me we didn't..." Jake swallowed hard. "Tell me I haven't..."

Beula chose that moment to snuggle up beside him, one arm draped across his chest.

Jake shook his head, clenched his jaw, ran his hands through his hair. He took her to mean that he'd already bedded her. Knuckling his eyes, he groaned.

You swore you'd never touch another woman, yet the very first one who came along...

Aw, Bess, can you ever forgive me?

Sitting up, he swung his legs over the side of the bed, intent upon getting dressed, getting out of this room, out of this *house*. But the alcohol, still surging through his veins, wouldn't allow it, and he fell back onto the mattress in a graceless heap.

He'd been booze blind on whiskey and white lightnin'. Had come undone in mugs of beer more times than he could count. But Jake had never been wine drunk, and its effects were more than mind numbing...they were mind-*boggling*.

It might just be simpler all round to let Carter catch him; he'd wrap a rope around Jake's sorry neck, and put an end to this running and hiding...and missing his Bess.

Chances of seeing her again are slim to none, but even if Lady Luck gives you another chance with her, how are you gonna face her, after what you just did with Beula?

Somewhere, off in the distance, a man was crying. Hard, dry, bone-racking sobs echoed through the room and bounced off the walls. *Sounds like that drunken sonofawhore is even more miserable than you are,* he thought. When he pressed the heels of his hands into his eye sockets, Jake felt the tears on his cheeks, and realized *he* was the miserable, drunken sonofawhore!

When Beula had shrugged into her fleecy robe and lit the bedside lantern, he didn't know, but it felt strangely warm and comforting against his bared chest as she hugged him tight. "Hush, now," she said, giving his temple a maternal kiss, "and tell Beula all about it."

Mamie had listened to her share of his pathetic past, but no *human* knew the details of Jake's history. He blamed the wine when the story poured out the way rushing water spills over the rocks in a river's shallows—the arrest and trial, the ride in the jailer's wagon, his escape, years on the run...and Bess.

They were leaning against the headboard by the time he finished, her arms around him, his head resting on her ample bosom. Between rocking him and kissing him, Beula made many promises: a good night's sleep, and the world would look rosy again; Bess would wait for him; he was too smart to get caught by any dunderheaded U.S. Marshal.... "Things're bound to get better, sugar," she insisted, "and I oughta know."

Jake believed she was telling the truth. Believed something else, too. He could survive just about anything, but he'd betrayed his Bess. How was he going to survive *that?*

"She's one lucky lady," Beula was saying, "to have a man like you so much in love with her."

Jake shook his head and knuckled his eyes. "A man like me," he repeated, disgust and shame echoing in his voice. "*I'm* the one who's lucky. She's the only woman ever loved me, just for myself."

He heard the pitiful sound of his own voice again, and it stopped him cold. Wine or no wine...enough was enough!

Jake wrenched himself free of her embrace and rubbed his aching temples. "What're you doin' here, Beula?"

She arched a black-penciled brow and smiled. "I live here, remember?"

Frowning hard, he met her eyes. "In this room?"

Her smile faded, as did the friendly tone in her voice. "It's a guest room...but it's in *my* house."

He wanted to lash out at her, to blame her for causing him to betray his private vow to be true to Bess. But there was no escaping it: she may have provided the wine, but Beula hadn't forced him to swallow it. She wasn't the reason he'd come to Gettysburg, she hadn't talked him into staying at Calico House. It was his doing, nobody else's.

"I'll head out at first light," he said quietly, drawing the covers up over his nakedness.

"No need to make any rash decisions, sugar," Beula said, getting out of bed and crossing to the door. "This is your room for as long as you can stay with us. I had no right to come in here uninvited." She stood in the open doorway. "I'm sorry."

Jake heaved a sigh. "What's done is done."

"One more thing before I go, though..." It seemed strange, Jake thought, that a woman with her reputation stood in the circle of glowing lamplight, like an angel in a heavenly beam. "Don't you worry your li'l head another minute, sugar," she said softly, "you didn't—"

His eyes locked on hers with hopeful expectation. "I didn't *what?*"

"More like *wouldn't*. You were ready and able—you just weren't willing."

Jake stared in quiet disbelief for a moment. Brow furrowed and lips taut, he whispered hoarsely, "You're sure?"

Beula laughed at that. "Take a good look at me, sugar," she said, arms spread wide. "If *I* don't know when a man has…'' Grinning, she added, ''Trust me. Nothing happened.''

He hung his head and closed his eyes. ''Thank God,'' he prayed aloud. ''Thank Almighty *God*.''

A moment of silence ticked by.

''Jake?''

He tried to focus on the leafy pattern of the rug between his feet. ''What.''

''Like I said…your Bess is some lucky woman.''

My Bess. I like the sound of that…. ''*I'm* the lucky one,'' Jake repeated.

But Beula never heard him, for she'd already closed the door.

''What are you doing here?''

The skinny old man leaned on the grimy handle of his broom and aimed a fiery glare at Lubbock's only in-residence minister. ''You ain't got claim to this alley, Atwood.'' Narrowing his watery blue eyes, Purdy added, ''Question is, what're *you* doing here?'' One brow high on his forehead, the town drunk rubbed arthritic fingers over his beard-bristled jaw and smirked. ''Seems to me the folks who pay your wages would be as interested as I am in what their preacher is doin' in the alley behind the saloon at three o'clock in the mornin'.''

Josh Atwood's arm shot out as if fired from a gun. ''I've had about enough of your sass,'' he growled, grabbing Purdy's collar. ''You've been a burr under my saddle for as long as I've known you.''

Though half Atwood's height and weight, Purdy stood his ground. His voice was calm and quiet, his watery eyes strangely sober when he said, ''That's 'cause I'm the only one 'round here who'll tell you to your face what you really are.''

Lip curled with disgust, Atwood tightened his grip on the shirt. ''And what would that be?''

''A bully what's been impersonatin' a holy man for ten long years, that's what.''

Eyes blazing with fury, Atwood whispered through clenched teeth, ''Why you no-account sot, I've got half a mind to—''

''Half a mind's about *all* you've got!'' Purdy interrupted, raising his chin a notch. ''You don't scare me none, Josh Atwood. Men like you never have scared me.''

Blinking, Atwood loosed his grip a mite. ''Men like me? What drunken foolishness are you spouting?''

''Men who'll use their size, their age, the power of their office to browbeat people.''

The preacher let Purdy go, turned on his heel and ran a hand through his hair. Shoulders slumped and bent slightly at the waist, as if the accusation itself was burdensome, he echoed, ''Browbeat.''

It was more a statement than a question; the tremorous timber of his voice telling Purdy that he realized his actions—at least on this night—had proven the drunk correct.

Neither man spoke for a long time.

''If it's a starin' contest you're after, Preacher-man,'' Purdy snarled, ''I'll win, on account-a I ain't got nothin' but this ole broom to call my own...no place to go, nobody to go *to*.'' He shifted his weight and leaned on the long, worn handle again, and tilted his gray-haired head, telling Atwood without words that in his mind, the preacher *did* have something to go home to. He nodded toward the rooms above the saloon. ''Don't rightly know why a man with a wife like Miss Polly would settle for one of them—''

This time, both of Atwood's arms shot out. ''Why, you miserable old bastard,'' he snarled, ''I'll teach you not to threaten me!''

''Reminds me of the old days,'' Purdy returned, ''when

you used to beat your nephew. Why, you'd whallop that young'un for so much as lookin' cross-eyed.''

He'd aimed his remark at the heart of the man, intending for it to sting…and it had, and the evidence was written all over Josh Atwood's strained, enraged face.

Purdy aimed the broom handle, too, and toppled the big man with one well-placed jab to Atwood's groin. The big man hit the hard-packed dirt with a loud *thud.*

While he lay writhing and moaning and cradling his manhood, Purdy bent to retrieve the object that had fallen from Atwood's pocket.

''Well, now,'' he said, palming it, ''what have we here?''

He took a few steps toward the street, where the moonlight wasn't blocked by buildings on either side of the narrow alleyway. ''Damn Sam!'' he said to himself, ''if that don't beat all.…''

Atwood had levered himself up on one elbow by now, and Purdy crouched beside him, nodding, a self-satisfied smile brightening his pale face. ''It all makes sense now.''

''What makes sense?''

''Your nephew didn't kill Horace Pickett ten years ago…''

Atwood hung his head and closed his eyes.

''*You* did.''

Deep-breathing exercises, it was said, were the latest in respiratory therapy. *If there's any truth in that,* Bess told herself, *I have the healthiest lungs this side of the Mississippi!*

True to her word, she'd stood at her window morning and night, scanning the horizon in the hopes of seeing Jake's familiar form. So many lonely weeks had passed since he'd left Foggy Bottom.

Bess had no reason to believe he'd return any time soon, or that he'd return at all. But she would continue to hope.…

She'd read his letter so many times that it felt more like cloth than paper. To protect it, she'd committed it to memory; to preserve it, Bess had pressed it into the pages of her Bible.

She sat in the window seat now, the chill late November wind ruffling the dark curls that framed her face, eyes closed as she recited her favorite part of his message: "Don't forget me, Bess."

Bess could picture him saying it, pale-blue eyes alight with love, sun-kissed hair gleaming, a tantalizing smile slanting his lips. He'd taken a big chance, signing his real name to that note, and she loved him all the more for it. *Don't forget me, Bess.*

"How *could* I?" she wondered aloud.

Leaning against the many-pillowed backrest, she pulled her long-fringed shawl tighter to fend off the effects of the crisp breeze, and prepared to watch the sun set in the West.

God, she decided, possessed a magical, artistic hand, for this day, He'd painted the skies with streaks of brilliant-orange and pale-pink, adding bands of yellow as bright as brass above a layer of steely blue.

The far-off cry of a hawk momentarily silenced the crickets' chirp and the toads' song. But soon, they joined again the chorus of katydids and cicadas. The Almighty Conductor led His harmonious symphony, adding the occasional bleat of sheep, the here-and-there low of cow, a spirited whinnying of a horse to the rhythm of the night. It was a peaceful world outside her window, and that peace lulled her into a contented slumber, thinking as she drifted off, *How much peace does Jake have tonight?*

She was awakened hours later by a mournful moan that blotted out the euphonious tones of the day, shattering the calm.

Bess sat up with a start and peered out the window. *A wolf? But how can that be?* she wondered, pressing her forehead to the cool glass, hoping to catch a glimpse of the creature that had cracked the quiet. She'd never heard anything like it at Foggy Bottom.

The caged wolf she'd seen as a girl in Baltimore had not made a sound, save the soft padding of its constantly pacing feet. But she'd heard wolves several years later, when she'd traveled to Texas and Wyoming with her father to inspect cows and bulls that would become part of the Foggy Bottom herd.

It was a sound like none other, and once heard, one that no one could forget....

A while back, there had been erratic reports of wolf sightings in the woods north of Freeland, but since no one could say for sure, they'd been dismissed as rumor. Bess considered the likelihood that, in her dreamlike state, she'd only imagined the eerie, bloodcurdling sound.

Glancing at the mantel clock, she realized she'd slept in her window seat for nearly two hours. Frowning, she wondered about that. She rarely required more than five hours of sleep at night; it simply wasn't like her to sleep during the day. Sighing, she rose, intending to change into her night dress and slip under the covers. *An extra hour or two of sleep couldn't do me any harm, could it?*

Leaving the window ajar, she crossed to the chiffarobe and opened its tall, mahogany doors. Bending, she removed a high-collared white gown from the top drawer.

Her hands froze above its handle.

Because there it was again...that hollow, keening cry.

Life on the farm had taught her to recognize and identify the sounds of the wild. This was not the wail of a dog, or the yap of a fox on the hunt. No animal *but* a wolf could produce a tone that was at once pitiful and poignant.

Bess ran back to the window and scanned the horizon.

Nothing.

After seeing the caged wolf in Baltimore, little-girl Bess

had made it her business to learn as much as she could about the species. Poring through hefty volumes in her father's library, she'd learned that wolves were intelligent, instinctual and cunning, with much to compare them to people. *Family* was of ultimate importance to Bess, and *family* was of great value to wolves, too. She respected the way the pack protected one another...cubs in particular. Admired, too, that like humans, wolves mated for life. When death took half of a pair, the survivor mourned as deeply as any human husband or wife.

Again, the rolling, lilting lamentation echoed over the farm, hovering and wavering like a thick, doleful fog.

The wolf was alone. Bess knew that much because there had been no response to his call. Had that been the reason for the spellbindingly sorrowful notes of his song?

The mental picture of the wolf she'd seen all those years before, flashed through her mind. She saw, too, the face of the wanted man on the poster—Jake—that she'd found that day in Philadelphia. What did they have in common?

Eyes as round and cold as ice that had, with one coolly level look, instantly permeated her mind, her heart, her soul. During the moments that their gazes and hers melded, she had read their thoughts, shared their emotions.

And concluded that they'd both wanted one and the same thing: freedom.

"It was an accident, Smitty, I swear."

The deputy's cackling laughter bounced off the stone walls of the jailhouse. "I had me a dollar for every time I heard that, I could buy me a new horse." The iron bars of the cell rang like a piano tuner's fork when he slammed the door. With calm deliberation, he made a regular production of turning the big black key in its lock.

Tossing the key ring into the top desk drawer, Smitty

paced back and forth in front of the bars. "You got some nerve, Preacher, I'll give you that."

Josh Atwood sat on the edge of the narrow cot, elbows on knees, head in his hands.

Stopping dead in his tracks, he threw both hands into the air. "Me 'n Yonker was takin' W.C. to the gallows when that jail wagon overturned." He stared at his prisoner. "And you would'a let him swing for a murder you committed...."

Atwood only continued to stare at some unknown spot on the gritty floor between his boots.

Smitty's face crinkled, as though he'd just inhaled a dreadful odor. "Yep, you got some nerve, all right."

Shaking his head and muttering under his breath, he headed across the room and settled into the worn seat of the wooden armchair. Propping his boot heels on the corner of the desk, he helped himself to one of the toothpicks Sheriff Carter kept in a shot glass on the ink blotter. "You have two choices, Preacher," he said, leaning back in the chair. "You can tell me your story, or you can wait 'til the sheriff gets back."

Atwood, still holding his head in his hands, said nothing.

Smitty's feet hit the floor one at a time and he sat up. "Don't it just beat all?" he said again, weather-worn hands folded on the desktop. "The sheriff's out east, followin' up on a lead that might he'p him bring in poor ole W.C., when Horace's real killer has been here in Lubbock, right under his nose, the whole damned time." He shook his head again. "If a judge and jury don't kill ya, Carter likely will. You know how many times he's left his wife and young'uns to go on a wild-goose chase after that boy?"

Sitting back again, he grabbed a stubby pencil and a sheet of paper from the desk drawer. "So what's it gonna be, Preacher? You want me to write down your account of what happened that night? Or is the sheriff gonna do it when he gets back?"

Atwood didn't move, save to heave a deep sigh. "Didn't know you could read or write, Smitty," he said in a quiet, spent voice.

"There's a lot you don't know, Preacher." He worked the toothpick to the other corner of his mouth. "I've known how to read an' write goin' on seven years now. But then, I don't suppose I would'a noticed much these past ten years, either, if I'd framed my brother's son for a murder that—"

Atwood was on his feet in a whipstitch, fingers wrapped tight around the thick black bars. "It *wasn't* murder, I tell you! It was—"

"Pardon me all the way to hell and back if I sound a mite sharp," Smitty interrupted. And in a high-pitched nasal whimper, he quoted Atwood: " 'It was an accident....' " The hard edge of his glare made it clear he didn't believe a word of it. The *tick-tick-ticking* of the big round clock on the wall drew his attention. "I got fifteen minutes afore I have to make my morning rounds." Pressing the rounded pencil point against the paper, he said, "Now, start talkin'...."

"B'lieve me, Miz Pickett, I'm sober as a judge, an' I promise you, I wouldn't ring your bell if what I had to say wasn't important."

The reed-thin woman in the high-collared black dress hesitated a moment, then opened the door wider and cringed slightly as Joe Purdy stepped into her dimly lit foyer.

Purdy held up a hand as she began moving toward the parlor. "Ma'am, I appreciate the invite, but I wouldn't want to soil your fancy settee. If it's all the same to you, I'd just as soon skip the pleasantries and get on with it."

Mrs. Pickett did not close the door. One pale, wrinkled hand remained on the brass knob as she said, "Very well, then, Mr. Purdy, state your business."

"W. C. Atwood didn't kill your husband."

She lifted her chin a notch and exhaled a sigh of frustration. "You said you weren't drunk, Mr. Purdy. You gave me your word, and—"

"I ain't had a drop since yesterday morning," he interrupted, standing a little taller. "The man who really killed Mr. Pickett is at the jailhouse right now, confessin' to the crime."

Her thin, graying eyebrows knitted in the center of her wrinkled forehead. "Are you daft? The killer is out *there* somewhere—" with her free hand, the widow gestured toward the bustling street "—on the loose! Has been for—"

"For ten long years," Purdy said softly, "for a crime he didn't commit."

She blinked, then blinked again as the weight of his words sunk in. "Someone has admitted it, you say?"

"Josh Atwood."

Lips taut, she narrowed her eyes. "You don't expect me to believe that Godly man could have committed cold-blooded murder!"

"He claims it was an accident. Said he never meant to kill your husband."

"An accident?" She closed the door and led the way into the parlor, where a teapot and two cups and saucers sat on the ornate cherrywood table in front of the sofa.

Purdy inspected the setup. "You expectin' company, Miz Pickett?"

She blushed deeply, then bit her lower lip. "No." Sighing, the widow added, "I have always believed in being prepared, is all. Now, how do you take your tea, Mr. Purdy?" she asked, lifting the lid of the gleaming silver sugar bowl. "One lump or two?"

Purdy perched on the edge of the armchair across from her. "One, thank you kindly."

A lone sugar cube landed in the bottom of the cup with a tiny *clink,* and an instant later was drowned in steamy, rusty-brown liquid. "Cream?"

"No, ma'am."

"Relax, Mr. Purdy." The barest hint of a smile lifted the corners of her mouth, "Despite what I'm sure you've heard about me, I don't bite," she said, grinning, "unless provoked."

He returned the smile, and with trembling hands accepted the cup. "Ma'am, if I ain't learned nothin' else in life, it's that nobody is what they seem to be."

Balancing the delicate china on her knee, the widow took a deep, shaky breath. She stared off into space, eyes vacant, as if remembering the moment when they told her that her husband was dead. "It was his eyes, I think, that made it easy to believe that young man had...that he'd..." The widow blinked and cleared her throat. "So Pastor Atwood did it, you say?"

"No, ma'am. Ain't me who says it. W.C.'s uncle himself says it. And if you don't believe me, you can ask him yourself." He gave a short, nervous laugh. "Smitty's got him locked up good an' tight down at the jail."

Daintily, Mrs. Pickett leaned forward and placed her cup and saucer on the gilded silver tray. "That won't be necessary, Mr. Purdy." Closing her eyes for a moment, she shook her head. "Now then, do tell me how this so-called 'accident' happened."

Purdy put his cup down, too. "You sure you're strong enough to hear?"

She sat up taller. "Mr. Purdy, my size and stature may make me appear weak and frail, but as we've already determined, appearances are deceiving."

"Well, it's just that according to the preacher, Mr. Pickett wasn't entirely blameless."

Shaking her head, she sent him a hard glare. "My husband and I had been together nearly thirty years when he was killed. I knew him better than anyone in this town. Now tell me what you know, or leave me in peace."

He cleared his throat and plunged in. "The preacher said he'd heard W.C. give your husband a dressing-down for scarin' Francine. Said he heard W.C. issue a threat of his own—'If I ever hear-tell of you threatening a woman again, I'll break your fat red neck.'" Purdy shrugged. "Well, that very night, the preacher and Mr. Pickett were, ah, well, let's just say they were in the same place at the same time when the preacher heard your husband threaten…*another* woman."

"You needn't fancy it up for me, Mr. Purdy. He was with a whore." Frowning, she stared at her hands, folded primly in her lap. "Wasn't he?"

The carriage clock on the mantel ticked five times before he said, "All I know for sure, ma'am, is that he was out back of the saloon when the preacher saw him."

Tears misted in her eyes and she managed a small smile. "You're very kind to try and protect me from the truth, Mr. Purdy. But the fact is, I know exactly what Horace was.…" She bit her lower lip, then quickly added, "…but I loved him anyway, more than anything in this world."

She took a long, slow sip of her tea. "Now please, do go on.…

"But wait," she interrupted. "You don't mean to say that *Pastor Atwood* was with one of those…that he'd been up- stairs in the saloon, too?"

"Like I said, ma'am, all I know for sure is the two of 'em were out back, in the alley. What went on before they got there, I can't say for sure. But the preacher claims he saw Mr. Pickett slappin' the woman around, says he saw him shove her to the ground. Says she'd hit her head, that she was crying and bleeding when he stepped in to put a stop to the beating." Purdy hesitated. "Guess it went pretty quick from a shoving match to a fistfight.…"

He took a deep breath before going on. "I reckon you know that the preacher was younger than your husband, he was bigger an' stronger, too.'' Another shrug. ''Preacher says he gave your husband a good sock in the jaw, hoping to knock him out, so's he could get the girls out of the alley and back upstairs, where they belonged. Only…only he hit him harder than he thought.''

''And when Horace fell,'' the widow interjected, ''he broke his fat red neck.''

Purdy nodded slowly. ''Yes'm. Least that's how the preacher tells it.''

She tidied the folds of her skirt, tucked a wayward tendril of white hair back into the severe bun at the nape of her neck. ''Then it happened just that way. I'm certain of it.''

And then the widow was on her feet, pacing back and forth in front of the marble fireplace. ''That poor young man,'' she said from behind her hands. ''Ten years on the run, and his own uncle the accuser!''

She stopped so abruptly that her skirt whirled around her ankles. ''But the pocket watch. The boy had Horace's watch in his possession when—''

''Don't rightly know how W.C. came by the watch they found on him, Mrs. Pickett, but it weren't your husband's. That much is for sure.''

''How do you know?''

''Because tonight, when me an' the preacher were goin' at it in the alley, a watch fell out of his pocket. It belonged to your husband. Atwood's had it all this time.'' He frowned, shook his head. ''Told me it was a reminder of exactly what kind of polecat he is…said that every time he looked at it, he said a prayer for Jake…and another one for his own sorry soul.…''

Eyes wide, she folded her hands beneath her chin. ''But how can you be sure it's Horace's watch?''

''There's an inscription in the lid.'' He scratched his bristled chin and frowned hard. ''If memory serves, it went something like 'From this day forth, my husband, my own.'"

Fingertips pressed to her lips, the Widow Pickett slumped into the nearest chair. "Dear Lord in heaven, I'm almost as much to blame for that poor boy's fate as the pastor is," she whispered, shaking her head. "It never occurred to me to tell them to look inside the watch, because those *eyes* of his..."

"W.C. led a hard life, Miz Pickett, and it turned him hard long before that night."

"Yes, yes, I know...lost his parents in that horrible fire, and went to live with the pastor and his wife." On her feet again, the widow resumed her pacing. "The watch! I remember thinking at first they'd need it for the trial—as evidence, you know? But afterward," she said, more to herself than to Purdy, "when I asked the sheriff if I could have it back, he said he'd given it to the boy, sort of as a cruel joke, when they locked him into the jailer's wagon. The sheriff promised I'd get it back once the..." Mrs. Pickett stared at her hands and sighed deeply. "Once the hanging was over, he said I'd get the watch back. But then..." She shrugged helplessly. "But then the boy ran off. I naturally assumed he'd taken the watch with him, that he would probably sell it to buy himself a gun, or bullets, or whatever...."

She looked up then, eyes wife and hopeful. "If Pastor Atwood has the watch, I really can get it back...."

"I imagine that's true, ma'am," Purdy agreed.

Suddenly, the widow's expression darkened. "That poor boy," she said softly. "All these years, he's been a fugitive, all because—" She clamped a hand over her lips. "If only I knew how to get in touch with him, I'd—"

"I know where he is."

"What?"

He shrugged. "I've been gettin' telegrams from nearly every city he's been in since leavin' here."

"And you never let on?" She shook her head again. "If you don't mind my asking, Mr. Purdy...if you were so close to the boy, why didn't you speak out on his behalf? Why didn't you tell them what you knew?"

Purdy got to his feet and faced her. "I tried, ma'am. I told 'em W.C. couldn't have killed your husband. I told 'em all about the things that boy had done for me...the clean clothes he brought me, the warm meals he'd sneak—" He chuckled, then shook his head sadly. "Name one person in this town who pays me any mind...'ceptin' as the town drunk."

The widow merely stared at him for what seemed a full minute, her silent appraisal causing him to shift from one crumpled boot to the other.

She nodded, then walked purposefully toward the foyer and took her shawl from a peg on the wall. "Mr. Purdy, will you kindly escort me to the telegraph office?" she asked, draping it over her narrow shoulders.

Purdy started for the door. "Be happy to, ma'am. But I don't get it. What're you plannin'—"

She jerked the door open and stepped aside, one hand inviting Purdy to exit, quickly. "What I'm planning," she announced, offering him her elbow, "is to send that poor young man a message. I want to be the one who tells him that his name has been cleared, that he's welcome to come home—if he still considers Lubbock his home, that is."

Purdy took her arm and they began marching up the street as she added, "And you, Mr. Purdy, are going to tell me where to send it!"

Chapter Twenty

It had been a long, hard ride, a fact that surprised Jake more than he cared to admit. He'd crossed Arizona's Yuma Desert before, on his way to Lubbock to clear his name, had learned the hard way how to prepare for such a trip: plenty of water and beef jerky, saddlebags of grain for Mamie.

Strange things could happen in the desert if a man didn't plan well, things that could cost him his life. And so Jake ate sparingly of the jerky, sipped cautiously from the lip of the canteen, carefully meted out Mamie's grain. Consequently, he stayed hungry and thirsty from the moment Mamie first trod onto the endless sea of sand.

The hunger burning in him had little to do an empty stomach. He missed Bess more now than he had in those first days, when the sheriff and the ex-deputy were hot on his heels. He'd led them on a dizzying chase, hoping to confuse them as he zigzagged across the country. Ever since he'd left Beula's whorehouse in Gettysburg, the idea had been to wear them out and frustrate them, make them think they'd done him in at long last, so that they could go home with a victorious tale to tell, and he could head east, to Foggy Bottom....

To *Bess*.

Obviously, he'd done something right, for he hadn't seen hide nor hair of them in months. Still, he couldn't be too careful or too patient; last thing he wanted was to lead them right back to Foggy Bottom and endanger the only real family he'd known since boyhood.

Mamie, head low and ears back, sauntered along at a slow, rolling pace. The soft *thud-thud* of hooves beating sand lulled him into a drowsy dream state, and he closed his eyes, more to conjure an image of Bess than to block out the unrelenting rays of the noonday sun.

Hot white fear made him snap them open again. "I can't see her," he whispered, "I've been gone so long, I can't even get a picture of her in my mind anymore!"

The admission ached inside him, doubling him over the saddle horn. She'd been the sole reason for his dogged determination to outrun Carter and Yonker. She'd been his incentive to keep going when winds howled and rains pelted and snow threatened to bury his last shred of hope. If he couldn't even *see* her...

He sat up, closed his eyes again and clenched his teeth, intent upon conjuring the image of her dark eyes, her sweet lips her creamy white skin.

But it was no use.

Try as he might, he couldn't summon her to memory.

If he couldn't call her image to mind—when there was nothing but the occasional scorpion and a cactus out here to occupy his mind—what must *Bess* be doing?

"She's moved on," he said aloud to himself. "And why shouldn't she? Didn't you tell her that if love came knockin', she oughta answer?"

Jake hung his head in sorrow as the agony of it welled up inside him. True enough, he'd written those words. But somewhere deep inside him, he'd hoped she wouldn't listen, that she'd wait for him.

Jake knew that she deserved a life free from worry and

fear, deserved to share it with a man who'd give her a home, and children, and—

"She deserves better than the likes of *you*, W. C. Atwood!"

His heart-renching bellow stopped Mamie in her tracks, and was quickly swallowed up by the dry grit and the sun-baked desert air. He gave the horse a soothing pat. "Sorry, girl," he said, "didn't mean to scare you."

Jake climbed out of the saddle, dug around in his rucksack. As Mamie nibbled oats from his cupped palm, Jake uncorked the canteen, tilted his head back and drank his fill. When his thirst was quenched, he dug a small metal bowl out of the pack, filled it with warm water, and gave Mamie a turn. She lapped greedily, nudging him for more when the bowl was empty.

"Don't you fret, girl," he said, stroking her forehead. "Pretty soon now, I'll see to it you get a proper meal and a good brushing, and all the water your belly can hold."

After recapping the canteen, he stowed the bowl and hoisted himself back into the saddle. "If we ride straight through and don't pamper ourselves," he said, patting the horse's right shoulder, "we'll be in Lubbock this time next week."

It was as though the horse understood, and agreed, for she stepped up her pace and continued due east.

"Easy, girl," he advised, "it's a long, long way to Texas from here. We've got to go sure 'n' steady if we want to make it alive."

Not that it matters, he thought, *'cause once we get there…*

Mamie dutifully slowed her pace. As they plodded along, he closed his eyes once more, and this time, he saw Bess's big eyes and sweet smile. Experience had taught Jake that if he let himself, he'd hear the lyrical notes of her laughter, feel the softness of her kisses, the tenderness of her touch.

He opened his eyes and focused on the drifting mounds of never-ending sand. "No point torturing yourself, man," he said. "Surely by now she's moved on."

His heartbeat doubled at the thought of her, giving to another man what she'd so lovingly, so willingly given him. He'd beat the man witless—if he ever got close enough—who dared put filthy hands on his woman!

"She's *not* your woman. Hasn't been for more'n a year now. Face up to it, and it'll go easier for you."

With a decisive nod, he pulled the brim of his hat lower on his forehead and squared his jaw. "It is what it is," he added glumly, "and the fact is, you're plumb loco. Why else have you been talkin' to yourself for the last hundred miles!"

Some other time, he might have chuckled at the confession. Some other place, the acknowledgment might have coaxed a grin, at least.

But the desert heat was beginning to take its toll, despite all his good planning.

Jake found himself alone in the world, this time with barely enough food and water to survive. He rode slowly, methodically, across the scorched sands, trying to ignore his parched, cracked lips and cheeks that were blistered by the scorching rays of the Yuma sun.

The fact that he seemed to have outwitted the sheriff and ex-deputy was of little comfort to him. Because sooner or later, *some* lawman or bounty hunter would catch up with him.

Jake took a deep breath and sat up straighter in the saddle. If they were going to get him anyway, it may as well be on his own terms. *Yep,* he thought, *you'll ride into Lubbock and give yourself up.* That way, at least, maybe he could die with a shred of dignity.

Die.

The word had never terrified him more than it did, now

that he knew how very much he would have had to live for, if only....

Jake gave Mamie's reins a slight tug and headed toward Lubbock.

Because even the hangman's noose was an easier fate to face than a lifetime without Bess.

Bess sat on the front porch and listened to the ongoing wail of the lone wolf. There was a chill in the air, and she acknowledged sadly that soon, the bright-blinking golden light of fireflies that lit the night would be dimmed by winter's determined approach.

Another season without Jake, she thought, hugging the small bundle in her arms.

A year ago, her father and brothers had said she should give up hoping Jake would ever return.

But a lot had happened in a year....

She'd known the moment she caught sight of Micah's dour expression when he returned late that afternoon that he'd brought home more than a supply of flour and cornmeal. Without even bothering to unload the wagon, he'd trudged up the walk and handed her the envelope that bore the name W. C. Atwood.

"I can't open this, Pa," she'd protested. "It's addressed to Jake."

"You're his wife in every way but one," he'd barked. "Open it!"

As she did, he'd added in a low growl, "If I knew for sure where he was, I'd hang him myself."

Hands trembling, Bess had slumped onto the parlor sofa and unfolded the telegram:

"W.C.," it said, "Pickett's killer is behind bars." It was signed "Josephus Purdy."

The dispatch had provided Bess with the first tangible

hope she'd had in months…hope that Jake was all right…
hope that he'd come back to her.

She left first thing next morning to send a telegram of her
own, care of Lubbock's sheriff. Certain that Jake would be
back in Texas by then, she watched as Stoney Frasier *click-
click-clicked* the simple message that would vibrate through
the wires between Baltimore and Lubbock—the only con-
nection between her and: "Come home. There's someone I
want you to meet."

That evening, and every evening since, she'd sat in this
very spot, watching the horizon. At first, she watched for
Stoney's son to ride up on his dapple gray to deliver Jake's
reply. When weeks passed with no sign of the boy, she began watching for Jake himself, thinking—*hoping*—that
maybe he'd decided to tell her in person what he might have
said in a telegram.

More than a whole lonely year had passed since she got
word that Jake had at last found his elusive freedom, yet she
continued to sit in the big rocker every sunset, staring at the
horizon. What choice did she have but to believe that one
day soon, his silhouette—tall and proud and unfettered by
the chains of his past—would appear in the distance.

She pictured their loving, joyous reunion, imagined his
jubilation at learning that he had a daughter.

They'd plan a wedding, a party afterward to celebrate
their union, then maybe build a little cottage near the manor
house, and in it, they'd get reacquainted, and he'd tell her
every detail of his life…including what the initials in his
name stood for.

Bess's shining dreams dulled a bit with each day that
passed without word from him. A week ago, on a night very
much like this one, she admitted the awful truth: she would
never see him again.

Still…something drove her to the front porch rocker every
day. Perhaps her father was right, maybe she *was* just tor-

turing herself, sitting here, looking for what would never arrive. But what choice did she have?

The baby squirmed, reached a tiny, pudgy-pink hand toward her mother's doting face.

Smiling past her tears, Bess tenderly held her three-month old daughter to her chest. "Maybe your daddy isn't coming back," she whispered, kissing the baby's cheek, "but I'll see him every day of my life…in your beautiful ice-blue eyes…."

Jake led Mamie down the center of the gritty road at a slow, even pace. He hadn't known what to expect, exactly, but it surprised him how little the town had changed.

The tidy row of buildings that ran down the center of Lubbock had been given a fresh coat of paint. There was a new sign on the feed and grain, the bank had changed names, and the old hotel was a restaurant now.

But music and laughter still filtered from the saloon, the steady sound of hammer meeting iron still rang from the blacksmith's shop. And the weathered rocker still sat on the porch of the Lubbock Sheriff's Office.

Jake headed for the livery stable, intent upon taking care of first things first.

He'd given it a lot of serious thought in the hundreds of miles, during the hundreds of hours it had taken to get from Arizona's west border to Texas: Mamie had been faithful and true to the end. She deserved to go to a good home, to a man who'd value her devotion and her loyalty, who'd appreciate just how far she'd go and just how much discomfort she'd tolerate for her master.

She wouldn't be sold, like common property. Instead, Mamie would be a gift, given in good faith to whatever man passed Jake's horsemanship test. And when he found that man, he wouldn't—couldn't say goodbye to his faithful companion. He would leave, quick and simple. It would be far less painful that way.

"That's some horse you've got yourself there," the liveryman said as Jake's feet hit the hay-strewn floor. "Ain't you a beauty," he continued, nuzzling her nose. "What's a purty li'l gal like you doin' with a dusty ole cowpoke like this?" He sent a gap-toothed grin in Jake's direction, then patted Mamie's forehead.

Jake watched Mamie's head dip low as the grizzled old fellow continued to shower her with affectionate praises. She'd always been skittish, wary of strangers, yet she hadn't so much as blinked when the liveryman approached, hadn't backed off when he reached out to scratch her whiskered chin.

"She could use a good brushin'," the man said. There was no mistaking the scolding tone in his voice. "And when was the last time she had herself some water? A bucket of oats?" He ran a leathered hand over her withers. "Man oughta be horsewhipped," he continued, "treatin' his horse this-a way."

"She's yours, if you want her."

"Horse like this?" He laughed. "I ain't got the askin' price."

Jake crossed both arms over his chest and willed himself to say it: "I have personal business," he began, "and Mamie, here, can't come along. All I'm askin' for her is your promise that you'll take good care of her...no rough ridin', no plows to pull.... She ain't overly fond of grass, but she'll eat it when pickin's are slim, and—"

"Mister," the liveryman interrupted, "no need to fret. I'll treat her good." He ruffled her bangs, as if to prove it. "But iffen you change your mind..."

Jake cleared his throat, pulled the hat lower on his forehead. "Well, time's a-wastin'," he said, and headed for the door.

''What-say we get you cleaned up all nice an' purty?'' he heard the liveryman say as he stepped onto the wooden walkway. ''An' after that, I'll rustle you up a feed bag full o' fresh oats.''

One down and one to go, Jake thought, frowning. His relief at providing Mamie with a caring owner waned as he headed for the sheriff's office. On the other side of that weathered door, his deadly fate awaited.

Stepping onto the porch, he paused beside the worn rocker. How many times had he seen the sheriff, sitting right there, chewing a toothpick and staring through narrowed eyes at the comings and goings in the street? Carter had held a tight rein on this town. From all outward appearances, that hadn't changed, either.

Jake wondered if Carter and his deputies would string him up at sundown, or make him wait until morning, so a proper crowd could be gathered to watch him die? Would they let him go to his Maker with a shred of dignity, or would they use fists and boots to take out ten years' worth of frustrations on him first?

Well, he thought as his hand wrapped around the doorknob, *you'll soon find out.*

Jake shoved the door open and stepped inside, and squinted to hurry his eyes into adjusting to the dim light.

''Well, I'll be damned,'' said a deep, gravelly voice from the shadows, ''if it ain't W. C. Atwood.''

He closed the door behind him and unholstered his sixshooter. ''One and the same,'' he said, laying the revolver on the sheriff's desk.

''Well, I'll be damned,'' the man repeated, stepping into the light.

Jake chuckled quietly and shook his head as he recognized the man. ''Joe Purdy, you sure are a sight for sore eyes.''

Purdy snickered. ''You sure ain't. You look like somethin' the dog drug in.''

Shoving his hat to the back of his head, Jake smiled.

"Didn't you get my telegram?" Purdy asked.

"Yeah. I got it. You saved my bacon again. Don't know how I'll ever repay you for warnin' me that Carter and Yonker were—"

Purdy held up a gnarled, arthritic hand. "Not *that* telegram, boy...the last one. The one the Widow Pickett paid for...I sent it more'n a year ago."

Frowning, Jake said, "The Widow Pickett? Why would she send me a telegram?"

The old man stood there, silently studying Jake's face for a long moment. In place of an answer, Joe said, "You been on the run all this time? Since leavin' Baltimore, I mean?"

"Yep." There wasn't much point in telling him what evils he'd seen, what tragedies he'd survived in the year since leaving Foggy Bottom. It would all end—if not this evening, then by morning—and there would be no more hiding, no more looking over his shoulder. It would be a blessed relief, once they slipped that noose around his neck and released the gallows' trapdoor....

Jake stood taller, lifted his chin. "But I'm all through running. I'm here to turn—"

"Set yourself down, W.C.," Purdy interrupted, pointing at the chair behind the sheriff's desk, "and take a load off. I got some news might just take you some gettin' used to."

His frown deepened. "I don't have time for one of your stories, Joe. Now tell me, where's the sheriff? We've got business—"

Purdy rolled the chair into the center of the room. "Set down, I tell you, and shut yer yap." He leaned his broom against the wall and pointed at the empty seat. "Set!"

"Lot of things have changed around here." He pointed at his bony chest. "This, for starters."

Jake grinned at the five-pointed star. "You're...you're a *deputy?*"

Purdy nodded. "I ain't had a drop to drink in over a year." He smiled and thrust out his chest. "And I took me a wife, too."

Shaking his head, Jake chuckled. "Well, don't that just beat all." One brow high on his forehead, he added, "I was wonderin' why you're all spruced up...no whiskers, clean duds, and—"

"And you're a free man, W.C."

The smile faded as Jake's mouth went dry. Heart pounding and pulse racing, he narrowed his eyes. "What did you say?"

"You heard me. You're a free man. Horace Pickett's real killer confessed." Purdy shrugged. "He's locked up good 'n' tight in the new jail out on the edge of town."

Jake screwed up his face, shook his head in disbelief. "Joe, I declare, you always did have the strangest dreams when you were drinkin'. You sure you haven't touched even a drop."

"I told you some stories, but I never told you a lie. I said I don't drink no more, and I meant it."

Eyebrows rising in disbelief, Jake grinned. "Well, I'm glad to hear it, but the fact is, true or not, you're spewin' nonsense. I'm not free yet, but I will be soon as I turn myself in and—"

"Will you *hush,* boy! I'm tellin' you true! You ain't a wanted man anymore." He paused, squinted one eye, and grinned. "I'll prove it. Tell me...when was the last time you saw your face on a Wanted poster?"

Jake removed his hat and ran a hand through his hair. "Now that you mention it, I don't rightly recall." He met Purdy's eyes. "But that doesn't mean—"

"It sure as shootin' *does!*"

Joe described what happened that night out behind the saloon. When he finished, Jake took up where Purdy left off, boots thudding across the board floor. "So...I'm *not* a wanted man?'' he said, more to himself than to Purdy. "I'm not a wanted man...." He could go home now, home to Foggy Bottom, and if Bess was free, as well...

"Ain't you the least bit curious to know who killed Pickett?"

It would take more than a few moments to align himself with the news. After so many years on the run, he wondered if he *could* adjust to life as a free man again. Curiosity raised its ugly head. "Yeah, I reckon I would."

"Then you'd better set your sorry self back down," Purdy insisted.

Jake smiled. "I believe I'll take the news just fine, standin' up."

"All right then, but don't say I didn't warn you."

"What did you do, Joe, trade whiskey for slow molasses? Spit it out, why don't you!"

"Was your uncle who done it," Purdy blurted.

"My..." Jake swallowed. "Uncle Josh? But...but he—"

"He admitted it, straight out. It's what I wired you...."

His uncle Josh?

Josh had lectured him that very day, after Jake warned Horace Pickett what might happen if he ever threatened a defenseless woman again. At the trial, *Josh* had testified that yes, he believed his nephew was capable of a hot-blooded crime. And, as he'd headed away from the witness stand, *Josh* had stopped, apologized—with tears in his eyes no less—for what he'd been forced to say.

"Where's this new jail?" he growled.

"Just east of town. Remember where the old Connor place used to be?"

Nodding, Jake jammed the hat back onto his head. "I'll be back by sundown."

Purdy grabbed his hat. "It's a slow day," he said, winking mischievously. "I'll ride over with you. The warden is Naomi's brother."

"Naomi?"

A slight flush colored Purdy's cheeks as he grinned. "The new Mrs. Purdy."

"Do I know her?"

Winking mischievously, Purdy said, "Let's just say the Widow Pickett ain't a widow anymore."

More had changed around here than he realized. "You don't say...."

"Well, let's not stand here yammerin'," Purdy said. "Let's get on over to the jail."

Jake nodded. "We have to stop over at the livery first. I have to see a man about a horse."

Chapter Twenty-One

Jake stared out the iron-barred window of a small office beside the infirmary and watched the men outside trudge single file across the hard-packed dirt, the stripes around their shoulders and the chains around their feet branding them prisoners of Lubbock Prison.

The blistering noonday sun beat down, glaring angrily from the whitewashed stone walls, deepening the bitter frowns of weariness on their hard-luck faces. Despite the heat, Jake shivered, for he knew that if not for his friend Joe Purdy, *he* might be shackled, wrist and ankle, awaiting the dreaded gallows like some of these men.

Many times on the trail, he'd been chilled to the bone by wintry weather; wind and snow and ice couldn't begin to compare with the bitter ache born of the knowledge that his uncle would spend another nine years in this cold, barren place.

According to the warden, Texas law had gone easy on Josh, taking into account his clean record, and all he'd done for the good folks of Lubbock. Instead of lynching him for Horace Pickett's death, they'd sentenced him to a decade behind bars…twelve months for every year that had passed since that fateful night.

I'd rather swing from the tallest tree than spend one day in this godforsaken place, Jake thought as the last of the men disappeared through a double-wide iron gate. He guessed the wall at twenty feet high, perhaps higher, topped off by a tangle of barbed wire. From his vantage point, Jake could see over it, to field and farm and stream. To view so much as the sunlit, cloud-dotted blue sky, the men who called this place home had no choice but to look straight up...as if into the eyes of God, Himself. If the prisoners prayed, did they ask for freedom from this place? And when no answer came, did their hearts cry out to Him for mercy?

They'd paved the road leading to the prison, brick by backbreaking brick. The many-hued flowers lining the drive had been grown from seed and planted by those same callused hands.

At first glance, a visitor might be fooled into thinking he'd mistakenly stopped at some wealthy rancher's mansion. But once beyond the bright-white entry doors, the tidiness and color stopped as abruptly as life within these walls. The place was gray and black, far as the eye could see.

He couldn't imagine what life here these past months had been like for his uncle, who often slept outside under the stars, saying that "sometimes, the confinement of the house smothers me!"

Jake shoved the unpleasant thoughts aside and focused instead on the deal he'd struck with the liveryman: the gap-toothed fellow got the price of a new horse for the time he'd spent feeding and grooming Mamie...and Jake got his devoted friend back.

He'd gotten Joe back, too, and Jake was acknowledging his gratitude about that when a pair beefy guards led a prisoner into the room. One elderly woman could have done the job—even without the shackles—yet these two seemed to delight in dragging and shoving the convict.

Jake stepped away from the window, and rubbed his eyes.

Surely the bright sunlight was playing tricks on him, for this frail, white-haired old man couldn't be his uncle.... The Josh Atwood Jake remembered was dark-haired, tall and broad-shouldered, hale and hardy. Had they brought him the wrong man?

One guard pushed the prisoner onto the seat of a rickety wooden chair as the other fastened his prisoner's chains to an iron ring bolted to the stone floor. "Warden says take all the time you want," he said to Jake. "Just bang on the door when you're through, and we'll take the miserable sum-bitch back to his cell."

The man lurched when the door slammed shut, winced at the metallic *click* of the key in the big black lock.

Could this debilitated being possibly be the man who'd delivered countless brutal beatings and harsh tongue-lashings? *Nah,* Jake corrected himself, *not this broken-spirited—*

And then their eyes locked, and Jake knew without a doubt that this was indeed his uncle Josh.

"Good of you to come, W.C."

He even sounds like a tired old man, Jake thought. He pulled up a chair, turned it around and swung a leg over its seat.

Josh managed a feeble smile. "You remind me of your pa, handsome and strong, cocksure of yourself...." Then, almost as an afterthought, "Have you seen your aunt Polly?"

"Not yet." And after a moment, "Wasn't it you who taught me to do first things first?"

Josh nodded. "Yes. I expect I taught you quite a few useless lessons." He inhaled a shaky breath. "Well, you be sure and pay her a visit on your way back to town. She'll be mighty proud to see how you turned out." He averted his gaze. "No thanks to me...."

There was no rancor in Jake's voice when he said, "Why'd you do it, Uncle?"

For a moment, Josh only sat there shaking his head. Jake was about to add a line of explanation to his question when his uncle said, "Because I'm a coward." He looked up, stared deep into his nephew's eyes and added, "That day in the store, when you defended Francine...you were more man back then than I'll be on the day I die...which won't be long, if God is truly a merciful Being."

Josh heaved a deep sigh. "There's no righting the wrongs I've done you, W.C., but I hope you can find it in your heart to forgive me before I meet my Maker."

Before he met his Maker? Jake's eyes narrowed slightly.

"I know I should have confessed sooner, but now that I have, you're a free man again."

If Josh ever had any intention of coming clean on his own, would he have waited ten years to do it? Jake didn't think so. He had Joe Purdy to thank for his freedom, not Josh Atwood.

Not so long ago, a thought like that might have driven him to do something vengeful and violent. But Bess had changed *that* about him just as surely as she'd changed his belief that he didn't deserve the love of a good woman.

When Jake told her what life had been like in Josh Atwood's house, he'd could see in her dark, loving eyes that his suffering hurt her, too. Somehow, she'd sensed he hadn't told the story to engender pity, and in her gentle, puppy-to-the-root way, Bess helped him puzzle out *why* his uncle changed. Didn't matter that no one held Josh accountable for the disaster that caused a young mother to lose her fingers; *Josh* blamed himself. What *did* matter, Bess insisted, was that *Jake* learn to forgive the man Josh had become because of it. Forgiveness, she'd taught him, was far more beneficial to the giver than to the receiver.

That day in the courtroom came back to Jake.

"Did you hear your nephew threaten Horace Pickett?" the prosecutor had asked.

Now Jake understood the heavy sigh, the long hesitation that came before Josh said, "Yes, I heard the threat."

"And do you believe your nephew is capable of such violence?"

He'd avoided Jake's eyes, and frowning, Josh had said, "All men are capable of such violence...."

His uncle's testimony had been carefully worded to cover his own tracks. And if Joe hadn't stumbled onto proof that it had been Josh who'd killed the banker, Jake would still be on the run...or dangling from a rope.

He could almost hear Bess's sweet voice, whispering, "Nothing will be gained by holding a grudge...except your own misery...."

"I could go easier, if I could take your forgiveness with me," Josh was saying.

"Go? What're you talkin' about?"

"I'm dying." Josh exhaled a long, shuddering sigh. "They say it's the cancer, that it's been eating at me for some time."

Jake frowned, swallowed. "There's nothing they can do? No medicine? No operation? No—"

He shook his head. "I'm as good as dead, nephew."

"There's nothing to forgive...Uncle Josh."

A moment of deafening stillness punctuated Jake's heartfelt statement. During most of the conversation, Josh had been staring at a crack in the floor between his boots. Slowly, his chin lifted from his chest and his eyes filled with tears. "I've been praying for your forgiveness, son. I don't deserve it, but it does my heart good to know the Almighty has answered my prayers."

I'm not your son, he wanted to say. But Jake held his tongue. What would be gained by lashing out at this shattered man? Even if he told Josh what he thought of him, all

the years Jake had spent running from the law would still
be just as gone. He shrugged, acknowledging that without
those years, he never would have met Bess. If he looked at
it that way, he owed Josh a debt of gratitude.

Enough precious time had been wasted. Jake saw no point
in sitting there jabbering when he could be on his way back
to her. "Are they treating you well? Do you have everything
you need?"

"Look in on your aunt now and then. That's all I need."

Jake nodded. That would be easy enough to promise.
"She'll be taken care of," he said. "You have my word on
it."

Josh went back to staring at the floor. "It's more than I
deserve. Thank you, W.C."

"No thanks necessary." Not knowing what else to say,
Jake banged on the big metal door.

"Will you be back?"

Jake shook his head. "Soon as I see to Aunt Polly, I'll
be headin' east."

"For good?"

Nodding, he said, "For good."

Josh sighed, and as the guards stood him on his feet, the
chains around his ankles clattered quietly. He looked deep
into Jake's eyes and extended his right hand.

Jake squeezed it between his own.

"I hope life is good to you, son, nobody deserves it
more."

He pictured Bess, the twins, Micah, Foggy Bottom.

Life could be good...if it wasn't too late.

It seemed to Jake he'd spent the better part of the past ten
years in a saddle. *When you climb down out of this one,* he
told himself, *you're not gonna set a horse again for a long,
long time.*

He'd headed east the moment the charges against him

were officially dropped, intent upon getting to Foggy Bottom quick as Mamie's hooves could carry him. But Mother Nature had other ideas: a flood in Oklahoma, lightning and torrential downpours in Arkansas. Mamie threw a shoe in Tennessee, and it had taken two days to trudge to the nearest town and find a blacksmith who could replace it. In Kentucky, the horse had stepped into a mole hole, nearly coming up lame. "Why don't you just sell the nag?" a local vet had asked as Jake waited impatiently for her strained muscle to heal. Already, the hours had become days, increasing his yearning to see Bess. "'Cause she saved my hide more'n once," had been his terse answer, "that's why!"

It was good going through West Virginia and Virginia...the extra month on the trail had given him more than enough time to plan what he'd say when first he saw his sweet Bess again. And so when he rode into Freeland, and spotted her going into the bank, Jake's heart pounded like a smithy's hammer as he tethered Mamie to the nearest hitching post. "Now, you behave yourself, girl," he said, patting the horse's rump, "and I promise to buy you a feed bag of oats when I'm through here...."

Won't Bess be surprised, he told himself, *when she finishes her business and sees me standin' here!* The minutes seemed like hours as he waited. Twice, he checked his pa's pocket watch, wondering as he studied the so familiar face what in tarnation could be taking her so long.

And then, at last, her surefooted bootsteps clicked across the marble bank floor. "Thank you, Mr. Abbott," came her musical voice. "You have a nice day now."

Ordinarily, the friendly banker would have walked her to the door, offered a similar greeting in return. But Jake didn't have time to wonder why Abbott's reply had been abrupt; he was too busy planning what he'd do when she stepped into the sunshine. Should he yell "Surprise"? No, he didn't

want to frighten her. Remove his hat? No, he wanted both
hands free to gather her to him.

And then, there she was, smack-dab in front of him.

First sight of her, after all this time apart, set his pulse to
pumping and his hands to trembling, and all the things he'd
rehearsed over the many miles between Texas and Maryland
were forgotten, blotted out by relief…and love.

She'd been in her usual hurry to get from one place to
the next, but when she saw him, Bess stopped walking so
suddenly that her skirts swirled around her ankles. She
looked up at him, dark eyes wide with questions. And anger?

"Jake," she whispered, "you—you came back."

If he didn't know better, he'd say she seemed disappointed by the fact! He forced the ugly thought from his
head, put both hands on her shoulders. "Course I came
back." It was all he could do to keep from grinding his lips
against hers, right there in the bank doorway, in broad daylight. But the heated glare emanating from her eyes stopped
him. "I said I would, didn't I?"

"You said you'd *try*.…"

To hell with what I said! Jake told her silently. *What I'm
about to say…what I hope you'll answer, that's all that
matters now.*

He decided to ignore her fury, and moved to pull her into
a hungry hug, but the bundle she held to her chest blocked
him.

Why hadn't he noticed it before?

He was about to suggest she put the confounded thing
down, give him a proper welcome home, when it moved,
emitted a small whimper.

A…a baby?

The blood froze in his veins.

Recalling that Bess told him she'd assisted Doc in delivering infants, how she'd brought a few children into the
world without his guidance, how she so often volunteered

to care for a friend's child, Jake's fear evaporated. His eyes bored into hers. "Whose young'un?"

In place of an answer, Bess pulled back the blanket that hid the baby's face. "Oh, Jake," she sighed, "isn't she just the most beautiful thing you've ever seen?"

If he counted them all up, he guessed he'd seen hundreds of calfs and foals. He knew how to birth 'em, if their mamas had trouble, knew what to feed 'em if the mamas wouldn't…or couldn't. But this was the closest he'd ever gotten to an infant in all his days. Why, what he knew about *human* babies he could put in one eye!

Tiny and pink, with fingers so small they reminded him of cat's whiskers, the baby seemed more fragile than an autumn leaf, more delicate than a thin skin of ice skimming a wintry pond. For an instant, an exhilarating possibility crossed his mind: he'd bedded her the day before leaving Foggy Bottom. Dare he hope it could it be…Bess, his woman; this child, *his?*

But rationality reared its ugly head, forcing him to consider the alternative. *The young'un is brand-new,* he told himself. Jake did some quick arithmetic, and the sum of his mental ciphering added up to heartbreak. *It doesn't look to me to be more'n a few days old, so it can't be yours.*

He slapped a hand to the back of his neck and shook his head. *You're a fool, a blamed fool. What made you think she'd wait a whole year for the likes of* you! *You told her not to wait; wrote in that damned goodbye note of yours that if love came knockin', she oughta—*

"Boy or girl?" he asked, more to get his mind off the awful facts than for any other reason.

"Girl. And I've named her—"

He didn't want to hear what she'd named the child born of another man's loins. "She's a beauty," Jake interrupted, "just like her mama."

"Jake," she began, a hand on his forearm, "how long have you been back?"

He pretended to have an itch that needed scratching, so he could free himself of her grasp. "Just rode into town." He forced himself to look away from the baby, into Bess's face. Motherhood, Jake decided, agreed with her. She was even lovelier than he remembered. Something about her had changed, for she glowed with serenity, seemed to be at peace with her new life.

"I wish you'd written...."

It wasn't an accusation. He could tell by the sweet light emanating from her eyes. So why did he feel he was being held accountable for some wrongdoing?

He wished he *had* found a way to get in touch with her, instead of working toward his goal of surprising the daylights out of her by simply showing up, because if he'd contacted her, maybe he could have stopped her, before she went and took up with the man who fathered the child... before he made a blamed fool of himself, heading east like there was no tomorrow....

Unable to cope with the idea that she'd shared herself with another man, Jake took a clumsy step backward. "I, uh, I have a few things... I, ah, promised her I'd...ah, before I head out."

Her dark eyes narrowed. "Head out? But Jake, you just got here. Pa and the twins would love to see—"

Pa and the twins? he ranted inwardly. *What about* you, *Bess? Wouldn't you love to welcome me home?*

But just how did he expect her to accomplish that, when she had a baby, a *husband?* Was the man waiting for her at Foggy Bottom? Did he share a bed with her in the room overlooking the corral? Or had he built her a house of her own?

Do you look at him the way you used to look at me? Jake wondered. He remembered the first time they made love, when she'd blushed and giggled, saying "I liked it, I liked it a lot!" Was she playful and loving with the man who had replaced him? *Do you kiss him and hold him like you—?*

"Everyone will be thrilled to see you, Jake. As luck would have it, I've been cooking your favorite stew all day. Why don't you—"

The picture of her moving about the house, cooking *his* stew for another man proved too much to bear. He held a hand up to silence her. "Can't talk now, Bess," he said around the lump in his throat. He glanced at Mamie, pawing the dirt. "My, um…I should get her some…she needs me to…"

He stomped toward his horse, hoisted himself into the saddle, and thundered away without another word.

Bess drove the team hard, crying all the way home, as if she thought with every jostle and jolt of the wagon she might be able to shake the painful ideas from her heart, dislodge the agonizing images from her mind. She'd hadn't expected to see Jake again, and her joy at the sight of him had been all-encompassing. But he'd put a quick end to that! He'd made it clear there was someone else, someone he'd made promises to, someone he needed to take care of.

"What's wrong, Bessie-girl?" Matt asked when she parked the wagon near the front gate.

"Nothing," she snapped, scooping the baby into her arms. "Put the groceries away for me, will you?"

Standing with arms crossed over his chest, he blocked her path. "I'll take care of that soon as you tell me what's ailin' you, big sister. You've got the horses lathered up like they've run a race, and both you and Li'l Bit there," he added, nodding toward the baby, "look like you've seen a ghost."

Shoulders slouching, she handed the baby to her brother

as his twin joined them. "What's goin' on?" Mark wanted to know.

"Tell us, Bess, or we'll send you to bed without any supper."

It was a threat she'd used on them dozens of times, unsuccessfully for the most part, but it inspired a sad little smile. "Jake's back," she said, slumping onto the bottom porch step, "and he brought a woman with him."

"A woman!" Mark demanded, fists clenched at his sides. "He *had* him a woman, and he's got responsibilities to her, right here at Foggy Bottom!"

"Somebody needs to teach that polecat a thing or two about doin' the right thing." Matt shifted the baby from one arm to the other.

"If we leave right now, we can probably catch him." Mark pounded a fist into an open palm. "Beat some sense into him."

Matt made a move to hand Bess the baby, but she grasped his sleeve instead. "Please, boys," she said, taking Mark's hand in her own, "haven't I been humiliated enough? Some folks in this town have labeled me a harlot, a brazen hussy for having had a child out of wedlock. And that sweet, innocent child," she continued, nodding toward her daughter, "has been branded a bastard." She shook her head vehemently. "If he doesn't want me, I don't want him, either."

"But, but he's the young'un's *father!*" Matt insisted, jabbing a finger into the air. "He owes you and Li'l Bit a—"

"He owes us nothing. He made me no promises, don't forget." The clock in the front hall gonged three times. Bess stood, took the baby from Matt's arms. "Do you love me, Matt? Mark?"

The twins exchanged a worried glance. "Course we do," Matt said. "And that's *exactly* why we're gonna hunt down that no good dog and pound the livin' daylights outta—"

"If you love me, you'll leave well enough alone. Now,

please, unload the wagon, will you? I'm going to put the baby down for a nap while I get supper on the table.''

''Way you look,'' Mark suggested, ''you oughta take a nap yourself.''

She sent them a sad, weary smile and kissed each of their cheeks, then trudged inside and slowly climbed the stairs.

At the sound of her closing bedroom door, Mark elbowed Matt. ''Betcha I can knock him on his butt before you can.''

''You're on!''

He'd been in the Freeland saloon all afternoon. Between swallows of whiskey, Jake wondered if Bess had made it back to Foggy Bottom safely.

Course she did, he told himself. *She knows that road like the back of her hand. Besides, it's barely more'n an hour's ride from here to the farm.*

Drumming his fingertips on the counter, he signaled the barkeep. ''Just leave the bottle this time,'' Jake said, slapping a silver dollar on the counter, ''it'll save us both a heap of time.''

The man held the bottle by its long, slender neck. ''Didn't your mama teach you you can't drown your sorrows in whiskey?''

''Maybe I can't drown 'em,'' Jake snarled, grabbing it, ''but I can numb 'em...if I'm lucky.''

The man leaned on the bar. ''Woman trouble?''

''You could say that—'' he carried the bottle to a table near the door, and used the toe of his boot to pull out a chair ''—but it'd be better all 'round if you didn't say it.''

The bartender held up his hands in mock surrender. ''Just tryin' to do the Christian thing,'' he told another customer.

''The Lord helps them what helps themselves,'' the drunken patron slurred. ''Leave 'im with his booze an' the she-devil that drove him to it.''

She was anything *but* a she-devil, and *that* was what had

driven Jake to the bottle! He downed another gulp of the alcohol, hoping it would deaden his ears to their ridiculous banter...deaden his heart to the news of Bess and her child....

He'd just tossed back his another jigger of whiskey when the twins barged into the saloon. "Jake Walker," one said, "we have business to discuss with you...*outside*."

"Well, would you look at what the wind blew in."

The Beckley boys stood beside his table, arms crossed over their chests, feet spread wide on the dusty floor.

"You've grown a lot in a year," Jake said, smiling. "Why, when I left here, you were barely bigger'n—"

Mark spoke first. "We're big enough to hurt you, if we have to."

Jake chuckled and poured himself another jigger of whiskey. "Now, now, boys. Why would you want to try an' do a fool thing like that?"

"'Cause you hurt Bess, that's why," Matt said. "And we're here to tell you, you've hurt her for the last time."

"*I've* hurt *her?*" Jake slammed a fist onto the table. "Don't make me laugh." He waved a hand in their direction, as if shooing away an annoying mosquito. "Now, git! Let me drown my sorrows in peace."

Matt leaned into Jake's face. "You think you've got sorrows? Let me tell you something about sorrows!" In a whip-stitch, he grabbed the man's shirt collar and brought him to his feet.

The men at the bar were on their feet, too, circling to watch the brewing fight. "My money's on the twins," said one.

"How much?" asked another.

"A dollar!"

And the barkeep shoved Jake's silver dollar forward. "Double or nothin'!"

"Put your money away, men," Jake growled. "I never fought a boy in my life, and I don't aim to start now."

"We ain't boys!" Matt insisted, tightening his hold on Jake's arm. "We're fifteen! What's the matter...you still yeller?"

Still yeller? "Look," Jake began, "I don't know what you're all riled up about, but—"

"Don't know what—" Matt knocked the hat off Jake's head. "I'll tell you what! You left Bess alone, to deal with those hens in town callin' her—"

"Matthew!"

Everyone turned toward the saloon's swinging doors, where Bess stood, babe in arms.

"I thought I told you two to mind your own business?" she huffed. "You promised me you'd stay out of this."

Jake looked from the twins to Bess and back again. The baby began to fuss, and he shook his head. He hadn't had time to drink enough whiskey to make him this confused, and yet...

Bess gently propped the child against her shoulder and patted its back. "What are you doing here?" she demanded, turning her wrath on Jake. "I thought your *woman* needed you?"

"My woman?"

And then it all began to make sense...the boys' rage, the agony in Bess's wide eyes as he left her in town earlier, her accusation just now that he'd ridden off to see to another woman's needs. What would she say if he told her that Mamie was that other woman?

Jake felt like a fool for having thought, even for a moment, that Bess hadn't waited for him. He should have known that a woman like her could never give her body to a man without first giving him her heart. Relief coursed through him. She'd been a virgin the first time he made love to her, and that child in her arms was *his*.

God, how I love that woman!

"You're the only woman in my life, Bess Beckley, and if you weren't so all-fired stubborn, you'd know it."

"B-but before…in town…you said—"

"I said my horse needed tending. Period." He held out his arms. "Now, will you bring that young'un over here and introduce her to her daddy?"

He wasn't the only one who knew the meaning of the word *relief*. Jake saw the proof of it shining in Bess's brown eyes. "This *young'un,*" she said, heading toward him, "has a name. Mary Ann…Mary for our ma and Ann for yours." Bess stood beside him so that he could look at his daughter.

He loved her so much at that moment that words failed him. She'd gone through plenty—alone—while he'd been running from the law. He'd spend the rest of his life making it up to her. "I—I—I'm so proud of you," he stammered. "You're the bravest woman I've ever known."

Bess blushed. "You talk as though I'm the first woman ever to have given birth!"

He looked deep into her eyes. "Well, you're the first woman to give *me* a child." Smiling, he shook his head. "Can I…is it all right if I hold her?"

Gently, Bess lay the baby in the crook of his arm.

"She's beautiful," he said, pressing a light kiss to Mary Ann's forehead. "But then, why wouldn't she be?" he added, meeting Bess's eyes.

Her blush deepened. "She has your eyes, Jake."

He lowered his head, drawing his big face closer to his daughter's tiny nose. "I'm never going to leave you, my sweet Mary Ann. You've got my word on it." He stood then, and handed the infant back to her mother. "I'll make the same promise to you, if you'll agree to be my wife…."

Immediately, Bess's eyes filled with tears. "You have a lot of explaining to do, Jake Walker." She leaned closer and whispered, "Or shall I say you have a lot of explaining to do…W. C. Atwood?'' A quiet laugh punctuated her question. ''No need to answer now, we have a lifetime to work out the details.''

''A lifetime,'' he said on a relieved sigh. Drawing them close in a tender embrace, he raised one eyebrow. ''But tell me…was that a yes?''

She nodded as one silvery tear rolled down her cheek.

He lifted the shot glass he'd just filled when Bess appeared in the doorway. ''Ladies and gentlemen,'' he announced, holding it aloft, ''a toast to my daughter…and the beautiful woman who gave her to me!''

Bar patrons raised their glasses, nodding their consent as Jake placed a loving kiss on Bess's waiting lips.

''Aw, gee,'' Mark said, feigning disgust. ''They're gonna ruin my appetite.''

Matt slung an arm over his brother's shoulders. ''Nah. Bess has been cookin' your favorite—beef stew with dumplings—and nothin' can spoil your appetite for *that*.''

Mark's head bobbed left, then right as they headed for the door. ''You make a good point,'' he said, grinning.

''See you at home, Bess,'' Matt called over his shoulder. ''And Jake? Don't you worry none…we'll hide Pa's shotgun the minute we get there.''

Jake tucked in one corner of his mouth and smiled sheepishly. ''Guess I have some fancy talking to do, eh?''

Wincing, Bess replied, ''As I said…we have a lifetime to work out the details.'' She stood on tiptoe and pressed a kiss to his chin.

''Now, how would you feel about tying Mamie to my wagon and driving your family *home?*''

Epilogue

Twenty-five years later

The quiet hour after supper had always been her favorite of the day. As a girl, she'd sit on this very porch, reading until the evening light faded, then listening to the songs of bugs and frogs as darkness pulled up over her world like a heavy black blanket.

As a young woman, her dreams had been spun here.

Today, it was where she counted her blessings.

And she had much to be grateful for…a beautiful home on a productive farm, physical and emotional vitality. There were her four healthy children, all grown, three of whom had youngsters of their own.

Two of those tykes now frolicked in the yard where she had played in as a child; the third slumbered peacefully in the room that had once belonged to her brother, Matt.

Her twin brothers had fought for the South during the Civil War, and thankfully, they'd both come home safe and sound. Jake fought at Gettysburg, too, and the Lord had seen fit to send him home to her…again.

Yes, there was much to be thankful for….

A hand over her mouth, Bess hid a grin, remembering

how, on the morning he'd returned to Freeland, she had mistaken his rambling promises about taking care of his horse...for promises made to another woman.

"What are you smiling about, pretty lady?"

In place of an answer, Bess held out her hand. And, as always, Jake instinctively wrapped it in his own. It wasn't necessary to look away from the children to know what she would read in his eyes if she turned her face toward him, and the mere thought of it swelled her heart.

"Johnny," she scolded gently, "don't climb so high. How will you ever get down?"

"Aw, Gramma," Mary Ann's four-year-old son complained, "don't be such a worrywart. I always get down, don't I?"

"Yes, yes you do...."

Sighing, she shook her head. "That namesake of yours is such a tease!" She squeezed Jake's hand. "He's so much like you, it's terrifying."

Jake chuckled, returned the squeeze. "And he's stubborn as the day is long. There's a morsel of *you* in him, too...."

Standing, Bess stooped, kissed his cheek, then walked to the porch rail to stare into the yard. How many nights had she leaned against this same bannister, looking past the sea of grass that separated the house from the river? How often had she peered into the darkening sky, ears tuned to the distant wail of the wolf?

It wasn't so very long ago that she'd come up with an explanation for the beast's mysterious and sudden disappearance. What she'd been hearing hadn't been a wolf at all, she convinced herself, but Jake's wild, wandering spirit, calling to her, pleading with her to wait for him.

She didn't dare share her theory with anyone—they'd have thought her daft!—but how else was she to interpret the fact that she'd heard the lamenting cry every night while

Jake had been gone…and hadn't heard it—not even once—since he'd come home again, home to stay?

Hours later, after the grandchildren had been bathed and tucked into their beds, Bess and Jake said good-night to their children, who'd come home to help them celebrate. Leaning on the rail surrounding the balcony outside their room, she glanced at her husband, slouched in the bentwood rocker that had been her father's, whittling a toy truck for their grandson.

He'd been a doting grandpa, a loving father, right from the start. Mary Ann and her sister Susan adored him to this very day. And their brothers, William—named for Jake's father, and Micah, named for hers—felt the same way.

"*Now* what are you smiling about?" he wanted to know.

She faced the yard once more, where her mother's birch trees continued to thrive in soil that everyone had been certain would kill them, where the red roses Bess had planted on her first anniversary still bloomed bright and bold from spring thaw to first frost.

Suddenly, Jake was behind her, sliding strong sure arms around her waist. "Tomorrow's the big day," he whispered into her ear.

"Every day I've spent with you has been a big day," Bess replied, leaning against his chest.

He kissed the back of her head. "I love you, too, pretty lady."

She turned, wrapped her arms around his barrel chest.

"Seems like just yesterday we were married."

"In a sense," she said, "it was."

"But…it's been twenty-five years!"

Bess nodded. "I know, I know, but I've come to the conclusion that I was born to be your wife. Every morning, when I wake up beside you, it's as though I'm seeing you for the first time, and I fall in love with you all over again."

He hid his face behind one big hand. "Aw, I bet you say that to all the cowboys...."

Pursing her lips, she said, "You know better. There's never been anyone but you."

She took a deep breath, let it out slowly. "You know that porcelain vase in the dining room?"

"The one on the mantel? With all the chips and cracks?"

"That's the one. Before I met you, *I* was like that vase, fractured and nicked. And then you came along, filling all the gaps with your love, the way rainwater fills crevices in clay soil. You softened my hard edges, made me stronger, and whole, and—"

"Remind me to send a prayer of thanks to your daddy."

Looking up into his face, Bess raised an eyebrow. "Oh, I like that! *I'm* the one who cooks your meals, cleans your house, raised your children, and—"

"—and keeps me warm at night," he said, pulling her closer. "Let's not forget how good you are at keeping me warm at night...."

"—and keeps you warm at night," she continued, her voice softly flirtatious. "I do all that, and you're thanking *my father?*"

Jake kissed the tip of her nose. "Well, without him, you wouldn't be here, now would you?"

She harrumphed. "Isn't that just like a man...Mama did all the work, and Pa gets the credit!"

His quiet laughter rumbled against her chest, and Bess tilted her face to accept his hungry kiss. When it ended, she asked, "What do you say we celebrate a little early?"

In one smooth move, Jake lifted her in his arms and followed the swath of moonlight that slanted across their room, gently depositing her on the feather mattress. And as if he were a bridegroom and she a bride, he leaned over her on the bed, nervous fingers untying the bow of her satiny robe. Slowly, he pushed it from her shoulders, let it fall open, exposing her breasts. Standing beside the four-poster, he shook his head. "I'll never get my fill of you, Bess," he rasped, "not even if I live to be a hundred."

She basked in his attentions, unashamed, unafraid, and beckoned him near with the crook of a finger.

Grinning seductively, he wiggled his eyebrows and climbed onto the bed.

She'd been calling him "Jake" since the day he arrived at Foggy Bottom; only when they were linked in lovemaking did she speak his given name.

She said it now: "Walker..."

He lay beside her, pressing kisses to her lips, across her cheekbones, down her throat. She knew what he was waiting to hear, and when the time was right, she would say it, as she'd been saying it for twenty-five years.

It was like a ballad between them, music that had begun during that first escapade in the sun-drenched hayloft that continued to this very coupling in their marriage bed, bodies merging like the notes of a harmonious song.

When the heated music of their lovemaking cooled, she snuggled close, her fingers combing damp hair from his forehead. It was time to sing the last note in their lusty song, to say the words he wanted...*needed* to hear.

Propping herself on one elbow, she kissed him. Kissed him again. "I love you, W. C. Atwood," she said, her voice filled with strong, abiding warmth, "and I always will."

* * * * *

This season, make your destination
England with four exciting stories from
Harlequin Historicals

On sale in December 1999,
THE CHAMPION,
The first book of *KNIGHTS OF THE BLACK ROSE*
by **Suzanne Barclay**
(England, 1222)

BY QUEEN'S GRACE
by **Shari Anton**
(England, 1109)

On sale in January 2000,
THE GENTLEMAN THIEF
by **Deborah Simmons**
(England, 1818)

MY LADY RELUCTANT
by **Laurie Grant**
(England, 1141)

Harlequin Historicals
Have a blast in the past!

Available at your favorite retail outlet.

HARLEQUIN®
Makes any time special ™

Visit us at www.romance.net   HHMED10

3 Stories of Holiday Romance from three bestselling Harlequin® authors

Valentine Babies

by

ANNE STUART

TARA TAYLOR QUINN

JULE McBRIDE

Goddess in Waiting by Anne Stuart
Edward walks into Marika's funky maternity shop to pick up some things for his sister. He doesn't expect to assist in the delivery of a baby and fall for outrageous Marika.

Gabe's Special Delivery by Tara Taylor Quinn
On February 14, Gabe Stone finds a living, breathing valentine on his doorstep—his daughter. Her mother has given Gabe four hours to adjust to fatherhood, resolve custody and win back his ex-wife?

My Man Valentine by Jule McBride
Everyone knows Eloise Hunter and C. D. Valentine are in love. Except Eloise and C. D. Then, one of Eloise's baby-sitting clients leaves her with a baby to mind, and C. D. swings into protector mode.

VALENTINE BABIES

On sale January 2000 at your favorite retail outlet.

HARLEQUIN®
Makes any time special ™